Single father s...
his child...

AT HI...
NANNY
NEEDED

Three heart-warming stories from
favourite authors: Cara Colter,
Melissa James and Teresa Hill

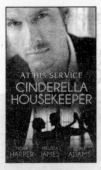

AT HIS SERVICE
CINDERELLA HOUSEKEEPER
FIONA HARPER · MELISSA JAMES · JACKIE ADAMS

Available in
July 2012

AT HIS SERVICE
HIS 9-5 SECRETARY
HELEN BROOKS · MICHELLE CELMER · JENNIE ADAMS

Available in
August 2012

AT HIS SERVICE
FLIRTING WITH THE BOSS
REBECCA WINTERS · ALLY BLAKE · BARBARA HANNAY

Available in
September 2012

AT HIS SERVICE
HER BOSS THE HERO
ALISON ROBERTS · ANNE FRASER · MOLLY EVANS

Available in
October 2012

AT HIS SERVICE
MILLIONAIRE'S MISTRESS
CATHY WILLIAMS · ANNE OLIVER · KELLY HUNTER

Available in
November 2012

AT HIS SERVICE
NANNY NEEDED
SARA CRAVEN · MELISSA JAMES · TERESA HILL

Available in
December 2012

AT HIS SERVICE:
NANNY NEEDED

CARA
COLTER

MELISSA
JAMES

TERESA
HILL

Mills & Boon, an imprint of Harlequin (UK) Limited, Eton House, 18-24 Paradise Road, Richmond, Surrey TW9 1SR

AT HIS SERVICE: NANNY NEEDED
© Harlequin Enterprises II B.V./S.à.r.l. 2012

Hired: Nanny Bride © Cara Colter 2009
A Mother in a Million © Melissa James 2007
The Nanny Solution © Teresa Hill 2009

ISBN: 978 0 263 90226 6

026-1212

Harlequin (UK) policy is to use papers that are natural, renewable and recyclable products and made from wood grown in sustainable forests. The logging and manufacturing processes conform to the legal environmental regulations of the country of origin.

Printed and bound in Spain
by Blackprint CPI, Barcelona

Hired: Nanny Bride

CARA
COLTER

Dear Reader,

By the time you read this, I will have experienced my first trip to Europe. I have never pictured myself as any kind of world traveller. I like to escape Canadian winters by going somewhere warm for a week or two every year, and that has been the extent of my travel ambition. So what convinced a non-adventuring homebody to move outside the comfort zone? Love, of course!

Rob and I have been invited to Denmark for the wedding of two of the people we care most about in the world. Mike is the son of wonderful friends, but he has become so much more to us: comedian, comrade, carpenter, co-worker. And Mike brought us Aline, a Danish girl he met while travelling. She has become a treasure in my life, bringing me the gifts of her depth, her incredible youthful energy and her creative abilities. In my line of work, Mike and Aline's love for one another, and the obstacles they've been prepared to overcome to have their happily-ever-after, have been a true inspiration.

This one is for you, Mike and Aline, and for everyone who believes in the power, hope and happiness love can bring to life.

With best wishes,

Cara

Cara Colter lives on an acreage in British Columbia with her partner, Rob, and eleven horses. She has three grown children and a grandson. She is a recent recipient of an *RT Book Reviews* Career Achievement Award in the Love and Laughter category.

Cara loves to hear from readers, and you can contact her, or learn more about her, through her website, www.cara-colter.com.

To Mike Kepke and Aline Pihl
'Love fills a lifetime'
August 9, 2008

CHAPTER ONE

JOSHUA COLE heard the unfamiliar sound and felt a quiver of pure feeling snake up and down his spine. So rare was that particular sensation that it took him a split second to identify it.

Fear.

He was a man who prided himself on moving forward, rather than back, in any kind of stressful situation. It had turned out to be a strategy for success in the high-powered world he moved in.

Joshua hit the intercom that connected his office to his secretary's desk in the outer lair. His office underscored who he had become with its floor-to-ceiling glass windows that overlooked the spectacular view of Vancouver, downtown skyscrapers in the foreground, majestic white-capped mountains as the backdrop.

But if his surroundings reflected his confidence, at this moment his voice did not. "Tell me that wasn't what I thought it was."

But the sound came again, through his closed, carved, solid walnut door. Now it was amplified by the intercom.

There was absolutely no mistaking it for anything but what it was: a baby crying, the initial hesitant sobs building quickly to strident shrieking.

"They say you are expecting them," said his receptionist, Amber, her own tone rising, in panic or in an effort to be heard above the baby, he couldn't quite be sure.

Of course he was expecting them. Just not today. Not here. Children, and particularly squalling babies, would be as out of place in the corporate offices of the company he had founded as a hippo at Victoria's Empress Hotel's high tea.

Joshua Cole had built his fortune and his company, Sun, around the precise lack of that sound in each of his exclusive adult-only resorts.

His office replicated the atmosphere that made the resorts so successful: tasteful, expensive, luxurious, no detail overlooked. The art was original, the antiques were authentic, the rugs came from the best bazaars in Turkey.

The skillful use of rich colors and subtle, exotic textures made Joshua Cole's office mirror the man, masculine, confident, charismatic. His desk faced a wall that showcased his career rise with beautifully framed magazine covers, *Forbes, Business, Business Weekly.*

But this morning, as always, his surroundings had faded as he intently studied what he hoped would become his next project. The surface of his desk was littered with photos of a rundown resort in the wilderness of the British Columbia interior.

He'd had *that* feeling as soon as he'd seen the photos. Moose Lake Lodge could be turned into an adventure destination for the busy young professionals who trusted his company to give them exactly what they wanted in a vacation experience. His clients demanded grown-up adventure plus five-star meals, spalike luxuries and all against the backdrop of a boutique hotel atmosphere.

The initial overture to Moose Lake Lodge had not gone particularly well. The owners were reluctant to talk to him, let alone sell to him. He had sensed they were wary of his reputation as a playboy, concerned about the effect of a Sun resort in the middle of cottage country. The Moose Lake Lodge had run as a family-oriented lakeside retreat since the 1930s, and the owners had sentimental attachments to it.

But sentiment did not pay the bills, and Joshua Cole did his homework. He knew buyers were not lining up for the place, and he was already strategizing his next move. He would up his offer tantalizingly. He'd convince the Baker family he could turn Moose Lake Lodge into a place they would always feel proud of. He'd visit them personally, win them over. Joshua Cole was very good at winning people over.

And he was passionate about this game, in all its stages: acquiring, renovating, opening, operating.

To that end Joshua had a resort in the Amazon jungle that offered rainforest canopy excursions, and one on the African savannah featuring photo safaris. And, of course, he still had his original small hotel in Italy, in the heart of Tuscany, where it had all started, offering a very grown-up winery and tasting tours.

Most recently Sun had opened a floating five-star destination for water lovers off the Kona Coast, on the Big Island of Hawaii.

Water lovers and kid haters.

Well, not all kid *haters*. Some of his best clients were just busy parents who desperately needed a break from the demands of children.

"WAHHHHHH."

As if that sound didn't explain it all. Even his own sister, Melanie, domestic diva that she had become, had accepted his offer to give her and her hubbie a much-needed break at the newly opened Sun in Kona.

No wonder, with a kid whose howls could register off the decibel chart.

How could his niece and nephew be here? His crammed calendar clearly said tomorrow. The plane was arriving at ten in the morning. Joshua planned, out of respect to his sister, to meet the plane, pat his niece on the head and make appropriate noises over the relatively new baby nephew, hopefully without actually touching him. Then he was planning on putting them, and the nanny they were traveling with, in a limo and waving goodbye as they were whisked off to a kid-friendly holiday experience at Whistler.

Holiday for Mom and Dad at the exclusive Kona Sun; holiday for the kids; Uncle Josh, hero-of-the-hour.

The baby screamed nonstop in the outer office, and Joshua's head began to throb. He'd given his sister and brother-in-law, Ryan, the adult-getaway package after the birth of the baby, stunned that his sister, via their Web cam conversations, always so vital in the past, could suddenly look so worn-out. Somehow, he hadn't exactly foreseen *this* moment, though he probably should have when Melanie had started worrying about her kids within seconds of agreeing to go to the Kona Sun for a week. Naturally, her brother, the hero, had volunteered to look after that, too.

He should have remembered that things never went quite as he planned them when his sister was involved.

"What is going on?" Joshua asked in a low voice into his intercom. His legendary confidence abandoned him around children, even ones he was related to.

"There's a, um, woman here. With a baby and another, er, small thing."

"I know *who* they are," Joshua said. "Why is the baby making that noise?"

"You know who they are?" Amber asked, clearly feeling betrayed that they hadn't wandered in off the street, thereby making disposing of them so much easier!

"They aren't supposed to be here. They're supposed to be—

"Miss! Excuse me! You can't just go in there!"

But before Amber could protect him, his office door opened.

For all the noise that baby was making, Joshua was struck by a sudden sensation of quiet as he pressed the off button on the intercom and studied the woman who stood at the doorway to his enclave.

Despite the screaming red-faced baby at her bosom, and his four-year-old niece attached to the hem of her coat, the woman carried herself with a calm dignity, a sturdy sea vessel, innately sure of her abilities in a storm, which, Joshua felt, the screaming baby qualified as.

His niece was looking at him with dark dislike, which took him aback. Like cats, children were adept at attaching themselves to those with an aversion, and he had spent his last visit to his sister's home in Toronto trying to escape his niece's frightening affection. At that time the baby had been an enormous lump under his sister's sweater, and there had been no nanny in residence.

The distraction of the baby and his niece's withering look aside, he was aware of feeling he had not seen a woman like the one who accompanied his niece and nephew for a very long time.

No, Joshua Cole had become blissfully accustomed

to perfection in the opposite sex. His world had become populated with women with thin, gym-sculpted bodies, dentist-whitened teeth, unfurrowed brows, perfect makeup, stunning hair, clothing that *breathed* wealth and assurance.

The woman before him was, in some ways, the epitome of what he expected a nanny to be: fresh-scrubbed; no makeup; sensible shoes; a plain black skirt showing from underneath a hideously rumpled coat. One black stocking had a run in it from knee to ankle. All that was missing was the umbrella.

She was exactly the type of woman he might dismiss without a second look: frumpalumpa, a woman who had given up on herself in favor of her tedious child-watching duties. She was younger than he would have imagined, though, and carried herself with a careful dignity that the clothes did not hide, and that did not allow for easy dismissal.

A locket, gold and fragile, entirely out of keeping with the rest of her outfit, winked at her neck, making him aware of the pure creaminess of her skin.

Then Joshua noticed her hair. Wavy and jet black, it was refreshingly uncolored, caught back with a clip it was slipping free from. The escaped tendrils of hair should have added to her generally unruly appearance, but they didn't. Instead they hinted at something he wasn't seeing. Something wilder, maybe even exotic.

Her eyes, when he met them, underscored that feeling. They were a stunning shade of turquoise, fringed with lashes that didn't need one smidgen of mascara to add to their lushness. Unfortunately, he detected his niece's disapproval mirrored in her nanny's expression.

Her face might, at first glance, be mistaken for plain.

And yet there was something in it—freshness, perhaps—that intrigued.

It was as if, somehow, she was *real* in the world of fantasy that he had so carefully crafted, a world that had rewarded him with riches beyond his wildest dreams, and which suddenly seemed lacking in *something,* and that *something* just as suddenly seemed essential.

He shrugged off the uncharacteristic thoughts, put their intrusion in his perfect world down to the yelps of the baby. He had only to look around himself to know he was the man who already had everything, including the admiration and attention of women a thousand times more polished than the one in front of him.

"My uncle hates us," his niece, Susie, announced just as Joshua was contemplating trying out his most charming smile on the nanny. He was pretty confident he was up to the challenge of melting the faintly contemptuous look from her eyes. Pitting his charm against someone so wholesome would be good practice for when he met with the Bakers about acquiring their beloved Moose Lake Lodge.

"Susie, that was extremely rude," the nanny said. Her voice was husky, low, as real as she was. And it hinted at something tantalizingly sensual below the frumpalumpa exterior.

"Of course I don't hate you," Joshua said, annoyed at being put on the defensive by a child who had plagued him with xoxo notes less than a year ago, explaining to him carefully each x stood for a kiss and each o stood for a hug. "I'm terrified of you. There's a difference."

He tried his smile.

The nanny's lips twitched, her free hand reached up and touched the locket. If a smile had been developing, it never materialized. In fact, Joshua wasn't quite sure if he'd amused her or annoyed her. If he'd amused her, her amusement was reluctant! He was not accustomed to ambiguous reactions when he dealt with the fairer sex.

"You hate us," Susie said firmly. "Why would Mommy and Daddy need a holiday from *us?*"

Then her nose crunched up, her eyes closed tight, she sniffled and buried her face in the folds of the nanny's voluminous jacket and howled. The baby seemed to regard that as a challenge to make himself heard above his sister.

"Why, indeed?" he asked dryly. The children had been in his office approximately thirty seconds, and he already needed a holiday from them.

"She's just tired," the nanny said. "Susie, shush."

He was unwillingly captivated by the hand that she rested lightly on Susie's head, by the exquisite tenderness in that faint touch, by the way her voice calmed the child, who quit howling but hiccupped sadly.

"I think there's a tiny abandonment issue," the nanny said, "that was not in the least helped by your leaving us stranded at the airport."

He found himself hoping that, when he explained there had been a misunderstanding, he would see her without the disapproving furrow in her forehead.

"There seems to have been a mix-up about the dates. If you had called, I would have had someone pick you up."

"I did call." The frown line deepened. "Apparently only very important people are preapproved to speak to you."

He could see how all those security measures intended to protect his time and his privacy were just evidence to her of an overly inflated ego. He was probably going to have to accept that the furrowed brow line would be permanent.

"I'm terribly sorry," he said, which did not soften the look on her face at all.

"Are those women naked?" Susie asked, midhiccup, having removed her head from the folds of her nanny's coat. Unfortunately.

He followed her gaze and sighed inwardly. She was staring at the Lalique bowl that adorned his coffee table. Exquisitely crafted in blue glass, and worth about forty thousand dollars, it was one of several items in the room that he didn't even want his niece to breathe on, though to say so might confirm for the nanny, who already had a low opinion of him, that he really did hate children.

He realized that the bowl, shimmering in the light from the window, was nearly the same shades of blue as the nanny's eyes.

"Susie, that's enough," the nanny said firmly.

"Well, they are naked, Miss Pringy," Susie muttered, unrepentant.

Miss Pringy. A stodgy, solid, librarian spinster kind of name that should have suited her to a T, but didn't.

"In your uncle's circles, I'm sure that bowl would be considered appropriate decor."

"And what circles are those?" Joshua asked, raising an eyebrow at her.

"I had the pleasure of reading all about you on the plane, Mr. Cole. *People to Watch*. You are quite the celebrity it would seem."

Her tone said it all: superficial, playboy, hedonist. Even before he'd missed her at the airport, he'd been tried and found guilty.

Joshua Cole had, unfortunately, been discovered by a world hungry for celebrity, and the fascination with his lifestyle was escalating alarmingly. It meant he was often prejudged, but so far he'd remained confident of his ability to overcome misperceptions.

Though he could already tell that Miss Pringy, of all people, looked as if she was going to be immune to his considerable charisma. He found himself feeling defensive again.

"I'm a businessman," he said shortly, "not a celebrity."

In fact, Joshua Cole disliked almost everything about his newly arising status, but the more he rejected media attention, the more the media hounded him. That article in *People to Watch* had been unauthorized and totally embarrassing.

World's Sexiest Bachelor was a ridiculous title. It perturbed him that the magazine had gotten so many pictures of him, when he felt he'd become quite deft at protecting his privacy.

Where had all those pictures of him with his shirt off come from? Or relaxing, for that matter? Both were rare events.

To look at those pictures, anyone would think he was younger than his thirty years, and also that he spent his days half naked in sand and sunshine, the wind, waves and sun streaking his dark hair to golden brown. The article had waxed poetic about his "buff" build and sea-green eyes. It was enough to make a grown man sick.

Joshua was learning being in the spotlight had a good side: free publicity for Sun for one. For another, the label *playboy* that was frequently attached to him meant he was rarely bothered by women who had apple-pie, picket-fence kind of dreams. No, his constantly shifting lineup of companions were happy with lifestyle-of-the-rich-and-famous outings and expensive trinkets; in other words, no *real* investment on his part.

The downside was that people like the mom-and-pop owners of Moose Lake Lodge weren't comfortable with his notoriety coming to their neck of the woods.

And sometimes, usually when he least expected it, he would be struck with a sensation of loneliness, as if no one truly knew him, though usually a phone call to his sister fixed that pretty quickly!

Maybe it was because the nanny represented his sister's household that he disliked being prejudged by her, that he felt strangely driven to try to make a good impression.

Just underneath that odd desire was an even odder one to know if she was evaluating him as the World's Sexiest Bachelor. If she was, she approved of the title even less than he did. In fact, she looked as if she might want to see the criteria that had won him the title!

Was it possible she didn't find him attractive? That she didn't agree with the magazine's assessment of his status? For a crazy moment he actually cared! He found himself feeling defensive again, saying in his head, *Miss Pringy wouldn't know sexy if it stepped on her.*

Or walked up to her and kissed her.

Which, unfortunately, made him look at her lips. They were pursed in a stern line, which he should have found off-putting. Not challenging! But the tightness around her lips only accentuated how full they were, puffy, *kissable*.

She reached up and touched the locket again, as if it was an amulet and he was a werewolf, as if she was totally aware of his inappropriate assessment of the kissability of her lips and needed to protect herself.

"I'm Danielle Springer, Dannie," the woman announced formally, the woman least likely to have her lips evaluated as kissable. She was still unfazed by the shrill cries of the baby. Again, he couldn't help but notice her voice was husky, as sensuous as a touch. Under different circumstances—very different circumstances—he was pretty sure he would have found it sexy.

At least as sexy as her damned disapproving lips.

"I was told you'd meet us at the plane."

"There seems to have been a mix-up," he said for the second time. "Not uncommon when my sister is involved."

"It's not easy to get children ready for a trip!" She was instantly defensive of her employer, which, under different circumstances, he would have found more admirable.

"That's why you're there to help, isn't it?" he asked mildly.

Her chin lifted and her eyes snapped. "Somehow I am unsurprised that you would think it was just about packing a bag and catching a flight."

She was obviously a woman of spirit, which he found intriguing, so he goaded her a bit. "Isn't it?"

"There's more to raising a child than attending to their physical needs," she said sharply. "And your sister knows that."

"Saint Melanie," he said dryly.

"Meaning?" she asked regally.

"I am constantly on the receiving end of lectures from my dear sister about the state of my emotional bankruptcy," he said pleasantly. "But despite my notoriously cavalier attitudes, I really did think you were arriving tomorrow. I'm sorry. I especially wouldn't want to hurt Susie."

Susie shot him a suspicious look, popped her thumb in her mouth and sucked. Hard.

Dannie juggled the baby from one arm to the other and gently removed Susie's thumb. He could suddenly see that despite the nanny's outward composure, the baby was heavy and Dannie was tired.

Was there slight forgiveness in her eyes, did the stern line around her mouth relax ever so slightly? He studied her and decided he was being optimistic.

He could read what was going to happen before it did, and he shot up from behind his desk, hoping Dannie would get the message and change course. Instead she moved behind the desk with easy confidence, right into his space, and held out the baby.

"Could you? Just for a moment? I think he's in need of a change. I'll just see if I can find his things in my bag."

For a moment, Joshua Cole, self-made billionaire, was completely frozen. He was stunned by the predicament he was in. Before he could brace himself or prepare himself properly in any way, he was holding a squirming, puttylike chunk of humanity.

Joshua shut his eyes against the warmth that crept through him as his eight-month-old nephew, Jake, settled into his arms.

A memory he thought he'd divorced himself from a long, long time ago returned with such force his throat closed.

Bereft.

"Don't worry. It's not what you think," Dannie said. Joshua opened his eyes and saw her looking at him quizzically. "He's just wet. Not, um, you know."

Joshua became aware of a large warm spot soaking through his silk tie and onto his pristine designer shirt. He was happy to let her think his reaction to holding the baby was caused by an incorrect assumption about what Jake was depositing on his shirt.

The baby, as stunned by finding himself in his uncle's arms as his uncle himself, was shocked into sudden blessed silence and regarded him with huge sapphire eyes.

The Buddha-like expression of contentment lasted for a blink. And then the baby frowned. Turned red. Strained. Made a terrifying grunting sound.

"What's wrong with him?" Joshua asked, appalled.

"I'm afraid now it is, um, you know."

If he didn't know, the sudden explosion of odor let the secret out.

"Amber," he called. The man who reacted to stress with aplomb, at least until this moment, said, "Amber, call 911."

Dannie Springer's delectable lips twitched. A twinkle lit the depths of those astonishing eyes. She struggled, lost, started to laugh. And if he hadn't needed 911 before, he did now.

For a time-suspended moment, looking into those amazing blue depths, listening to the brook-clear sound of her laughter, it was as if disaster was not unfolding around him. It was as if his office, last sanctuary of the single male, had not been invaded by the enemy that represented domestic bliss. He might have laughed himself, if he wasn't so close to gagging.

"Amber," he said, trying to regain his legendary control in this situation that seemed to be unraveling dismally, "forget 911."

Amber hovered in the doorway. "What would you like me to do?"

"The children haven't eaten," Miss Pringy said, as if she was in charge. "Do you think you could find us some lunch?"

How could anyone think of lunch at a time like this?

Or put Amber in charge of it? Even though Amber disappeared, Josh was fairly certain food was a question lost on her. As far as Joshua could see, his secretary survived on celery sticks.

Did babies eat celery sticks?

For a moment he felt amazed at how a few seconds could change a man's whole world. If somebody had told him when he walked into his office, he would be asking himself questions about babies and celery sticks before the morning was out, he would not have believed it.

He would particularly not have believed he would be contemplating celery sticks with that odor now permeating every luxurious corner of his office.

But he, of all people, should know. A few seconds could change everything, forever. A baby, wrapped in a blue hospital blanket, his face tiny and wrinkled, his brow furrowed, his tiny, perfect hand—

Stop! Joshua ordered himself.

And yet even as he resented memories of a long-ago hurt being triggered so easily by the babe nestled in his arms now, he was also aware of something else.

He felt surprised by life, for the first time in a very, very long time. He slid his visitor a glance and was painfully aware of how lushly she was curved, as if *she* ate more than celery sticks. In fact, he could picture her digging into spaghetti, eating with robust and unapologetic appetite. The picture was startlingly sensual.

"I'll just change the baby while we wait for lunch."

"In here?" he sputtered.

"Unless you have a designated area in the building?" she said, raising an eyebrow at him.

Joshua could clearly see she was the kind of woman you did not want to surrender control to. In no time flat, she would have the Lalique bowl moved and the change station set up where the bowl had been.

It was time to take control, not to be weakened by his memories but strengthened by them. It was time to put things back on track. The nanny and the children had arrived early. The thought of how his sister would have delighted in his current predicament firmed his resolve to get things to exactly where he had planned them, quickly.

"The washroom is down the hall," Joshua said, collecting himself as best he could with the putty baby trying to insert its pudgy fingers in his nose. "If you'd care to take the baby there, Miss Pringy—"

"Springer—" she reminded him. "Perhaps while I take care of this, you could do something about, er, that?"

A hand fluttered toward the Lalique. He knew it! She was eyeing the table for its diaper changing potential!

"It's art," he said stubbornly.

"Well, it's art the children aren't old enough for."

Precisely one of his many reservations about children. Everything had to be rearranged around them. Naturally, he needed to set her straight. It was his office, his business, his life. No one, but no one, told him how to run it. She and the children were departing as soon as he could arrange the limo and reschedule their reservations by a day.

But when she took the evilly aromatic baby back, after having fished a diaper out of a huge carpetbag she was traveling with, he was so grateful he decided not to set her straight about who the boss was. After she looked after the baby change, there would be plenty of time for that.

Dannie left the room, Susie on her heels. In a gesture

he was not going to consider surrender, Joshua went and retrieved his suit jacket from where it hung on the back of his chair, and gently and protectively draped it over the bowl.

"Thank you," the nanny said primly, noticing as soon as she came back in the room. A cloud of baby-fresh scent entered with her, and Jake was now gurgling joyously.

"Naked is not nice," Susie informed him.

"Well, that depends on—" A look from the nanny made him take a deep breath and change tack. "As soon as we've had some lunch, I'll see to changing the arrangements I've made for you. You'll love Whistler."

"Whistler?" Miss Pringy said. "Melanie never said anything about Whistler. She said we were staying with you."

"I'm not staying with him," Susie huffed. "He hates us. I can tell."

He wondered if he should show her all those little x and o notes, placed carefully in the top drawer of his desk. No, the nanny might see it as a vulnerability. And somehow, as intriguing—and exasperating—as he found her, he had no intention of appearing vulnerable in front of her.

"Don't worry," Joshua told Susie, firmly, "No one is staying with me, because I don't want—"

"Don't you dare finish that sentence," Miss Springer told him in a tight undertone. "Don't you dare."

Well, as if his life was not surprising enough today! He regarded her thoughtfully, tried to remember when the last time anyone had told him what to do was, and came up blank.

And that tone. No one ever dared use that tone on him. Probably not since grade school, anyway.

"Amber," he called.

She appeared at the doorway, looking mutinous, as if one more demand would finish her. "Lunch is on the way up."

"Take the children for a moment. Miss Pringy and I have a few things to say privately."

Amber stared at him astounded. "Take them where?"

"Just your office will do."

Her lips moved soundlessly, like a fish floundering, but then wordlessly she came in and took the baby, holding him out carefully at arm's length.

"You go, too," Miss Pringy said gently to Susie.

It was a mark of her influence on those children, that with one warning look shot at him, Susie traipsed out of the room behind Amber, shutting the door with unnecessary noisiness behind her.

"You weren't going to say you didn't want them in front of them, were you?" Miss Pringy asked, before the door was barely shut.

It bothered him that she knew precisely how he had planned to finish that sentence. It bothered him the way she was looking at him, her gaze solemn and stripping and seemingly becoming less awed by him by the second.

Much as he disliked his fledgling celebrity status, Joshua had to admit he was growing rather accustomed to awe. And admiration. Women *liked* him, and they had thousands of delightful ways of letting him know that.

But no, Miss Pringy looked, well, *disapproving*, again, but then she shook her hair. It was not the flirtatious flick of locks that he was used to, and yet he found himself captivated. He found himself thinking she was really a wild-spirited gypsy dancer disguised, and unpleasantly so, as a straitlaced nanny.

"Look," he said doggedly, "I've made arrangements for you to stay at a lovely resort in Whistler. They organize child activities all day long! Play-Doh sculpture. Movies. Nature walks. I just have to change everything up a day. You should be out of here and on your way in less than an hour."

"No," she said, and shook her hair again. Definitely not flirtatious. She was *aggravated*.

"No?" he repeated, stunned.

"That's not what Melanie told me, and she is, after all, my employer, not you."

Until the moment his sense of betrayal in his sister increased, Joshua had been pleasantly unaware he still harbored it.

His older sister had been with him in those exhilarating early days of the business, but then she'd broken the cardinal rule. It was okay to date the clients; it was not okay to fall head over heels in love with them!

Then she'd decided, after all these years of wholeheartedly endorsing the principles and mission of Sun, that she *wanted* kids.

That was okay. He felt as if he'd forgiven her even though over the past few years it felt as if he had been under siege by her, trying to make him see things her way. His sister had made it her mission to get him to see how great a relationship would be, how miraculous children were, how empty a life without commitment and a relationship and a family was.

She sent him e-mails and cell phone videos of Susie, singing a song, cuddling with her kitty, pirouetting at her ballet classes. Lately, Jake starred in the impromptu productions. The last one had shown him being particularly disgusting in his desperate attempts to hit his own mouth with a steadily deteriorating piece of chocolate cake gripped in his pudgy hands.

Mel's husband, Ryan, a busy and successful building

contractor, a man among men, fearless and macho, was often in the back ground looking practically teary-eyed with pride over the giftedness of his progeny.

For the most part, Joshua had managed to resist his sister's efforts to involve him in her idea of a perfect life. Was the arrival of her children some new twist in her never-ending plot to convince him the life he'd chosen for himself was a sad and lonely place compared to the life she had chosen for herself?

"Why did you invite the children here just to send them away?" Dannie demanded.

"Play-Doh sculpture is nothing to be scoffed at," he insisted.

"We could have done that at home."

"Then why did you come?"

"Melanie had this idea that you were going to spend some time with them."

Joshua snorted.

"She was so delighted that they were going to get to know you better."

"I don't see why," he said.

"Frankly, neither do I!" She sank down on the couch, and he suddenly could see how tired she was. "What a mess. Melanie said I could trust you with the lives of her children. But you couldn't even make it to the airport!"

"She gave me the wrong day!"

"Nothing is more important to your sister than the well-being of Susie and Jake. Surely she couldn't have made a mistake?" This last was said quietly, as if she was thinking out loud.

Joshua Cole heard the doubt in her voice, and he really didn't know whether to be delighted by it or insulted.

"A mistake?" he said smoothly. "Of course not. I said I'd make arrangements for you and the children's accommodations immediately."

Rather than looking properly appreciative, Miss Pringy was getting that formidable look on her face again.

"Mr. Cole," she said sternly, "I'm afraid that won't do."

Joshua Cole lived in a world where he called the shots. "Won't do?" he repeated, incredulous.

"No," she said firmly. "Packing the children off to a hotel in Whistler will not do. That's no kind of a vacation for a child or a baby."

"Well, what is a vacation for them?" he asked. Inwardly he thought, *anything*. If she wanted tickets to Disneyworld, he'd get them. If they wanted to meet a pop star, he'd arrange it. If they wanted to swim with dolphins, he'd find out how to make that happen. No cost was too high, no effort too great.

"They just want to be around people who love them," she said softly. "In a place where they feel safe and cared about. That is what Melanie thought they were coming to or she would never have sent them."

Or gone herself, he thought, and suddenly, unwillingly, he remembered his sister's tired face. No cost was too high? How about the cost of putting himself out?

Had he led Melanie to believe he was finally going to spend some quality time with her kids? He didn't think so. She hadn't really asked for details, and he hadn't provided any. He wasn't responsible for her assumptions.

But Joshua was suddenly very aware that a man could be one of the world's most successful entrepreneurs, moving in a world of power and wealth, controlling an empire, but still feel like a kid around his older sister, still *want* her approval in some secret part of himself.

Or maybe what he wanted was to be worthy of her trust. Something in him whispered, *Be the better man.*

Out loud he heard himself saying, without one ounce of enthusiasm, "I guess they could come stay with me."

Danielle Springer looked, understandably, skeptical of his commitment.

Too late he realized the full ramifications of his invitation.

Miss Pringy, the formidable nanny with the sensual lips and mysterious eyes would be coming to stay with him, too.

And if that wasn't bad enough, he was opening himself up to a world that might have been his, had he hung on instead of letting go of a different baby boy in a lifetime he had left behind himself.

His son.

He wanted to be a better man, worthy of his sister's trust, but who was he kidding? He'd lost faith in himself, in his ability to do the right thing, a long time ago. His sister didn't even know about the college pregnancy of his girlfriend.

He found himself holding his breath, hoping Dannie Springer would not be foolish enough to say yes to his impulsive invitation, wishing he could take it back, before it drew him into places he did not want to go.

"Obviously, we have to stay somewhere for now," she said, her enthusiasm, or lack thereof, matching his exactly. "I'm not subjecting the children to any more travel or uncertainty today."

But his whole world suddenly had a quality of the

uncertain about it. And Joshua Cole did not like it when things in his well-ordered world shifted out of his control. He didn't like it one little bit.

CHAPTER TWO

DANNIE sat in the back seat of the cab, fuming. *The next time I see Melanie, I'm going to kill her,* she decided.

Thinking such a thought felt like a terrible defeat for a woman who prided herself on her steady nature and unflappable calm, at least professionally. To think it toward Melanie showed how truly rattled Dannie was. Melanie, in just a few short months, had become so much more than an employer.

But the truth was that a steady nature was not any kind of defense against a man like Joshua Cole. He was a complete masculine, sexy package, with that brilliant smile, the jade of those eyes, the perfect masculine cut of his facial features, the way he carried himself, the exquisitely expensive clothing over the sleek muscle of a toned body. All of it put together would have been enough to rattle Mother Theresa!

Dannie had known Melanie's brother was attractive. She had seen two pictures of him in the Maynards' home. Not that those pictures could have prepared her for Joshua Cole in the flesh.

Melanie's two framed photos showed her brother through the lens of an ordinary family. Nothing extraordinary about Joshua at twelve, on the beach, scrawny, white, not even a hint of the man he would become. In fact, whatever had been behind that impish grin seemed to be gone from him entirely.

The other picture showed Joshua in a college football uniform, posed, looking annoyingly cocky and confident, again some mischief in him that now seemed to be gone. Though he was undeniably good-looking, that photo showed only a glimmer of the self-possessed man he now was.

"He never finished college," Melanie had said, with a hint of sadness, when she had seen Dannie looking at that picture. For some reason Dannie had assumed that sadness was for her brother's lost potential.

Melanie had seemed to see Joshua as the exasperating kid brother who was an expert at thwarting her every effort to interfere in his life with her wise and well-meaning sisterly guidance. From Melanie's infrequent mentions of her brother, Dannie had thought he managed a hotel or a travel agency, not that he was the president and CEO of one of the world's most up-and-coming companies!

So, the article in *People to Watch* had been a shocker. First, the photos had come a little closer to capturing the pure animal magnetism of the man. The little-boy mischief captured in his sister's snapshots was gone from those amazing smoky-jade eyes, replaced with an intensity that was decidedly sensual.

That sensuality was underscored in the revealing photos of him: muscled, masculine, at ease with his body, oozing a self-certainty that few men would ever master.

Melanie had certainly never indicated her brother was a candidate for the World's Sexiest Bachelor, though his unmarried status seemed to grate on her continually.

Again, the magazine portrayal seemed to be more

accurate than the casual remarks Melanie had tossed out about him. The magazine described him as powerful, engaging and lethally charming. And that was just personally. Professionally he was described as driven. The timing of the openings of his adventure-based adult-only resorts was seen as brilliant.

In the article, his name had also been paired with some of the world's wealthiest and most beautiful women, including actress Monique Belliveau, singer Carla Kensington and heiress Stephanie Winger-Stone.

By the time he'd stood them up at the airport, Danielle Springer, the steady one, had already been feeling nervous about meeting Joshua Cole, World's Sexiest Bachelor, and had developed a feeling of dislike for him, just *knowing* he would exude all the superficial charm and arrogance of a man who had the world at his feet. He would move through life effortlessly, piling up successes, traveling the globe, causing heartbreaks but never suffering them.

She had already known, before the plane landed, that Melanie had made a terrible mistake in judgment sending them all here. That knowledge had only been underscored by the fact the Great One had not put in an appearance at the airport, and she had not been able to penetrate the golden walls that protected him from the annoyances of real life.

Which begged the question: Why *hadn't* she jumped at the opportunity to go to Whistler when he had offered it? It was more than the fact small children and hotels rarely made a good combination, no matter how "child-friendly" they claimed to be.

It was more than the fact that the children were exhausted and so was she, not a good time to be making decisions!

It was that something about him had been unexpected.

He had not been all arrogance and charm. Something ran deeper in him. She had seen it in that unguarded moment when she had thrust Jake upon him, something in his face that said his life had not been without heart-break, after all.

Stop it, she told herself sternly. They would spend the evening with him. Tomorrow, rested, she would regroup and decide what to do next. The original plan no longer seemed feasible. Spend a week with him? Good grief!

What she was not going to do was call Melanie and Ryan, who needed this time together desperately. At a whisper of trouble, Melanie would come home.

Still, could it really be in the best interests of the children to spend time with their uncle? He'd made it clear he was uncomfortable with children. In fact, his success was based on the creation of a child-free world! There was no sense seeing anything noble in his sudden whim to play the hero and spend time with the niece and nephew he'd invited here in the first place.

And how about herself? How much time could any woman with blood flowing through her veins spend with a man like that without succumbing?

Not, she reminded herself sourly, that there would be anything to *succumb* to. He was rich and powerful and definitely lethally charming. There had been no pictures in the article of him accompanied by women like her.

Women like her: unprocessed, unsophisticated, slightly plump.

She touched the locket on her neck and felt the ache. Only a few weeks ago, the locket would have protected her. *Taken.*

Brent had given it to her before leaving for Europe. "A promise," he'd said, "I will return to you."

Perhaps it would be better to take the locket off, now
that it represented a promise broken. On the other hand
perhaps it protected her still, reminding her of the fick-
leness of the human heart, and especially of the fickle-
ness of the *male* human heart.

And besides, she wasn't ready to take it off. She still
looked at the photo inside it each night and felt the ache
of loss and the stirring of hope that he would realize he
had made a mistake....

Though all along maybe the worst mistake had been
hers. Believing in what she felt for Brent, even after
what she had grown up with. Her own parents' split up
had been venomous, their passion had metamorphosed
into full-blown hatred that was destructive to all it had
touched, including their children. Maybe especially
their children.

Thank God, Dannie thought, for the Maynards, for
Melanie and Ryan, for Susie and Jake. Thank God she
had already been welcomed into the fold of their household when this hurricane of heartbreak had hit her. She
would survive because they gave her a sense of family
and of belonging, a safe place to fall when her world
had fallen apart.

Bonus: loving them didn't involve one little bit of risk!

Though since Brent's call from London, "I'm so
sorry, there's someone else," now when Dannie saw the
way that Melanie and Ryan looked at each other, she
felt a startling stab of envy.

"Hey, lady, are we going somewhere, or are we just
sitting here?" the cabbie asked her, waiting for her instructions, impatient.

"When you see the horrible yellow car, follow it,"
Dannie said. Delivering the variation on the line
"Follow that car" gave her absolutely no pleasure.

"A yellow car?" he said, bemused. "Do you think you could be a little more specific?"

Dannie looked over her shoulder. "It's coming now."

The cabbie whistled. "Okay, lady, though in what world a Lamborghini is horrible, I'm not sure."

"Totally unsuited for children's car seats," she informed him. The horrible yellow car, with its horrible gorgeous driver passed them slowly.

A man like that could make a woman rip a locket right off her neck!

She snorted to herself. A man like that could cause a heart to break just by being in the same room, a single glance, green eyes lingering a touch too long on her lips... Joshua's eyes were probably always making promises he had no intention of keeping.

Unattainable to mere mortals, she reminded herself with a sniff. Not that she was a mortal in the market! Done. Brent had finished her. She had given love a chance, nurtured her hopes and dreams over the year he'd been away, *lived* for his cards and notes and e-mails and been betrayed for all her trouble.

Terrible how that vow of being *done* could be rattled so easily by one lingering look from Joshua Cole! How could his gaze have made her wish, after her terrible Brent breakup, that she had not made herself over quite so completely? Gone was the makeup, the fussing over the hair, the colorful wardrobe. On was about fifteen pounds, the result of intensive chocolate therapy!

She was *done,* intent on making herself invisible and therefore safe. How could she possibly feel as if Joshua Cole had *seen* her in a way Brent, whom she had pulled out all the makeover tricks for, never had?

The sports car was so low, she could look in the window and see Jake, his brand-new car seat strapped in securely, facing backward, his black hair standing straight up like dark dandelion fluff.

She refused to soften her view of Joshua Cole because he had insisted on the car seat to get the baby home. Once you softened your view of a man who was lethally charming, you were finished. That's what *lethally* meant.

Besides, there hadn't been enough room in that ridiculous car to put her and Susie to ride with him.

A car like that said a lot about a man. Fast and flashy. Self-centered. Single and planning to stay that way.

Since she was also single and very much planning to stay that way *for the rest of her life, a poor spinster nanny in the basement room*, it was probably unfair to see that as a flaw in him.

Except the car meant he was a *hunter,* on the prowl. Didn't it?

"What does a car like that mean to you?" she asked the cab driver, just in case she had it wrong.

"That you can have any girl you want," he muttered. *Bingo.*

"If he opens her up, I'm not going to be able to keep up with him," the cabbie warned.

"If he opens her up, I'm going to kill him," she said. "He has a baby in there." *My baby.* Of course, Jake was not officially her baby. Unofficially he had won her heart and soul from the first gurgle. Now, post-Brent, she had decided Jake might be the only baby she ever had.

Emotion could capsize her unexpectedly since Brent had hit her with his announcement, and she felt it claw at her throat now, defended against it by telling herself that sweet little baby boy was probably going to be lethally charming someday, just like his uncle.

Twice, in the space of five minutes, steady, dependable Dannie had thought of killing people.

That's what heartbreak did: turned normal, reliable people into bitter survivors, turned them into what they least wanted to be. In fact, it seemed to her, her recent tragedy had the potential to turn her into her parents, who had spent their entire married lives trying to kill each other.

Figuratively. Mostly.

"You shouldn't say you're going to kill people," Susie told her, a confirmation of what Dannie already knew. Susie was hugging the new teddy bear that had arrived in her uncle's office along with the car seat. The teddy bear did not seem to have softened the child's view of her uncle at all.

In Susie's view, Uncle Josh was the villain who had torn her mother away from her. A teddy bear was not going to fix that.

A lesson Uncle Josh no doubt needed to learn! You could not buy back affection.

The car seat and the teddy bear had arrived within minutes of a quiet phone call. Dannie had heard him giving instructions to have a baby crib set up at his apartment. In the guest room with the Jacuzzi. Which begged the question not only how many guest rooms were there, but why did you need a guest room with a Jacuzzi?

Obviously, for the same reason you needed a car like that. Entertaining.

Still, she had gotten the message. He spoke; people jumped.

And he'd better not even think of trying that with her! She might have been the kind of person who jumped before Brent's betrayal. She was no longer!

They arrived at a condominium complex not far from his office building, and Dannie tried very hard not to be awed, even though a guest room with a Jacuzzi should have given her ample time to prepare herself for something spectacular.

She was awed, anyway. Even though Melanie and Ryan certainly had no financial difficulties, she knew she was now moving in an entirely different league.

The high-rise building appeared to be constructed of white marble, glass and water. The landscaping in front of the main door was exquisite: lush grass, exotic flowers, a black onyx fountain shooting up pillars of gurgling foam.

She was fumbling with her wallet when Joshua appeared at the driver's window, baby already on his hip, and paid the driver. He juggled the baby so he could open the door for her. There was no sense noticing his growing comfort with the baby!

Instead, she focused on the fact that if the great Joshua Cole was aware he had parked the horrible yellow thing in a clearly marked no-parking zone, it didn't concern him.

But she'd do well to remember that: rules were for others.

A doorman came out of the building to move the car almost instantly. Another unloaded her luggage from the trunk of the cab.

Joshua greeted both men by name, with a sincere warmth that surprised her. And then he was leading her through a lobby that reminded her of the one and only five-star hotel she had ever stayed at. The lobby had soaring ceilings, deep carpets over marble tile, distressed leather furniture.

For all that, why did it feel as if the most beautiful

thing in the room was that self-assured man carrying a baby, his strength easy, his manner unforced?

Few men, in Dannie's experience, were really comfortable with children. Brent had claimed to like them, but she had noticed he had that condescending, overly enthusiastic way of being around them that children *hated*.

She hoped it was a sign of healing that she had remembered this flaw in her perfect man!

It was a strange irony that, while Joshua Cole had not made any claims about liking children and in fact radiated unapologetic discomfort around them, he was carrying that baby on his hip as if it was the most natural thing in the world to be doing.

Joshua chose that moment to glance down at the bundle in his arms. She caught his look of unguarded tenderness and felt her throat close. Had she just caught a glimpse of something so real about him that it made her question every other judgment she had made?

What if the World's Sexiest Bachelor was a lie? What if the sports car and clothes and office were just a role he'd assumed? What if he was really a man who had been born to be a daddy?

Danger zone, she told herself. What was wrong with her? She had just been terribly disappointed by one man! Why would she be reading such qualities into another that she barely knew?

Besides, there was no doubt exactly why men like Joshua Cole were so successful with women. They had charm down to a science.

It made it so easy to place them in the center of a fantasy, it was so easy to give them a starring role in a dream that she had to convince herself she did not believe in anymore.

Enough of fantasies, she told herself. She had spent the entire year Brent was away building a fantasy around his stupid cards and e-mails, reading into them growing love, when in fact his love had been diminishing. She was a woman pathetic enough to have spent her entire meager savings on a wedding dress on the basis of a vague promise.

Joshua went to a door off the bank of elevators and inserted a key.

The door glided open, and Dannie tried not to gawk at the unbelievable decadence of a private glass elevator. How was a girl supposed to give up on fantasy in a world where fantasy became reality?

The glass-encased elevator eased silently upward, and even Susie forgot to be mad at her uncle and squealed with delight as they glided smoothly higher and higher, the view becoming more panoramic by the second.

The problem with elevators, especially for a woman trying desperately to regain control of suddenly undisciplined thoughts, of her *fantasies,* was that everything was too close in them. She could smell the tantalizing aroma of Joshua, expensive cologne, mixed with soap. His shoulder, enormously broad under the exquisite tailoring of his suit jacket, brushed hers as he turned to let the baby see the view, and she felt a shiver of animal awareness so strong that it shook her to the core.

The reality of being in this elevator with a *real* man made her aware that for a year Brent had not been real at all, but a faraway dream that she could make into anything she wanted him to be.

Had she ever been this aware of Brent? So aware that his scent, the merest brush of his shoulder, could make her dizzy?

She forced her attention to the view, all too aware it had

nothing to do with the rapid beating of her heart. She could see the deep navy blue of an ocean bay. It was dotted with sailboats. Wet-suited sailboarders danced with the white capped waves. Outside of the bay a cruise ship slid by.

All she could think was that she had made a terrible mistake insisting on coming here with him. She touched her locket. *Its* powers to protect seemed measly and inadequate.

To be so *aware* of another human being, even in light of her recent romantic catastrophe, was terrible. To add to how terrible it was, she knew he would not be that aware of her. Since the breakup call, she had stripped herself of makeup, put away her wardrobe of decent clothes, determined to be invisible, to find the comfort of anonymity in her role as the nanny.

The elevator stopped, the doors slid open, and Dannie turned away from the view to enter directly into an apartment. To her left, floor-to-ceiling glass doors that spanned the entire length of the apartment were open to a terraced deck. Exotic flowering plants surrounded dark rattan furniture, the deep cushions upholstered in shades of lime and white. White curtains, so transparent they could only be silk, waved gracefully in the slightly salt-scented breeze.

Inside were long, sleek ultramodern white leather sofas, casually draped with sheepskins. They formed a conversation area around a fireplace framed in stainless steel, the hearth beaded in copper-colored glass tile. The themes of leather, glass and steel repeated themselves, the eye moving naturally from the conversation area to a bar that separated the living area from a kitchen.

The kitchen was magazine-layout perfect, black cabinets and granite countertops, more stainless steel, more copper-colored glass tiles. A wine cooler, state-of-the-art appliances, everything subtle and sexy.

"Don't tell me you cook," she said, the statement coming out more pleading than she wanted.

He laughed. "Does opening wine count?"

Oh, it counted, right up there with the car and the Jacuzzi, as a big strike against him.

Thankfully, it really confirmed what she already knew. She was way out of her league, but vulnerable, too. And the apartment gave her the perfect excuse.

Was he watching her to see her reaction?

"Obviously," she said tightly, "we can't stay here. I'm sorry. I should never have insisted. If you can book us a flight, I need to take the children home."

But the very thought made her want to cry. She told herself it wasn't because his apartment was like something out of a dream, that it called to the part of her that wanted, dearly, to be pampered, that wanted, despite her every effort, to embrace fantasy instead of reject it.

No. She was tired. The children were tired. She couldn't put them all back on a plane today. Maybe tomorrow.

"A motel for tonight," she said wearily. "Tomorrow we can go home."

"What's wrong?"

Everything suddenly seemed wrong. Her whole damned life. She had never wanted anything like the elegance of this apartment, but only because it was beyond the humble dreams she had nurtured for Brent's and her future.

So why did it feel so terrible, a yawning emptiness that could never be filled, that she realized she could never have this? Or a man like him? She hadn't even been able to hold the interest of Brent, pudgy, owlish, *safe*.

Joshua Cole had the baby stuffed under his arm like a football, and was looking at her with what could very easily be mistaken for genuine concern by the hopelessly naive. At least she could thank Brent for that. She wasn't. Hopelessly naive. Anymore.

"Obviously, I can't stay here with the children. They could wreck a place like this in about twenty minutes." The fantasy was about being pampered, enjoying these lush surroundings; the reality was the children wrecking the place and her being frazzled, trying to keep everything in order.

Reality. Fantasy. As long as she could keep the two straight, she should be able to survive this awkward situation.

"That's ridiculous," he said, but uncertainly.

"Dic-u-lous," Susie agreed, her eyes lighting on a pure crystal sculpture of a dolphin in the center of the coffee table.

Dannie took a tighter hold on Susie's hand as the child tried to squirm free. She could already imagine little jam-covered fingerprints on the drapes, crayon marks on the sofas, wine being pulled out of the cooler.

"No," she said. "It's obvious you aren't set up for children. I'd have a nervous breakdown trying to guard all your possessions."

"They're just possessions," he said softly.

Of course he didn't mean that. She'd already seen what he drove. She'd seen him eyeing that bowl in his office with grave concern every time Susie had even glanced in its direction. It was time to call him on it.

"You're less attached to all this than the bowl in your office?" She congratulated herself on just the right tone of disbelief.

"I can move anything that is that breakable."

"Start with the wine," she said, just to give him an idea how big a job it was.

"The cooler locks. I'll do it now." As he moved across the room, he said over his shoulder, "I'll send for some toys as a distraction."

She had to pull herself together. She had to make the best decision for the children. The thought of moving them again, of cooping them up in a hotel room for the night suddenly seemed nearly unbearable.

They would stay here the night. One night. Rested, she would make good decisions tomorrow. Rested, she would be less susceptible to the temptations of his beautiful world. And his drop-dead-gorgeous eyes. And the brilliant wattage of his smile.

Which was directed at her right now. "What kind of toys should I get?" he asked her. He came over and gave her the key to the wine cooler, folded her hand around it.

She desperately wished he had not done that. His touch, warm and strong, filled with confidence, made her more confused about reality and fantasy. How could a simple touch make her feel as if she'd received an electric jolt from fingertip to elbow?

She'd given him an out, but he wasn't taking it. She could see he was the kind of man who made up his mind and then was not swayed.

There was no point in seeing that as admirable. It was mule-stubbornness, nothing more.

"What toys?" he asked her again. He was smiling wickedly, as if he knew the touch of his hand had affected her.

Of course he knew! He radiated the conceited confidence of a man who had played this game with many women. Played. That's why they called them playboys. It was all just a game to him.

"Princess Tasonja!" Susie crowed her toy suggestion. "And the camping play set. I have to have the tent and the backpack. And the dog, Royal Robert." Seeing her uncle look amenable, she added a piece she coveted from a totally different play set. "And the royal wedding carriage. Don't get Jake anything. He's a baby."

He took his cell phone out of his pocket and tried to dial with his thumb while still holding the baby. Apparently, he was going to have someone round up all the toys his niece had demanded.

"I wouldn't bother with Princess Tasonja, if I were you," Dannie managed, in a clipped undertone as Susie slipped free of her hand and skipped over to the sofa where she buried her face in a copper-colored silk pillow. Dannie was pretty sure the remnants of lunch were on that face.

"Why not?"

Why bother telling him that Susie's attention would be held by the Princess Tasonja doll and her entire entourage for about thirty seconds? Why not let him find out on his own that attempts to buy children's affection usually ended miserably? Susie would become a monster of demands once the first one was met.

That was a lesson he probably needed to learn about the car, too. Any woman who would be impressed with such a childish display of wealth was probably not worth knowing.

Her own awed reaction to this apartment probably spoke volumes about her own lack of character!

"I suspect you think it's going to keep her occupied— Susie do not touch the dolphin. But it won't. Unless you are interested in playing princess doll dress up with her, the appeal will be strictly limited."

He clicked the cell phone shut. "What do I do with her if I don't buy her toys?" he asked.

"You are a sad man," she blurted out, and then blushed at her own audacity.

"I don't do kids well. That doesn't make me *sad*." He regarded her thoughtfully and for way too long.

Swooning length.

"You don't just work for my sister," he guessed. "You hang out with her, sharing ideas. Scary. I'm surprised she doesn't have you married off ." He looked suddenly suspicious. "Unless that's why you're here."

"Excuse me?"

"My sister has been on this 'decent girl' kick for a while. She better not be matchmaking."

"Me?" Dannie squeaked. "You?" But suddenly she had a rather sickening memory of Melanie looking at her so sadly as she'd dealt with her news about Brent, as if everyone had expected it *except* her.

Joshua's look grew very dark. "Do you have a boyfriend?"

"Not at the moment," she said coolly, as if she'd had dozens of them, when she'd had only one serious relationship, and the greatest part of that had been by long distance. "But you needn't worry, Mr. Cole. Your sister would know me well enough to know that you are not my type!"

He had the nerve to look offended, as if he just naturally assumed he was every woman's type, the title of World's Sexiest Bachelor obviously having gone straight to his handsome head. "Really? And what is your type?"

She could feel heat staining her cheeks to a color she just knew would be the most unflattering shade of red ever. "Not you!"

"That isn't really an answer."

"Studious, serious about life, not necessarily a sharp

dresser, certainly not materialistic." She was speaking too fast, and in her panic describing a man she knew was less than ideal to a T.

"Priests aren't generally available," he said dryly.

"I meant someone like a college professor." Which was what Brent had been. Rumpled. Academic. Faintly pre-occupied all the time. Which she had thought was adorable!

"Your ideal man is a college professor?"

"Yes!" How dare he say it with such scorn?

"Miss Dannie Springer, don't ever take up poker. You can't lie. You're terrible at it."

"As it happens, I don't like poker, and neither does my ideal man." With whom her whole relationship, in retrospect, had been a lie, concocted entirely by her, sitting at home by herself making up a man who had never existed.

"The college professor," he said dryly.

"Yes! Now, if you'll entertain Susie for a bit, it's time for Jake to have a bath." Of course, it wasn't anywhere near time Jake had a bath, but she had to get out of this room and this conversation. She doubted Mr. Playboy of the World knew anything about baby bath times. Or college professors for that matter! But he seemed to know just a little too much about women, and his look was piercing.

"Entertain Susie?" he said, distracted just as she had hoped. "How? Since you've nixed Princess Tasonja."

"Try noughts and crosses."

He frowned. "Like those notes she used to give me? Before she hated me? That were covered with x's and o's that meant hugs and kisses?"

Dannie steeled herself. He was not *really* distressed that he had fallen into his niece's disfavor. His world was way too big that he could be brought down by the little things.

"Noughts and crosses," she said. "Tic-tac-toe."

He looked baffled, underscoring how very far apart their worlds were, and always would be.

"Get a piece of paper and a pencil, Susie will be happy to show you how it works," she said.

"You mean a piece of paper and a pencil will keep her as entertained as the princess?"

"More."

"Do I let her win?" he asked in a whisper. He shot his niece a worried look.

"Would that be honest?"

"For God's sake, I'm not interested in honest."

"I'm sure truer words were never spoken," she said meanly, getting back at him for being so scornful of her college professor.

"I'm interested in not making a little girl cry."

"It's about spending time with her. That's the important part. Not winning or losing."

"I have a lot to learn."

"Yes, you do, Mr. Cole," she said, aware of a snippy little edge to her voice.

"You have a lot to learn, too," he said, quietly, looking at her with an unsettling intensity that she would have done anything to escape.

"Such as?" she said, holding her ground even though she wanted to bolt.

"The college professor. Not for you."

"How would you know?"

"I'm an astute judge of people."

"You aren't! You didn't even know whether or not to be honest playing noughts and crosses."

"Not miniature people, the under-five set. But you,

I know something about you. I wonder if you even know it yourself."

"You know nothing about me that I don't know about myself!" she said recklessly. To her detriment, part of her wanted to hear what he had to say. How often, after all, did an invisible nanny get to hear love advice from the World's Sexiest Bachelor?

But he didn't say a word, just proved exactly why he was the World's Sexiest Bachelor. He lifted her chin with the tip of his finger and looked deep into her eyes. Then he touched her lip with his thumb.

If it was possible to melt she would have. She felt like chocolate exposed to flame. She felt every single lie she had ever told herself about Brent. Dannie yanked away from him, but he nodded, satisfied that he did know something she didn't know herself.

Except now she had an idea.

That she was as weak as every other damn woman he'd ever met. Not that he ever had to know that!

"You're in the bedroom at the end of the hall," he said, as if he hadn't shaken her right to the core. "I had the crib set up in there. Is that okay?"

"Perfect," she said tightly, and she meant it. A pint-size chaperone for weaklings, not that she needed to worry about this man sneaking into her room in the dead of night. That was fantasy.

Of the X-rated variety, and she didn't mean tic-tac-toe, either.

"Hey, Susie," he said turning from her, after one last look that seemed more troubled than triumphant, "do you want to play noughts and crosses?"

Susie glared at him, clearly torn between personal dislike and the temptation of her favorite game. "All right," she said grudgingly.

Danielle marched down the hall with the baby. The room at the end had the same spectacular views and windows as the rest of the apartment.

The decorating was so romantic it was decadent, the whole room done in shades of brown, except for the bed linens that were seductively and lushly cream colored, inviting in that sea of rich dark chocolate.

Her suitcases were on the bed. How that had happened she wasn't quite sure. A crib had been set up for Jake, too.

Through a closed door was a bathroom, with the Jacuzzi.

A jetted tub built for two.

"We have to get out of here," she confided in the baby as she took his plump, dimpled limbs out of his clothes. The fact that Joshua thought his sister might be matchmaking—and that she could not say with one hundred per cent certainty that Melanie was not—just added an element of humiliation to the urgency she felt to go.

Was Melanie matchmaking? She frowned, thinking back over her conversations with her employer. As eager as Mel was to have everyone in the world enjoy the same state of wedded bliss she lived in, she had always been reserved about Brent.

Dannie assumed because she had never met him.

She had assumed Mel's eagerness to have her join her children with their uncle had only been her effort to help her nanny over her heartbreak, to give her a change of scenery. A hidden agenda? Wouldn't that be humiliating?

But Mel had never alluded, even subtly, to the possibility she considered her nanny and her brother to be anything of a match.

Because we so obviously are not, Dannie thought, and detected just a trace of sulkiness in that conclusion.

As always, the baby worked his magic on her sour mood, her tendency toward dour introspection. Dannie put about two inches of water in the gigantic tub, and Jake surrendered his little naked self gleefully into the watery playpen.

When the baby began to laugh out loud, she was drawn in, and she laughed back, splashing his little round tummy with warm water until he was nearly hysterical with joy.

"Do I take myself and life way too seriously, Mr. Jake?"

What if Mel *had* sent her here with some kind of hidden agenda? So what? What if she just played along?

"Oh, Dannie," she chided herself, "that would be like playing patty-cake with a powder keg."

Jake recognized the term, cooperatively held out his hands and crowed.

Relax, she ordered herself. *If you still know how,* and then sadly, *if you ever knew how.*

CHAPTER THREE

"PATTY cake, patty cake, baker's man, bake me a cake as fast as you can."

Dannie's voice and her laughter, intermingled with happy shouts from the baby and splashing noises, floated down the hallway to where Joshua sat opposite Susie on the couch.

Who would have imagined the serious, rather uptight nanny could sound like that? So intriguingly carefree?

Not that that was the truth about her. No, the truth was what he had *felt* when he had touched her lip—

"Tic, tac, toe," Susie cried and drew a triumphant line though her row of crosses.

Susie was trouncing him at noughts and crosses.

Something unexpected was happening to him. Given that his carefully executed schedule had gone out the window, he felt unexpectedly relaxed, as if a tightly wound coil inside of him was unwinding. Watching his niece, whose tongue was caught between her teeth in fierce concentration, listening to Dannie and the baby, he felt a *feeling* unfurling inside him.

It couldn't possibly be yearning.

He had the life every man worked toward, success beyond his wildest dreams, the great car, the fabulous apartment, gorgeous women as abundant in his life as apples on a tree. Just as ready to be picked, too.

And yet all of that paled in comparison to a baby's laughter and a little girl playing noughts and crosses. All that paled in comparison to the softness of a woman's lip beneath his thumb.

His sister, diabolical schemer that she was, would be thrilled by this turn of events.

What had he been thinking when he had touched Dannie's lip? When he had said to her with such ridiculous confidence, "I know something about you. I wonder if you even know it yourself."

The truth was he hadn't been thinking at all. Thinking belonged to that other world: of deals, successes, planning. That other world of accumulating more and more of the stuff.

The stuff that had failed to make him feel as full as he felt in this moment.

No, the truth was that thought had abandoned him when he touched her. Something deeper had temporarily possessed him.

He had seen her, not through his mind, but with his heart. He had seen her and *felt* the lie she had told him about the college professor. How could she even kid herself that she would ever be happy with a staid life?

From the second she had appeared in his office, she had presented the perfect picture of a nanny. Calm, controlled, prissy.

And from the beginning, he had seen something else. A gypsy soul, wanting to dance. That is what he knew about her that she did not know about herself.

That the right man—and probably not a college professor—was going to make her wild. Would make her toss out everything she thought she believed about herself. Under that costume of respectability she wore beat the drum of passion.

Stop, he told himself. *What is wrong with me?*

"I win," Susie said, carefully checking the placement of her crosses. "Again. You're dumb."

He stared at her, and then started to laugh. Yesterday he would have disagreed, probably argued, but today, since he had done one extremely dumb thing after another, starting with inviting them here, and ending with touching Dannie Springer's most delectable lip, he knew Susie was right.

"Let this be a lesson to you," he said. "Don't drop out of school."

"I don't even go to school yet," Susie informed him. "But when I do, I will love it. I will never ever stop going. I will go to school until I am one hundred."

That was precisely how he had felt about college. From the first day, he'd had a sense of arrival. This was where he belonged. He loved learning things. He loved playing football. He loved the girls, the parties, all of it.

And then, in his senior year, along came Sarah. They were "the" couple on campus. The cool ones. The ones everyone wanted to be. She played queen to his king. Looking back, something he rarely did, what they had called love seemed ridiculously superficial.

And in the end it had been. It had not stood up to the test life had thrown at it. Despite the fact they had taken every precaution, Sarah was pregnant.

Funny how, when he'd found out, he'd felt a rush, not of fear, but of excitement. He'd been willing to do whatever it took to give his baby a family, a good life.

Sarah had been stunned by his enthusiasm. "I'm not keeping it."

To this day, he could feel the bitterness, a force so real and so strong, he could nearly taste it on his tongue, when he remembered those words and the look on her face when she'd said them. "It."

He'd actually, briefly and desperately, considered keeping the baby himself. But reality had set in, and reluctantly he had gone along with Sarah. He'd stuck with her through the pregnancy and the birth.

It was a boy.

And then he'd made the mistake.

He'd held his son in his arms. He had felt the incredible surge of love and protectiveness. He had felt that moment of connection so intense that it seemed nothing else in his life but that moment had ever mattered.

He had known, *I was born to do this.*

But it was too late. He'd held his baby, his son, his light, for about five minutes. And then he'd let go. He had not met the adoptive parents.

Every other reality had faded after that. Nothing mattered to him, not school, not life, not anything at all. His grief was real and debilitating.

Sarah, on the other hand, had chosen not to see the baby, and she moved on eagerly, as if nothing had happened. He was part of what she left behind, but really, he had continued with her throughout the pregnancy out of a sense of honor and decency. But he had never forgiven her the "it."

He dropped out of college a month before he was supposed to graduate, packed a backpack, bought a ticket to anywhere. He'd traveled. Over time, he had come to dislike going to places with children. The sound of their laughter, their energy, reminded him of what he was supposed to be and was not.

When he'd come across Sarah's obituary a few years ago, killed in a ski accident in Switzerland, he had taken his lack of emotion as a sign he'd been a man unworthy of raising that child, anyway.

"Are you all right?"

He hadn't seen her come down the hallway, but now Dannie was standing in the doorway, Jake wrapped up in a pure white towel, only his round, rosy face peeking out, and a few spikes of dark hair.

Her blouse was soaked, showing off full, lush curves, and she looked as rosy as the baby.

Dannie looked at home with Jake, comfortable with her life. Why was she content to raise other people's children, when she looked as if she'd been born to hold freshly bathed babies of her own?

"All right?" he stammered, getting up from the couch. "Yeah. Of course."

But he wasn't. He was acutely aware that being around these kids, around Dannie, was making him feel things he had been content not to feel, revisit places he had been relieved to leave behind.

All he had to do was get through the rest of tonight. Tomorrow he'd figure out how to get rid of them, or maybe she would decide to go.

That would be best for everyone involved, and to hell with his sister's disapproval.

Though what if Mel cut her own vacation short? She needed it.

"Are you sure you're all right?" Dannie asked, frowning.

He pulled himself together, vowed he was not going back to the memory of holding his baby. He could not revisit the pain of letting that little guy go and survive. He couldn't.

He was going to focus totally and intensely on this moment.

He said, with forced cheer, "As all right as a guy can be whose been beaten at noughts and crosses by a four-year-old, thirty-three times in a row."

Because of his vow to focus on the moment, he became acutely aware of what it held. Dannie. Her hair was curling from the moistness, her cheeks were on fire, her blouse was sticking to her in all the right places.

He glanced at Susie, who was drawing a picture on the back of a used piece of paper, bored with the lack of competition.

Her picture showed a mommy, a daddy, a child suspended between their stick arms, big smiles on their oversize heads.

Despite his vow, the thought hit him like a slug. The world he had walked away from.

His son would have been three years older than his niece. Did he look like Susie? Worse, did he look like him?

He swore under his breath, running a hand through his hair.

"Mr. Cole!"

Susie snickered, delighted at the tone of voice he'd earned from her nanny.

"Sorry," he muttered, "Let's go get something to eat." His mind wandered to the thought of Danielle eating spaghetti. "There's a great Italian restaurant around the corner. Five-star."

Dannie rolled her eyes. "Have you ever taken a baby and a four-year-old to a restaurant?"

No, he wanted to scream at her, *because I walked away from that life.*

"So, we'll order pizza," he snapped.

"Pizza," Susie breathed, "my favorite."

"Pizza, small children and white leather. Hmm," Dannie said.

"I don't care about the goddamned leather!" he said.

He expected another reprimand, but she was looking at him closely, way too closely. Just as he had seen things about her that she might have been unaware of, he got the same feeling she saw things like that about him.

"Pizza sounds great," she said soothingly.

Glad to be able to move away from her, to take charge, even of something so simple, he went and got a menu out of the drawer by the phone.

"What kind?" he asked.

"Cheese," Susie told him.

"Just cheese?"

"I hate everything else."

"And what about you, Miss Pringy? Can we order an adult pizza for us? The works?"

"Does that include anchovies?"

"It does."

"I think I'm in heaven," she said.

He looked at her wet shirt, the beautiful swelling roundness of a real woman. He thought maybe he could be in heaven, too, if he let himself go there. But he wasn't going to.

She glanced down at where he was looking and turned bright, bright red. She waltzed across the space between them, and placed the towel-wrapped baby in his arms.

"I need to go put on something dry."

The baby was warm, the towel slightly damp. A smell tickled his nostrils: something so pure it stung his eyes.

He realized he'd had no idea what heaven was until

that moment. He realized the survival of his world probably depended on getting these children, and her, back out of his life.

She wanted to go. He wanted her to go.

So what was the problem?

The problem was, he suspected, both of them knew what they wanted, and neither of them knew what they needed.

Dannie reemerged just as the pizza was brought to the front desk. She was dressed casually, in black yoga pants and a matching hoodie, which, he suspected, was intended to hide her assets, and which did nothing of the sort. Her figure, minus the ugly black skirt, was amazing, lush.

Her complexion was still rosy from the bath. Or she was blushing under his frank look.

He had to remember she was not the kind of woman he'd become accustomed to. Sophisticated. Experienced. *Expecting* male admiration.

"I'll just run down to the lobby and pick up the pizzas," he said. He glanced at her feet. They were bare, each toenail painted hot, exotic pink.

He turned away quickly. College professor, indeed! He'd *known* that's what she was hiding. What he hadn't known was how he, a man who spent time with women who were quite comfortable sunbathing topless, would find her naked toes so appealing.

Would have a sudden vision of chasing her through this apartment until she was breathless with laughter.

What would he do with her when he caught her?

He almost said the swear word out loud again. Instead he spun on his heel and took the elevator down to the lobby. He took his time getting back, cooling down, trying to talk sense to himself.

He might as well not have bothered. When he returned to the apartment, she was in the kitchen, scowling at his fridge.

"This is pathetic," she told him.

"I know." He brushed by her and set the pizza down. He tried not to look at her feet, snuck a peek, felt a funny rush, the kind he used to feel a long time ago, in high school, when Mary Beth McKay, two grades older than him, had smiled at him.

It was obviously a lust for the unobtainable.

She was studying his fridge. "No milk. No juice. No ketchup."

"Ketchup on pizza?" he asked.

"I'm just making a point."

"Which is?"

"Your fridge is empty." But it sounded more like she had said his life was empty.

Ridiculous. His life was full to overflowing. He worked twelve-hour days regularly and sixteen-hour days often. His life was filled with constant meetings, international travel, thousands of decisions that could be made only by him.

His life was million-dollar resorts and grand openings. The livelihoods of hundreds of people depended on him doing his work well. His life was flashy cars and flashier women, good restaurants, the fast lane. So why was he taking her disapproving inventory of his fridge as an indictment?

"Do you have peanut butter?" she asked, closing the fridge and opening a cabinet.

"On pizza?" he asked, a bit defensively. "Or are you making a point again?"

"Just thinking ahead," she said. "Breakfast, lunch." She took a sudden interest in a sack of gourmet coffee, took it out and read the label. "Until you make arrangements for us to go. Which you probably will, immediately after you've seen the children eat pizza."

"Give me some credit," he said, though of course that was exactly what he wanted to do. Feed them pizza, talk to his assistant who made all his travel arrangements, get them gone. "Do you want wine? As you've seen, my beverage choices are limited."

"No, thank you," she said. *Primly.*

Good for her. A glass of wine would be the wrong thing to add to the mix. Especially for her. She'd probably get drunk on a whiff of the cork.

They had no high chair, so he held the baby on his lap and fed him tidbits of crust and cheese. She'd been right about the mess. Despite his efforts, Jake looked as if he'd been cooked inside the pizza.

His cell phone rang during dinner, Susie, her lips ringed in bright-red tomato sauce, scowled at him when he fished it out of his pocket.

"My Daddy doesn't answer his phone when we eat," she informed him.

"I'm not—" he swallowed *your daddy* at the warning look on Miss Pringy's face and shut his phone off "—going to, either, then."

When was the last time he'd done anything for approval? But there was something about the way those two females were beaming at him that made him think he'd better get back in the driver's seat. Soon.

Maybe after supper.

Immediately, whoever had tried his cell phone tried his landline. The answering machine picked up.

"Mr. Cole, it's Michael Baker. If you could get back to me as soon as—"

He practically tossed the tomato-sauce stained baby

to Dannie. Susie, noticing the nanny's hands were full, decided she had to have a pencil, right then. She jumped up from her seat.

"No," Dannie called. "Susie, watch your hands."

But it was too late. A pizza handprint decorated his white sofa.

"Michael," he said to the owner of Moose Lake Lodge, "good to hear from you."

Susie was staring at the pizza smudge on his couch. She picked up the hem of her shirt and tried to wipe it off. Out of the corner of her eye, she saw Dannie moving toward her.

"I can fix it myself!" she screamed. "I didn't mean to."

"Just a sec," he put the phone close to his chest. "It's nothing," he told the little girl. "Forget it."

But Susie had decided it was something. Or something was something. She began to howl. Every time Dannie got near her, she darted away, screaming and spreading tomato sauce disaster. Dannie, encumbered by the baby, didn't have a hope of catching her.

"Sorry," he said into the phone. How could one little girl make it sound like World War III was occurring? How could one little girl be spreading a gallon of pizza sauce when he could have sworn the pizza contained a few tablespoons of it at the most? The baby, focused on his sister, started to cry, too. Loudly.

He was going to take the phone and disappear into his den with it, but somehow he couldn't leave Dannie to deal with this mess. He sighed.

Regretfully he said, "I'll have to call you back. A few minutes."

He went and took the baby back from Dannie, and sat on the couch, never mind that the baby was like a pizza sauce squeeze bottle. His shirt was pretty much toast, anyway.

"I want my mommy," Susie screamed. And then again, as if he might have missed the message the first time. "I want my mommy!"

He didn't know where the words came from.

He said, "Of course you want your mommy, honey." He probably spoke with such sincerity because he dearly wanted her mommy right now, too. Here, not soaking up the sun in Kona, but right here, guiding him through this sticky situation.

Something in his voice, probably the sincerity, stopped Susie midhowl. She stared at him, and then she came and sat on the couch beside him.

He held his breath. The baby took his cue from his sister, quieted, watched her intently, deciding what his next move would be.

Susie leaned her head on Joshua's arm, sighed, popped her thumb in her mouth, and the room was suddenly silent except for the sound of her breathing, which became deeper and deeper. Her eyes fluttered, popped open and then fell shut again. This time they didn't reopen.

The baby regarded his sleeping sister, sighed, burrowed into his uncle's chest and slept, too.

"What was that?" Joshua whispered to Dannie.

"Two very tired kids," she said. "Susie has been acting up a bit ever since she heard her parents were planning a vacation that did not include her."

His fault. Sometimes even when a guy had the best of intentions, things went drastically wrong.

"I'm sorry," he said.

"I actually think it's good for them to experience a little separation now and then. It'll help them figure out the world doesn't end if Mel and Ryan go away."

"What now?" he said.

"Well, if you don't mind a few more pizza stains, I suggest we just pop them into their beds. I can clean them up in the morning."

She held out her arms for the baby, who snored solidly through the transfer. Then he picked up his niece.

Who was just a little younger than his son would be.

And for the first time in his life, he put a child to bed. Tucked clean sheets around little Susie, so tiny in sleep. So vulnerable.

Who was tucking his son in tonight? Was the family who adopted him good enough? Kind? Decent? Fun-loving? People with old-fashioned values and virtues?

These were the thoughts he hated having, that he could outrun if he kept busy enough, if he never let himself get too tired or have too many drinks.

He left Susie's room as if his feet were on fire, bumped into Dannie in the hall outside her room where she had just settled Jake.

"Are you okay?" she asked.

"Oh. Sure. Fine. Why wouldn't I be okay?"

She regarded him with those huge blue eyes, the eyes that *expected* honesty, and he had the feeling if you spent enough time around someone like her, you wouldn't be able to keep the mask up that kept people out.

"You just look," she tilted her head, studied him, "as if you've seen a ghost."

A ghost. Not quite.

"A kind of a ghost," he said, forcing lightness into his tone. "I'm remembering what my home looked like before pizza."

She smiled. "I tried to warn you. I'll have it cleaned up in a jiff."

"No, we'll clean it up." In a jiff. Who said things like that? Probably people with old-fashioned values and virtues.

A little later he tossed a damp dishcloth in the sink. He was a man who had trekked in Africa and spelunked in Peru. He had snorkeled off the coast of Kona and bungee jumped off the New River Gorge Bridge in West Virginia.

How was it something so simple—tracking down all the stains and moving all the items that were delicate and breakable—seemed oddly *fun,* as if he was fully engaged, fully alive for the first time in a long time?

Is that what a woman like her would make life like? Fun when you least expected it? Engaging without any trinkets or toys?

Was it time to find out?

"Do you want that glass of wine now?" he asked her, when she threw a tomato-sauce-covered rag into the sink beside his. "You're off duty, aren't you?"

"I'm never off duty," she said, but not sanctimoniously. Still, she was treating the offer with caution.

Which was smart. As his niece had pointed out to him earlier, he wasn't smart. Plain old dumb.

"It's more than a job for you, isn't it?" he asked, even though he knew he should just let her get away to do whatever nannies did once the kids were asleep.

She blinked, nodded, looked away and then said in a low, husky voice, filled with reverence, "I love them."

He felt her words as much as heard them. He felt the sacredness of her bond with his niece and nephew and knew how lucky his sister was to have found this woman.

But how had it happened that Dannie loved the children enough, apparently, to put her own college-professor dreams on hold, her own dreams for her life, her own ambitions?

He wanted to say something, and he didn't. He didn't want to know anymore about what she was giving up for other people's children.

"I think we should go tomorrow," she said, taking a deep breath. "I know your intentions are good, but the children really need to be someplace where they can romp. Someplace not so highly vulnerable to small hands, pizza sauce, the other daily catastrophes of all that energy."

Her eyes said, *I need to be away from you.*

And he needed to be away from her. *Fast.* Before he asked more questions that would reveal to him a depth of love that shone like water in a desert, beckoning, calling.

"I'll go make the arrangements," he said coolly. "I have to return a phone call, anyway."

"I'll say good-night, then, and talk to you in the morning."

He nodded, noticing she did not go back to her room but slipped out onto the terrace. He watched her for a moment as she stood looking out at darkness broken by lights reflecting in the water, stars winking on overhead. The sea breeze picked up her hair, and he yearned to stand beside her, immerse himself in one more simple moment with her.

Moments, he reminded himself harshly, that were bringing up memories and thoughts he didn't want to deal with.

Unaware she was being watched, she turned slightly. He saw her lift the chain from around her neck, open the locket and look at it.

There was no mistaking, from the look on her face, that she had memories of her own to deal with. And he didn't want to know what they were!

He walked away from the open patio doors, and

moments later he shut the door of his home office. He waited for the familiar surroundings to act as a balm on him, to draw him back into his own world.

But they didn't. He thought of her standing on the deck with the wind lifting her hair. The fact that he suddenly didn't want her to go was all the more reason to make the arrangements immediately. Thinking of them leaving filled him with relief. And regret. In nearly equal proportions.

He glanced at his watch. It had been less than eight hours since she had arrived in his office.

His whole world had been turned topsy-turvy. He had revisited a past he thought was well behind him. He was feeling uncertainties he didn't want to feel.

He needed the safety and comfort of his own world back.

He dialed Michael Baker's number.

Michael sounded less guarded than he had in the past, almost jovial.

"It sounded like you had your hands full," he said to Joshua.

"My niece and nephew are here for a visit."

"My wife and I were under the impression you didn't like children," Michael said.

"Don't believe everything you read," Joshua said carefully, sensing the slightest opening of a door that had been firmly closed.

"We had decided to just tell you no," Michael said. "Moose Lake Lodge is not at all like any of your other resorts."

Baker said that in a different way than he had said it before, in a way that left Joshua thinking the door was open again. Just a little bit. Just enough for a shrewd salesman to slip his foot in.

"None of my resorts are ever anything like the other ones. They're all unique."

"This is a family resort. We're kind of hoping it always will be. Does that fit into your plans?"

To just say *no* would close the door irrevocably. He needed to meet with the Bakers. He needed them to trust and like him. He was certain he could make them see his vision for Moose Lake Lodge. Hikes. Canoe and kayak adventures. Rock climbing. The old retreat alive with activity and energy and excitement.

Whether that vision held children or not—it didn't— was not something Joshua felt he had to reveal right now.

"I could fly up tomorrow," Joshua said. "Just meet with me. I'm not quite the superficial cad the press makes me out to be. We'll talk. You don't have to agree to anything."

"You might be making the trip for nothing."

"I'm willing to risk it. I'd love to see it. It's a beautiful place in the pictures." He always did his homework. "Just being able to have a look at the lodge would be great. I understand your grandfather logged the trees for it and built it nearly single-handedly, with a block and tackle."

Hesitation. "Maybe we have been hasty in our judgments. We really don't know anything about you."

"No, you don't."

"It probably couldn't hurt to talk."

"That's how I feel."

"No lawyers, though. No team. Unless—"

"Unless what?"

"How long are your niece and nephew with you?"

A few more hours. "It hasn't quite been decided."

"Look, why don't you bring them up for a few days? Sally and I will get to know you, and a little about your plans for Moose Lake. The kids can enjoy the place. This is the first year we haven't booked in families, because we're trying to sell and we didn't want to disappoint anyone if it sold. We're missing the sound of kids."

It was an answer to a prayer, really, though how anybody could miss the sound that had just filled his apartment, Joshua wasn't quite sure.

Still, the situation was shaping up to be win-win. He could give the kids the vacation he'd promised his sister. He could woo the owners of the Moose Lake Lodge.

It occurred to him he should ask the nanny if she thought the trip would be in the kids' best interests, but she had a way of doing the unpredictable, and she probably had not the least bit of concern in forwarding his business concerns.

She might even see it as using the children.

Was he using the children?

The little devil that sat on every man's shoulder, that poked him with its pitchfork and clouded his motives, told him of course not!

Told him he did not have to consult the nanny. He was the children's uncle! Susie had wanted a camping toy. This was even better! A real camping experience.

"We'll be there tomorrow," he said smoothly. "I'll land at the strip beside the lake around one." He was juggling his schedule in his head. "Would two days be too much of an inconvenience?"

"Two days? You mean fly in one day, and leave the next? That's hardly worth the trip. Why don't you make it four?"

He couldn't make it four. His schedule was impossible to squeeze four days out of. On the other hand, if he stayed four days, he could send the kids home knowing their mother and father would be only a day or two behind them. He could claim he had given them a real holiday.

Plus he could have four whole days to convince the Bakers that their lodge would be safe in the hands of Sun.

"Four days," he agreed smoothly. "It sounds perfect."

"We'll be at the runway to pick you up."

Joshua put down the phone and regarded it thoughtfully. The usual excitement he felt as he moved closer to closing a deal was strangely absent. Somehow he thought maybe he had just created more problems than he had solved.

CHAPTER FOUR

DANNIE woke up and stretched luxuriously. The bed was phenomenal, the linens absolutely decadent. She snuggled deeper under the down comforter, strangely content, until she remembered the day held nothing but uncertainty.

Had Joshua booked them tickets for home? Why did she feel sad instead of happy? Was she falling under the charm of all the *stuff*? The luxurious rooms, the million-dollar views?

Or was it his charm she was falling under? She thought of the smoke and jade green of those eyes, the deep self-assuredness in his voice, the way his thumb had felt, on her lip.

Whatever remained of her contentment evaporated. She felt, instead, a certain queasiness in her stomach, similar to what she felt on a roller coaster as it creaked upward toward its free fall back to earth. Was it anxiety or excitement or some diabolical mixture of both?

She touched her locket, reminding herself where these kinds of thought led. She was not even over Brent. How could she possibly be thinking about a roller-coaster ride with another man?

"Fantasy," she reminded herself sharply. "Whatever

is going on in your thoughts with Joshua Cole is not real, even if he did touch your lip." Sadly, she suspected the same was true of her relationship with Brent.

Created largely in her own mind. Was that why Melanie had sometimes looked at her with ill-disguised sympathy, as Dannie had added yet another picture to her "possible honeymoon" file? Had everyone known, long before she had, that a good relationship was not conducted from three thousand miles away and oceans apart?

Normally she would have looked in her locket when she first woke up and allowed herself to feel a longing for what was not going to be, but today she just let it settle back in the hollow of her neck, unopened.

Jake gurgled from his crib, she sat up on her elbows and watched him pull himself to his feet, begin his joyous morning bounce.

The wonderful thing about children was they did not allow one to dwell for too long in the realm of mind, they called you out of those twisting, complicated caverns of thought. They invited you to dance with the now, to laugh, to enjoy every simple pleasure. Jake was especially good at this, gurgling at her, holding out his arms, practicing a new song.

"Ba, bab, da, da, boo, boo, doo."

She could not resist. It was the first morning in a long time that she did not feel like crying. Maybe she'd start opening that locket less often! In fact, Dannie threw back the covers, went and hefted Jake from his crib, danced around the room to his music. Her bedroom door burst open and in flew Susie in her Princess Tasonja pajamas, the new bear tucked under her arm. She made for the bed and began jumping.

Normally Dannie would not encourage jumping on

the bed, but the children were on holidays. For another few hours, anyway. This might be as good as it got.

She threw her own caution to the wind, and baby in arms, jumped on the bed with Susie. They jumped and then all fell down in a heap of helpless giggles.

The room grew very quiet. She realized they were no longer alone. Dannie, upside down in the bed, tilted her head just a little bit.

Joshua Cole stood in the doorway, a faint smile tickling his lips. Unlike them, he was not in pajamas, though dressed more casually than he had been yesterday, in crisp khaki hiking pants, a pressed shirt. He had obviously showered and shaved, his golden-brown hair was darkened by the damp, his face had that smooth look of a recent close encounter with a razor that made Dannie want to touch it, to see if it felt as soft as it looked.

He took a sip of steaming coffee, drawing her eyes to his lips. She wondered how he'd feel if she waltzed over and put her thumb on his lips!

She wondered how *she'd* feel.

Like an idiot, probably. World's Sexiest Bachelor could pull off such nonsense with panache. World's Frumpiest Nanny, not so much.

Naturally, he had caught her at her frumpy best.

Her pajamas were baggy red flannel trousers with a drawstring waistline. She had on a too-large man's white T-shirt that fit comfortably over her extra protective padding. Too late, she remembered the shirt claimed she'd gotten lei'd in Hawaii.

His eyes lingered there for a touch too long. "Have you been to Hawaii?" he asked.

"No, I'm afraid I haven't. This was a gift from a friend."

"Ah. You'd love it there."

How would you know what I'd love? she thought grumpily. No two worlds had probably ever been further apart than his and hers. However, if Hawaii was even a fraction as gorgeous as this apartment, he was probably right.

"The air there smells like your perfume," he said softly.

She went very still. It was a line, obviously. The lame line of a guy whose lame lines had scored him lots of points with women a lot more sophisticated than her.

"I'm not wearing perfume," she said, letting the grumpiness out.

"Really?" He looked genuinely astounded, as if he'd meant it about Hawaii smelling like her.

She resisted an impulse to give her armpits a quick, subtle sniff. And then she realized that she was having this intimate conversation while lying upside down with a baby on her tummy.

She scrambled to sitting, juggling Jake. Her hair was flying all over the place, hissing with static, and she ran a self-conscious hand through it, trying to tame it.

He took another sip of his coffee. "Maybe it's your hair that made me think of Hawaii."

The flattery was making her flustered. A different woman, which she suddenly found herself wishing she was, would know how to respond to that. A different woman might giggle and blink her eyes and talk about skinny-dipping in the warm waters of the Pacific. With him.

Even *thinking* about skinny-dipping made her blush. Thinking of skinny-dipping anywhere in the vicinity of him made her feel as if she should go to confession. And she wasn't even Catholic!

Besides, she was sworn off men. And romance. And most certainly off skinny-dipping! Though it did seem like a bit of a shame to swear off something before even trying it.

Having thoroughly rattled her, he smiled with cat-that-got-the-cream satisfaction.

"I'm having some breakfast sent up," he said. "Fruit, yogurt. Any other requests?"

"I have to have Huggi Bears for breakfast," Susie told him.

"She doesn't," Dannie said firmly. "Yogurt is just fine. If you'll excuse us for a minute, I'll make myself presentable. And the children. Of course."

"I thought you were quite presentable. Don't feel you have to dress for breakfast. I want you to feel at home here."

"Why? We're leaving."

"Until you do," he said smoothly, and then shut the door quietly and left them alone.

A few minutes later she had the children washed and dressed. Dannie actually found herself lamenting the lack of choice in the clothing she had brought, but wore the nicest things she had packed, a pinstripe navy blue blazer and matching slacks. Like most of her clothes, the slacks were protesting her weight gain and were just a touch too snug. Thankfully the blazer covered the worst of it! The outfit was decidedly businesslike, almost in defiance of his invitation to make themselves at home. At the last moment she added a hint of makeup, ridiculously grateful there was some in her bag left over from her last trip.

He was being particularly charming this morning. That would come naturally to him. She needn't be flattered by it. Or worse, wonder what he wanted. She had nothing a man like that would want, even with the addition of mascara!

When she came out, the breakfast bar had been set up with platters of fresh fruit and croissants. Several child-size boxes of cereal, including Huggi Bears were available. There were choices of milk, chocolate milk or juice, the coffee smelled absolutely heavenly.

What would it be like to live like this? To just snap your fingers and have a feast including Huggi Bears delivered instantly?

It would make a person spoiled rotten, she thought. Emphasis on the *rotten*.

Or make them feel as if they had died and gone to heaven, she thought as she took a sip of the coffee. It was even richer and more satisfying than it had smelled.

It renewed her commitment to taking the children home. Before she was spoiled for real life. Before she started wanting and expecting luxuries she was never going to have.

"Let's take it out on the terrace," he suggested. He took the baby from her with more ease than she would have expected after just one day. When she joined him outside, he was spooning yogurt into Jake who was cooperatively opening his mouth like a baby bird waiting for a worm.

Susie had chosen one of the tiny boxes of Huggi Bears. It was the annoying kind that claimed it could be used as a bowl, but never quite worked properly. Still, Susie insisted she had to have it out of the box, and by the time Dannie had it opened along all the dotted lines and had poured the milk, she was cursing Joshua's charm and good looks, which made her feel as clumsy as if she were trying to open the box with elephants' feet instead of hands!

She made herself focus on the view, which was spectacular in the early morning light. The sea breeze was fresh and scented. She wondered what Hawaii smelled like.

She ordered herself just to enjoy this place and this moment, but it proved to be impossible. She needed to know what happened next. It was just her nature.

"So, may I ask what arrangements you've made for the children and me?" The thought of traveling again so soon exhausted her. The thought of staying here with him was terrifying.

It gave new meaning to being caught between a rock and a hard place.

"Well," he said, and smiled widely, "I have a surprise for you."

Danielle was one of those people who did not care much for surprises. It was part of being the kind of person who liked to know what was going to happen next.

"I'm flying out to look at a property for a few days. It's called the Moose Lake Lodge. Susie mentioned camping, so I thought she'd love it. All of us. A vacation in the British Columbia wilderness."

"We're going camping?" Susie breathed. "I love camping!"

"You don't know the first thing about camping," Dannie said.

"I do so!"

She was staring at Joshua with a growing feeling of anger. So this was why he'd been so charming this morning! Smelled like Hawaii, indeed. Her hair made him think of Hawaii. Sure it did!

"Are you telling me or consulting me?" she asked dangerously.

He pondered that for a moment. "I'd really like for you to come."

It was an evasive answer. It meant he hadn't booked them tickets home.

"The real question is *why* would you want to drag two children and a nanny along on a business trip?"

"It's not strictly business."

She raised an eyebrow and waited.

"You know as well as I do Melanie will kill me if I send the kids home after I promised her I'd give them a holiday."

It still wasn't the whole truth. She could feel it.

"Say yes," Susie said, slipping her hand into Dannie's and blinking at her with her most adorable expression. "Please say yes. Camping."

Everything in her screamed no.

Except for the part of her that screamed yes.

The part of her that *begged* her to, just once, say yes to the unexpected. Just once to not know what the day held. To not have a clue. To just once embrace a surprise instead of rejecting it.

To leave the safe haven of her predictable, controlled world.

What had her controlled world given her so far? Despite her best efforts, she had ended up with her heart broken, anyway.

"What do you mean, *you're* flying?" she asked, looking for a way to ease into accepting, not wanting to say an out-and-out yes as if the promise of an adventure was more than poor, boring her could refuse.

Not wanting to appear like a staid nanny who'd been offered a rare chance to be spontaneous.

"I have a pilot's license," he said. "I fly my own plane."

There was that feeling in her stomach again, of a roller coaster chugging up the steep incline. "Is that safe?" she demanded.

"More safe than getting in your car every day," he said. "Did you know that you have more chance of dying in your own bathroom than you do of dying on an airplane?"

Who could argue with something like that? Who could ever look at their own bathroom in the same way after hearing something like that?

That was the problem with a man like Joshua Cole. He could turn everything around: make what had always seemed safe appear to be the most dangerous thing of all.

For wasn't the most dangerous thing of all to have died without ever having lived? Wasn't the most dangerous thing to move through life as if on automatic pilot, not challenged, not thrilled, not engaged?

Engaged. She hated that word with its multitude of meanings. She thought she had been engaged. For the first time she did not touch her locket when she thought about it.

She took a deep breath, squeezed Susie's hand. "All right," she said. "When would you like us to be ready?"

Dannie had never flown in a small plane before. Up until getting on the plane, her stomach had been in knots about it. But watching Joshua conduct extremely precise preflight checks on the aircraft calmed her. The man radiated confidence, ease, certainty of his own abilities.

The feeling of calm increased as she settled the children, Jake in his car seat, and then she took the passenger seat right beside Joshua.

She loved the look on his face as he got ready to fly, intensely focused and relaxed at the very same time. He had the air of a man a person could trust with their life, which of course was exactly what she was doing.

The level of trust surprised her. At this time yester-day, getting off an airplane after having read about him, she had been prepared to dislike him. When he hadn't arrived at the airport, she had upgraded to intense dislike.

But after seeing him in his own environment, and now in charge of this plane, she realized the mix-up at the airport probably had been Melanie's. Joshua gave the impression of a man who took everything he did seriously and did everything he did well.

Still, to go from being prepared to dislike someone to feeling this kind of trust in less than twenty-four hours might not be a good thing. She might be falling under his legendary, lethal charm, just like everyone else.

Of course she was! Why else had she agreed to fly off into the unknown with a man who was, well, unknown?

She did touch her locket then, a reminder that even the known could become unknown, even the predictable could fail.

Before she really had time to prepare herself, the plane was rumbling along the airstrip and then it was lifting, leaving the bonds of gravity, taking flight.

Dannie was surprised, and pleasantly so, to discover she liked small airplanes better than big ones. She could watch her pilot's face, she could feel his energy, he did not feel unknown at all. In fact, she had a sense of knowing him deeply as she watched his confident hands on the controls, as she studied his face.

He glanced at her, suddenly, and grinned.

For a second he was that boy she had seen in the photo on the beach, full of mischief and delight in life. For a second he was that football player in the other photo, confident, sure of his ability to tackle whatever the world threw at him.

Something had changed him since those photos were taken. She had not been aware he carried a burden until she saw it fall away as they soared into the infinite blue of the sky.

"You love this," she guessed.

"It's the best," he said, and returned his attention to what he was doing. And she turned hers to the world he had opened up for her. A world of such freedom and beauty it could hardly be imagined. Joshua pointed out landmarks to her, explained some of the simpler things he was doing.

An hour or so later he circled a lake, the water dark denim blue, lovely cabins on spacious tree-filled lots encircling it. Wharves reached out on the water. Except for the fact it was too early in the year for people to be here, it looked like a poster for a perfect summer. Still, she was actually sorry when the flight was over.

A car waited for them at the end of the runway, and introductions were made. Sally and Michael Baker were an older couple, the lines of living outdoors deeply etched in both their faces. They were unpretentious, dressed casually in jeans and lumber jackets. Dannie liked them immediately.

And she liked it that Joshua did not introduce her as a nanny, but said instead that his sister had sent her along because she didn't trust him completely with her children!

The Bakers had that forthright and friendly way about them that made children feel instantly comfortable. Jake went into Sally's arms eagerly.

"I think he's been waiting all his short life to have a grandmother," Joshua said.

"He doesn't have a grandmother?" Sally asked, appalled.

"The kids paternal grandparents are in Australia. My mom and dad were killed in an accident when I was growing up."

Melanie had told Dannie her parents were gone, but never the circumstances. Dannie had assumed they were older, and that they had died of natural causes. Now she wondered if that was the burden he carried, and she also noted how quickly he had revealed that to the Bakers.

There was a great deal to know about this man. But to know it was to invite trouble. Because even knowing that he'd lost his parents when he was young caused a growing softness toward him.

"That must have been very hard," Sally clucked, her brown eyes so genuinely full of concern.

"Probably harder on my sister than me," he said. "She was older."

Suddenly Dannie saw Melanie's attitude toward her brother, as if he was a kid, instead of a very successful man, in a totally different light.

Michael packed their things in the back of an SUV, and they drove toward the lake. Soon they were on a beautiful road that wound around the water, trees on one side, the lake, sparkling with light, on the other.

Then they came into a clearing. A beautiful, ancient log lodge was facing the lake at one end of it, gorgeous lawns and flower beds sweeping down to the sandy shores. Scattered in on the hill behind it were tiny log cabins of about the same vintage.

"It's beautiful," Dannie breathed. More than beautiful. Somehow this place captured a feeling: summer laughter, campfires, water games, children playing tag in the twilight.

A children's playground was on part of the huge

expanse of lawn before the beach, and Susie began squirming as soon as she saw it.

"Is that a tree fort?" she demanded. "I want to play!"

Sally laughed. "Of course you want to play. You've been cooped up in a plane. Why don't I watch the kids at the park, while Michael helps you two get settled?"

Dannie expected some kind of protest from Susie, but there was none. As soon as the car door opened, she bolted for the playground.

Michael and Joshua unloaded their bags, and they followed Michael up a lovely wooden boardwalk that started behind the main lodge, wound through whispering aspens, spruce and fur. The smell alone, sweet, pure, tangy, nearly took Dannie's breath away. The boardwalk came to a series of stone stairs set in the side of the hill, and at the top of that was the first of about a dozen cabins that looked through the trees to the glittering surface of the lake.

The cabin had a name burned on a wooden plaque that hung above the stairs to the porch.

Angel's Rest.

There were a pair of rocking chairs on the covered, screened-in front porch. The logs and flooring were gray with age, the chinking and the trim around the paned window was painted white. A window box was sadly empty. Dannie could imagine bright red geraniums blooming there. A worn carpet in front of a screen door said Welcome.

Michael opened the door, which squeaked outrageously and somehow only added to the rustic charm. He set their bags inside.

It occurred to her she and Joshua were staying together, under the same roof. Why was it different from how staying under the same roof had been last night?

The cabin was smaller, for one thing, everything about it more intimate than the posh interior of Joshua's apartment. This was a space that was real. The decades of laughter, of family, soaked right into the cozy atmosphere.

"This is our biggest cabin," Michael said. "There's two bedrooms down and the loft up. Sometimes the kids sleep on the porch on hot nights, though it's not quite warm enough for that, yet."

"How wonderful there's a place left in the world where it's safe enough for the kids to sleep out on an unlocked porch," Dannie said.

Michael nodded. "My daughter and her kids usually take it for the whole summer, but—" He stopped abruptly and cleared his throat. "Dinner is at the main lodge. See you there around six. There's always snacks available in the kitchen if you need something before then."

And then he closed the door and left them.

Alone.

The cabin was more than quaint, it was as if it was a painting entitled *Home*. There were colorful Finnish rag rugs over plank flooring. An old couch, with large faded cabbage roses on the upholstery, dominated the living room decor. Inside, where the logs had not been exposed to the weather, they were golden, glowing with age and warmth. A river rock fireplace, the face blackened from use, had two rocking chairs painted bright sunshine yellow, in front of it.

Maybe it was that feeling of home that made her venture into very personal territory. Standing in this place, with him, made her feel connected to him, as if all the warmth and love of the families who had gathered in this place had infused it with a spirit of caring.

"I can't believe I've worked for Melanie for months

and didn't know about your parents. I knew they had passed, but I didn't know the circumstances."

"It was a car accident. She doesn't talk about it."

"Do you?"

He shrugged. "We aren't really talkers in our family."

"Doers," she guessed.

"You got it." Without apology, almost with warning. No sympathy allowed. Don't go there. To prove the point, he began exploring the cabin, and she could tell his assessment of the place was somewhat clinical, as if he was deliberately closing himself off to the whispers of its charm.

He was studying the window casings, which were showing slight signs of rot, scowling at the floors that looked decidedly splintery. He went up the stairs to the loft.

"I'll take this room," he called.

She knew she shouldn't go up there, but she did. She went and stood behind him. The loft room was massive. The stone chimney from downstairs continued up the far wall, and there was another fireplace. A huge four-poster bed, antique, with a hand-crafted quilt took up the greater part of the space.

He was looking under the bed.

"Boogeymen?" she asked.

He hit his head pulling out from under the bed, surprised that she was up here. "Mice."

The shabby romance of the place was obviously lost on him. "And?"

"Mouse free. Or cleaned recently."

She was afraid of mice. He was afraid of caring. Maybe it was time for at least one of them to confront their fears.

"Joshua, I'm sorry about your parents. That must

have been incredibly hard on you." She said it even though he had let her know it was off-limits.

He went over and opened a closet door, peered in. She had a feeling he was already making architectural drawings, plans, notes.

"Thanks," he said. "It was a long time ago."

"What are your plans for this place?" she said, trying to respect his obvious desire not to go there. "If you acquire it?"

"I want to turn it into a Sun resort. So that means completely revamping the interiors of these cabins, if we kept them at all. Think posh hunting lodge, deep, distressed leather furniture, a bar, good art, bearskin rugs."

She actually felt a sense of loss when he said that.

"For activities," he continued, "overnight camping trips, rock climbing, hiking, a row of jet skis tied to a new wharf."

She winced at that.

"Five-star dining in the main lodge, a lounge, some of the cabins with their own hot tubs."

"Adult only?" She felt her heart sinking. How could he be so indifferent to what this place was meant to be?

"That's what we do."

"What a shame. This place is crying for families. It feels so empty without them."

"Well, that's not what Sun does."

"Is it because of your own family?" she asked softly, having to say it, even if it did cross the boundaries in his eyes. "Is that why you cater to people who don't have families around them? Because it's too painful for you to go there?"

He stopped, came out of the closet, looked at her with deep irritation. "I don't need to be psychoanalyzed. You sound like my sister."

She had hit a nerve. She saw that. And she saw that he was right. Staying at his place, seeing him with the children, riding in his airplane, being alone in this cabin with him had all created a false sense of intimacy.

She was the nanny, the employee. She had no right to probe into his personal life. She had no right to think of him on a personal level.

But she already was! How did you backpedal from that?

"I'm sorry, Mr. Cole," she said stiffly.

The remote look left his face immediately. He crossed the room to her, she was aware how much taller he was when he looked down at her.

"Hey, I didn't mean to hurt your feelings."

"You didn't."

"Yes, I did. I can see it in your face."

"I'm sure you're imagining things."

"No, I'm not."

"Now you're being too personal, Mr. Cole."

He stared at her. "Are we having a fight?"

"I think so." Though after what she'd grown up with, this wouldn't even qualify as a squabble.

He started to laugh, and then surprisingly so did she, and the sudden tension between them dissipated, only to be replaced with a different kind of tension. Hot and aware. She could feel his breath on her cheek.

"Please don't call me Mr. Cole again."

"All right, Joshua."

"Just for the record, I didn't start running adult only resorts because of my parents." For a moment there was a pain so great in his eyes she thought they would both drown in it.

It seemed like the most reasonable thing in the world to reach out and touch his cheek, to cup his jawline in her palm and to rest her fingertips along the hard plain of his cheekbones.

His cheek was beginning to be ever so slightly whisker roughened. His skin felt unexpectedly sensual, cool and taut, beneath the palm of her hand.

He leaned toward her. For a stunning moment she thought he was going to tell her something. Something important. Maybe even the most important thing about him.

And then, the veil came down in his eyes, and something dangerous stirred in that jade surface. He was going to kiss her. She knew she should pull away, but she was helpless to do so. And then he reeled back as if he had received an electric shock, looked embarrassed, turned back to his inspection of the cabin.

She was way too aware of that big bed in this room, of the fireplace, of the pure and rugged romance of it.

"Uncle! Dannie!" Susie burst through the door downstairs. "Isn't this place the best? The best ever? You have to come see the tree fort. Sally said maybe I could sleep in it. Do you want to sleep in it with me?"

Now, that would be so much better than sleeping in here, with him. Even though she would be in a different room, this loft space was so open to the rest of the cabin below it. She would be able to imagine him here even as she slept in another room. She might even be pulled here, in the darkest night, when the heart spoke instead of the head.

Her eyes went once more to the bed. She was aware that Joshua had stopped and was watching her.

"Where are you?" Susie called.

"Up here. But coming down." Away from temptation.

Dannie ran down the steps, relieved by the distraction of the children.

Her job, she reminded herself sternly, her priority.

"Do you want to pick a bedroom?' she asked Susie.

"No, I want to *camp* in the tree fort. It's the best," Susie said, hugging herself and turning in delirious circles. "Moose Lake Lodge is the best!"

"The best," Dannie agreed halfheartedly, knowing the future of Moose Lake Lodge rested with someone who had quite a different vision of what *best* was.

But why did she feel that underneath that exterior of a cool, professional, hard-hearted businessman, Joshua was something quite different?

"I have to change," Dannie said, suddenly aware her suit was hopelessly wrong for this place. Luckily, in anticipation of a holiday, she had packed some casual slacks and T's. "Pick a room," she told Susie, "just in case you don't like camping in the tree fort."

Susie rolled her eyes at that impossibility but picked out a room. Then Dannie grabbed her suitcase and ducked into the other one.

Her mind went to that encounter with Joshua in the loft. If that kiss had been completed would she know who Joshua *really* was? Or would she be more confused than ever?

She saw herself in the old, faintly warped mirror. The first thing she noticed was not the extra ten or fifteen pounds of sadness that she carried, but the locket winking at her neck.

She touched it, then on impulse took it off and tucked it into the pocket of her suitcase. She told herself the gesture had no meaning. The locket was just too delicate for this kind of excursion.

Unwelcome, the thought blasted through her mind that she was also way too delicate for this—still fragile, still hurting.

And despite that, she would have kissed him if he had not pulled away! She put on a fresh pair of yoga pants and a matching T-shirt, regarded her reflection and was a little surprised to feel voluptuous rather than fat.

That assessment should have convinced her to put the locket back on, a constant reminder of the pain of engaging.

But she didn't. She left it right where it was.

CHAPTER FIVE

THE thing Joshua Cole loved about flying was that it was a world accessed only through absolute control, through a precision of thought and through self-discipline that only other pilots fully understood. Flying gave a sense of absolute freedom, but only after the strictest set of rules had been adhered to.

Business was much the same way. Hard work, discipline, precision of thought, all led to a predictable end result, a tremendous feeling of satisfaction, of accomplishment.

But relationships—that was a different territory altogether. They never seemed to unfold with anything like predictability. There was no hard-and-fast set of rules to follow to keep you out of trouble. No matter what you did, the safety net was simply not there.

Take the nanny, for instance. Not that he was having a relationship with her. But a man could become as enraptured by the blue of her eyes as he was held captive by the call of the sky.

He had seen something in her when they flew that he had glimpsed, too, when she had come out of her bedroom at his apartment, with Jake wrapped in that pure white towel, her blouse sticking to her, the laughter still shining in her eyes. Dannie Springer had a rare ability to experience wonder, to lose herself in the moment.

Something about her contradictions, stern and playful, pragmatic and sensitive, made him feel vulnerable. And off course. And it seemed the harder he tried to exert his control over the situation the more off course he became.

For instance, when he could feel her probing the tragedy of his parents' deaths, he had done what he always did: erected the wall.

But the fact that he had hurt her, while trying to protect himself, had knocked that wall back down as if it was constructed of paper and Popsicle sticks, not brick and mortar and steel, not any of the impenetrable materials he had always assumed it was constructed of.

In the blink of an eye, in as long as it took to draw a breath, he had gone from trying to push her away to very nearly telling her his deepest truth. He'd almost told her about his son. He had never told anyone about that. Not even his sister. To nearly confide in a woman who was virtually a stranger, despite the light of wonder that had turned her eyes to turquoise jewels while they flew, was humbling. He prided himself on control.

And it had gone from bad to worse, from humbling to humiliating. Because that flash moment of vulnerability had made him desperate to change the subject.

And he had almost done so. With his lips.

And though he had backed away at exactly the right moment, what he felt wasn't self-congratulatory smugness at his great discipline. No, he felt regret.

That he hadn't tasted the fullness of those lips, even if his motives had been all wrong.

"Just to get it over with," he muttered out loud.

He heard her come back into the main room below him and was drawn to the railing that overlooked it.

She had changed into flared, stretchy pants that rode low on the womanly curves of her hips. She was wearing sandals that showed off those adorable toes.

Just to get it over with? Who was he kidding? He suspected a person never got over a woman like Dannie, especially if he made the mistake of tasting her, touching his lips to the cool fullness of hers. If he ever got tired of her lips—fat chance—there would be her delectable little toes to explore. And her ears. And her hair, and her eyes.

Just like a baby, wrapped in a blue blanket, those eyes of hers, turquoise and haunting, would find their way into his mind for a long, long time after she was the merest of memories.

Only, though, if he took it to the next level. Which *he* wasn't going to. No more leaning toward her, no more even thinking of sharing his deepest secrets with her.

He barely knew her.

She was his niece and nephew's nanny. Getting to know her on a different level wouldn't even be appropriate. There were things that were extremely attractive about her. So what? He'd been around a lot of very attractive women. And he'd successfully avoided entanglement with them all.

Of course, with all those others he had the whole bag of tricks that money could buy to give the illusion of involvement, without ever really investing anything. It had been a happy arrangement in every case, the women delighted with his superficial offerings, he delighted with the emotional distance he maintained.

Dannie Springer would ask more of him, expect more, deserve more. Which was why it was such a good

thing he had pulled back from the temptation of her lips
at exactly the right moment!

He hauled his bag up to the loft, changed into more-
casual clothes and then went back down the stairs and
outside without bothering to unpack. He paused for a
moment on the porch, drinking it in.

The quiet, the forest smells, the lap of waves on the
beach stilled his thoughts. There was an island in the
lake, heavily timbered, a tiny cabin visible on the shore.
It was a million-dollar view.

Which was about what it was going to take—a
million dollars—take or give a few hundred thousand,
to bring Moose Lake Lodge up to the Sun standard.

He had seen in Dannie's face that his plans appalled
her. But she was clearly ruled by emotion, rather than
a good sense of business.

Maybe her emotion was influencing him, because
preserving these old structures would be more costly
than burning them to the ground and starting again.
And yet he wanted to preserve them, refurbish them,
keep some of that character and solidness.

The playground would have to go, though. He could
picture an outdoor bar there, lounge chairs scattered
around it. A heated pool and a hot tub would lengthen
the seasons that the resort could be used. A helicopter
landing pad would be good, too.

And then the squeal of Susie, floating up from the
playground he wanted to destroy, was followed by the
laughter of Dannie. He looked toward the playground.
He could clearly see the nanny was immersing herself
in the moment again, chasing Susie up the ladder into the
tree fort, those long legs strong and nimble. Susie burst
out the other side of the fort and slid back to the ground,
Dannie didn't even hesitate, sliding behind his niece.

If he knew women with more to offer than her, he suddenly couldn't think of one. He could not think of one woman he knew who would be so comfortable, so happy, flying down a children's slide!

A little distance away from Dannie and Susie, Sally was sitting on a bench with Jake at her feet. He had a little shovel in his hand, and was engrossed in filling a pail with fine sand.

Joshua wondered how he was going to tear the playground down now. Without feeling the pang of this memory. That was the problem with emotion. He should have stuck to business. He should never have brought the children here. Of course, without the children he doubted he would have been invited here himself.

For a moment, watching the activity at the playground, Joshua felt acutely the loss of his parents and the kind of moment they would never share with him. He felt his vision blurring as he looked at the scene, listened to the shouts of laughter.

He missed them, maybe more than he had allowed himself to miss them since they had died. He remembered moments like the one below him: days at the beach in particular, endless days of carefree laughter and sunshine, sand and water.

He had a moment of clarity that felt like a punch to his solar plexus.

I wanted to keep my son so I could feel that way again. A sense of family. Of belonging. Of love.

The thought had lived somewhere deep within him, waiting for this exact moment of vulnerability to burst into his consciousness. When he had given up his son, he had given up that dream. Put it behind him. Shut the door on it. Tried to fill that empty place with other things.

And not until this very moment was he aware of how badly he had failed. He snorted with self-derision.

He was one of the world's most successful men. How could he see himself as a failure?

His sister knew what he really was.

And so did he. A man who had lost something of himself.

He shook off the unwanted moment of introspection. Though he had planned to move away from the group at the playground and go in search of Michael to begin to discuss business, he found himself moving toward them instead.

With something to prove.

Just like kissing Dannie might get it out of his system, might prove the fantasy was much more delightful than the reality could ever be, so was that scene down there.

That happy little scene was just begging to be seen with the filters removed: the baby stinking, Susie cranky and demanding.

Sally looked up and smiled at him as he crossed the lawn toward them. "Glad you arrived," she said. "I was just going to see about dinner."

And then she got up and strolled away, leaving him with Jake. After a moment considering his options, Joshua sat down on the ground beside his nephew. Just as he'd suspected: reality was cold and gritty, not comfortable at all.

And then he looked through a plastic tub of toys, found another shovel and helped Jake fill a bucket.

Just as he'd suspected: boring.

And then he tipped the bucket over and saw the beginning of a sand castle. Jake took his little shovel and smashed it, chortling with glee.

Susie arrived, breathless. "Are you making something?"

Dannie's long length of leg moved into his range of vision. She was hanging back just a bit. Sensing, just as he did, that something dangerous was brewing here.

He looked up at her. He didn't know why he noticed, but the locket was missing. Just in case he hadn't already figured out something dangerous was brewing here.

He handed her a bucket, as if he was project manager on a huge construction site. *Thatta boy,* he congratulated himself. *Take charge.* "Do you and Susie want to haul up some water from the lake? We'll make a sand castle."

Before he knew it, he wasn't bored, but he was still plenty uncomfortable. Take charge? Working this closely with Dannie, he was finding it hard to even take a breath, he was so aware of her! She kept casting quick glances at him, too. It was so junior high! Building a Popsicle bridge for the science fair with the girl you had a secret crush on!

Not that he had a secret crush on her!

The castle was taking shape, multiturreted, Dannie carefully carving windows in the wet sand, shaping the walls of the turrets.

She had the cutest way of catching her tongue between her teeth as she concentrated. Her hair kept falling forward, and she kept shoving it impatiently back. It made him wonder what his fingers would feel like in her hair, a thought he quickly dismissed in favor of helping Susie build the moat and defending the castle from Jake's happy efforts to smash it with his shovel.

Before he knew it, his discomfort had disappeared, and happiness, that sneakiest of human emotions, had slipped around them, obscuring all else. It was as if fog, turned golden by morning sun, had wrapped them in a world of their own. Before he knew it, he was laughing.

And Dannie was laughing with him, and then Susie was in his arms with her thumb in her mouth, all wet and dirty and sandy, and the baby smelled bad, and reality was strangely and wonderfully better than any fantasy he had ever harbored.

Something in him let go, he put business on the back burner. For some reason, though he was undeserving of it, he had been given this gift. A few days to spend with his niece and nephew in one of the most beautiful places he had ever seen or been.

A few days to spend with a woman who intrigued him.

By the next day, he and Dannie settled into a routine that felt decidedly domestic. It should have felt awkward playing that role with her, but it didn't. It felt just like walking into the cottage Angel's Rest had felt, like coming home.

Sally prepared the most wonderful food he had ever eaten: old-fashioned food, stew and buns for supper the evening before, biscuits and jam for breakfast, thick sandwiches on homemade bread for lunch.

The lodge, magnificently constructed, always smelled of bread rising and baking and of fresh-brewed coffee. In the chill of the evening last night, there had been a fire going, children's board games and toys spread out on the floor in front of it.

The second day unfolded in endless spring sunshine. They played in the sand, they went on a nature walk, he rowed the kids around in the rowboat. When the kids settled in for their afternoon naps, he and Dannie sat on the front porch of Angel's Rest.

"Kids are exhausting," he told her, settling back in his chair, glad to be still, looking at the view of the little cabin on the island. "I need a nap more than them."

"You are doing a great job of being an uncle. World's Best Builder of Sand Castles."

Somehow that meant more to him than being bestowed with the title of World's Sexiest Bachelor.

"Thanks. You're doing a great job of…being yourself." That made her blush. He liked it. He decided to make her blush more. "World's Best Set of Toes."

"You're being silly," she said, and tried to hide her naked toes behind her shapely calves.

Today she was wearing sawed-off pants he thought were called capris. They hugged her delicious curves in the most delightful way.

"I know. Imagine that. Come on. Be a sport. Give me a peek of those toes."

She hesitated, took her foot out from behind her leg, and wiggled her toes at him.

He laughed at her daring, and then so did she. He thought it would be easy to make it a mission to make her laugh…and blush.

"I love the view from here," Dannie told him, hugging herself, tucking her toes back under her chair. "Especially that cabin. If I ever had a honeymoon, that's where." She broke off, blushing wildly.

If there was one thing a guy as devoted to being single as he was did not ever discuss it was weddings. Or honeymoons. But his love of seeing her blush got the better of him.

"What do you mean *if?*" he teased her. "If ever toes were made to fit a glass slipper, it's those ones. Some guy is going to fall for your feet, and at your feet, and marry you. You'll spend your whole honeymoon getting chased around with him trying to get a nibble of them. I'm surprised it hasn't happened already."

Even though the teasing worked, her cheeks staining to the color of crushed raspberries, the thought of some lucky guy chasing her around made him feel miserable.

"Oh," she said, her voice strangled, even as she tried to act casual, "I've given up Cinderella dreams. Men are mostly cads in sheep's clothing."

Her attempt at being casual missed, and then she touched her neck, where the locket used to be.

"How right you are," he said, but he felt very sorry about it, and he knew he was exactly the wrong guy to correct her misconceptions. Who had lured her and the kids here veiling another motive, after all?

Who looked at her lips and her toes and her hair and fought an increasingly hard battle not to steal a little taste, no matter what the consequences?

He knew he shouldn't ask. But he did, anyway. "Did he hurt you badly?"

"Who?" she croaked, wide-eyed.

He sighed. "The professor."

Her hand dropped away from her neck. "I'm embarrassed to be so transparent."

"Good. I hope it makes you blush again. Did he?"

She contemplated that for a moment and then said quietly, "No, I hurt myself."

But he doubted if that was completely true, and he felt a sudden murderous desire to meet the jerk that had hurt her. And another desire to see if he could chase the sudden sadness from her eyes. With his lips.

But something kept him from giving in to the little devil that sat on his shoulder, prodding him with the proverbial pitchfork and saying with increasing force and frequency, *Kiss her. No one will get hurt.*

The thought was in such contrast to the innocence of playing tag in the trees until they were breathless with laughter, in such contrast to the wholesome fun of wading and splashing along the shorelines of a lake too cold yet to swim in.

He was not looking forward to another night in the cabin with her, once the children were in bed, but the angel that sat on her shoulder must have been stronger than the devil on his.

Because after another incredible supper, fresh lake trout cooked by Sally, Dannie announced she and Susie would be sleeping in the tree fort. Ridiculously, he heard himself saying he would join them.

He had the worst sleep of his life in the tree fort, with Susie between his and Dannie's sleeping bags, the baby in a huge wicker basket at their heads, cooing happily from his nest of warm blankets.

Dannie was so close, he could touch that incredible hair, but he didn't. She was so close he could smell the Hawaiian flower scent of her. He lay awake looking at the incredible array of stars overhead, and listening to her breathing, and in the morning, he felt cold and cramped and more alive than he had felt in a long, long time.

He woke up looking into Dannie's sleep-dazed turquoise eyes, and wondered how on earth he was ever going to go back to life as he had known it.

The carefree stay here at Moose Lake Lodge was about as far from his high-powered life as he could have gotten. He didn't check his Blackberry, there was no TV to watch. No Internet.

He had a new reality and so much of it was about Dannie: her eyes and her lips and the way she tossed her hair. How she looked with her slacks rolled up and smudged with dirt, hugging the womanliness of her curves, her bare toes curling in warm sand.

He saw the way she was with those kids: patient, loving, genuine. He came to look forward to her intelligence, the playful sting of exchanged insults.

He was acutely aware Dannie was the kind of woman that men, superficial creatures that they were, overlooked. But if a man was looking for a life partner—which he thankfully was not—could he do any better than her?

That morning, after the exquisite pleasure of a hot shower after a cold night, over pancakes and syrup, Sally told them she and Michael would mind the kids for the day.

"The only one who hasn't had any kind of a holiday, a break from responsibility, is Dannie. This is your last full day here. Go have some fun, you two."

His niece had been so right about him, Joshua thought. He was just plain dumb.

He turned to Dannie, humbled by Sally's consideration of her. This morning Dannie was wearing a red sweatshirt that hid some of the features that made his mouth go dry, but the jeans made up for it.

The dark denim hugged her. It occurred to him that skinny butts were highly overrated. It occurred to him that was a naughty thought for a man who was going to try his hand at being considerate.

"The whole time I've been thinking how enjoyable this experience is," Joshua admitted, "you've been doing your job, minding children."

"Oh, no," Dannie protested, "I don't feel like that at all. I once heard if you do a job you love, you'll never work a day in your life, and that's how I feel about being with Susie and Jake."

Again, Joshua was taken with what a prize she was going to make for someone. And again he was taken aback by his own reaction to that thought. Misery.

Before someone else snapped her up, could he put his own priorities on hold long enough to show her a good time? Could he trust himself, not forever, but for one day? To put her needs ahead of his own? To be considerate, instead of a self-centered jerk?

"Sally's right," he decided firmly. "It's time for your holiday."

Dannie was looking wildly uncomfortable, as if she didn't really want to spend time with him without the buffer zone of two lively and demanding children.

Which was only sensible. He was tired of her sensible side. He was annoyed at being bucked when he'd made the decision to be a better man, to be considerate and a gentleman.

"I have had a holiday, really," she insisted. "How can I eat food like Sally's, and stay in a place as beautiful as Angel's Rest and not feel as if I've had a holiday? I loved it better than a stay at a five-star resort. No offense to five-star resort owners in the vicinity."

"No," Sally said, firmly. "Today it's your turn. You have some grown-up time. Why don't you and Josh take a canoe over to the island? I'll pack you a picnic. Josh should look at it anyway, since it's part of the Moose Lake Lodge property. Many a honeymoon has taken place at that cabin!"

Despite Dannie claiming to be cynical about relationships, he did not miss the wistful look in her eyes when she heard that she had been so right about the island being an idyllic setting for a honeymoon! Joshua, good intentions aside, wasn't sure he was up to grown-up time with Dannie on an island where people had their honeymoons!

Still, he didn't miss the fact that Sally and Michael, though no business had been discussed, must be opening just a little bit to the idea of him acquiring the Lodge for Sun since they were encouraging him to see all that comprised it.

In search of perfect adventures for the clients of Sun, and in keeping with his fast-paced single lifestyle, Joshua had tried many activities, including some that might be considered hair-raising like bungee jumping and parasailing.

None of those activities had ever really fazed him, but an hour later, out in the canoe with Michael, brushing up on his canoeing skills, Joshua felt the weight of responsibility. He had canoed before, but never in waters that could kill you with cold if you capsized and had to stay in them for any length of time.

Michael assured him the island was only a twenty-minute paddle across quiet waters.

"I'll keep an eye on you," he promised. "If something goes wrong, I'll rescue you in the powerboat."

Joshua was not sure he could imagine anything that would be more humiliating than that, especially with Dannie sharing the boat with him. He was also aware Dannie's presence, besides making him aware of not wanting a rescue, made him feel responsible for another human being, something that was also new in his free-wheeling bachelor existence.

In a way it was ironic, because he shouldered tremendous responsibility. The business decisions he made literally affected the lives and livelihoods of hundreds of people.

That kind of responsibility didn't even seem real compared to having a life in his hands. Naturally he'd had his own life in his hands many times before, but if he got himself in trouble, he was the only one who suffered the consequences. Maybe the truth was he didn't really even care.

Strangely, both feelings—of not wanting to make a fool of himself in front of her and of feeling responsible for her safety—made him feel not weakened, but strengthened. Like he was manning up, assuming the ancient role of the protector, the warrior. He would never have guessed that role could feel so satisfying.

Trust Dannie not to let him relish the role for too long! He got her settled in the front of the boat—the non-control position in a canoe—and gave her a paddle for decorative purposes. He issued dire warnings about the tipiness of the contraption they were setting out in, and then he settled into his own position of navigator, course setter, and head paddler.

He was so intent on his duties, he noticed only peripherally that her red sweatshirt matched the red of the canoe, and that her rear in those jeans was something worth manning up for!

But before they were even out of the protected bay that sheltered the lodge, she turned to him in annoyance. Her cheeks were flushed with exertion, which she was bringing on herself by trying to pull the boat single-handedly through the water with her paddle!

"Look, I think this is a team activity. I'm not really the kind of girl who wants to sit in the front of the boat and look pretty, but I think we're paddling out of sync."

In other words she wasn't the kind of girl he'd gotten accustomed to.

In other words, maybe he'd been going it alone a little too much. He wasn't even sure he could play on a team anymore.

But to his surprise, as soon as he relaxed control, as

soon as he began to work with her instead of trying to do it all himself, the canoe began to cut through the water with silent speed and grace, an arrow headed straight for that island.

"That's better," she said, looking over her shoulder and grinning at him.

He wasn't quite sure when she had transformed, but somewhere in the last few days she had gone from plain to beautiful. The sun had kissed pale skin to golden, she had given up all effort to tame her luscious hair, and it curled wildly around her face, her expression seemed to become more relaxed each second that they left the children behind them.

"You are pretty," he stammered, and was amazed how he sounded. He, who had escorted some of the world's most beautiful and accomplished women, sounded like a schoolboy on his first date.

In answer, she scraped her paddle across the surface of the water, and deliberately splashed him with the icy cold lake water.

Now he could see the gypsy he had glimpsed in her before, dancing to life, especially when she laughed at his chagrin. Dannie said, with patent insincerity, "Oops."

Now, in this moment, he could see the truth of who she was, shining around her. This is what he had glimpsed when he had touched her lip with this thumb, a very long time ago, it seemed. This is what he had known about her that she had not known about herself. That she was made to dance with life, to shine with laughter, to blossom.

And in that he recognized another truth.

It was not her who was becoming transformed. It was him.

"Don't rock the boat," he said grumpily. And somehow it sounded like a metaphor for his life. Joshua Cole, entrepreneur who performed feats of daring and innovation in business, and who embraced adventure in the scant amount of time he allowed for play, did not rock the boat in that one all-important area.

Relationships. He did not even risk real involvement. He saw women a few times, and at the first hint they wanted more he made an exit. At the first sign of true intimacy of the emotional variety he was out of there. He was willing to play the game with his wallet, but he did not take chances with his heart.

Because his heart had been battered and bruised. When his parents had died, people had told him time would heal all wounds. When he had agreed with Sarah that the best thing for that baby would be to allow him to go to a loving family who were emotionally and financially mature, who were prepared for a child in every way, he had thought time would eventually lessen the ache he felt over that decision.

Maybe he had even believed that time *had* eased the pain. But he had only been kidding himself.

Outrunning something was not the same as healing. Not even close.

"Land ho," Dannie called, as they drew close to the island.

He looked at her face, shining with enthusiasm for the day, and he felt his guard slip away. He made a decision, just for today, he would engage as completely as he was able.

For her. So she could enjoy one day of being irresponsible, of having fun without the kids.

They landed the canoe, gracelessly, coming as close to tipping it as they had come yet, though thankfully the

waters off the island were shallow enough that he didn't
have to worry about her dying of hypothermia in them
if they did capsize. Still, even with her jeans rolled up,
she was wet to her knees.

He lifted the picnic basket Sally had packed for
them and followed Dannie up the shoreline and left the
basket there.

"I can't wait to see it," she said, and started up the
path that led to the cabin. She stumbled on a root, and
he reached out his hand to steady her. Somehow he
never took his hand away. Hers folded into his as if it
was absolutely meant to be there.

There was a well-worn path to the cabin, which was
as quaint up close as it had been from far away. Like
Angel's Rest, it had a name plaque hanging at the
entrance to the covered, vine-twined porch.

"Love's Rhapsody," she read out loud. "Isn't that
lovely?"

"Corny," he said, deciding then and there the sign
was coming down the minute he owned the place

"Should we go in?" she asked. There was something
about her wide-eyed wonder in the little cabin that was
making him feel edgy.

"Well, yeah, it's not a church. Besides, I might own
it one day. I might as well see how much money I'd have
to throw at it to keep it."

She reacted as he had hoped, by glaring at him as if
he had desecrated a sacred site. It was important that she
know that distinction existed between them. He cynical
and pragmatic, she soft and dreamy. It was important
she know that that distinction existed between them, so
the wall was up.

And a man needed a wall up in a place like this! He
needed a wall up when he was beginning to feel all

enthused about playing the protector and warrior. When he felt strangely uncertain if they should enter that sanctuary. What if whatever was in there—the spirit of romance—overcame them? What if he was helpless against it?

Annoyed with himself for so quickly breaking his vow to make the day about her instead of about him, Joshua pushed past her and shoved open the door.

His first reaction to the interior was one of relief, because the cabin was dark and musty smelling. There was absolutely nothing in it to speak of. An old antique bed, with the mattress rolled up, and the linens stored, a little table, a threadbare couch and a stone fireplace just like the one at Angel's Rest.

And yet, the fact there was so little in here, seemed to highlight that there was something in here, unseen.

"Look," she whispered, wandering over to one of the walls. "Oh, Joshua, look."

Carved lovingly into the walls, were names. Mildred and Manny, April 3, 1947, Penelope and Alfred, June 9, 1932. Sometimes it was just the couple's name, other times a heart and arrow surrounded it, sometimes a poem had been painstakingly cut out in the wall. It seemed each couple who had ever honeymooned here had left their mark on those walls.

It was hard not to be moved by the testament to love, to commitment. There really was nothing at all of material value in this cabin.

And yet there was something here so valuable it evaded being named: a history of people saying yes to the adventure of beginning a life together.

In this funny little cabin, it felt as if it was the only adventure that counted.

Cynicism would protect him from the light shining

in her eyes. But what of his vow to let her have the day she wanted?

So, when they left the cabin he took her hand again, despite the fact he wanted to shove his into his pockets, defending against what had been in there. Strangely, holding her hand seemed to still the uncertainty in him.

The island was small. They walked around the whole thing in an hour. He soon forgot his discomfort in the cabin, and found himself making it about her with amazing ease. But then, that's what being with her was like: easy and comfortable.

With just the faintest hint of sexual awareness, tingling, that added to rather than detracted from the experience of being together.

Finally they returned to the beach and opened Sally's picnic basket. She had sent them hot dogs and buns, matches and fire starter.

They gathered wood, and he lit the fire, feeling that *thing* again, the shouldering of the ancient role: *I will start the fire that will warm you.*

Obviously, the corniness from the cabin was catching!

With hot dogs blackening on sticks over an open fire, and the magic of the cabin behind him, he found himself taking a tentative step forward, wanting to be more but also to know more. Soon she would go her own way, and he would go his. It made the exchange seem risk-free.

"Tell me why you're content to raise other people's children," he said, touching the mustard at the edge of her mouth with his finger, putting that finger to his own lips, watching her eyes go as wide as if he had kissed her.

"I told you, it's a job I love. I never feel as if I'm working."

"But doesn't that make you think you are ideally suited to be a mother yourself, of your own children?"

Maybe that was too personal, because Dannie blushed wildly, as if he had asked her to be the mother of his children!

He loved that blush! Before her, when was the last time he had even met a woman who still blushed?

"It's because of the heartbreak," he guessed softly, looking at the way she was focusing on her hot dog with sudden intensity. "Will you tell me about it?"

This was exactly the kind of question he *never* asked. But suddenly he really wanted to know. He knew about things you kept inside. You thought they'd gone away, when in fact they were eating you from the inside out.

"No," she said. "You're burning your hot dog."

"That's how I like them. What was his name?"

She glared at him. Her expression said, *leave it.* But her voice said, reluctantly, "Brent."

"Just for the record, I've always hated that name. Let me guess. A college professor?"

"It's not even an interesting story."

"All stories are interesting."

"Okay. You asked for it. Here is the full pathetic truth. Brent was a college professor. I was a student. He waited until I wasn't in any of his classes to ask me out. We dated for a few months. I fell in love and thought he did, too. He had a trip planned to Europe, a year's sabbatical from teaching, and he went."

"He didn't ask you to go?"

"He asked me to wait. He made me a promise."

Joshua groaned.

"What are you making noises for?"

"If he loved you he would never, ever have gone to Europe without you."

"Thank you. Where were you when I needed you? He promised he would come back, and we'd get married. I took the nanny position temporarily."

"No ring, though," Joshua guessed cynically.

"He gave me a locket!"

"With his own picture inside? Thought pretty highly of himself, did he?" It was the locket she'd worn when he first met her. That she'd put away. What did it mean that she had taken it off?

That it was a good time for her to have this conversation? He knew himself to be a very superficial man, the wrong person to be navigating the terrifying waters of a woman's heartbreak. What moment of insanity had gripped him, encouraged her confidences? But now that she'd got started, it was like a dam bursting.

"At first he e-mailed every day, and I got a flood of postcards. It made me do really dumb things. I...I used all my savings and bought a wedding gown."

Her face was screwing up. She blinked hard. Maybe wheedling this confession out of her hadn't been such a good idea after all.

"It's like something out of a fantasy," she whispered. "Lace and silk." She was choking now. "It was all a fantasy. Such a safe way to love somebody, from a distance, anticipating the next contact, but never having to deal with reality.

"Can I tell you something truly awful? Something I don't even think I knew until just now? The longer he stayed away, the more elaborate and satisfying my fantasy love for him became."

She was crying now. No mascara, thank God. He patted her awkwardly on the shoulder, and when that didn't seem to give her any comfort, or him either, he threw caution to the wind, and his hot dog into the fire. He pulled her into his chest.

Felt her hair, finally.

It felt as he had known it would feel, like the most expensive and exquisite of silks.

It smelled of Hawaii, exotic and floral. This was why he was so undeserving of her trust: she was baring her soul, he was being intoxicated by the scent of her hair.

"Actually," she sniffed, "Brent was the final crack in my romantic illusions. My parents had a terrible relationship, constant tension that spilled over into fighting. When I met Brent, I hoped there was something else, and there was, but it turned out to be even more painful. Oh, I hope I don't sound pathetic. The I-had-a-bad-childhood kind of person."

"Did you?" he asked, against his better judgment. Of course the smell of her hair and her soft curves pressed into his body made him feel as if he had no judgment at all, wiped out by sensory overload. And yet even for that, he registered her saying she'd had a bad childhood and he ached for her. There were things even a warrior could not hope to make right.

"Terrible," she said with a defeated sigh. "Filled with fighting and uncertainty, making up that always filled us kids with such hope and never lasted. It was terrible."

"Maybe that's why you're so invested in children. Giving them the gift of happiness that you didn't have. You do have that gift, you know. So engaged with them, so genuinely interested in them."

"Did you have a good childhood?" she asked, and her wistfulness tore through the barriers around his heart that usually kept him from sharing too deeply with anyone.

"Camelot," he said. "I can't remember one bad thing.

I often wonder if every family is only allotted so much luck, and we used ours up."

"Oh, Joshua," she said softly.

"My parents were crazy about each other. And about us. We were the fun family on the block—my dad coaching the Little League team, my mom filling the rubber swimming pool for all the neighborhood kids. And it was all so genuine. I see parents sometimes who I think are following a rule book, thinking about how it all looks to other people, but my folks weren't like that. They did these things with us because they loved to do it, not because they wanted to *look* like great parents."

"And because of that they were great parents."

"The best," he remembered softly. "Every year for three weeks they rented a cottage on the seashore. We had these long days of swimming and playing in the sand, we had bonfires out front on the beach every night. There wasn't even a TV set. If it rained, we played Monopoly or Sorry or cards."

He realized he had never felt that way again. Ever. Not until he had come here.

And to feel that way was to leave yourself open to a terrible hurt.

Was he ready?

A sudden sound made him jerk up from her. Without his noticing, so engrossed in protecting her and comforting her, and sharing his own secret memories with her, the wind had come up on the lake.

Some warrior. Some protector! He had not tied the canoe properly. It had yanked free of its mooring, the sound he had heard was it crashing into a rock as it bounced away from the small island.

He ran for the water, plunged in, could not believe the cold and stopped.

"Leave it," Dannie cried.

Good advice. He should let the canoe go, but every-thing about Moose Lake Lodge said the Bakers were op-erating on a shoestring. He'd been entrusted with their canoe.

"I can't," he shouted at her, moving deeper into the water. "Can you imagine how the Bakers will react if the canoe drifts back there, empty? What about Susie?"

He took a deep breath and moved deeper into the water, felt her movement on the beach behind him.

"Stay there," he called. "I've got it under control."

He was used to speaking, and people listened. Naturally, Dannie did not. He heard her splash into the water, her shocked gasp as the icy water filled her shoes.

It made him desperate to get that canoe before they were both in deep trouble. He was up to his waist, he lunged forward, and just managed to get the rope that trailed off the bow of the boat.

He pulled it back toward shore, grabbed her elbow as he moved by, steering her in the right direction.

"I told you not to come in," he said.

"I was trying to help!" she said, unrepentant.

"Now we're both wet." But what he was thinking was it had been a long time since he had been with the kind of woman who would plunge into that water with him. He knew a lot of women who would have stood on shore, unhelpfully hysterical or more worried about her haute couture than him!

Still, they both could have got in trouble and it would have been his fault. He was aware of freezing water squeezing out of his shoes and that, wet up to his chest, his teeth were chattering wildly and in a most unmanly way.

Except for the fact it might save the Bakers some

distress, his rescue was wasted. When he inspected the canoe it had a hole the size of his fist in the bottom of it from where it had smashed into a rock.

He inspected her, too. She was wet past her waist, had her arms wrapped around herself. She was reacting to the cold in a very womanly way, and he did his best not to whistle with low appreciation.

Think, Joshua snapped at himself.

He was stranded on an island. With a beautiful woman. Who was shivering, and who had hair that smelled of Hawaii.

They were both going to have to get these wet clothes off quickly. And not in the way any red-blooded man wanted to have the first disrobing happen.

But because the May wind was like ice as the spring day lengthened and chilled, if they didn't get out of these wet clothes, there was a real chance of hypothermia.

There was only one option.

They were going to have to seek shelter in the honeymoon cabin.

Just his luck that he was going to end up half-naked in the honeymoon cabin with Dannie Springer. Maybe it was because he was shaking with cold that he couldn't quite figure out if he had landed in the middle of a dream or a nightmare.

CHAPTER SIX

DANIELLE SPRINGER had been in a few awkward situations, but this one definitely rated as Most Embarrassing, especially given the fact she was in the company of Most Sexy. If she hadn't known that about him before, she certainly couldn't miss it now that she had seen his soaked clothes mold every inch of his fine male body.

What had started off as a day full of potential, was now quickly declining toward disastrous, as quickly as darkness was sweeping over the small island.

She had broken down in front of him, shared confidences she never should have shared. When the canoe had ripped away, she'd been devastated. He had been in the middle of telling her important things, *real* things about himself. Thankfully, his own confidences had snapped her out of her self-pitying recital of woe.

Watching him push out into the water to save the canoe, she had thought sadly, only Dannie Springer would be alone on an island with a man like that, lamenting her last, lost boyfriend. It was no excuse that Joshua had encouraged her. That's what men who were successful with women did. That was their secret weapon. They listened.

Except it was becoming increasingly difficult to see Joshua in the light of his playboy reputation.

Especially after the way he had looked talking about his family, the tenderness in his voice, he seemed like the most real man she had ever met. Poor Brent seemed like a comic book character in comparison. Joshua Cole seemed genuine. That's why the *trust* element was there, despite the fact she had known him only a matter of days. That's why she had let her guard down, when she of all people, jilted, should have her guard up higher.

When had she decided it would be okay to trust him with her heart? It was the way he looked at her, compassionate intensity darkening the shade of green of his eyes. Something she interpreted as *interest,* hot, male and intoxicating was brewing just beneath the calm surface.

Yet for all that male energy—sure and strong—the way he had conducted himself over the past few days was nothing short of admirable. He was a man navigating a foreign land with the children, and yet he was doing it with grace and openness.

Even the way he plunged into the water after that canoe spoke to character. It was him, supposedly the self-centered bachelor, not her, the supposedly compassionate nanny, who had considered how others would react to the empty canoe showing up somewhere.

Dumb to plunge into the water after him, because what was she going to do? But somehow, ever since they'd gotten in that canoe together, she had felt the delicious sense of teamwork. She had plunged into the water almost on instinct. They were in this *together*.

But she was paying for her altruism now.

They were in the honeymoon cottage where hundreds of couples had shyly taken off their clothes for each other for the very first time.

And not a single one of them like this, she thought dourly. Not a single one of them because they were in imminent danger of shivering to death.

"Embarrassing," she muttered out loud.

"Forget embarrassment," he said, glancing back at her from where he was crouched in front of the fireplace, feeding little sticks into it, coaxing a bright blaze to life.

He had peeled off his sodden trousers as if it was the most natural thing in the world. Of course, for him, World's Sexiest Bachelor, it probably was.

Except for the part where he'd warned her he was doing it, giving her time to turn around.

Except for the part where he'd unearthed a container full of bedding, snapped off the lid, and tucked a blanket around himself.

He should have looked like an idiot with his flowing red tartan blanket tied in a knot at his taut stomach. Instead he looked like a chieftain, his shoulders and chest bare, his arms rippling with sinewy strength. There was a warrior cast to his face, remote and focused, as he had turned his attention to getting a fire going in the old stone fireplace.

"I can't get my jeans off," she wailed.

"What?"

"I can't get them off," she said, annoyed he was making her say it again. He had heard her the first time!

The soaked denim, which had probably been a touch snug to begin with, was stuck to her now. Her hands were so cold she couldn't make them do one thing she wanted them to do.

He turned and looked at her. "Are you asking me to help you get your pants off, Miss Pringy?"

"No!" Then with sudden rueful understanding, she said, "You like making me blush, don't you?"

"If I was considering a new hobby that would be it. I could while away hours at a time thinking up things like—"

"Now is not the time for games, Joshua! I'm just telling you I'm stuck. Just hand me a blanket."

He came across the room toward her, without the covering she had ordered, and his own blanket slipped. She held her breath, shamelessly hopeful, but he stopped and reknotted it, moved toward her.

"Just relax," he said soothingly, looking at the situation with what struck her as an annoying bent toward the analytical. She had the button undone on her jeans, and the zipper down. She had wrested the uncooperative, sodden, freezing fabric about three inches down her hips and there it was stuck, hard.

"It's because you're tense," he decided.

Taking off my pants in a room with the World's Sexiest Bachelor, and I'm tense. Go figure.

"It's because my hands are too cold." It was true her hands felt as if they had turned into icy basketballs at the ends of her wrists. But there was another problem. She was just going to have to admit it and get it over with.

"The jeans might have been a little too tight to begin with. Marginally."

"They looked fine to me," he said, apparently thinking about it. "More than fine. Great." She might have been thrilled that he'd noticed in different circumstances.

As it was, the jeans had been a bit of a challenge to get on, and that's when they'd been dry. What little devil of vanity had made her think her rear end looked good enough in them to put up with a tiny bit of discomfort?

"Look, no matter how reasonable a choice they were when they were dry, they won't come off now. They won't fit over my hips. There, am I blushing enough for you?"

His lips twitched.

"Don't laugh," she warned him.

"I won't," he said, but she could tell he was biting the inside of his cheek. Hard. He didn't speak for a minute, containing himself. "Let me help," he finally managed, and then choked. "I sound like a butler."

"Only one of us here would know what that sounded like," she warned him, but it was too late.

He was laughing, moving toward her with singleness of purpose written all over him.

"Don't touch me!" There. Self-preservation finally rising to the occasion. Where had that fine attribute of character been when she had been sobbing her heart out in his seemingly sympathetic ear?

"I can't help you without touching you."

"I don't need your help." That was a lie obvious to both of them. "You're laughing at me."

"I'm trying not to."

"Try harder."

"Okay." He crouched down, and was looking at the area where the soaked jeans were bound up around the wideness of her hips. Oddly enough, the way his eyes rested there, briefly and with heat, before returning to her face did not make her feel like a whale. At all. In fact, his laughter seemed to have died, too.

"Yes, you do," he said firmly, "need my help."

"Okay, then." She was shaking too hard to deny it any longer. She closed her eyes hard against her humiliation. "Just be quick."

"That's the first time I've ever heard that in this particular situation," he muttered.

"We are not in a *situation*," she warned him, "or not one you've ever been in before."

"You're absolutely right about that," he said.

His hands settled around the jeans. Her skin was so cold she actually felt scorched from the heat of his hands. She had to resist an impulse to wiggle into that warmth. Instead she made herself stand rigidly still. She opened her eyes just enough to squint at him undetected through the veil of her lashes.

He yanked with considerable strength, enough that she saw that lovely triceps muscle in his arm jump into gorgeous relief. Unfortunately the jeans did not budge, not a single, solitary fraction of an inch.

"Your skin feels like ice-cold marble," he noted clinically.

Somehow in her imagination, she had imagined him saying softly, *Your skin is like silk that's been heating in the sun, soft and sensual.*

When had she imagined such a thing? Practically every damn minute since she had met him, a dialogue of lust and wanting running just below her prim surface.

"Can't you relax?"

"I doubt it," she moaned, and then made the confession that made her humiliation complete. "You're going to have hurry. I think I have to go to the bathroom."

"Dannie, it would be really inadvisable for you to get us laughing right now. Really."

"Believe me, I am nowhere close to laughing." But his lips were twitching again. How had she ever thought he was handsome? He wasn't. He was like an evil leprechaun.

"Someday you'll see the humor in this," he assured her. "You'll tell your kids about it."

No, she wouldn't. Because a story like that would begin with, "Did I ever tell you how I met your dad?"

And he was not going to be the father of her children. Though suddenly she was aware she had a secret self that not only conducted entire conversations just out of range of her conscious mind, but *wished* things. Impossible things.

Green-eyed babies.

She told herself she had just gotten over another man. This was rebound lust, nothing more. But she was very aware of quite a different truth. There never had been another man, really, just a convenient fantasy, a risk-free way to play at love, a safe way to withdraw from the game while pretending to be engaged in it.

Joshua tugged again. The wet, cold, thick fabric shifted a mean half inch or so.

"Ouch. Who invented denim? What a ridiculous material," she complained.

"There's a reason they don't make swimsuits out of it," he agreed, and then broke it to her gently. "You're going to have to lie down on the bed. Hang on. I'll cut the mattress open."

He found a knife and cut the strings that were wrapped tightly around the mattress, a defense against mice.

Mice, which had probably been her greatest fear until about thirty seconds ago. Now her greatest fear was herself!

"Maybe you could just cut the jeans off," she said. She shuffled over to the bed, the jeans just down enough to impair her mobility, no dignified waltz across the cold cabin floor for her. She left great puddling footsteps in her wake.

"I'll keep that in mind as a last resort, but I might cut you by accident, so we'll try this first. Lie down."

Why didn't her fantasies *ever* work out? Every woman in the world would die to hear those words from his lips. "Don't get bossy," she said, so he'd never guess how great her disappointment was at the *way* he said that.

"Hey, if you could have followed simple instructions in the first place, you wouldn't be in this predicament."

She turned around and flopped down on the mattress, her knees hanging over. "I wasn't letting you go in that water by yourself."

"Why not?"

The truth blasted through her. *I think I'm falling in love with you. For real, damn it, not some romantic illusion I can take home and satisfy with buying dresses and planning honeymoons I know are never going to happen.*

Out loud she said, "The team thing. Okay, pull. Pull hard."

Real, she scoffed at herself. She was getting more pathetic by the day. You did not fall in love with a man in four days. Unless you were a Hollywood celebrity, which she most definitely was not.

She felt his hands, scorching hot again against the soft flesh of her hips and looked at the frown of concentration marring his handsome features.

It felt real, even if it wasn't. Of course, people who heard little voices swore that was real, too.

"Hang on," he said. He took a grip and pulled. The jeans inched down. Finally he was past the horrible hip obstacle, but now his hands rested on the top of her thighs, his thumbs brushing that delicate tissue of pure sensitivity on her inner leg. Thankfully, the skin was nearly frozen, not nearly sensitive enough to make her reach up grab his ears and order him huskily to make her warm.

He tugged again. His hands moved from the thigh

area and the jeans reluctantly parted from her frozen, pebbled skin. He yanked them free triumphantly, held them up for her to see, as if he was a hunter holding up a snake he had killed and skinned just for her.

"My skin looks like lard, doesn't it?" she demanded, watching his face for signs of revulsion. If she had seen any, she would have gotten up and marched straight back into that lake!

He was silent for a long moment. "Alabaster," he said softly.

"Huh!" Nonetheless, she was mollified for a half second or so until she thought of something else. "I hope I don't have on the panties that say Tuesday."

"Uh, no, you don't."

Suddenly she saw why he delighted so in making her blush, because when she saw that brick red rise up from his neck and suffuse his cheeks, she felt gleeful.

"Wednesday?" she asked, shocked at herself.

"I am trying to be a gentleman!"

Of course he was. And it didn't come naturally to him, either. One little push, and he wouldn't be a gentleman at all.

But did she know how to handle that?

"Here's a blanket," he said, sternly, handing it to her.

She glanced down before she took the blanket from him. Plain white, the perfect underwear for the nanny to have her encounter with the billionaire playboy! Of course the encounter was tragic, rather than romantic. She really didn't have what it took to start a fire that she didn't know how to put out!

She wrapped the blanket around herself, lurched off the bed, nearly tripped in the folds.

He reached out to steady her. "It's okay," he said softly. "Don't be embarrassed."

She looked at where his hand rested on her arm. There was that potential for fire again. She pulled her arm away. "I have to go to the bathroom. Now can I be embarrassed?"

"Yeah, okay. Everybody on the planet has to go to the bathroom about four times a day, but if you want to be embarrassed about it be my guest." And then he grinned at her in a way that made embarrassment ease instead of grow worse, because when he grinned like that she saw the person he *really* was.

Not a billionaire playboy riding the helm of a very successful company. Not the owner of a grand apartment, and the pilot of his own airplane.

The kid in the picture on the beach, long ago.

And in her wildest fantasies, she could see herself sitting around a campfire, wrapped in a blanket like this one, her children shoulder to shoulder with her, saying,

"Tell us again how you met Daddy."

She bolted out of the cabin, then took her time trying to regain her composure. Finally she went back in.

He had pulled the couch in front of the fire and patted the place beside him. "Nice and warm."

Cottage. Fire. Gorgeous man.

In anyone else's life this would be a good equation! She squeezed herself into the far corner of the couch, as far away from him as she could get.

He passed her half a chocolate bar.

She swore quietly. Cottage. Fire. Gorgeous man. Chocolate.

"Nannys aren't allowed to swear," he reprimanded her lightly.

"Under duress!"

"What kind of duress?" he asked innocently.

She closed her eyes. *Don't tell him, idiot.* Naturally her mouth started moving before it received the strict instructions from her brain to shut up. "You'll probably think this is hilarious, but I'm finding you very attractive."

At least it wasn't a declaration of love.

"It's probably a symptom of getting too cold," she added in a rush. "Lack of oxygen to the brain. Or something."

"It's probably the way I look in a blanket," he said, deadpan.

"I suppose there is that," she agreed reluctantly, and then with a certain desperation, "Is there any more chocolate?"

"I find you attractive, too, Dannie."

She blew out a disbelieving snort.

He leaned across the distance between them and touched her hair. "I can't tell you how long I've wanted to do this." His hands stroked her hair, his fingers a comb going through the tangles gently pulling them free. He moved closer to her, buried his face in her hair, inhaled.

She was so aware this was his game, his territory, he *knew* just how to make a woman melt. Spineless creature that she was, she didn't care. In her mind she took that stupid locket and threw it way out into Moose Lake.

What kind of fire she could or could not put out suddenly didn't matter. So close to him, so engulfed in the sensation of his hands claiming her hair, she didn't care if she burned up on the fires of passion!

She turned her head, caught the side of his lip, touched it with her tongue. He froze, leaned back, stared at her, golden light from the fire flickering across the handsome features of his face.

And then he surrendered. Only it was not a surrender at all. He met her tentativeness with boldness that took her breath away. He plundered her lips, took them captive, tasted them with hunger and welcome.

She knew then the totality of the lie she had told herself about loving another, about pining for another.

Because she had never felt this intensity of feeling before, as if fireworks were exploding against a night sky, as if her heart had started to beat after a long slumber, as if her blood had turned to fire. There was not a remnant of cold left in her.

Burn, she told herself blissfully, *burn.*

"I've wanted to do that for a long time, too," he whispered, his voice sexy, low and hoarse. "You taste of rain. Your hair smells of flowers, you do not disappoint, Danielle."

She tasted him, rubbed her lips over the raspiness of whiskers, back to the softness of his mouth, along the column of his neck. She gave herself permission to let go.

And felt the exquisite pull of complete freedom. She went back to his mouth, greedy for his taste and for the sensation of him. She let her hands roam his bare skin, felt the exquisite texture of it, soft, the hardness of male muscle and bone just beneath that surface softness.

His breathing was coming in hard gasps, almost as if she knew what she was doing.

She both did and didn't. The part of her that was knowledge knew nothing of this, she was an explorer in unmapped terrain. But the part of her that was instinct, animal and primal, knew everything about this, knew just how to make him crazy.

She loved it when she felt him begin to tremble as

her lips followed the path scorched out first across his naked chest with her hand.

"Stop," he said hoarsely.

She laughed, loving this new wicked side to herself. "No."

But he pulled away from her, back to his own side of the couch. As she watched him with narrowed eyes, he ran a hand through the spikiness of his hair that looked bronze in the firelight.

"We aren't doing this," he said, low in his throat, not looking at her.

She laughed again, feeling the exquisiteness of her power.

"I'm not kidding, Dannie. My sister would kill me."

"You're going to mention your sister *now?*"

"She always comes to mind when I'm trying to do the decent thing," he said sourly.

"I'm a grown woman," she said. "I make my own decisions."

"Yeah, good ones, like following me into the water when it was completely unnecessary." She moved across the couch toward him. He leaped out of it.

"Dannie, don't make this hard on me."

"I plan to make it very hard on you," she said dangerously, gathering her own blanket around her, sliding off the couch.

"Hey, I hear something."

She smiled. "Sure you do."

"It's a powerboat!"

She froze, tilted her head, could not believe the stinginess of the gods. They were stealing her moment from her! She had *chosen* to burn.

And now the choice was being taken away from her!

There was no missing his expression of relief as the

sound of the motor grew louder out there in the darkness. With one last look at her—gratitude over a near miss, wistful, too, he grabbed his blanket tighter with one fist, and bolted out the door.

As soon as he was gone, the feeling of power left her with a slam. She flopped back on the couch and contemplated what had just transpired.

She, Danielle Springer, had become the tigress.

"Shameless hussy, more like," she told herself.

She was not being rescued in a blanket! Her state of undress suddenly felt like a neon Shameless Hussy sign! She tossed it down and grabbed her jeans from where he had hung them on a line beside the fire.

They were only marginally drier than before, and now beginning to stiffen as if someone had accidentally dropped a box of starch in with the laundry.

Nonetheless, she lay back down on the bed and tried valiantly to squeeze them back on.

She had just gotten to that awful hip part when he came back in the door.

"Don't look," she said huffily. "I'm getting dressed. I plan to maintain my dignity." As if it wasn't way too late for that!

He made a noise she didn't like.

She let go of her jeans and rolled up on her elbow to look at him. "What?"

"That was Michael in the boat. The bottom of the lake is really rocky here and he can't see because it's too dark. He said if we'd be okay for the night, he'd come back in the morning."

"And you told him we'd be okay for the night?" she said incredulously. It was so obvious things were not okay, that her self-discipline had unraveled like a spool of yarn beneath the claws of a determined kitten.

"That's what I told him."

"Without asking me?"

"Sorry, I'm used to making executive decisions."

She picked up a pillow and hurled it at him. He ducked. She hurled every pillow on that bed, and didn't hit him once. If there had been anything else to pick up and throw, she would have done that, too.

But there was nothing left, not within reach, and she was not going to get up with her jeans half on and half off to go searching. Instead she picked up her discarded blanket, and pulled it over herself, even over her head.

"Go away," she said, muffled.

It occurred to her, her thirty seconds of passion had done the worst possible thing: turned her into her parents! Loss of control happened that fast.

And had such dire consequences, too. Look at her mom and dad. A perfect example of people prepared to burn in the name of love.

She peeked up from the blanket.

In the murky darkness of the cabin, she saw he had not gone away completely. He had found a stub of a candle and lit it. Now he was going through the rough cabinets, pulling out cans.

"You want something to eat?" he asked, as if she hadn't just been a complete shrew, made a complete fool of herself.

Of course she wanted something to eat! That's how she handled pain. That's why the jeans didn't fit in the first place. She yanked them back off, wrapped herself tightly in the blanket and crossed the room to him. If he could pretend nothing had happened, so could she.

"This looks good," she said, picking up a can of tinned spaghetti. If he noticed her enthusiasm was forced, he didn't say a word.

"Delicious," he agreed, looking everywhere but at her, as if somehow spaghetti was forbidden food, like the apple in the garden of Eden.

CHAPTER SEVEN

"DELICIOUS," Dannie said woodenly. "Thank you for preparing dinner."

Hell hath no fury like a woman scorned, Joshua thought, trying not to look at Dannie. He'd been right about her and spaghetti. Her mouth formed the most delectable little *O* as she sucked it back. No twisting the spaghetti around her fork using a spoon for her.

The ancient stove in the cabin was propane fired, and either the tanks had not been filled, because there was going to be no season this year at Moose Lake, or it had just given out in old age. He'd tried his luck with a frying pan and a pot over the fire, and the result was about as far from delicious as he could have made it. Even on purpose.

"Everything's scorched," he pointed out.

Something flashed in her eyes, vulnerable, and then closed up again. Truthfully it wouldn't have mattered if it was lobster tails and truffles. Everything he put in his mouth tasted like sawdust. Burnt sawdust.

The world was tasteless because he'd hurt her. Insulted her. Rejected her.

It was for her own bloody good! And if she didn't quit doing that to the spaghetti his resolve would melt like sugar in boiling water.

He made the mistake of looking at her, her features softened by the golden light of the fire and the tiny, guttering candles, but her expression hardened into indifference and he could see straight through to the hurt that lay underneath.

She plucked a noodle from her bowl, and he felt that surge of heat, of pure wanting. He knew himself. Part of it was because she was such a good girl, prim and prissy, a bit of a plain Jane.

It was the librarian fantasy, where a beautiful hellcat lurked just under the surface of the mask of respectability.

Except that part wasn't a fantasy. Unleashed, Danielle Springer was a hellcat! And the beauty part just deepened and deepened and deepened.

He wanted back what he had lost. Not the heated kisses; he'd had plenty of those and would have plenty more.

No, what he wanted back was the rare trust he felt for her and had gained from her. What he wanted back was the ease that had developed between them over the past few days, the sense of companionship.

"Want to play cards?" he asked her.

The look she gave him could have wilted newly budded roses. "No, thanks."

"Charades?"

No answer.

"Do you want dessert?"

The faintest glimmer of interest that was quickly doused.

"It's going to be a long evening, Dannie."

"God forbid you should ever be bored."

"As if anybody could ever be bored around you," he muttered. "Aggravating, annoying, doesn't listen, doesn't appreciate when sacrifices have been made for her own good—"

She cut him off. "What were the dessert options?"

"Chocolate cake. No oven, but chocolate cake." Just to get away from the condemnation in her eyes, he got up, his blanket held up tightly, and went and looked at the cake mix box he had found in one of the cupboards.

He fumbled around in the poor light until he found another pot, dumped the cake mix in and added water from a container he had filled at the lake. He went and crouched in front of the fire, holding the pot over the embers, stirring, waiting, stirring.

Then he went and got a spoon, and sat on the couch. "You want some?" he asked.

"Sure. The girl who can't even squeeze into her jeans will forgive anything for cake," she said. "Even bad cake. Fried cake. I bet it's gross."

"It isn't," he lied. "You looked great in those jeans. Stop it." And then, cautiously, he said, "What's to forgive?"

"I wanted to keep kissing. You didn't."

"I need a friend more than I need someone to kiss. Do you know how fast things can blow up when people go there?" He almost added *before they're ready.* But that implied he was going to be ready someday, and he wasn't sure that was true. You couldn't say things to Dannie Springer until you were sure they were true.

Silence.

"Come on," he said softly. "Forgive me. Come eat cake." He wasn't aware his heart had stopped beating until it started again when she flopped down on the couch beside him.

He filled up the spoon with goo and passed it to her, tried not to look at how her lips closed around that spoon. Then he looked anyway, feeling regret and yearning in equal amounts. He'd thought watching her eat spaghetti was sexy? The girl made sharing a spoon seem like something out of the *Kama Sutra*.

The cake was like a horrible, soggy pudding with lumps in it, but they ate it all, passing the spoon back and forth, and it tasted to him of ambrosia.

"Tell me something about you that no one knows," he invited her, wanting that trust back, longing for the intimacy they had shared on the lakeshore. Even if it had been dangerous. It couldn't be any more dangerous than sharing a spoon with her. "Just one thing."

"Is that one of your playboy lines?" she asked.

"No." And it was true. He had never said that to a single person before.

Still, she seemed suspicious and probably rightly so. "You first."

When I put that spoon in my mouth, all I can think is that it has been in your mouth first.

"I was a ninety-pound weakling up until the tenth grade."

"I already knew that. Your sister has a picture of you."

"Out where anyone can see it?" he asked, pretending to be galled.

"Probably posted on the Internet," she said. "Try again."

There was one thing no one knew about him, and for a moment it rose up in him begging to be released. To her. For a moment, the thought of not carrying that burden anymore was intoxicating in its temptation.

"Sometimes I pass gas in elevators," he said, trying for a light note, trying to be superficial and funny and irreverent, trying to fight the demon that wanted out.

"You do not! That's gross."

"Real men often are," he said. "You heard it here first."

"Wow. I don't even think I want to kiss you again."

"That's good."

"Was it that terrible?" she demanded.

Could she really believe it had been terrible? That made the temptation to show her almost too great to bear. Instead, he gnawed on the now empty spoon. "No," he said gruffly, "It wasn't terrible at all. Your turn."

"Um, in ninth grade I sent Leonard Burnside a rose. I put that it was from Miss Marchand, the French teacher."

"You liked him?"

"Hated him," she said. "Full-of-himself jock. He actually went to the library and learned a phrase in French that he tried out on her. Got kicked out of school for three days."

"Note to self—do not get on Danielle Springer's bad side."

"I never told anyone. It was such a guilty pleasure. Your turn."

"I don't floss, ever."

"You *are* gross."

"You mean you could tell I didn't floss?" he asked sulkily. "I knew if you really knew me, you wouldn't want to kiss me."

And then the best thing happened. She was laughing. And he was laughing. And they were planning cruel sequences that she could have played on full-of-himself Lennie Burnside.

It grew very quiet. The fire sputtered, and he felt warm and content, drowsy. She shifted over, he felt her head fall onto his shoulder. Even though he knew better, he reached out and fiddled with her hair.

"The part I don't get about you," she said, after a long time that made him wonder if she'd spent all that time thinking of him, "is if you had such a good time with your family on family holidays, why is your own company geared to the young and restless crowd?"

The battle within him was surprisingly short. He had carried it long enough. The burden was too heavy.

He was shocked that he *wanted* to tell her. And only her.

Shocked that he wanted her to know him completely. With all his flaws and with all his weaknesses. He wanted her to know he was a man capable of making dreadful errors. He wanted to know if the unvarnished truth about him would douse that look in her eyes when she looked at him, dewy, yearning.

"When I was in college," he said softly, "the girl I was dating became pregnant. We had a son. We agreed to put him up for adoption."

For a long time she was absolutely silent, and then she looked at him. In the faint light of the fire, it was as if she was unmasked.

What he saw in her eyes was not condemnation. Or anything close to it.

Love.

Her hand touched his face, stroked, comforting.

"You didn't want to," Dannie guessed softly. "Oh, Joshua."

He glanced at her through the golden light of the dying fire. She was looking at him intently, as if she was holding her breath. Her hand was still on his cheek. He could turn his head just a touch and nibble her thumb. But it would be wrong. A lie. Trying to distract them both from the real intimacy that was happening here, and from her deepest secret, which he had just seen in her eyes.

"No, I didn't want to. I guess I wanted what I'd had before, a family to call my own again, that *feeling*. I cannot tell you how I missed that feeling after Mom and Dad died. Of belonging, of having a place to go to where people knew you, clean through. Of being held to a certain standard by the people who knew you best and knew what you were capable of."

He was shocked by how much he had said, and also shocked by how easily the words came, as if all these years they had just waited below the surface to be given voice.

"What happened to the baby?" Dannie asked quietly.

"Sarah didn't want to be tied down. She wasn't ready to settle down. I considered, briefly, trying to go it on my own, as a single dad, but Sarah thought that was stupid. A single dad, just starting in life, when all these established families who could give that baby so much stability and love were just waiting to adopt? My head agreed with her. My heart—"

He stopped, composing himself, while she did the perfect thing and said nothing. He went on, "My heart never did. Some men could be unchanged by that. I wasn't. I couldn't even finish school. I tried to run away from what I was feeling. I had abandoned my own son to the keeping of strangers. What kind of person did a thing like that?

"I traveled the world and developed an aversion for places that catered to families. Wasn't there anywhere a guy like me could get away from all that love? I kind of just fell into the resort business, bought a rundown hotel in Italy, started catering to the young and hip and single, and became a runaway success before I knew what had hit me."

Her hand, where it touched his cheek, was tender. It felt like absolution. But he knew the truth. She could not absolve him.

Silence for a long, long time.

And then she said, "Funny, that your company is called Sun. If you say it, instead of spell it, it's kind of like you carried him with you, isn't it? Your son. Into every single day."

That was the problem with showing your heart to someone like Dannie. She saw it so clearly.

And then she said, "Have you considered the possibility that what you did was best for him? That he did get a family who were desperate for a child to love? Who could give him exactly what you missed so much after your parents died?"

"On those rare occasions that I allow myself to think about it, that is my hope. No, more than a hope. A prayer. And I'm a man who doesn't pray much, Dannie."

"Have you ever thought of finding him?" she asked softly.

"Now and then."

"And what stops you?"

"How complicated it all seems. Just go on the Internet and type in *adoption* to see what a mess of options there are, red tape, legal ramifications, ethical dilemmas."

Dannie wasn't buying it, seeing straight through him. "You must have a team of lawyers who could cut to the quick in about ten minutes. If you haven't done it, there's another reason."

"Fear, then, I guess," he said, relieved to make his

truth complete, wanting her to know who he really was. Maybe wanting himself to know, too. "Fear of being rejected. Fear of opening up a wanting that will never be satisfied, searching the earth for what I can't have or can't find."

"Oh, Joshua," she said sadly, "you don't get it at all, do you?"

"I don't?" He had told her his deepest truth, and though the light of love that shone in her eyes did not lessen, her words made him feel the arrow of her disappointment.

A woman like Dannie could show a man who was lost how to find his way home. Like being in a family, she would never accept anything but his best. Like being in a family, she would show him how to get there when he couldn't find his way by himself.

For the first time in a very, very long time, the sense of loneliness within him eased, the sense that no one really knew him dissipated.

"When you gave your son up for adoption, it wasn't really about what you needed or wanted, Joshua," she said gently. "And it isn't now, either. It's about what he needs and wants. What if he wants to know who his biological father is?"

And suddenly he saw how terribly self-centered he had always been. He had become more so, not less, after he had walked away from his baby seven years ago. He had layered himself in self-protective self-centeredness.

And he was so glad he had not taken that kiss with Dannie to where it wanted to go.

Because he had things he needed to do, roads he needed to travel down, places he needed to visit. Places of the heart.

For a moment, sitting here by the fire, exchanging

laughter and confidences, eating off the same spoon, slurping spaghetti, he had thought it felt like homecoming.

Now he saw he could not have that feeling, not with her and not with anyone else, not until he had made peace with who he was and what he had done.

A long time ago he had given his own flesh and blood into the keeping of strangers. He had tried to convince himself it was the right decision. He had rationalized all the reasons it was okay. But in the back of his mind, he had still been a man, self-centered and egotistical, *knowing* that child would have disrupted his plans and his life and his dreams.

Ironically, even after he'd made the decision that would supposedly set him free, he had been a prisoner of it.

Dannie had seen that right away. *Sun. Son.*

A nibbling sense of failure, of having made a mistake in an area where it really counted, had chased him, and chased him hard. He had barely paused to catch a breath at each of his successes before beginning to run again. He had lost faith in himself because of that decision.

And no amount of success, money, power or acquisition had ever absolved him.

But Dannie was right. It was about the child, not about him. If he found out if his boy was okay, then would the demons rest? If he was able to put the needs of that babe ahead of his own, then was he the man worthy of what he saw in Dannie's eyes?

Joshua realized when he had come back into this cabin, after Michael had roared away in the motorboat, leaving them here together until morning, he had thought his mission was to get her to trust him again, the way she had when she had told him about her disastrous nonrelationship with the college professor. The way she had when she had told him about a wedding gown that she had spent all her money on and that she would never wear.

But now he saw that mission for what it was: impossible.

He could not ask anyone else to place their trust in him until he had restored his trust in himself, his belief that he could be counted on to do the right thing.

Where did that start? Maybe his journey had begun already, with saying yes to the needs of his niece and nephew. And then again, maybe that didn't count, since he'd had an ulterior motive.

Maybe his journey had begun when he had backed away from Dannie, backed away from the soft invitation of her lips and the hot invitation of her eyes, because he had known he was not ready and neither was she.

And maybe he could win back his trust in himself by taking one tiny step at a time. Was it as simple—and as difficult—as adding his name to an adoption registry, so that his son would know if he ever wanted him, he would be there for him?

"Thank you for trusting me," Dannie said softly.

The last of the embers were dying, and her voice came at him out of the darkness.

"Dannie, you are completely trustworthy," he said. And he wondered if someday he was going to be a man worthy of that.

But he had a lot of work to do before he was. The darkness claimed him, and when he woke in the morning, it was to the sound of a powerboat moving across the lake. His neck hurt from sleeping on the couch; he could not believe how good it felt to have her cuddled into him.

Trusting.

He sighed, put her away from him, got up and pulled his stiff slacks from where they were strung in front of the now-dead fire.

Trust. He could not even trust himself to look at her, did not think he was strong enough to fight the desire to say good morning to her with a kiss.

Dannie barely spoke on the way back across the water. Neither did he. There was something so deep between them now it didn't even need words. That was what he wanted to be worthy of.

They had barely landed when Susie greeted them, by dancing between the two of them, and throwing her sturdy arms around their knees, screeching as if it was Christmas morning. Even the baby seemed thrilled to see them.

Worthy of this kind of love.

"Were you okay over there?" Sally asked. "What a terrible thing to happen."

"We were fine, but I think the canoe is beyond repair," Joshua said. "I'll replace it."

Sally made a noise that sounded suspiciously close to disgust. "I'm not worried about *stuff*," she said annoyed. "Stuff can be replaced. People can't."

A little boy in a blue blanket. Never replaced. Not with all the stuff.

"I've made a farewell breakfast," Sally said, turning away from them and leading the way back to the lodge. "Come."

With Susie holding his one hand, as if he completely deserved her love and devotion, and the baby in the crook of his arm, he followed Sally up to the lodge. Dannie trailed behind, lost in her own thoughts.

Sally had made a wonderful feast: bacon, eggs,

pancakes, fresh-squeezed juice. For them. For people she barely knew. Still, she looked a little sad and Joshua realized that was part of the magic of this place. It made everyone who came here into family, it made every farewell difficult.

He had not once discussed business with Michael, and suddenly he was glad. He had not made any promises he could not keep.

Trust. It was time to be a man he could be proud of. That Dannie would be proud of. That maybe his son would be proud of one day.

"I have a confession to make," he said, when the remnants of breakfast had been cleared away. Susie was in front of the fire, playing with an old wooden fire engine, out of earshot.

He looked Michael in the eye. "Michael, I was trying to get rid of my niece and nephew when you called. They'd arrived in my life because of an error in dates. I didn't want them there. They made me feel inadequate and uncomfortable. But when I got the feeling that they might improve my chances of acquiring the lodge, I jumped at your invitation and I brought them with me. I was going to play devoted uncle to manipulate your impressions of me."

He glanced at Dannie, could not read the expression on her face. Had he disappointed her again?

"Instead of *using* them, as I'd intended," he continued, "the lodge gave me a chance to spend time with them and really enjoy them, and I'm very thankful to you and Sally for that opportunity."

No one looked at all surprised by his confession, as if he had been totally transparent all along. No one looked angry or betrayed or hurt.

Somehow he had stumbled on the place that was *family,* where everyone saw you as you were, and while they hoped the best for you, always saw the potential, they never seemed to judge where you were at in this moment.

"So, Joshua, what are your plans for the lodge if you acquire it?" Michael asked, but his voice conveyed a certain reluctance to discuss business.

Joshua was silent. Then he said words he did not think he had said in his entire business career. "I thought I knew. But I don't. I can't make you any promises. I don't know what direction Sun is moving in."

He glanced at Dannie. He knew she had heard the truth. It was not about Sun right now. It was about son.

Michael sighed and looked at his hands, Joshua could clearly see he was a man with the weight of the world on his shoulders.

Dannie, always intuitive, saw it, too.

"Why are you selling Moose Lake Lodge?" Dannie asked. "You obviously love this place so much. To be frank, I can't even picture the place without you two here."

It was the kind of question Joshua would never have asked in the past. It was the kind of question that blurred the lines between professional and personal.

On the other hand, hadn't those lines been blurring for days now? He felt grateful it had been asked. He felt as if the right decision on his part needed the full story and all the facts.

Sally shot Joshua a look, clearly wondering if he would use any weakness against them. She glanced at her husband. He shrugged, and she covered his big work-worn hand with hers.

It was a gesture of such tenderness, some connection between them so strong and so bright, that Joshua felt his eyes smart.

Or maybe it was just from the fire smoking in the

hearth. Or from several days so far out of his element. Or from falling in love with Dannie Springer.

He looked at her again, saw her watching Sally with such enormous compassion. Remembered her over the past few days, laughing, playing with the kids, running into the lake right behind him when the boat had broken free.

A woman a man could share the burdens with, just as Sally and Michael so obviously had shared theirs over the years. A woman a man could go to as himself, flawed, and still feel valued. *Worthy.*

He had said it in his own mind. He was falling in love with her. He waited for the terror to come.

But it didn't. Instead what came was a sense of peace such as he had not felt for a very long time.

"We're selling, or trying to sell, for a number of reasons," Sally said, her voice soft with emotion. "Partly that we're too old to do the place justice anymore." She stopped, distressed, and he watched Michael's hand tighten over hers.

"It's mostly that our daughter is sick," Michael said gruffly. "Darlene has an aggressive form of a degenerative muscle disorder. She practically grew up here, but she can't come here anymore. She's got three little kids and she's a single mom.

"Pretty soon she's going to need a wheelchair. And if she's going to stay in her own home, everything has to be changed, from the cabinets to the door handles. She's going to need a special lift system to get in the bathtub. She's going to need a modified van. She's going to need us."

Joshua heard the unspoken: it was going to take more money than they knew how to raise to take care of their daughter as her health deteriorated.

Michael got up abruptly and walked out into the clear brightness of the morning, a man prepared to do the right thing, no matter how hard it was, no matter what it cost him, no matter what he had to let go of.

"Sorry," Sally said, watching him go, pain and love equal in her eyes. "It's hard for a man to care as much as he does and to find himself helpless."

It really confirmed everything Joshua already knew about love. It could slay the strongest man. It could tear the flesh from his bones. It could leave him trembling and unsure of the world.

He looked at Dannie. She was staring into the fire.

He saw her hand had crept into Sally's. Such a small thing. Such a right thing.

He felt sick to his stomach. He wanted the Moose Lake Lodge, and he wanted it badly. But he wasn't going to take advantage of these fine people's misery.

Except they needed the money.

And they only had one way to get it.

To sell what they loved most. Their history. Their memories.

Why did his whole life feel all wrong ever since the nanny had put in an appearance?

Only a few days ago, Joshua Cole had been sure of his identity: businessman, entrepreneur. Maybe he'd even embraced the playboy part of it a little bit because it had allowed him to fill up his life with superficial fun but never required anything *real* of him.

Today he was sure of nothing at all, least of all his identity.

Later that morning, his bags packed beside him, Joshua watched Dannie and the kids from the safety of the porch on Angel's Rest. They were walking the beach one last time with Sally, Dannie carrying the baby, her feet bare in the cold sand. He acutely felt, watching that scene, the emptiness of his own life.

He had filled it with stuff instead of substance.

He watched Dannie pull something from her pocket. He saw her reach inside herself for strength, and then she sent that small object hurtling out into the water, further than he could have imagined she could throw.

He saw the glint of gold catching in the sun, before the object completed its upward arch and then plummeted to the lake and slipped beneath the surface with nary a ripple.

From here he could hear Dannie's laughter. And understood that she was free.

He was glad to get on the plane an hour later. His world. Precision. Control. He hoped for freedom as great as he had heard in Dannie's laughter.

But instead of feeling a joyous release as the plane took off, he was acutely aware there would be no more running. He could not fly away from the truths he had to face. They would just be waiting when he landed.

It occurred to him that maybe he would never find his own son. Or maybe he would find him, and the family would choose not to have contact.

But he was aware that he could reclaim his faith in himself in other ways.

Joshua Cole knew his heart was ready.

And he was surprised to find he did have a simple faith, after all. It was that once a heart was ready, the opportunities would come. And once a man was ready, he would take them.

CHAPTER EIGHT

THEY were saying goodbye. Dannie couldn't believe it had happened this fast. She had wanted to tell Joshua she admired him for telling Sally and Michael the truth. She wanted to ask him how he planned to help them, for surely he did.

And she had wanted to thank him for telling her about his son.

But somehow, during that short flight back to Vancouver from Moose Lake Lodge, the opportunity had never come. Aside from the fact his expression had been remote and focused, not inviting any kind of conversation, Jake had been terribly fussy.

Susie had a delayed reaction to the fact they had left her for the night without consulting her, and her upset had intensified when she had not been able to find Michael to tell him goodbye.

Now she was behaving outrageously. Bits of stuffing from the teddy bear Joshua had given her on their first day with him was soon floating in the air, landing in handfuls in the front seats of the aircraft.

Joshua didn't even seem to notice, but no wonder when he landed, he asked them to wait, and then disappeared into the terminal.

When he came back out he told them he had arranged their flight home. A chartered plane would take them to Toronto, a car and driver would meet them and take them to his sister's house.

He took Dannie's hands in both his own. For a moment she thought he was going to kiss her, but he didn't. In some ways the look in his eyes was better than a kiss.

Trusting. Forthright.

"I'll be in touch as soon as I can," he said. "I have some things I need to look after first. I don't know how long it will take, but when it is done, I promise, I will come for you."

Words eerily like those Brent had spoken.

Would she do it again? Build a fantasy around a few words, a vague promise? But when she returned his look, she found herself believing. This time it was real.

But the lifestyles-of-the-rich-and-famous flight home, the growing geographical distance between them, played with her mind. Nothing about this private plane ride seemed *real*.

Was it possible Joshua Cole had divested her from his life?

Was it possible he had left the story in the middle? Was it possible Dannie might never know what happened to Sally and Michael? To Sun and Moose Lake Lodge?

Was it possible he would make that journey of the heart, his decisions about his son, alone? By himself?

He was the playboy. Lethally charming. Had she fallen, hook, line and sinker, for that lethal charm, or had she really seen the genuine Joshua Cole, the one he showed no one else?

Melanie and Ryan arrived home a day later, tanned and relaxed, more in love than ever.

Their affection and respect for each other seemed, impossibly, to have deepened. Susie's behavioral problems evaporated instantly once her secure family unit was back the way she wanted it to be.

Dannie had never felt on the outside of that family quite so much. She had never felt so uncertain of her own choices.

Part of her waited, on pins and needles, jumping every time the phone rang. Because when she thought back on her time with Joshua, it seemed as if it had been exquisitely solid, an island in the land of mist that her life had been. It seemed as if those days at Moose Lake Lodge might have been the most real thing about her entire life.

It felt as if what she had been when she was with him, alive and strong and connected to life, had been the genuine deal. She was sure he had felt it, too.

He had shared his secret self with her. He had told her about his son. Every time she thought of the way he had looked as he told that story, lost and forlorn, and yet so brave and so determined, she felt like weeping. She felt as if she wanted to be there for him as he took the next steps, whatever he decided those would be.

She had been sure he would call. Positive that his promise meant something. She had felt as if he needed her to navigate the waters he was entering, as if she could be on his team as surely as when they had paddled the canoe together.

When he did not call, for one day and then another, her self-doubt returned in force. When a week passed with no call, Dannie condemned herself as the woman who could spin a romance, a fantasy out of the flimsiest of fabrics.

Brent had given her a locket with his picture in it. He had made vague promises. Naturally he was coming home to marry her.

Joshua Cole, World's Sexiest Bachelor, in a moment of complete vulnerability had told her his deepest secret. Naturally that meant he was throwing over all the women he'd been paired with in the past!

He was giving up actresses and singers and heiresses for the nanny! Of course he was! Dannie even took her wedding dress out of its wrapper and laid it on her bed, allowed herself to look at it wistfully and imagine herself gliding down the aisle, *him* waiting for her.

But as the days passed and it became increasingly apparent he wasn't, Dannie found comfort in chocolate rather than her wedding dress!

"Okay," Mel said finally. "Tell me what on earth happened to you, Dannie?"

"What do you mean?"

"You're gaining about a pound a day! You're not the same with the children as you were before. It's as if you've decided to be an employee instead of a member of our family. I miss you! What's going on?"

"It's the whole Brent thing," Dannie lied. *The whole romance thing. The whole life thing.*

But Melanie stared at her, and understanding, totally unwanted, dawned in her eyes.

"It's not Brent," she guessed softly. "It's my brother. What has Josh done to you?"

"Nothing," Dannie said, quickly. Obviously way too quickly.

"I'm going to kill him," Mel said.

Dannie had a sudden humiliating picture of Mel phoning her brother and reaming him out for having done something to her nanny.

The one he had probably forgotten existed as soon as he'd divested himself of her at the airport!

"You didn't do a bit of matchmaking, did you? You

didn't think your brother and I would make a good pair, did you?" Dannie asked, remembering Joshua's embarrassing conclusion on their first meeting.

"Of course not," Melanie said quickly and vehemently, her eyes sliding all over the place and landing everywhere but on her nanny's face.

"You did!" Dannie breathed.

"I didn't. I mean not officially."

"But unofficially?"

"Oh, Dannie, I just love you so. And him. And you both seemed so lonely and so lost and so devoted to making absolutely the wrong choices for yourselves. I thought it couldn't hurt to put you together and just see what happened. I thought it couldn't do any harm. But it did, didn't it?"

Harm? Dannie thought of her days with Joshua, of the delight of getting to know him, and herself. Even if he never called, could those days be taken away from her? Could what she had glimpsed in herself fade away?

Only if she let it.

"I'm going to kill him," Melanie said again, but with no real force.

"You know what, Melanie?" Dannie said slowly, as understanding dawned in her. "Your brother didn't do anything to me. I do things to myself."

"What does that mean?" Melanie asked, skeptical.

"It means I have an imagination that fills in the gaps where reality leaves off."

As she said it, Dannie's understanding of herself grew. She was too willing to give her emotions into the keeping of other people. She was too willing to rearrange her whole world around a possibility, to put her whole life on hold while she *waited* for someone else to call the shots.

It was not admirable that she was willing to put her whole world and her whole life on hold in anticipation of some great love, some great event in the future! She'd done it with Brent on very little evidence, and now on even less evidence—only four days—she was going to waste time mooning over Joshua Cole?

No, he could have his car and his airplane and his fancy apartment and his five-star resorts. He could have heiresses and actresses and rock stars, if that was what made him happy. Love wanted the beloved to be happy. It didn't demand ownership!

Besides, Dannie missed the girl she had been, ever so briefly, in that canoe. Not a girl who *waited* for life to happen, but someone who participated fully, someone who had discovered her own strength and insisted on pulling her own weight.

While Melanie watched her, Dannie took the ice cream she was eating and washed it down the sink.

"That's it," she told her friend and employer. "No more self-pity. No more being victimized. I have a life to live!"

"I'm still going to kill him," Melanie muttered.

"Not for my benefit, you're not," Dannie said firmly.

The next day, her day off, she took the wedding gown to a local theatrical company and donated it to their costume department. They were thrilled to have it, and frankly she was thrilled to see it go. That's where that fantasy concoction of silk and lace belonged, in a world of make-believe. And that's where she was living no longer.

And then she went and signed up for canoe lessons at a place called Wilderness Ways Center. And while she was there, she noticed they had a class in rock climbing, and their own rock wall, so she signed up for that, too.

She took to her activities intensively, spending every free minute at the centre.

The loveliest and most unexpected thing happened. Danielle Springer had been waiting her whole life to fall in love. And she did.

She fell in love with herself.

She fell in love with the laughter-filled woman who attacked climbing walls and finicky canoes with a complete sense of adventure. She fell in love with the woman, whom she recognized had always been afraid of life, suddenly embracing its uncertainties.

She had always been a good nanny, and she knew that, but suddenly she felt as if she was a great nanny, because she was passing on this new and incredible sense of adventure and discovery to the children.

As the cool, fresh days of spring turned to the hot, humid days of summer, she found herself right out there jumping through the sprinkler with Susie, immersed in the wading pool with Jake.

She was teaching her young charges what she was learning: that life was a gift. An imperfect life, a life that did not go as planned, was no less a gift. Maybe a surprising life was even more of one.

The strangest thing was the more she danced with the gypsy spirit she was discovering in herself, the less she needed a man to validate her! When Joshua Cole had touched her lip with his thumb, he had told her he knew something of her that she did not know of herself.

But now she did! She knew she was strong and independent and capable. And fun loving. And full of mischief. And ready to dance with life! The irony, of course, was that men, who had always treated her as invisible, liked her. They flocked to her! They flirted with her.

The phone started ringing for her all the time. Now

that she could have anything she wanted, and anyone, she was surprised how much herself was enough. She liked how uncomplicated it was to live her own life, pursue her own interests, immerse herself in her job and her everyday pleasures. Something as simple as lying on the fragrant back lawn at night looking with wonder at the stars filled her to the top.

She was just coming in the door from her kayak lesson, when Melanie told her she had a phone call.

"It's Joshua," Melanie said, eyebrows raised, not even trying to hide her hope and delight that her brother might be coming to his senses.

Dannie picked up the phone. Despite how she had made herself over, her heart was hammering in her throat.

"How are you?" he asked.

Such a simple question. And yet the sound of his voice, alone, familiar, deep, masculine, tender, made her call him, in her own mind, "beloved."

"I'm fine, Joshua." Before she could ask how he was, he started talking again.

"Mel says you've been keeping really busy. Canoeing and rock climbing."

"I've been staying busy," she said, keeping her voice carefully neutral so he would not hear the unspoken, *I wish you could do it with me.*

"She says the guys are calling there all the time for you."

Was that faint jealousy in the World's Sexiest Bachelor's voice? Dannie laughed. "Not *all* the time."

His voice went very low. "She says you don't go out with any of them. Not on dates, anyway."

"Joshua! Your sister shouldn't be telling you anything about my private life."

"She can't resist me when I beg," he said.

Who could? "Why are you begging for information about me?"

"You know why."

Yes. She said nothing, afraid to speak, afraid to believe, afraid this was a test of all her resolve to not live in her fantasies but to create a dynamic reality for herself in the here and the now.

"Dannie, I couldn't call you until I had looked after certain things. Until I had done my very best to clear away any baggage, any heartache that would have kept me from being the man you deserve."

She wanted to tell him he was wrong, that he had always been the man she deserved, but something in her asked her to wait, to listen, and most of all, to believe.

"When I got back from Moose Lake Lodge, I thought of what you had said, about putting the ball in my son's court. Doing what he needed, instead of what I thought I needed or wanted. I discussed the options with one of my lawyers. After a lot of discussion we finally agreed to register with an agency that specializes in triad reunions. That means all three parties, the child, the adoptive family and the birth parents, have to want a contact or a meeting or a reunion. Until all three pieces are in place, nothing happens."

She could hear the emotion in his voice. She felt so proud of him. She felt as if she had never loved him more.

There was a long, long silence. Finally he spoke, whispered a single word.

"Dannie."

He couldn't possibly be crying. He couldn't. Not the strong, totally in control playboy. Not the World's Sexiest Bachelor. Not one of the world's successful entrepreneurs and resort visionaries.

Her Joshua, the one she had always seen, while the rest of the world bought the role he was playing, was capable of this great tenderness, this great vulnerability, this final unmasking.

"Dannie," Joshua choked out, "they were waiting for me."

"Oh, Joshua," she breathed his name, and then again in confirmation that he was exactly who she had known he was. "Oh, Joshua."

The tears of joy were coursing down her own cheeks.

"I've spoken to his parents on the phone. And him. It's funny, I had not grieved the death of his mother, until I had to tell him she was gone."

"Joshua." Again his name came from her lips like a celebration, like a prayer.

"I've arranged to meet my son and his adoptive parents this weekend. They live in Calgary. His name's Jared. I—" he stopped, hesitated, his voice still hoarse with emotion "—I'd like you to come with me."

"Why?" she said. It was a hard question to ask, when everything in her just wanted to say *yes*. Scream yes.

But his answer was everything. Everything. If he wanted her to come with him because of her skills as a nanny, it didn't count. It wasn't what she wanted. It wasn't even close. The seconds before he answered were easily the longest of her life.

"I want you to come with me because this is the most important thing I've ever done, and I cannot imagine doing it without you. I want you to come with me because I trust you more than I trust myself," he said, and then softly, ever so softly, "I want you to come because I think I could fall in love with you. I think I'm halfway there, already."

She couldn't speak through the tears.

"Dannie, are you there?"

"Yes."

"Will you?"

The question asked more than whether she would accompany him to meet his son for the first time.

It asked her to take a chance on this crazy, unpredictable, potential-for-heartbreak thing called love all over again.

"Will I? Oh, Joshua, I'm just like them." She took a deep breath. It did not stop her voice from shaking. "I've been waiting for you."

She didn't even know how true that was until she spoke the words. She hadn't even realized all of it—the canoeing and rock climbing, the boldly saying yes to life, all of it had been about being ready.

Being the kind of woman ready to fall in love—sure of herself and her place in the world first.

Not being *needy*, but being strong. Not needing another person to complete her, but bringing her whole self to a union.

It was true, she had been waiting for Joshua. It was just as true that she had been waiting for herself.

CHAPTER NINE

I'VE been waiting for you.

The words, and his memory of them, had been like a lifeline through the past few days. He held on to them, he held on to the beauty of what he had heard in Dannie's voice.

Joshua Cole had been the prime player in million-dollar deals. He had taken a company from nothing and turned it into something. He single-handedly ran an empire valued in billions, not millions.

And yet all that paled in comparison to how he felt about meeting his son. And about seeing Dannie again.

It was as if, in all his world, only two things mattered. Only two things had become important.

And both those things were all about *the* thing. Love.

He waited at the Calgary International airport for Dannie, nervously holding a bouquet of flowers for her. He had purchased flowers for dozens of women, and it had never caused him so much anxiety, choosing each bloom personally, debating over daisies or roses, baby's breath or lily of the valley.

He saw Dannie coming through the door of the security area, and was astonished by the changes in her, knew that daisies were *exactly* right, unpretentious, simple, earthy, beautiful, hardy.

Dannie looked as if she was twenty pounds lighter than she had been the first time he'd seen her. Gone was any vestige of the frumpalumpa. Today she was dressed in a white tailored silk shirt, a blazer, amazing low-riding jeans. He was aware he wouldn't have any problem peeling those jeans off her if they got wet!

Not that he wanted his mind to be going there since he was working so hard at being the man she deserved. Decent. Considerate. Strong. A man of integrity and honor.

Her hair was, thankfully, the same jet-black gypsy tangle. She had made no effort to tame it, and it sprang around her head in sexy, unruly curls that his fingers ached to touch. She was tanned and healthy looking, her turquoise eyes subtly shaded with makeup that made them pop.

He saw the man who came out the door ahead of her glance back, knew enough about male body language to know he was interested.

Hey, buddy, I saw her first.

And that was the truth. He had *seen* her, even before she had done one single thing to be seen.

Joshua saw that though Dannie had always radiated calm, a ship confident of riding out the storm, now there were layers to that calm. He saw the confidence in her. And the purity of her strength. And he knew he had never needed it more.

She saw him, and he didn't think for as long as he lived, he would ever forget the look in her eyes. More than welcome. More than joy. Bigger.

Homecoming.

She flew into his arms, no reservations, and he

picked her up and swung her around, felt his own welcoming answer to the look in her eyes, felt how right her sweet weight was in his arms, as if she belonged there, her softness melting into the firmness of his chest.

Finally, he put her down and gazed at her, silent, wonder filled. He touched her hair, just to make it real.

"Tonight is just you and me," he said, picking up her bag, realizing he couldn't just stand there staring at her forever, even if that's what he wanted to do. "We're going to meet Jared and his mom and dad for lunch tomorrow at their house, and if that goes okay, we're going to go to the zoo."

"How are you doing?" she asked, seeing right through the illusion of control reciting the itinerary was supposed to give him!

He smiled at how she could see right through the confidence of the designer suit, and the take-control businessman attitude.

Just as he had seen her before anyone else had, she had seen him.

"Terrified," he whispered. Not just about Jared, either, but about making a mistake with her. Funny, he who had been classified as a playboy, felt he had no skill at being real. But he needn't have worried.

"What do you want to do tonight?" he asked, his voice faintly strangled.

It sounded hilarious, like a teenage boy fumbling his way through his first date. He felt like a teenage boy, as if he wanted to get this so right. Before her arrival, he'd picked up the newspaper and been scanning it, looking for exactly the activity that would bring them back to the people they had been on that island several weeks ago.

There were a number of live shows in town. Five-star restaurants had been recommended to him. But he had not bought tickets or made reservations because he didn't want it to have that awkward-first-date feeling.

Even though that's probably what it was, he felt way past that.

"Let's order a pizza in the hotel," she said, burying her nose in the bouquet, "and watch a movie in your room."

So simple. So perfect. Like daisies. Like her.

"Um," he actually felt shy, embarrassed. "I booked you a separate room. I didn't think—" He was actually blushing, he could feel it.

She threw back her head and laughed. "You were right, Joshua, you are going to have to woo me. I'm not like the other girls."

"You aren't," he said ruefully. "Not a single soul I know could use the word *woo* seriously like that."

"Well, I intend to be wooed. I'm not just falling into the sack with you."

It was his turn to laugh, to tell the little devil on his shoulder to forget peeling off those pants anytime soon.

That night they sprawled out on his bed in his room, eating pizza and watching movies, and he remembered how it had been that night with her in the cabin.

Exhilarating. But comfortable, too.

At eleven she kissed him good-night, her lips tender and full of promise. But then she went to her own room.

The next morning she insisted they find a rock-climbing wall, because she said the tension was boiling off him.

By the time she'd beaten him to the top of that wall three times, he didn't have any energy left, never mind any tension.

They went shopping together. He was going to buy Jared a teddy bear, but she rolled her eyes at that, and told him seven-year-old boys did not like teddy bears.

Which was a relief, because then he got to look at the really fun stuff like remote control cars and footballs, skateboards and video games. He wanted to buy everything. Dannie, guiding him calmly through the jagged mountain terrain of the heart, told him to choose one.

And so they arrived at Jared's house at lunchtime, he with one remote control car, wishing he had a boxload full of toys to hide behind. He looked at the house, gathering evidence that somehow, despite himself, all those years ago, he had managed to do the right thing.

It was an ordinary house on an ordinary street, well kept, tidy, *loved*. Behind the picket fence, peeping through the leaves of a mature maple tree, he could see a platform in a tree, looking over the yard. A bicycle leaned up against the side of the house. A volleyball lay in the neat grass.

It pleased Joshua more than he could have said that the yard and the house indicated his son had enjoyed an ordinary life, an ordinary family, a life very different than the one Joshua could have given him if he'd hung on instead of letting go.

A better life, he thought, surveying the yard one more time, feeling Dannie's hand tightening in his, a life where everyone had put Jared first. Even the man who had been unaware that he had done so.

Joshua had never in his life been as afraid as he was when he rang that doorbell. A dog barked from inside. A golden retriever, delirious with happiness greeted them first. A lovely woman came to the door, in her early thirties, a redhead with an impish grin and warm green eyes. Behind her stood her husband, as wholesome looking as apple pie, the guy next door who built the tree house and threw the baseballs until dark, and who probably got up predawn to coach the peewee hockey team.

And then the world went still.

Jared ran into the room, all energy and joy. By now, Joshua had seen his son's picture, but it did not prepare him for how he felt. It seemed as if energy streamed off the boy, pure as sunshine. Jared was sturdy, with auburn hair and green eyes that danced with mischief, the confidence of a child who had known only love.

He skidded to a halt, ruffed the dog's ears, gazed at Joshua with intent curiosity.

"You look like me," he decided, "I couldn't really tell from the picture. Hey, Mom, can I get a frog?"

Until that moment, it felt to Joshua as if his life had been a puzzle, the pieces scattered all over the place.

But with those words, *Hey, Mom, can I get a frog* and the sudden laughter that chased the awkwardness from the room, it was as if the pieces drew together and slid firmly into place.

It seemed as if that moment, and all of life, was infused with light, as if, in spite of the efforts of people, rather than because of them, everything had turned out exactly as it was meant to be.

Introductions were made, but they were an odd formality in this group of people that somehow already were, and always would be a family.

The entire weekend, they did nothing special, and yet everything was special. Eating barbecued burgers in the Morgans' backyard, playing Frisbee with the dog, touring the zoo, sitting on the edge of his son's bed, trying to read him a story through the lump in his throat.

Joshua Cole, who had specialized in giving ordinary people spectacular experiences made the humbling discovery that ordinary experiences were made spectacular by the people you shared them with, by the addition of one secret ingredient.

Love.

He discovered that sometimes a man had to work at love.

But most of the time it was just brought to him, even though he might be completely undeserving of it.

"I can't think when I've had a more perfect weekend," Joshua said as he strolled through the airport with Dannie on Sunday night. Her hand in his felt perfect, too.

"Me, neither," she said.

In a few moments, the miles would separate them. How could he make the ache less, take away the sense of loss? Not just for himself, which was the way the old Joshua thought, but for her?

He stopped in front of a jewelry store counter, and they looked at a display of sparkling diamond necklaces together. "Pick one," he said. "Any one. To remember this weekend by."

"No," she said.

"Come on," he said. "To remember me. To show you how much I care for you and am going to miss you until we meet again."

"No," she said, more firmly than the first time.

Too expensive, he thought, not appropriate for their first weekend together, though he had given far more expensive gifts for far less.

"How about one of those, then?" he said, pointing to a glittering display of diamond tennis bracelets.

"Joshua, no!"

"Hey," he said, "I'm wooing you!"

"No," she said, almost gently, as if she was explaining the timetables to a three year old. "That's wowing. There's a difference. I don't need anything to remember this weekend by, Joshua."

"How am I supposed to woo you with an attitude like that?" he asked, pretending to be grouchy.

"For you, Joshua, the easiest thing would be to shower me with gifts, with all the *stuff* money can buy. But that's not what I want. I want the hardest things from you. I want your time. I want your energy. I want you fully engaged. I want *you*. You can't win me by throwing your wealth at me."

He scowled at that. The weekend had gone so well he thought he'd already won her. He could now clearly see that wasn't true.

That she was going to make him work for her heart, and that she planned to give him a run for his money. He could clearly see that he was going to have to win her the old-fashioned way.

And suddenly it felt like the most exciting challenge of his whole life. Better than any of it. Better than buying resorts, better than flying airplanes, better than thrill seeking, better than traveling to the seven wonders of the world.

She was trying to tell him there was no destination. It was all about the trip. And the truth was, he couldn't wait. He felt as if she was leading him to the eighth wonder of the world.

Which existed for each man within the unexplored and unmapped territories of his own heart.

"Dannie," Melanie said, "could you just say yes? My brother is driving me crazy."

They were both standing at her picture window, looking out at the front lawn. Overnight three hundred plastic pink flamingos had appeared on it, splashes of color against the first winter's snow. They spelled out, more or less, DANNIE.

"It's been six months," Melanie said. "He's more insanely in love with you every day. Just say yes."

"I don't really know if the flamingos fit the criteria. He used money."

"He had to have rented them! Or borrowed them. Maybe he even stole them. He didn't buy them. And I bet he was out there himself in the freezing cold spelling your name in tacky plastic birds. If that isn't love, nothing is. Say yes."

"To what?" Dannie said innocently. "He hasn't asked me anything yet."

Dannie smiled at Melanie, allowed herself to feel the tenderness of the flamingos planted in a declaration of love for her. When she had challenged Joshua to woo her, without great displays of wealth and power, nothing could have prepared her for how that man rose to a challenge!

The only exception she had made to her proviso about his using his wealth was plane tickets. Even she had to admit that it was pretty hard to woo someone unless you saw them.

So, he flew to Toronto, and he flew her to Vancouver, or they met in Calgary to have time with Jared and the Morgans.

Melanie was right. Her brother was crazy, but in the most phenomenal way. Never had a woman been wooed the way Danielle Springer was being wooed.

While the weather had still been good, they had attended rock-climbing and canoeing schools together.

To his consternation, Dannie insisted on paying her own tuition. She asked him to donate his offering to the classes Wilderness Ways offered to the Boys & Girls Club.

He had found a guitar—he claimed it had been given to him, so that it was still within her rules of wooing— and sang to her outside his sister's house. He neither knew how to play or how to sing. Listening to him murder a love song had been more endearing than him offering to take her to a concert in Vancouver, which she had said no to, firmly, when he had flashed the very expensive tickets in front of her.

He had made her a cedar chest with his own hands, when she had refused the one he had wanted to buy for her after she had admired it at an antique store they had been browsing through. He didn't know how to build anymore than he knew how to sing, the chest a lopsided testament to his love.

He was slowly filling it with treasures, not a single one that money could buy. The chest held his mother's wedding ring and his grandmother's handmade lace. It held a bronzed baby shoe—his—and a baby picture of Jared. He was giving her his history.

He had made her a locket to replace the one she had thrown away, only his was made out of paper maché and contained his thumb print. She had worn it until it threatened to disintegrate, and then she had put it in the chest with her other treasures.

He had baked her cookies shaped like haphazard hearts and that had tasted strongly of baking soda. One of their most romantic evenings had been over his home-cooked spaghetti, perfecting the art of eating the same noodle, both of them sucking one end of it until their lips met in the middle.

He had sent her dental floss, special delivery, claiming he was a reformed man.

"Is that used?" Melanie had asked, horrified when Danielle had opened the package.

"Never mind," Danielle had said, tucking the envelope in her chest of treasures. "I will show it to my children one day. I will say, 'Your father gave me plaque.'"

"You're as disgusting as him," Melanie griped. "What children? Has he asked you?"

"Not yet."

"He better get on with it. I'm reporting him to the post office if he sends anything else like that."

When he flew in for the weekends, he taught her how to fish on a little canal near Melanie and Ryan's house, and when it froze over, he taught her how to skate. They never caught a single fish, though they caught a frog for Jared, and then had to figure out how to get it to him. Joshua ended up chartering a plane so he didn't have to smuggle the little green creature through airport security.

Dannie never was able to skate without him holding her up, and it just didn't matter. They went for long walks and on star-gazing expeditions. When they passed some children with kittens in a box outside a grocery store, under a huge sign that said Free, he picked out the cutest one for her.

She named it Rhapsody.

When he flew her to Vancouver, she brought him terrible poems that she had written herself, and cooked him disastrous meals. She admired the flowers he was growing for her on his terrace, since he wasn't allowed to buy her anything. They rode the Skytrain, and explored Stanley Park. They spent evenings in the Jacuzzi, in bathing suits.

When they went to Calgary they went on picnics with the Morgans and rode bicycles with Jared on the network of trails. They threw baseballs in the backyard and built a roof on the tree platform so they could sleep out there at night. Joshua proved again he was no builder. That roof leaked like a sieve, which only added to the fun!

They took Jared to the public pools that had waves and waterslides, and they hung out at the libraries that offered story time. They caught bugs for his frog, Simon, and took the golden retriever to obedience class.

Joshua and Jared took ski lessons at the Olympic Park, and she perfected the art of drinking hot chocolate in the ski lodge.

"There he is," Melanie said, looking past the flamingos. She snorted with affection. "The great playboy arrives. If he doesn't ask you this weekend, I'm disowning him."

"You said that last weekend," Dannie reminded her.

"The difference is this weekend I mean it."

"Look, Melanie," Dannie said softly, "he brought you a surprise."

Joshua was getting out of a small sports car, obviously a rental, trying to convince an eight-foot-long toboggan to get out with him. And then a little boy tumbled out of the front seat.

"Ohmygod," Melanie said, and turned wide tear-filled eyes to Dannie. "Is that my nephew?" She didn't wait for an answer, but went out the front door in her sock feet, tripping over pink flamingos in her haste to meet the little boy who looked just like her brother had once looked.

Every day they spent together seemed magical, but that one more so. They took the kids tobogganing, Susie had an instant case of hero-worship for her older cousin.

When they got home, Melanie took the kids under her wing, then handed her brother an envelope. "Enough's enough," she said sternly. "I'll mind the children."

Joshua opened the envelope. Inside it was a map. Danielle could hardly look at him, suddenly shy, wondering if he, too remembered the last time someone had offered to mind the children for them.

They followed the map outside of the city, through the ever deepening darkness and the countryside to a little cabin.

It was inside the cabin that Dannie realized he was in on it. How else could it be completely stocked with tinned spaghetti and boxed cake mix?

He made her a dinner, and then as the fire roared in the stone hearth, he poured the cake mix into a pot, mixed it with water, and cooked it over the fire.

"I don't want any of that," she said.

"Come on. You're just way too skinny."

It was true, but for the first time in her life, she wasn't skinny on purpose. She was skinny because she was so happy there was not a single space in her that food could fill.

Tonight, she thought, looking through the door to the bedroom of the tiny cabin. Tonight would be the night. She leaned forward and kissed him.

Normally he would have kissed her back, but tonight he didn't.

"I can't do it anymore," he said. "I can't kiss you and not have you."

"I know," she said. "It's okay. I'm wooed. Let's go to bed."

"Ah, no."

"What do you mean, no?" she asked stunned.

"Dannie, that's not how an old-fashioned wooing ends."

"It isn't?"

"No," he said and got down on one knee in front of her. "It ends like this." He freed a ring box stuck in his pocket. "Dannie, will you marry me? Will you be mine forever? Will you have my children and be a part of the family that includes my son? And my niece and nephew?"

"Yes," she whispered.

Then he kissed her, but when she tried to get him into that bedroom he wouldn't allow it.

"Nope. You have to wait until the wedding night."

"I do?"

"Yeah."

"Give me the fried cake," she said glumly. She shared the spoon with him. It didn't taste half bad.

"Don't you want to see what's in the box?" he teased.

She'd actually forgotten to look at the ring. The truth was the ring did not mean anything to her. How could it compare to the ring he'd made her out of tinfoil and glue that was in her box of treasures? How could it have the same value as these wonderful days of wooing? Oh, she was going to miss this.

Of course, being married meant it was all going to be replaced. With something better. Much better. She realized she was *starved* for him. For more of him. For his body and for his tongue and for his lips and for his hands all over her.

Her eyes skittered to that bedroom door again. Was he really going to make her wait?

"Open it," he insisted handing her the box.

The lid was very hard to pry open. When she did get it open, she saw why. Instead of a ring, there was a piece of paper folded up to fit in there. Carefully, she unfolded it, tried to understand the legal terms printed on it.

Finally, she got it. Joshua had given her the deed to Moose Lake Lodge.

"I cannot imagine not having you as a full partner in every single thing I do, my confidante, my equal. This is yours, Dannie, to run as you see fit."

She was smiling through her tears.

"How long is it going to take you to plan a wedding?" he asked. "I want you to have it all. The dress, the flower girls, the cathedral, the—"

"No," she said. "No, I don't want any of that. That's all about a wedding, and nothing about a marriage." She began to blush. "Joshua, I can't wait much longer."

"For what?" he said with evil knowing.

"You know."

"Tell me."

So she whispered her secret longings in his ear.

"You're right," he said. "I think we need to do something fast. My honor is at stake. What do you have in mind, then?"

"A quick civil ceremony. As soon as we can get the documents in place."

He laughed. "I forgot you already have a dress."

"I don't," she said. "I'm marrying you in a snowsuit so that we can go straight to our honeymoon."

"You've given that some thought?" he asked, raising a wicked eyebrow at her.

"I'm afraid I have," she confessed, blushing. "I want to have our honeymoon at Moose Lake Lodge at the honeymoon cabin."

"It's snowing up there!" he said.

She smiled. She could not think of one thing—not

one—that she would love better than being snowbound in a little cabin with him.

"I know," she said happily. "I know."

"I don't even know how you get to the cabin in the winter. I'm not canoeing you across the lake in the snow!"

"Joshua?"

"Yes?"

"I trust you to think of something." She paused, and whispered, "I trust you."

"You wouldn't if you knew the perverted thoughts I was having about your toes."

But she saw the words were her gift to him. The one he needed and wanted more than any other. She put her head on his shoulder and found the warmth of his hand.

"I trust you," she whispered again. "With my forever after."

EPILOGUE

JOSHUA COLE stood behind Angel's Rest at Moose Lake Lodge. It was a rare moment alone, and the sounds of summer—a vigorous game of football, laughter, the shouts of children down on the beach— drifted up to him.

He held a rose to plant and a spade, and he looked for the perfect place in the rugged garden that had been started there. Four years had passed since he had first laid eyes on this place, and first acknowledged the stirrings of his own heart.

Four years had not changed much about Moose Lake Lodge. It remained stable while all around it changed.

Dannie had an innate sense for what the world wanted: a family place, a home away from home, a place basically untouched by modern conveniences, by technology, by all those things like TV sets and computers that put distance between people who shared the same homes.

Moose Lake Lodge had become Sun's first family resort. It was not a runaway financial success, but it stood for something way more important than financial success. It was his favorite of all the Sun resorts.

"Susie, Susie Blue-Toes."

His son, Jared, now eleven, was down there torment-
ing his niece, refusing her command to be called Susan
now that she had reached the mature age of eight. His
nephew, Jake, now four, had the same contempt for the
new baby that his sister had once had for him. Sally and
Michael managed the place, their three grandchildren
had come to live here with them since the death of Sally
and Michael's daughter, Darlene, in the spring.

Moose Lake Lodge seemed a natural place for those
children, since they had been able to spend so much
time here with their mother. The only real change Sun
had ever made to the lodge was to make Angel's Rest
completely wheelchair accessible, so that Darlene could
spend her last few summers here.

In the folds of what had become a family.

His son, Jared, and the Morgans, came every year for
the whole summer. Joshua never stopped learning from
the Morgans' generosity of spirit, from how they had
included him in their lives without a moment's pause or
hesitation. From them he had learned that love expanded
to include; if it contracted to exclude it was no longer love.

Melanie and Ryan had fallen in love with Moose
Lake Lodge from their first visit. They were entrenched
in the cabin called Piper's Hollow for every long
weekend and every summer. Susie and Jake acted as if
they owned the whole place.

No one wanted a pool. Or a new wharf. Or jet skis.
No one wanted new furniture or an outdoor bar.

No one who came here wanted anything to change.

This summer was the baby's first year here. Joshua
had worried his daughter, only four months old, was too
young for cold nights and onslaughts of mosquitoes, for
late nights around the campfire, for noisy children all
wanting to hold her. Dannie had laughed at him.

Dannie, who had come into her own in ways he had not even imagined a woman could come into her own: shining with beauty and light, with laughter and compassion. Somehow Dannie was always at the center of all this love, the spokes around which the wheel turned.

As he thought of her, he heard her shout, turned for a moment from the flower bed, to see if he could catch a glimpse of her.

And there she was, hair flying, feet bare, slender and strong, those long legs flashing in the sun, with every kid in the place trying to catch her and wrest that football from her.

Sometimes he wished her curves back. He remembered her lush full figure when he had first met her.

But she said that once a woman had known love, chocolate just didn't do it anymore. Only four months after the baby, she was back to her normal self.

He turned again to the flower garden that Sally had just planted in Darlene's memory and found an empty place in the rich dark soil. He got down on his hands and knees and began to dig, the sounds of shouting and laughter like music in the background.

Every life, he thought, had a period of Camelot in it, a time overflowing with youth and energy, a time that shimmered with creation and abundance and love.

Joshua had experienced that in his boyhood, and thought he'd lost his chance to have it again, for good, when he had given up Jared.

He'd chased it, tried to manufacture its feeling through the Sun resorts.

But in the end Camelot came to those who did not chase it. It came through grace.

Joshua put the rose in the hole he had made in the ground, tenderly patted the dirt back into place around it, sat back on his heels and admired the buds that promised pure white blooms. To get to Camelot, an ordinary man had to become a knight, to ride into the unknown with only one weapon: a brave heart.

A heart that had faith that all would be good in the end, even if there was plenty of evidence to the contrary.

A heart that that knew a man could not always trust circumstances would go his way, but if he was true, he would always be able to trust himself to deal with those circumstances.

In Camelot, there was only one truth. Money did not heal wounds. Nor did possessions. The biggest lie of all was that time did.

No, here in Camelot, Joshua found comfort in the greatest truth of all: love healed all wounds.

When a man's world burned down and there was nothing left, out of the ashes of despair and hurt and fear, love grew roses.

"Dad-O." The voice drifted up the hill, the name his son Jared had chosen to call him. "Are you coming? Our team needs you."

Joshua gave the rose one final pat, got to his feet, looked across the lake to where a little cabin, Love's Rhapsody, waited. It would probably have to wait awhile yet for them to return there, but just looking at it, he remembered.

Chasing Dannie. Kissing her toes until they were both breathless with wanting. Fusing together to create the boundless miracle that was life.

"Dad-O!" Jared had an eleven-year-old's impatience. And he would never say what he really meant. That he was anxious to spend every second he could with his father before summer ended.

"Coming," Joshua called, and went down the creaking

old boardwalk stairs, two at a time, to a world that was beyond anything he could have ever dreamed of for himself. To a world that was better than any man had a right to dream of for himself.

It was a world that had waited for him when he was lost. Sometimes he called it Camelot.

But he knew its real name was Love.

* * * * *

A Mother
in a Million

MELISSA
JAMES

Dear Reader,

From the day my husband encouraged me to write, in 1991, I knew I wanted to be a romance writer. Why? Because from the time I could read romances were what I loved, from *Heidi* and *Little Women* to *Sense and Sensibility* and the other romantic classics. And with Mills & Boon I can write about issues that concern women, while uplifting them with the kind of happy ending we all dream of having for ourselves and our children.

I hope you enjoy Noah and Jennifer's story. A happy ending for a man trapped in a life beyond his control, and a woman who no longer believes a happy ending is possible for her, it was the kind of challenge I revel in. If a loved one of yours has gone missing, even for a few days, then I believe you will love this story.

Melissa

Melissa James is a mother of three, living in a beach suburb in New South Wales, Australia. A former nurse, waitress, shop assistant, perfume and chocolate demonstrator—among other things—she believes in taking on new jobs for the fun experience. She'll try at least anything once to see what it feels like—a fact that scares her family on regular occasions. She fell into writing by accident, when her husband brought home an article stating how much a famous romance author earned, and she thought, *I can do that!* She can be found most mornings walking and swimming at her local beach with her husband, or every afternoon running around to her kids' sporting hobbies, while dreaming of flying, scuba diving, belaying down a cave or over a cliff—anywhere her characters are at the time!

To two wonderful loving mothers—my own, Mary, and my mother-in-law, Rosalie—and to Tania, a mother at last after so many years of suffering. There are many roads to motherhood…

CHAPTER ONE

Hinchliff, northern New South Wales, Australia

"No! Naughty Timmy. Give back to Rowdy!"

"Make me, loser!"

"I tell Daddy, *bad* boy!"

"Go on, baby," came the taunting older child's voice. "See if Dad cares. See if he even hears you!"

Jennifer March sighed, and laid her latest handmade quilt on her lap. The family next door were at it again. They'd only moved in seven days ago, but she'd heard little except the fighting and yelling. She'd crossed the fence four times to introduce herself, but returned home in silence when she heard the fights or discipline happening at the time.

Given small towns, she could know all about them now, if she chose to; but with all the gossip and speculation she'd endured in her past, she'd preferred to close off confidences, and wait for the people next door to come to her.

So far she'd waited in vain. Maybe they weren't the kind of people to want to introduce themselves to the only neighbour they had—but the kids at least weren't private. The boundary fence lying between her five-acre lot and theirs seemed to be a preferred place to, um, sort out their differences. It wasn't as if she wanted to hear their private business every day.

Yeah, right. You're going to get involved sooner or later, an inner voice taunted, not quite bitter nor truly resigned, but something in between. It kind of sounded like Mark, before he'd walked out the final time. *I can't believe you've lasted seven days without waltzing in there to help. Pollyanna strikes again. Go and make everyone's lives better...isn't that why you moved here, to fix Uncle Joe's life after Aunt Jean died?*

She was done fighting with phantoms. Mark could think what he wanted—he would, anyway. If she'd moved here first to help Uncle Joe get through the worst of his grief, she'd also come to escape. Escape the pity...escape her sisters, all having healthy babies around her...

"Daddy *care!*" The baby voice, trembling with emotion, broke into her thoughts. He sounded heartbreakingly like Cody...he must be around three, the same age Cody had been.

They might have played together, though Cody would have been five now.

The familiar lump thickened in her throat, and her eyes stung—but she breathed slowly, in and out, willing control and calm. She'd done her crying. She'd miss Cody until her last breath, would miss being a mother for the rest of her life; but she was making something of herself—

"Yes, Rowdy, Daddy *cares.*" The gravelly voice, grim and tired, pulled Jennifer from the familiar up-down spiral of grief and slow healing.

Scarring isn't healing, Jen, Mark would have said. *Get it right.*

"Timothy Brannigan, I'm ashamed of you," the man went on, in a weary mantra. "Teasing a three-year-old. I only asked you to look after your little brother for half an hour while I make up an ad for work. Why did you steal his blanket?"

Before she knew it Jennifer had drifted to the window, watching from behind the curtain. She shouldn't be interested—she should mind her own business...but it wasn't as if entertainment was everywhere up here. Two TV channels, and that was only when the wind was in the right direction or it didn't rain, and the only radio was country music or talkback. *Old man's radio and yee-hah music,* she'd thought when she'd first moved up here from Newcastle for a fresh start. *This really is a two-horse town—two of everything, no more and no less.*

Like these two houses up on the hill overlooking the sea. Twin houses, old and rambling, each on long, thin five-acre blocks five hundred metres from the ocean and three kilometres from town: isolated enough for peace, beautiful enough to fill the spirit.

"I didn't steal it! He was putting it in his mouth, and it's *gross,* Dad." The boy's voice whined as he looked up at his father. "It stinks. Look at the—"

The tall, brown-haired man—he had lovely hair with shimmering golden highlights, even if it was rather shaggy and unkempt—put his hand on the child's shoulder and said in his deep, rumbling voice, "It might be gross to you, Tim, but Rowdy's only little. Now give it back. I'll wash it tomorrow when I do a load." He leaned toward the object of dispute. "It is pretty stinky, isn't it? Rowdy, it gets washed tomorrow."

"Yeah, Timmy," came the baby voice, with cute triumph. "So give back Rowdy's banket!"

"Oh, *have* your stupid baby blanket, then. Get sick, see if I care!"

Tears erupted from the little boy as his brother shoved him along with the blanket to the ground. "Dad-*dee!* Timmy *bad!*"

The pitiful wails were muffled as the man swung the boy up into his arms. Weariness laced his every word as he said, "Tim, time out in your room. Fifteen minutes by the kitchen timer."

"Who cares? There's nothin' to do in this dump anyway! I hate it here. *I hate it!*"

The boy, who looked about seven or eight, stomped off down the hill from the ring of trees where the children had been playing, toward the house next door. The man buried his face in his baby son's soft mess of hair. The little boy's arms wrapped around him; childish hands patted his shoulder blade. The son comforting the father.

From behind the window Jennifer ached, watching the tableau. Poor children—and poor father. He looked exhausted—as stressed as his children appeared to be.

"Where's their mother?" she muttered, aching for them. And wasn't there another child…a girl? She knew she'd seen a tangle-haired moppet wandering around once or twice, golden hair and big blue eyes, like a messy Shirley Temple.

As if in answer, a tiny sniff came from somewhere above Jennifer's head, and then another.

Twisting around under the open sash, she peered through the window. The tangle-haired moppet was up one of Jennifer's trees, a dirty thumb in her mouth and her bright blue eyes like big, serious saucers as she contemplated Jennifer.

A five-year-old girl was fifteen feet up her tree.

Panic skittered through her. Jennifer couldn't climb—she'd always been the dollies and tea party kind of little girl, never causing her parents a moment's worry—about her safety, at least. They'd always known where she was, what she was doing—but she was the youngest of four children, the homebody child, and her mother had always been there to watch over them.

Where was this child's mother?

Interfering or not, Pollyanna or not, she had to do something… "Hello," she called to the girl, smiling in a way she hoped didn't show her terror. "I'm Jennifer."

The child's mouth tightened around her thumb. She sucked on it with the fury of childhood fear of strangers.

"That's a—a nice tree, isn't it?" Jennifer blathered on as she climbed out the window and walked slowly toward the child. She wouldn't have a clue if it was a nice tree or a killer straight from Hobbiton's Old Forest at the moment, but she had to talk, to connect to the little girl to get her down. "It's my favourite one in the yard."

Nothing.

She craned her neck, looking up at the branch. The little girl was so tiny, and the tree so high... "What's your name?" she asked, beginning to feel desperate—and the little girl's eyes were filling with tears. If her sight blurred and she panicked—

Please God, I couldn't take another ambulance trip with a dying child!

"Would you like a cookie?" she cried suddenly, remembering the six-month squirrel's store of cookies in her freezer: her store of rewards and treats for the day-care kids she had four days a week. "Or I could give you some crackers with—with Vegemite? Or chocolate spread?" she asked, thinking of her hidden stash of PMS-rescue spread: the one without nut traces in it, since four-year-old Amy was violently allergic to nuts. For all she knew, this child could be, too.

The little girl's face lit up. "I *like* choc'lit," she confided in a piping voice, as if it were a state secret.

"I have milk, too." Jennifer felt as if she'd scored a major victory.

"*Choc'lit* milk?"

She couldn't help laughing. "I can make chocolate milk, just for you," she agreed, thinking of her other PMS-rescue: her ice-cream syrup. "How does that sound? Is it worth coming down the tree for all that?"

"You said cookie." Her voice was muffled. "A big, fat cookie with choc'lit?"

"You really like chocolate, don't you?" Jennifer said, smiling. "Yes, they're big, fat cookies with *tons* of chocolate chips."

Cody's favourite had been choc-chip cookies, too. Except that Cody wasn't coming back to dunk them in milk and make a mess all over his high chair. Now Ben and Amy and Sascha and Jeremy and Shannon and Cameron sat in that chair—at least in the daytime.

Filling the void with other people's children might be pathetic as Mark had claimed, but at least the void didn't scream at her day and night with its howling emptiness. During the day she had baby hands in hers, big, trusting eyes looking up at her for guidance, fun and games and safety…she was a day-care mother now, and she'd found in the past eighteen months that second-best was far better than nothing at all.

She asked the child, "So is two cookies and chocolate milk worth coming down the tree? Or—or—" she frantically reached for inspiration "—I could make you some spaghetti?"

Please, just come down before you fall!

"S'getti?" The little girl sounded ecstatic. "I *like* s'getti."

"Spaghetti and cookies and milk it is, then. What's your name?" she asked again. "I can't make spaghetti and share cookies unless I know your name," she added, laughing. Hoping she would gain the child's trust.

"Cilla," the child said, with a lisp Jennifer didn't know was natural, or caused by the thumb still in her mouth. "Priscilla Amelia Brannigan."

"Well, Priscilla Amelia Brannigan, would you like to come into my kitchen for cookies and chocolate milk and spaghetti?" To her intense relief the little girl smiled, pulled her thumb from her mouth and turned to climb down the tree, with a natural agility Jennifer envied.

From the corner of her eye, she saw movement down the hill. The older boy—Tim—was climbing out his bedroom window.

It seemed the man next door had no control over his children whatsoever. It had been less than five minutes, she was sure of that. Surely he must have *seen* the child was feeling so rebellious he wouldn't obey orders for long?

Then a rush of pity filled her, remembering the exhausted, overwhelmed man clinging to a three-year-old for comfort.

Before she knew it she was waving the boy over, with a conspiratorial air. Hoping he would come out of curiosity, if nothing else. Someone had to help that poor man—*I mean, the poor children.*

"Catch me!"

On instinct, her arms reached out—and a moment later, her arms were full of warm, silky-soft skin, and the scent of muddy child and baby shampoo filled her head.

She minded other people's children every day, held them when they hurt or to carry them around—so what was it about this child's touch that choked her up so tight she couldn't *breathe?*

She put Cilla down to the ground with care, before she dropped her; the trembling, when it came, was bone-deep.

"Cookie?" The hopeful voice woke her from the half-dreaming world of loss. Big, trusting eyes were shining as she looked up at Jennifer.

She pulled herself together, as she'd done every day of the past eighteen months, when she'd decided she could either sink into terminal depression, or try to make something good from the ashes of her life. "Cookie," she said, smiling. "Let's go wash your face and hands first."

A little warm hand slipped into hers. "Timmy wants a cookie, too." Cilla pointed to the boundary fence, where a very dirty face was peeking through the wooden rail slats.

Again, though she held other children's hands almost every day, the feel of Cilla's hand in hers filled her heart with her sweet trust, poignant with memory—with the need for motherhood she must deny for the rest of her life.

Stop it. She turned her face, and smiled at the wary, hostile little boy peering at her as if he expected her to yell at him. "So you're Tim," she said gravely.

The boy nodded, his chin pushed out. Pugnacious and ready to fight. "I'm eight," he said aggressively, as if she was about to argue the fact.

"I'm Jennifer, your neighbour. I bet you like spaghetti and choc-chip cookies, too." She grinned down at Cilla as her brother scrambled over the fence in record time—and, watching the child, Jennifer realised how thin he was. Lean, hungry, wary with suffering and only eight...

She'd had every intention of sending Tim back to his room to wait out the fifteen minutes of wholesome discipline, telling him the food would be waiting when he'd obeyed his father. As a child-care worker, she knew reinforcing parental commands was vital. Yet Jennifer found herself saying, "Then come on in."

Yeah, right, Jen. You were never going to send him back.

Her mouth curved into a determined smile as she led the way in.

Somehow she didn't think Tim would take well to being told to wash his face and hands; so she led Cilla into the bathroom, and hoped he'd get the message.

He didn't. They returned to the kitchen to find him sitting at the table. The look on his face was daring her to even *think* about ordering him to the bathroom.

But she'd had a better idea, based on the reactions of Shannon, the livewire child she minded every Tuesday and Thursday. With a lifted brow, she tossed a warm wet cloth on the table *splat* in front of him, and stood there, waiting. *Do it.*

Tim didn't move to touch the cloth. He folded his arms and waited, his expression matching hers. *Make me.*

A tiny tug at her hand made Jennifer look down at Cilla. Her little face—so pretty, now she could see it without smudges everywhere—was hopeful. "I'm *very* hungry...and I washed."

Jennifer smiled. "You're right, Cilla." She opened the fridge and freezer, got out plates, and put two cookies in the microwave to soften while she made up the chocolate milk.

One glass. One plate.

She settled Cilla with her snack. "There you are, sweetie."

She turned back to put away the food on the bench. "I wouldn't even think about it if I were you, Tim," she remarked placidly.

A stifled gasp told her she'd been right; he'd been about to steal Cilla's food and run.

"The milk and cookies will be out on this bench for another thirty seconds—and remember, you can come back every day for more…if you wash first," she announced to no one in particular, and checked her watch. "Twenty-two…twenty-five…"

Thwap! She gasped as the washcloth landed on the curve of her neck and shoulder.

She ought to have *known* a fighter like Tim wouldn't be able to resist! She fought to keep calm, but a laugh burst out of her. Turning, she saw a clean face filled with mischievous challenge and wary defensiveness, unsure if he was about to be disciplined by a stranger.

She plucked the cloth from her shoulder and threw it back, landing right on his head.

Cilla laughed and clapped, spitting cookie bits all over the table. "Get her back, Timmy!"

Tim grinned and threw the cloth. He laughed when Jennifer staggered back, coughing and wiping her mouth as if the dirt from his face had gone in.

Cilla choked on enchanting laughter when Jennifer threw the cloth at her. She tossed it on to Tim, who threw it at Jennifer.

The room erupted in laughter and dirty wet-washer attacks.

From outside the back door, a sleepy Rowdy on his hip, Noah Brannigan watched the scene. He'd seen Tim heading for the fence, and came to fetch him back—but now all he could do was stare through the screen, with a joy so poignant it was almost pain. Tim was *laughing*.

It had been exactly three years since he'd seen his boy so— *little.* A child having fun, just because he could. No reason…

And Cilla was here, too—*Cilla,* so shy she never spoke to

him, her own dad, without her thumb in her mouth, and who never talked to strangers. Cilla had been disappearing every day since they moved from Sydney to Hinchliff, and Noah hadn't been able to find her. He only wished he understood why Cilla had become so silent, so reclusive.

She wasn't merely speaking now; she was *shrieking* with joy, her big eyes alight as she spat cookie crumbs across the table. She took her turn tossing the grubby washcloth at the woman, who cried foul with a grin and tossed it at Tim, who dodged it and caught it with one hand, throwing it back at their neighbour. The woman, after a pitiful attempt at dodging in turn, took it on the chin. Literally. Her face was alight with mirth.

Who'd have thought his kids would finally find laughter in a game of tag-teaming with a dirty face cloth?

"They're having fun, Daddy," Rowdy whispered from Noah's shoulder.

"Yes, they are," he whispered back, the gratitude a deep ache inside him.

"Want cookie, too. Want—" Rowdy wriggled down from his hip and raced inside, sure of his welcome. "Rowdy want cookie," he announced.

Jennifer March—he'd heard about her from Henry, the local mechanic and jack-of-all-fixing, and one of the best gossips in town—had peeled the wet cloth from her face, and turned to Noah's son with a flitting expression he couldn't identify. It lasted only a moment, before she smiled and took his hand. "Then we'd better get you washed, Rowdy, and you and Tim can both have your cookies."

Almost casually, she tossed the washcloth a final time at Tim, and poked her tongue out in cheeky victory as she led Rowdy into the bathroom.

Noah knew enough about the woman next door, from the people in town. She was divorced, in her late twenties, and the only provider of child-care in town. Yet, from the moment he'd seen her in the distance, he'd refused to go over to introduce himself and the kids, as good manners demanded. Even from that distance, there was *something*...

A quiet, restful woman who could often be seen wearing simple cotton sundresses and sandals, her hair almost always in a loose plait. She seemed to have a natural connection to the children she minded; they followed her around like the Pied Piper—and his kids felt it, too, even from a distance. The laughter and games emanating from the house up the hill drew the kids to play at the ring of trees near the boundary fence every day.

But for him, she wasn't restful. There was something about her...

He had little choice now but to go inside—and unless he could hide the way he looked at Jennifer March, disaster would follow the introduction. For the past three years, Tim's terrified preoccupation that his dad would remarry had reached epic proportions. He'd appointed himself his father's personal watchdog, using his worst behaviour to scare off any woman who came within thirty feet of Noah, unless she was old or married. If a woman got up the courage to flirt with him, his son's pitiful, terror-filled nightmares were more than Noah could stand. *Make her go away, Dad, or Mummy will never come home...*

Little did Tim know; there was no question of his remarriage for a long time. While Belinda was missing she couldn't sign divorce papers, and until seven years had passed, he was as bound to his marriage as if Belinda was still sharing his life and bed. He could force a divorce—but at what cost? Peter and Jan wouldn't allow him to divorce their daughter without causing a fuss the size of Uluru, and Noah refused to allow anything to damage the kids further.

So he was stuck in this limbo, needing help but unable to reach out to any woman who could mother the kids for another four years. Even if Noah *wanted* a woman in his life, Tim would never accept a woman that wasn't his mother. Poor little man, he'd suffered so much the past three years. The child psychologist said the acting out was a combination of grief and terror of losing him, his only security. He'd counselled patience—that this would be a long-term problem until Tim could stand at Belinda's grave and begin to find healing through closure.

The counsellor was right. Tim still checked inside every passing car, looked in every store or on the street, for signs of Belinda. Noah had lost that luxury over a year ago. He was too busy trying to keep his family together and pay off debts; but somehow he'd find a way to make things better.

This woman was already making things better. Tim and Cilla were smiling again—and though he ached to be a part of it, he wasn't about to blunder in and kill it.

Jennifer March didn't know he existed, and was showing uncomplicated kindness and fun to his kids. She was showing Tim that some women could show kindness to him without being a threat to his security, and he could almost kiss her for that…

Don't think of kissing. Don't think of her as a woman at all!

When she returned from the bathroom, she was still leading Rowdy by the hand…and that look was on her face again. The soft eyes held their own internal struggle.

Jennifer March had ghosts she was refusing to show in front of his kids…yet the hidden pain held Noah with unwilling fascination. Everything she did held his attention, from the smile that lit up her whole face to the gentle sway of her hips as she walked.

She put Rowdy in the high chair beside the table, and strapped him safely in. "Right, boys, it's time for your cookies."

Cilla sniffled. Noah's gaze swivelled to his daughter. She'd lowered her eyes to the table top, her thumb shoved in her mouth; and he ached for his daughter's inability to ask, like a normal child. Following her big brother's example of silence, and expecting nothing. He hated that Cilla and Tim weren't normal kids—but he didn't have the weapons for that particular fight. It was all he could do to keep the family together.

Until those final few months after Rowdy's birth, when the post-natal depression took her over, Belinda had been a fantastic mother. She'd have known how to fix Tim and Cilla. She wouldn't have made one fumbling mistake after another.

Jennifer March had already turned to Cilla, with a smile and wink—and Noah caught his breath with the gentle sweetness of those thick-lashed blue eyes and curving pink lips. "I think someone's still hungry." The words held conspiratorial fun, not rebuke; and Cilla responded to it. The thumb stayed in, but she nodded, smiling around the hand half-shoved inside.

Jennifer turned back to the bench, her hair swinging around her shoulder as she did. Shiny brown hair half-spilled from a loose plait reaching her shoulder blades. She had a dusting of freckles across a slightly long nose, and across lightly tanned oval cheeks. Her figure, encased in plain jeans and a purple T-shirt, was ordinary—curvy without being slender or voluptuous.

There was nothing spectacular about Jennifer March: just an average woman. Yet as she looked down at Cilla, her smile— so tender and caring—made her something deeper, richer than beautiful. The sight of her with his kids did something, not just to his body, but to his heart. Like a funny tug, warm and soft. Safe, and yet—

He shook his head to clear it. He didn't like the stray thoughts he'd been getting about her. He hadn't been with a woman since Belinda's disappearance three years ago, and he didn't *want* his body to wake up from its somnolence. It was a complication he didn't need.

It seemed he had no choice. He'd moved to Hinchliff for change—and he'd got it. He was living next door to a woman he already found compelling. The worst part was, she hadn't even said a word to him yet. What would happen once they met? And if Tim picked up on it…

Get over yourself, Brannigan. She might not even like you.

He wasn't stupid enough to think he was a prize to any woman. He was still putting a new architectural and building business in place after having to sell off his Sydney operation to pay the debts, most of which he'd only discovered after Belinda was gone; he had three kids he was barely coping with. If only he'd *seen* the depth of Belinda's depression.

"Hmmm." Jennifer checked her watch as she put more cookies in the microwave, and stirred chocolate sauce into the milk. "You know what, Priscilla Amelia? It's almost lunchtime. I think it's time I made that alphabet spaghetti for everyone."

"Yeah!" Rowdy cried, who knew what the alphabet was from *Sesame Street,* and loved spaghetti in any form. "Alpaget p's'getti!"

"Then more cookies?" Cilla mumbled around her thumb.

"Then more cookies," Jennifer replied. Her mouth twitched, but she kept a straight face. "We'd better let your mum and dad know where you are, though. Tim, could you—"

"My mummy's dead," Cilla said without expression—just stating a fact.

Noah, knowing what was about to happen, closed his eyes, and sent up a desperate, heartfelt prayer for help, knowing it wouldn't help. Nothing could.

About to say something—probably an apology, but what a *terrible* introduction to his family!—Jennifer was interrupted by Tim's snapping, "Mummy's *not* dead! She was sad, and she went away for a while. She'll come back!"

Cilla just looked at Tim, her big eyes holding a world of unspoken sorrow. She didn't say anything—she knew Tim would.

"Shut up, thumb-sucker. She will find us, she will!" Tim yelled. "Even if we're like *days* away from home now! Nana and Pa know where we are. She said she'd come back."

"I don't got a mummy," Rowdy said, his big, trusting eyes on Jennifer, who was hurrying to bring the cookies over.

"Yeah, that's 'cause you made her run off, loser," Tim

muttered. He crammed a cookie in his mouth, gulped down the milk and turned to get out of the house.

His mother's son: when things get too hard, bolt…

Noah rapped on the old, ratty screen door before Tim could make his getaway. "Hello," he called. "I see my kids have found free food with all their usual skill." He made the tone joking—or tried to, but it fell as flat as the atmosphere inside the big, homey old country kitchen.

Tim's look was pure accusation. He knew he was about to be disciplined, and attack was his best form of defence.

Half of Cilla's hand disappeared into her mouth; the pitiful shaking came back. Within moments she, too, would disappear—and Noah had no way to cure her. It scared the living daylights out of him every time she went missing, and if he tried to make her understand he wasn't angry, just terrified, it led to tears and heartbreaking apologies. *I'm sorry I'm a bad girl, Daddy. Please don't go away like Mummy!*

"Come on in, Mr. Brannigan, and have a cookie. I'm just about to warm a new batch for the kids," Jennifer said with utter calm—and the evil spell disintegrated as if it had never been. Her gaze on him was more compelling than words. *Help me out here.* "Would you like a cup of tea or coffee with that? Or maybe you want chocolate milk, too?"

Caught out by the teasing, Tim sniggered at his father. "Dad makes the *worst* chocolate milk," he mock-complained. "He makes it so milky you can't find the chocolate."

"Then maybe I'd better get another bottle of chocolate sauce out, and show him how it's done?" she suggested, smiling as if the eruption over Belinda's disappearance had never taken place. "Or does he spill the milk, too? Mr. Dropsy Brannigan?"

Cilla giggled… *Cilla giggled.*

Noah wanted to take Jennifer March in his arms—no, to go into her arms, lay his head on her shoulder and thank her from his soul for the gift she'd just given Cilla. His serious, hurting baby was laughing, and he wanted to shout with joy.

"Actually, it's *Noah* Dropsy Brannigan," he said, gruff with the emotion filling his throat.

"I'm very pleased to meet you, Mr. Noah Dropsy Brannigan." As the kids giggled again, Jennifer smiled and pulled out a chair for him. "I'm Jennifer March."

The gentle, light-up-the-room smile had finally turned his way, and it socked him in the guts with its power. Was it her, or this place? Like a wave of a fairy godmother's wand, like they'd been transported to a magical place where no pain existed, his family had become *normal* from the moment they'd stepped inside Jennifer March's door.

Looking at her, he also felt normal…just an ordinary guy for once…and it was good.

He smiled, wondering if she'd known his name all along, as he had hers. The bush telegraph of local gossip ran pretty fast in country towns. "Pleased to meet you, too, Ms Jennifer *I make great chocolate milk* March."

The kids laughed again—they'd laughed *with* him as well as *at* him…

His kids were laughing, just like any other kids.

As he sat at the plain wooden chair, a scent surrounded him: chocolate, vanilla and cookies, furniture polish and fresh air. The walls were scattered with Wiggles posters, times tables and fun alphabet pictures as well as simply framed long-stitch pictures of old houses. The floor in the next room had a big, fluffy old rainbow rug that just begged kids to play on it.

Despite the seeming absence of a child—maybe it was with its father right now?—Jennifer March must be a mother. No day-care place he'd used in Sydney felt like this house. It had the aura and scent of old-fashioned love and motherhood and comfort—of *home*.

It was an aura the kids were responding to with instinctive

enthusiasm. All three of them kept their eyes on Jennifer as if she'd disappear if they didn't—especially Cilla and Rowdy, neither of whom could remember Belinda.

Tim was another, infinitely sadder matter. Although it was obvious he liked Jennifer's cookies and her gentle way of dealing with his rebellion, the wariness in his eyes, as they flicked between Jennifer March and his dad, told its tale. The adored mother he'd done his best to protect from her depression had left them with a fourteen-year-old girl, walked out of the house and never returned…

But she would always be his mum. Tim was still on guard, protecting the family as Belinda had asked him to. It was a sacred vow to him. *Watch the kids until I get back, honey.*

Instead of playing at soldiers with toys, Tim was a soldier in a war without detente. That his little son should know such weary fear and endless vigilance at eight years old made Noah want to weep tears of blood. So many useless nights of little sleep, trying to work out a way to heal him. Trying to work out *why* Belinda had ever left.

But these days, he understood the need to run away from your life, no matter how much you love your family. But that she'd never returned, never once checked on the kids she adored—

Only one answer made sense, but how could he *know?* If in three long years—one thousand and forty-five days—he'd had a letter, just one call, he might *believe…*

On the three-year anniversary of Belinda's disappearance he couldn't stand it anymore. He'd sold the house in western Dural and headed seven hundred kilometres north of Sydney to Hinchliff. Selling everything off paid the debts he still hadn't cleared. He'd bought the house next door for little more than a song, hoping the change of scene and people—and distance from Belinda's obsessive, eternally grieving parents—would help bring his family some closure.

But now, seven hundred kilometres from Sydney and all its

sad memories, he knew it would take nothing less than a miracle to bring the Brannigan nightmare to an end.

But then, hadn't he just witnessed a miracle, right here in Jennifer March's kitchen? His kids were *playing* for the first time in three years…and he was terrified to take them home, and face the reality that was just too damn painful.

CHAPTER TWO

NOAH *DROPSY* BRANNIGAN had the worst kind of smile.

The kind that made her forget what she was doing, right in the middle of doing it.

That was bad. Really bad—because she hadn't had that kind of reaction to a man since Mark McBride had walked into her life when she was seventeen. And he'd walked right back out seven years later, three months before Cody had his final attack, and all the medication in the world hadn't been enough to make him breathe again.

Her right fist clenched hard to stop the shaking. She looked down at it in the usual half-disbelieving revulsion. It had been happening for two years, just like that. Why was it only *one* of her hands trembled? It was as if she were having a one-sided brain malfunction. She'd done all she could to return to a normal life. She'd accepted the past—and her future. She was a genetic Cystic Fibrosis carrier, and until they found a cure, she couldn't risk having more kids. Mark, a recessive carrier, was long gone, living a far less complicated life.

Her world was slow, placid and serene. She didn't want anything more to complete it. She was happy enough.

So why did her right hand continue to betray her this way?

"Where the alpaget p's'getti?"

The sound of the baby voice worked on the shaking as if it

were medicine. Jennifer found she could look up again; she even smiled. "I'm sorry, Rowdy. I promised, didn't I? Alphabet spaghetti, coming right up." Trying to prove her control had returned, she pulled her pot drawer open with more force than necessary; and because it was an old dovetailed drawer without protective wheels and pulleys it flew out hard, too fast to stop.

She landed in a heap on the floor with the big old drawer on top of her, the sound of pots clanking against the tiled floor hurting her ears, the wind knocked out of her and pain shooting up from her tailbone to her back and palms.

All three kids burst into giggles. "Look at her! She got pots all over her!" Rowdy chortled.

The drawer was lifted from her within seconds, and her hands taken in a warm, strong clasp. "Are you okay, Jennifer? Do you hurt anywhere? Can you stand up?"

"I—don't know. I think—" No…she wasn't thinking, because she *couldn't* think. His hands enveloping hers made her feel strange…mushy and warm and safe. And—and—

Strong hands. Builder's hands, sturdy and capable, like his body…lithe and muscular and—and dependable.

Yes, you fooled yourself just the same way with Mark, didn't you?

"Jennifer? Should I get a doctor?"

Dazed, she stared up at Noah. His strong brown face was filled with concern, his eyes—oh, they were deep, warm brown, almost like maple syrup: a shade darker than his sun-kissed hair. So gentle, yet so—*powerful*. Like his smile…

"No, I'm okay," she said, but heard the breathlessness: an instinctive female-touching-attractive-male reaction she hadn't felt in years.

She was on her feet again. How did that happen? One moment she was on the floor, her hands in Noah's, and now she was standing.

"Are you sure you're okay? You don't seem very steady." He

put a hand at her back as he turned her to a seat. "Maybe you should sit down?"

It was only then she realised one of her hands still clung to his; she couldn't stop looking at him. A dim part of her acknowledged what he was saying—yes, *unsteady* was a good term for her shaky grip on uprightness. But she didn't know if that was due to the fall, or the effect this man was having on her.

"Apart from my lacerated dignity, I'm fine," she said ruefully, smiling at him, "and, um, sitting down might hurt more than it would help right now."

"Gotcha." He grinned, and her breath caught again.

"Thank you…Noah," she said softly, wondering why she'd ever preferred chocolate syrup on pancakes to maple; it was the most beautiful colour, um, taste, um—

"Dad, stop it *now!*"

The words were a reprimand, a command. Jennifer watched as Noah's eyes clouded over with a pain that seemed older than he was himself, sadder than the world should have to carry.

His wife. His children's mother. Oh God, help her, what had she been *thinking? He's a married man, no matter where his wife is. If he hasn't divorced her, he isn't free.*

He released his hold on her and turned to Tim, gentle and sad, yet with a dignity she found compelling to watch. "Tim, you're being rude and ungrateful. We're in Jennifer's house, eating her food, and she hurt herself. She needed help."

From stark-white, the boy flushed, and looked down at the table. "You didn't have to—" He didn't say it, but the words almost shimmered in front of them all: a neon sign of resentment. *You didn't have to touch her.*

With those words, Jennifer had gone from friend to enemy in the eyes of a small child who wanted his mummy home again.

"Yes, I did." Noah was gentle, and unutterably weary; as if it was an argument they'd danced their way through many times before. "And if you don't know why, I've failed to teach you any good manners. Jennifer's been kind to you all. Did you expect me to leave her on the floor, hurt?"

Tim didn't look up, didn't speak; but Noah's quiet dignity and strength as he dealt with his rebellious son mesmerised her. The *love* for his ungracious, hurting child all but shimmered from him, giving him an aura as warm and caramelly as his eyes.

Still, she ached for this family Ring Around the Rosie, which could go nowhere but to the eventual falling down. Yet she knew better than to interfere. What she didn't know would definitely hurt her in this case—or it would hurt others. It wasn't her place to blunder in.

Strange, but it felt as if Noah's lost wife was standing in the room with them. Her presence in Tim's heart was so real, so vivid Jennifer could almost see her.

"Tim, apologise to Jennifer," Noah was saying, his voice both gentle and inflexible.

"No! I don't want her stupid spaghetti anyway. This place *sucks!*" Shoving his chair back with ferocious force, Tim bolted from the house.

The chair tottered and fell to the floor with a crash that almost seemed an anti-climax.

Cilla sucked on her thumb as if her life depended on it. Rowdy just stared at his father with a sympathy more deep and heartfelt than any three-year-old should know. "We get Timmy, Daddy?" he asked quietly, as if it was something they'd done many times before.

Not knowing what else to do, Jennifer picked up a pot from the floor and crossed to the sink to fill it with water for the pasta.

"Jennifer—ah, Ms March—"

Hearing the anguished awkwardness of an apology unspoken—of the distance he was forced to put between them—she turned to smile at him. "I have spaghetti sauce all ready, Mr. Brannigan. I just need to heat it. Why don't you leave Cilla and Rowdy here with me, and spend some time with Tim?"

Noah's face darkened. He said nothing, but she could feel the indecision, fear and hope.

"I'm a qualified child-carer, Mr. Brannigan, as well as your neighbour. As you might have noticed, I run a day-care centre from home. I'm licensed to have up to six children here at a time," she said, in her most professional tone. "Feel free to call Fred Sherbrooke, the local police sergeant, to verify my capability. The number's on the wall beside the phone."

His jaw hardened. "I can't afford to pay you."

So that was the reason for his hesitation. How hard it must have been for him to say that. She clenched her fists against the useless wish to cover his hand with hers. Cilla or Rowdy could tell Tim of it later, and it was obvious the boy was threatened—or scared—enough. "We're neighbours, Mr. Brannigan, and I invited you all for lunch. I'm not going anywhere else today. I've been to my Sunday service." *Please go. Your son needs you! Can't you see he needs you to run after him?*

She'd said all she could without crossing the line. The rest was up to him.

With a short nod, he got to his feet. "Thank you."

"Spaghetti will be waiting for you both, if Tim wants to come back," she called after him as he ran down the back stairs.

The screen door swung shut: the only answer she received.

After a short silence where Jennifer scrambled to say something, the only noise was of Cilla sucking her thumb with greater force.

"Are we ready for spaghetti?" she finally asked with a brightness they all knew was overdone. Cilla wrapped her thumb-sucking hand around her nose, covering half her face—and little Rowdy looked up at Jennifer with big, candid eyes.

"Timmy gets mad a lot," he said quietly.

Two hours later, having called Tim's phone every ten minutes—it was switched off again—having been to every place Tim had run to since they'd moved here, combing every tree, every inch of the beach, even driving a few miles in each direction of the Pacific Highway, Noah called Sergeant Sherbrooke to tell him Tim had disappeared again.

Fred didn't make the joke about needing a leash for his kids this time, or ask which trees he'd checked out so far. The jokes had stopped when Fred had checked the COPS database, and found out about Belinda—and Noah didn't know which he hated more, the jokes or the awkward silences filled with pity.

He'd given the details to Fred and Mandy, the uniformed woman with him. She'd said in a town the size of Hinchliff it would only take an hour or two. Since it was Sunday, more recruits were available to make the calls, and to get out and search in all the likely kid places.

Noah trudged toward the house next door to get Cilla and Rowdy before heading back out to look everywhere a second time, and try again.

From experience, he knew Tim would only return in his own time and way—Noah hoped to God he would, anyway. He couldn't fool himself he was overreacting, when he wasn't. This constant fear was so much harder to take for its not being groundless. Every time Tim ran away or Cilla vanished, another chunk of him seemed to crumble into dust. His life revolved around keeping his family together, but it just kept disintegrating before his eyes.

As he drew nearer to the March house, a squeal of laughter lifted his soul for a moment—just a moment. Why the hell had he shown up here earlier today? Jennifer had proven herself capable of dealing with his kids—far more than he was—and Tim would still be here, safe and happy, if he hadn't stuck his nose in.

If he could, he'd turn and leave at this moment, leave Cilla and Rowdy here, laughing and joyous, and help the townfolk to find Tim; but it wasn't up to him. Jennifer—Ms March—had a life of her own to live, and it didn't include unlimited, unpaid babysitting.

No matter how *happy* she made his kids.

A shriek filled the air, followed by the slamming of the screen door. Jennifer came flying out, her long plait streaked with garish rainbow shades of paint, screaming with laughter. Cilla and Rowdy followed within moments, brandishing paint-brushes aloft in teasing threat.

Jennifer—he couldn't think of her as Ms March, looking like that—caught sight of him. She grinned and waved as she bolted past him and into the ring of trees halfway to the boundary fence, squealing like the proverbial stuck pig, arms waving madly. "You can't get me again!" she cried, dodging between trees at little-kid pace.

Cilla and Rowdy bolted straight past him, yelling, "We're gonna get you!"

After playing dodge-paintbrush for a few minutes she allowed them to "get" her, falling to the ground and allowing them to daub her with yet more riotous colours. Cilla and Rowdy were yelling like victorious warriors as they dug the paintbrushes into her hair and face.

"Wait, wait!" she cried after a minute or two, with a massive grin. "You win!"

The kids gave blood-curdling bellows, sitting on her belly, holding their paintbrushes aloft as if they were Excalibur. "We're the champions!" they chortled while she mock-bucked, trying to get up.

When it came to children, Jennifer March obviously gave no thought to her dignity—and his kids responded to her brand of fun like winter buds finding sunlight and rain.

Earlier, when assuring Noah he could trust Jennifer with his kids, Fred had told him she lived alone. Why *wasn't* she a mother? So what if she was divorced? She was pretty and gentle and fun-loving, so why hadn't some other man snapped her up long before now?

Then, remembering the flashes of sadness in her eyes, he knew there must be a compelling reason why she was spending her life minding other people's kids instead of having her own.

He shook himself. It wasn't his place to find out Jennifer March's past. He had enough trouble trying to work out how to make his kids happy; and from bitter experience he knew he was no good at working out what a woman was thinking, let alone how to make her life work.

He'd get past this brief fascination with Jennifer March, become friends with her, and the man in him would go back to sleep. He had no choice but to believe that.

Sudden tugging at his jeans made him look down. "Daddy, did you see? Daddy, we won!"

Seeing his little son's eager excitement, Noah grinned and swung Rowdy up on his hip. "I saw, matey. You and Cilla are the paint warriors! Yah!" He gave his best attempt at a blood-curdling scream of victory.

"Aaah, Daddy, ouch!" Rowdy covered his ears, grinning.

But Cilla's thumb shoved back in her mouth as she looked at her father; her eyes were big with a fear he *couldn't* have inspired in her. He'd never even been able to bring himself to tap her hand, his fragile little girl. *Why* was she frightened of him? What was it that made him such a damn *failure* with his kids?

The feminine voice called out cheerfully, "Right, who wants to turn my boring pink Play-Doh into a rainbow?"

"Me! Me! C'mon, Cilla, let's go!" Rowdy wriggled until Noah let him down—and Cilla was smiling again, her eyes filled with an excitement he couldn't manage to rouse in her with all his play ideas.

"Sit at the table. I'll come in a minute and get it down for you. Just grab more paper and keep painting until I get there," Jennifer called after them as both ran for the house.

When they'd gone, she came to him—too close—and laid a hand on his arm, her multihued face filled with concern. "You couldn't find Tim?"

Something flashed through him at the touch, just as it had earlier when he'd lifted her to her feet. He didn't know what it was, besides the obvious male reaction to a pretty woman in his vicinity—and he didn't want to know. It was useless anyway. He'd met the woman for the first time three hours ago and she was already babysitting for him and—

Feeling sorry for him.

Yeah, let's help the emotional basket case before he screws his kids up any worse than he already has.

He pulled his arm out from under her hand, hoping the move was subtle, so she wouldn't think he was running scared. "He'll come home when he's ready. He always does." His mouth tightened. *That's it, tell the woman your son disappears all the time, why don't you?*

"If he does this—" she hesitated "—does he have a phone?"

"Yes," he sighed, and ran a hand through his hair. "It's off."

"I see," she said quietly, and he had the feeling she really did see—too much. "Did you call Fred Sherbrooke?"

"Of course I did. Tim's only eight," he snapped.

"Of course you did. Stupid question," she murmured; but something in her voice made him look closer at her. Well, he'd wanted the concern and pity gone from her face, hadn't he? Mission accomplished. Beneath the mess of paint streaks, the pretty, gentle face was emotionless, but the lack of expression was a touch overdone. "I'd better take the plastic off the Play-Doh for the kids, and put it on the Formica table. I'll be right back."

The distance lay between them like the universe, or a time paradox. She was here, yet she wasn't. He got the point; he even appreciated it. She could keep as much distance from him as she liked, so long as she was good to his kids.

"No need. I'll take the kids off your hands." He almost winced at the flat hardness of his tone. "You've done more than enough already."

"And I'm a stranger," she said, still neutral. "But I promised them. You're welcome to take some of the Play-Doh and paint home for the kids, if you prefer. I have plenty here." She turned and strode for the house, not a single feminine sway about it.

That much he understood. He'd made her angry, but she wasn't going to talk about it, because despite all she'd done for him, they were strangers.

She was a stranger who'd been nothing but kind to him, and he'd not only rebuffed her kindness, he'd thrown it back in her face. He'd doused her in cold water: a punishment that belonged to other times and other people. She hadn't interfered.

He watched her go, conscious of a wish to call her back and apologise.

You owe her that much, at the very least. And you're good at apologies—remember? You had good experience every time you got it wrong with Belinda.

Wishing he had a clue what made women tick, he sighed and walked in after her.

Inside the kitchen, the withdrawn woman she'd been with him moments before had vanished. She was warm and laughing again as she packed a lump of Play-Doh and a small package of paints for the kids.

Was she in such total control of her emotions as this? Could she be? Heaven knew if she was he'd bottle whatever it was she had, and drink it every day. If he could show his kids nothing but warmth and laughter, Tim and Cilla might actually want to hang around with him.

"Here you are, Play-Doh and paint and brushes. If you lay it on a sheet of plastic, and watch them—"

"I have a play mat," he said, breaking into her words with a curtness she didn't deserve, and again, her face closed off. "I'm sorry," he sighed, turning away. "I'm worried."

"You wouldn't be human if you weren't." Her voice was strange as she added, too soft for the kids to hear, "I know you don't think so at the moment, but you *are* a good father. It's obvious how much you love your kids. Tim will come home."

"You don't know anything about what I'm thinking or feeling," he snapped, wanting to hit himself within moments. "Look—"

"It's okay, Mr. Brannigan," she said quietly. "I don't appreciate others prying into my personal business, either. I obviously crossed the line. I'm sorry, too."

He nodded, relief filling him at the understanding that didn't descend to pity; but then, looking into her eyes—soft and pretty and glimmering with a world of pain unspoken—he said gruffly, "Too many people knew my business back home."

After a long silence, she said in almost a whisper, "You're not the only one."

She'd turned away before he could ask and on second thought, he didn't want to know. It wasn't as if *he* could help; he couldn't even keep his kids at home. "We'd better go."

She nodded, her head drooping a little. "I'll keep an eye out here. I'll call Fred if Tim comes home, okay?"

He wanted to thank her for the help, but all he could see was Jennifer standing alone, watching through windows for his son because she had nothing else to fill her Sunday nights…or any nights.

For the first time in a long time, he wondered if the peace of being alone could replace the feeling of little arms around his neck; if the quiet of no kid fights was worth rising and eating, cooking and cleaning for one only. She seemed so alone…yet she hadn't said a word.

"Goodbye," she said softly.

On impulse, he took her hand in his. "Thank you for everything, Jennifer."

She didn't answer, but the stiffness of her back at his touch spoke a thousand words—and this time, he wished he couldn't read a woman.

She wanted him to take his kids and leave.

Leave her alone in this empty house: a home made for fun and family and laughter and love, holding one solitary woman with sadness in soft blue eyes and no one to give all that joy and laughter to…

Suddenly, for no reason he could fathom, he said, "I like a quiet glass of wine in the back paddock at night when the kids are asleep. If you'd like to join me tonight, I'd—"

She whirled back around to face him, eyes burning with fury that didn't even seem funny with the paint still daubing her face and hair. She snapped before he could finish the sentence, "You're right, Mr. Brannigan, I don't know much about you— but I do know you have a wife, wherever she is."

The fury swamping him, the overwhelming anger at the judgment when he was scared out of his mind for Tim, was too white-hot to think about how he'd put the invitation. "I might not win the world's greatest father award, or the world's strongest moralist, but you can at least acquit me of adultery. I chose not to bring up my private business in casual conversation with a stranger while my kids were listening—" he quickly turned his head to check where Cilla and Rowdy were completely absorbed in painting, before he went on in a low voice "—especially with Tim still needing to believe his mum will come home. But in three years, Belinda hasn't used a credit card, hasn't touched her bank accounts, hasn't been seen anywhere. Even if she'd left *me,* she was a devoted mother and daughter, and she hasn't contacted her kids or her parents. The police marked her file 'presumed dead' over a year ago."

She caught her breath—a little, strangled gasp. "I'm *sorry,*" she whispered, her soft-tanned face pale with shock.

He barely heard the apology; his chest heaving as if he'd run a race, he said, low, "Just so you know, the offer was my way of thanking you for minding the kids and for your hospitality. There's nothing I can do to repay you for today, but I wanted to give back—maybe friendship. I have nothing else to give a woman. Whatever you might think of me, I wouldn't sink so low as to hit on a neighbour I've just met, especially when you've been kind to me and my kids."

No longer pale, a deep, burning blush filled her face. Her eyes glimmered with tears. "I don't want repayment…Noah," she whispered. With an averted face, she held out her hand. "Can we go back a few minutes? I'd love a glass of wine…"

Just like that, his fury evaporated. Remembering everything she'd done for him today, all the kindness he'd just thrown in her face as a punishment for a misunderstanding not of her making. With a rueful smile, he took her hand. "Friends?"

"Yes, please." She still couldn't look at him—and her hand was shaking.

What to say? He didn't know her well enough to know in what way he'd upset her most—he only knew he felt like a first-class loser right now. "Jennifer…"

"What time will I come over?" she said softly. "I wouldn't want to come too early, and upset Tim."

Tim. He'd wasted fifteen minutes here that he could have spent searching for his son…

"Try about nine. I have to go now. Kids, we have to find Timmy, and get some dinner." He snapped his fingers, and Cilla and Rowdy got to their feet. They never argued or disobeyed his orders when Tim disappeared again; they knew he must be found.

At that moment, the phone rang. As Jennifer moved to answer it, he packed up the presents she'd given him for the kids, and tilted his head toward the door.

"Noah, wait!"

He turned back, seeing a radiant smile covering her face. "Tim's been found."

CHAPTER THREE

IT WAS almost half-past nine when he finally walked out his back door.

Watching from where she sat on a rocking swing on her side verandah, Jennifer waited another minute before rising to her feet. She didn't want to seem anxious—as if she saw him and ran for him. As if she saw him as something more than just a new neighbour.

As if he were a man she felt compelled to reach out to, to be with, even when the reminders of his runaway wife cast a shadow so dark she could barely see the man he'd been.

A runaway wife, a runaway son…but she refused to judge him as the cause of both. After all, Mark had run from her, too; and the *gentleness* with which Noah treated his kids— the hurt in his eyes, the shadows of the past—showed the man he was.

A man who wanted to be her friend. A man who *needed* a friend right now—and oh, she'd been there. Holding it all in, aching sometimes for just *one* person to understand…

I can understand. I've been there—well, almost.

So, they'd be friends. Right. She could do that.

She jumped the low fence and came to where he stood waiting for her, halfway up a grassy hill overlooking the sea. A deeper shade of darkness in the summer night; a man lost in the past.

The kicking of her pulse as she drew closer made a mockery of her thoughts on friendship.

It was obvious she'd have to be very careful. Noah Brannigan was more than a harassed single dad struggling to make things right in an impossible situation; he was far from the average man. He'd already shown he could see through the shutters covering her eyes to the pain she kept hidden beneath. If he saw the unwilling pull he held over her already...if he realised she'd spent an hour working out which of her shabby old sundresses to wear tonight—whether to replait her hair after she'd washed the paint out of it, or if it would look too obvious to wear it out.

So many years since she'd been through this kind of anticipatory torture; a lifetime since she'd *wanted* to think about it. Her life had been *safe*—then a man tapped on her back door, wanting his adorable, hurting kids back, and changed her world with a single smile.

"Hi."

Even his voice held power over her, as warm as the night, as dark as the gravel road leading to their houses. She was glad night concealed her blush. "Hi."

The darkness of his hand swept sideways. "There's a blanket there, if you can see it. I brought crackers and cheese, too. I hope you like white wine?"

"I do," she agreed cautiously, hoping it wasn't *very* dry. "I don't like reds."

"Lucky pick, then." A soft chuckle filled the air. "Hold on." With a click, the soft light of a double-halogen camping lantern blurred the darkness, and she could see his face. "I was saving the batteries until you came. I have mosquito repellent as well."

She watched him light the coil, wondering how she could be absorbed by so simple a thing. How could he make her tremble without touching her, or even looking at her? "Please, get comfortable," was all he said.

She sank down onto the rug, and opened the small basket.

"A night-time picnic. I've never had this experience," she said, knowing she was babbling but unable to stop it.

"It's not much."

Sensing his embarrassment beneath the neutral tone, she relaxed and smiled up at him. "It's the experience that counts, not what you eat." She waved a hand heavenward. "Look at it, Noah." Wanting to say his name for no reason she could discern; just wanting to. "The clear, clean sky, the stars. The sound of the ocean, the smell of the grass. Wine and cheese."

"And thee. It's almost poetic." With a grin, he sat down facing her. "Are you always so positive?"

She chuckled. "I know, it's annoying. My—" she hesitated before she said it "—my ex-husband used to call me Pollyanna." *And not in an admiring way, either.*

Noah relaxed with the reference to Mark, and she guessed he'd already known about the divorce. Henry the mechanic or June, the postmistress had passed on the gossip when they found out where he lived, no doubt. "Cynicism is everywhere these days. It gets old quickly. Don't underestimate simple happiness."

Touched, she smiled at him. "Thanks for inviting me tonight."

"Thanks for coming." He smiled back, turning her insides to warm jelly. "I love it out here at night, but it's good to have adult company. Don't get me wrong—I love my kids—but this hour of peace before bed…"

"You don't need to explain, I work with kids all day," she said, trying to laugh. "I usually sit on my back verandah for an hour about this time."

Shut up, Jennifer. You're sounding breathless again. It's enough to send the man running.

An awkward silence fell between them: two people trying to not try too hard. People who didn't know each other, yet had so much unspoken already. Strangers with far too many things to *not* say.

"You couldn't have had a worse introduction to my family," he said abruptly, when the silence became unbearable. "You and your uncle Joe both."

He was crumbling a cracker in his hand, it was so tense.

"Please." Acting on impulse, she laid a hand over his, stilling the movement. "You must have seen how much I enjoyed playing with the kids today, and as for Uncle Joe—" she grinned then "—Tim's turning up there was almost inspired. He adores having anyone visit his junkyard, let alone a boy totally fascinated by all the rusty rubbish he's got there. Tim made his day by asking all those questions. Uncle Joe said he was welcome back any time—and he meant every word."

Instead of relaxing with the reassurance, Noah shrugged. "I guess I'll know where to find him from now on, at least."

"Is that so bad?" she asked gently, hearing the underlying grimness in the words.

He poured wine into two glasses. "So long as he doesn't bother your uncle, I suppose it's all right."

She sensed that wasn't what Noah wanted to say, but after her gaffe this afternoon, she knew better than to push the issue. "Uncle Joe's been pretty lonely since Aunty Jean died two years ago, and my cousins all moved to Sydney or Brisbane for work. He doesn't see his own grandchildren more than twice a year—and though I visit him every week, I'm not a junkyard kind of girl," she laughed. "I suspect Tim's about to be adopted."

"I suspect he'll love it. A million places to hide."

"But always safe," she said softly, trying to soften whatever hardness lay beneath the light words. Wanting to heal the festering hurt so deep inside him, even though she knew she couldn't. "Uncle Joe will make sure he won't hurt himself."

As if he sensed her anxiety, Noah smiled at her. "True." He handed her a glass of wine. "Have you always run day-care centres?"

Willing to follow his lead—and wanting to talk of things

other than the kids he loved dearly yet worried him so much—
she nodded. "I did my diploma straight out of high school, then
went for the full degree by correspondence while doing a
nursing degree. I also keep up my Advanced First Aid. I always
planned to open my own place—but with rental and insurance,
let alone hiring staff, it was more than I could afford in the
Newcastle area."

Ah, so that was where she was from? Noah had wondered—
she seemed to be so much a *part* of this place. "Is that where
you grew up?"

"Yes. A born and bred Novocastrian—my parents still live
in Swansea, by the ocean."

"My parents still live out west of Dural in Sydney," he said
abruptly, almost adding, *so did Belinda's parents.* He and
Belinda had started school together, grown up on the same
street and had been together from the age of fifteen.

He didn't want to think about Belinda—it was like running
on a treadmill, exhausting him and ultimately, going nowhere.
"They're travelling around the country now, though. How many
kids do you have every day?"

And why don't you have any kids of your own?

"I have three to four children each day, usually. I have a
licence for up to six kids, but since I work alone, I won't over-
burden myself. Not that there's many kids in Hinchliff who
have working mothers who need me to give full-time care."
She laughed again, the sound sweet and clear in the late
summer night.

The aura of summer shimmered in the air around her. She
was like the tiny purple star-flowers blossoming amid the warm
grass waving in the wind: unexpected and lovely. A piece of
old-fashioned prettiness dotting the uniformity of unending
blades of grass that was his life.

Watching her walking to him in the thin white dress, her plait
falling over one shoulder, she'd seemed the embodiment of a

country night. She'd seemed to float toward him rather than walk in the soft moonglow, glimmering like a gentle beacon.

And he still wanted her. He wanted to hover around her aura like a lost moth, to slip inside it and feel her contentment and quiet joy in life. He wanted to sit here and drink in her face, to keep *feeling* her hand on his and this time, not let go...

Pulling away was too damn hard at this moment. It had been too long since he'd felt the night-heat of a woman's touch—a woman who wanted him, too.

And she did. It was in those soft blue eyes of hers, in the curve of her mouth...in the way she leaned into his lightest touch. In the breathlessness of her words when he was close to her, and the slight tremble when they touched. It was in the dress she wore, and the soft vanilla scent on her skin, a perfume she hadn't been wearing when they'd met. In the tendrils of loose hair escaped from her plait, half-curling around her face. In the gloss on her lips—lips she kept wetting with her tongue when she looked at him.

Jennifer wanted him, too—so much she didn't even seem to know how to hide it.

It couldn't happen. He wouldn't let it. The last thing he needed was the demands of a relationship, and the last thing his kids could cope with was a new mother-figure in their lives—especially Tim.

But even though flirting with danger was wrong, stupid, still he did it. Turning his hand beneath hers, not lifting or threading his fingers through hers, but feeling the soft warmth of palm to palm. "So you came here to start your business?"

Her gaze dropped to where their hands weren't quite linked— and slowly, her fingers moved; just a fraction, the tiniest, most tentative caress he'd ever known. Terrified and sweet, it acted on him like he'd downed the whole bottle of wine at a gulp.

As did her soft, breathless voice, saying all her words didn't. "I needed a fresh start after Mark and I divorced. Uncle Joe needed family close by—he's well physically and fine mentally, but he's getting older, you know? I came to visit, saw an opportunity since there was no other day-care providers here and ended up staying."

It took him almost a minute to work out what he'd asked, what she'd said in reply. He was too lost in the newfound wonder. His mind was caught up in the beating of his pounding pulse, in the sudden rush of hot wanting. She'd moistened her lips again. Her gaze fluttered down to his mouth, then back to his eyes, with a fugitive feminine shyness that left him drunk on need.

He had no experience in coping with this sudden rush of hot wanting; he'd never been with any woman but Belinda. Though he'd had the years of flirting and parties, it'd all revolved around Belinda; he didn't know how to play the game with a new woman.

He didn't think Jennifer knew how, either.

Both of them sat there, two feet apart, hands barely touching. Bowled over by this slamming of want and neither one knowing what to do with it—

Who was he fooling? They both knew what they wanted to do…it was the *consequences* of giving in to the desire they didn't know how to handle.

"What do you do with your life? Besides bringing up your kids?" Her voice held the aching femininity of a woman's desire.

He forced words from a closed-up throat. "I'm an architect and builder. I had a business in Sydney—the whole home-building package from start to finish." He didn't add that he'd had to sell off the Sydney business to pay off debts. It wasn't Belinda's fault—he ought to have seen her suffering. But lost in building up the business, then maintaining its prestige and success, he'd relied on Belinda's strength to keep the homefront going smoothly. He'd noticed she was buying a lot more things, sure, but they were doing well—why shouldn't she enjoy it? And if their married life had lost its intimacy since a few months before Rowdy's birth, he'd thought time and patience would fix it.

The full extent of her problems had only burst on him after she'd disappeared…and when the demands for payment had come, one after the other, from dresses and shoes to Internet gaming sites.

Jennifer's laugh burst in on his thoughts, feminine, unsteady, *wanting.* "And you moved to *Hinchliff?* What will you do in a town with two thousand residents?"

Glad to be diverted, he grinned. "Yeah, not that many opportunities for that kind of work here—so I thought I'd start up a renovation business. I'll be offering designs to suit any type of extension, for any era of house. And I could still offer new building services as well. There are a few new estates going up on the highway north and south of Ballina. That's not too far from here." He hesitated, knowing what he needed to say, to ask, but hating to put it on her. Still feeling the warmth of their semi-linked hands bringing him to life, touching a part of him he'd thought dead until a week ago. Until he'd seen Jennifer. "Of course, with Cilla and Rowdy too young yet for school, I'll only work part-time during the day. I can design at night."

Her eyes thoughtful, she nodded. "I—" Her hesitation was as obvious, as strong as his. "I have places for them both in day-care on Monday, Wednesday and Fridays if you need that? I run the centre until six at night, so if you need to work back, Tim's more than welcome to come over those days after school, as well."

Contact established; danger signs put on the tracks and they were running on a line heading for a broken track over a cliff. He knew it; she knew it; and still they plunged ahead.

After a short silence, she rushed on, her voice uneven. She pulled her hand from his, showing her nervousness—and no wonder, with the amount of times he'd shut her out today. "It'd be a business arrangement of course. I—I only have three kids on those days…and I don't charge that much…"

"Jennifer." To his surprise, he'd already laid his hand back over hers. "Thank you. I was hoping you'd have space. It's hard dragging the kids everywhere, as I had to in Sydney—and as for Tim—" He sighed. "I think he'd like it—especially if I'm not there to complicate things."

"I think it was me who complicated things," she said quietly, looking down at her lap, but she didn't move her hand from beneath his.

"We both complicated it," he admitted, just as quiet.

The wanting, the desire all but shimmered between them, and they were barely touching.

She looked up. "I think it's best for Tim if I go back home. I think we both have enough ghosts to deal with."

Aching to touch his lips to the curve of her neck, or to the exposed shoulder just beneath him….to lift her face to his—all he could do was nod. He knew she was right, but hearing the words filled him with resentment. He *wanted* Jennifer, damn it—just as she wanted him; but he was barred from the normal male-female attraction games, because of this damned *limbo*. Would he never stop paying the price for a few months of emotional blindness?

Am I giving Tim security and stability by being alone, or bowing to an insecure child's demands, and making things worse for the whole family? Cilla and Rowdy need a mother figure in their lives…and Tim needs it more than both of them together.

Why had he never thought of that before?

"I'd better go," she whispered, but she still didn't move her hand.

"Daddy!"

Noah scrambled to his feet. "It's Tim," he said tersely.

"Daddy! Daddy!"

He bolted to the house, through the kitchen and down the hall in to the big, blue room Tim shared with Rowdy. Even though it was a four-bedroom house, Tim didn't like sleeping alone. Though he'd never admit it, his baby brother's presence, his tiny snores and the comfort of Rowdy's *Sesame Street* posters and baby mobiles and teddy bears gave him a sense of continuity and safety. "It's okay, matey, I'm here."

He lifted his sobbing son into his arms, holding him close: the only time Tim would allow Noah into his space. He whispered inane words of comfort, caressing Tim's spiky shock of streaky hair, his palm wet with the sweat drenching his child. Tim was shivering, wracked with the terror again. Noah held him and rocked him, realising anew why he lived alone. Aching for the pain that never went away, locked inside a father's anguish that made him want to promise anything to make his little boy better, if only for a few hours.

"Daddy," he mumbled, lost in a world between sleeping, waking and the fear that walked with him night and day. The fear that separated him from all the other kids at school, made him different, because nobody else's mummy had *disappeared*. If Belinda had died, Tim would have accepted it by now, moved on and begun to heal; but there was nowhere to go when your mother was a missing person. There was no end, no closure or healing, just unending pain and the terror that it was your fault she didn't want to come home.

It was a burden too heavy for any little boy to carry around and still be normal.

"I'm here, matey. I'll always be here," he swore now to his son, wishing it didn't feel like a damned lie—that Tim could believe it. But he didn't and Noah didn't: the fragility of life and belonging was a lesson burned onto their skins with a branding iron.

Promises were something too easily broken. Belinda had proven that.

"Make her go away, Daddy…" Tim buried his face in Noah's shoulder, heaving with sobs too hacking to be an act to get his way.

Noah sighed, knowing this time, it was a promise he couldn't make. "I can't, matey," he whispered back, throat thick with pain as he kissed Tim's forehead. "She's our neighbour—and she'll be minding Cilla and Rowdy while I work."

The hiccups came thick and fast. "No, Daddy," Tim sobbed. "Mummy will never come home if—if…"

Tim couldn't even say it, couldn't finish the words.

Noah ached and burned with guilt piling on guilt, because this time he couldn't say he didn't want or like the woman who was threatening Tim's peace of mind. No matter how hard he tried, he couldn't lie to his son about this—because he *did* want Jennifer, and it would show every time he saw her. He wanted her even now, when he should be resenting her intrusion into his mind and body at the worst possible time.

Worst of all, he *liked* her—and this time Tim knew the danger was real. With his radar tuned in to his father day and night, needing him as much as he punished him, he'd sensed the danger even before Noah had.

There was nothing he could say to reassure his son, and the nightmares, the fear, would just go on and on.

Some instinct alerted him. He turned his head.

Jennifer stood in the doorway, her face white, eyes glistening with the tears spilling over in silence. A shaking hand, fisted tight, covered her mouth as she looked at Tim.

Slowly she lifted her gaze to Noah. He couldn't move, couldn't breathe. He could feel her driving need to reach out, to help them both—but if she did, Tim would know they'd been together, and he'd never feel safe again.

There was nothing she could do to help this, nothing she could say. It was over before it began. For half an hour they'd reached out to the fire—now it was burning an innocent child.

Without a sound she vanished, leaving only sadness and regret in her wake.

Jennifer was sitting on the picnic blanket, downing her second glass of wine when he came back. He stopped a few feet from her. Waiting for an explanation as to why she was still there.

Feeling like a complete idiot—why *hadn't* she gone home,

instead of sitting here drinking his wine?—she said, sounding lame even to her ears, "Is—is he all right now?"

"No." A terse word. "He's in my bed. I just came out to pack up the picnic before wild mice get to it."

"I'll do it." She scrambled off the blanket.

"No, Jennifer. Please, just go," he said quietly. "If he wakes up and comes out—"

She nodded, feeling even worse, if it were possible. "I just needed to know he was—"

So awkward, all these silences. Saying everything but the things they needed to say.

"He won't be all right until Belinda comes back...or her body's found." He went on, the words bursting from him. "It's not like a death. That's bad enough. But *this* is like permanent purgatory. The pieces of my life are jagged, and they keep cutting me—and cutting Tim, Cilla and Rowdy—over and over." He swiped a hand across his face, as if pushing the intensity and despair from his features. "There's nowhere to go, no way to move on. In Tim's mind, healing is disloyalty—even moving here feels to him like I've accepted her death. How do I tell him he's wrong to keep hoping, to keep looking for her in every car, bus or train? How do I say 'it's not Mummy' every time the phone rings and he runs for it? What if Belinda *is* alive and comes back? I know he's told Cilla that, too, so she feels the same even though she can't remember Belinda. Rowdy just doesn't understand. So we just exist, waiting for her, waiting for news—for anything that gives us permission to live without this damned hope and fear and *guilt* eating us all alive."

There was nothing more useless than unwanted tears. She gulped them back, but oh, how she *wanted* to wrap her arms around him right now, to let him know he didn't have to be so alone with all this pain...that she understood more than he knew.

But touching him was taboo, and her fascinated stare must be embarrassing him.

Jennifer closed her eyes against the force of this beautiful, tortured man. "I should have gone home. I'm sorry...I was worried."

"By now you must be worrying you're living next door to a basket case. I'm sorry, Jennifer." Another weary swipe of his hand over his face. "It might be a relief for me to talk, but you don't need to hear it."

"Maybe you needed to say it," she said quietly, giving him what she could. Unable to reach out because of a simple truth: she was utterly fascinated by this man, and touching him, even in comfort, was too dangerous. "And maybe saying it to a stranger felt cleansing."

"Maybe, but you're not a stranger," he muttered, his eyes intense on her.

Slowly she nodded. Accepting the rebuke, and the danger, without his speaking of either. They weren't strangers—but they couldn't be anything more than that.

"Jennifer."

Slowly she looked up, compelled by the starkness in his voice. Those jagged pieces of his life were ripping at him again. She knew—oh, how she *knew*...

He didn't look at her. His whole attention seemed focussed on packing up the little basket. "Even if Belinda's dead—and I believe she is—I have nothing left to give. You probably can't understand..."

Hearing the words *hurt,* even if she'd known it before she'd even seen him. Even if she knew all the reasons why she, too, had so little to give. Why she might take a lover, but never a husband—and as her life with Cody had been, Noah's life didn't allow for brief flings.

"To have a child you can't kiss better, you can't heal no matter how hard you try, kills you piece by piece," she said softly, "but you can't stop hoping, can't stop trying. You have no choice but to put them first—even when you worry you're spoiling them or making a rod for your back later." She smiled and shrugged, and before he could ask her how she knew so much, she handed him the picnic blanket she hadn't even known she was folding, and turned away. "Bring Cilla and Rowdy over whenever you need to work. Doesn't matter what days, okay? No notice needed."

"Jennifer…" In the darkness, a hand—that sturdy, dependable brown hand—reached out to her, and she ached to touch him one final time.

A wave crashed below them. The tide was right in, attacking the sandstone walls below them. It was a lonely sound.

She shook her head, trying to smile. "Best not to."

His gaze was deep and intense. "I can't do all the taking. It's not in me."

"You aren't," she assured him quietly. "You're paying me. I'm saving money to have my verandah rebuilt bigger, and get a new cubby house for the kids, a portable one." She flushed as she said it, though why, she had no idea. "I've been thinking of selling up and moving into town—it'll be closer for the kids…well, most of them…"

"We both know you're still the one giving the most in this arrangement." His voice was grim. "So I'll design and build your verandah and cubby house for you. Just pay for the materials. No charge for labour, not while you're minding the kids. I need to start up my business again, heaven knows—" he didn't even crack a smile as he said it "—and it can serve as local advertising at the same time."

She heard the prickly note in his voice. She couldn't find it in her to blame him; his day would reach any sane man's limits. "If it serves us both, all I can say is thank you, Noah."

"Good." Only then did he smile—and it was as if he'd cracked apart the wall of isolation she'd been trying to build. "If I get some really big work in the interim—"

Knowing what he couldn't say, she nodded. "Of course, you

have a family to support. To finish up before and after work will be fine. The kids are still with you then. We can alternate dinners, maybe. One night I cook, another you can bring it home."

"Thank you, Jennifer. I don't know how to say…" His voice trailed off. Husky, but not with desire: rough with the gratitude of a man who'd carried his burdens alone too long.

And though she knew that, still she thought of what she couldn't have, and blushed. "I have to go. Good night, Noah."

Pollyanna strikes again, her inner voice taunted as she walked away without looking back.

She was setting herself up for a fall; it was as inevitable as the tide coming in below her feet. After two years of wandering through a half-dreaming existence, she was alive again—and it hurt. The worst part of it was until she could change the person she was, she had no choice in it. Within a day she knew Noah Brannigan had the power to destroy her, yet she couldn't do a thing about it without hurting his beautiful children, or making his suffering worse.

Heart against conscience, and the pull of needing children. No, she had no choice—and she knew whatever price she'd pay for her decision, she went into it with her eyes open.

She hoped.

CHAPTER FOUR

Six weeks later

"JENNY! Jenny, we're here!"

As she sipped her morning coffee, she found herself smiling at Rowdy's enthusiastic interruption to her routine. Usually this was her quiet time before the other kids arrived, but Tim, Cilla and Rowdy weren't "other" kids. What it was about them that called her so strongly, she only wished she knew. She loved all the children she cared for but the Brannigans had broken through the eggshell-thin wall of self-protection around her heart. Perhaps it was because the family needed her so much.

No, the Brannigan *children* needed her. Noah only needed her child-minding skills.

Apart from the days she had the kids, he'd been over only twice in the past six weeks—to draw up the plans, and show them to her. He'd called to let her know the local council had approved the plans, and again to let her know he'd be starting work today.

He was cutting and assembling her new cubby house in his yard, and would bring it over when it was done. "I thought it'd be a joint project I could do with Tim," he'd told her in a gruff voice. She didn't know if the odd note was because he was using an excuse to avoid her—or because Tim was refusing to hammer in a single nail when his father was around.

He might not be running off quite so much—only twice since the night they'd met—but that didn't mean he wasn't going to keep punishing Noah for his invisible crimes.

She didn't flatter herself that it was *her* influence that stopped Tim running off. She only wished she knew what it was—

Rowdy erupted into the kitchen with a big, glowing smile, sure of his welcome. He ran straight into Jennifer's arms with all the confidence he'd shown from the first day. Knowing he was loved. "Jenny, I'm here! Are you happy?"

"Of course, very happy," Jennifer chuckled as she hugged him. He always stated the obvious, and asked the same thing every day. "Are you hungry?"

He nodded with vigour, though Jennifer was sure Noah would have fed all of them before coming over. "Toast and Vegemite!"

She hugged him again, and swung Cilla up onto her other hip, giving her a big kiss before she answered. "Sorry, sweetie, no can do. I have three other kids coming soon." Whenever she gave him the spread, it seemed to give him a massive burst of energetic chatter and climbing she couldn't cope with when she had other children to watch.

It was the only time he fulfilled the nickname Tim told her Noah had given him soon after his birth—the baby who constantly made noise. She often wondered if he'd quietened down by nature or necessity. Tim and Cilla needed so much more than he did...he seemed such a happy child, but she watched him, just in case.

As Tim walked through the door with far more caution than the other kids showed, she suggested, "How about baked beans and cheese on toast?"

That was Tim's favourite, but Rowdy tended to emulate Tim—at least when Tim wasn't angry or screaming. Rowdy was perpetually good-natured.

Tim grinned and nodded. "Thanks," he said: a reluctant concession to manners, and as gruff as his father always was when he felt overwhelmed.

Cilla made a tiny sound.

Jennifer smiled down at Cilla, hiding the ball of emotion the non-request engendered. After six weeks of constant invitation, the little girl still didn't have the courage to ask for anything she wanted. "Chocolate spread and mashed banana for Cilla, of course."

The glowing smile was reward enough.

Noah knocked on the door, polite and withdrawn—the constant reminder of the wall between them. "Good morning, Jennifer."

"Good morning, Noah," she returned, grave and just as polite. Trying to smile as normal, but if she did, he'd smile back, and she'd forget what she was doing—and Tim would see it.

"I just made coffee. Would you like some?" she offered as he walked through to the little-used front door, and put barrier tape across it, in preparation for tearing out the front verandah.

He turned back from his task. "Yes, thank you."

It took all she had not to gulp—Tim was watching—but Noah's simple good manners made her feel as if she'd just endured three rounds with a kickboxing champion. She clung to the memory of their night together as dearly as if they'd made love: it was all she was likely to have. Remembering his rare smile, the way his hand turned beneath hers in a promise unspoken...

She put Cilla down after another gentle kiss, and got Rowdy into the high chair, strapping him in. "I'll just get the kids set first."

She turned away from the sight of him as if he was just another father dropping off his kids, or a tradesman working on her house. A crazy infatuation, an unrequited attraction.

So why did she always feel as if he'd touched her, when he never did? He hadn't touched her once, nor even come close to her, from that first night. Why was it he could break years of self-sufficiency and good sense with a look, or a smile—or even by the lack of them?

"Jen? Here's the baked beans." Noah's personal watchdog stood in front of her, waiting. Watching. On guard.

She blinked and smiled at Tim. "You're such a good help." She smiled down at the boy, feeling his hunger for the closeness of touch, and his fear and loathing of it. Poor little man needed a mother so much, even more than Cilla and Rowdy did; but he barricaded himself from the simple joy of a hug because she was a woman, and therefore a threat to his security. His mother was no more than a distant memory; his vow was all he had left of Belinda.

With a sense of fatality she made the breakfast. Child-carer, just the child-carer…

That coffee was a long time coming.

Noah muttered words he'd never use in front of the kids as he tore up one plank after the other, glad for something heavy and physical to do. He'd work himself to exhaustion, if that's what it would take to quieten the screaming demands of his body, the whispers of his heart.

Every time he saw her now, her pretty face, her tenderness and unassuming grace filled him like the thrumming of a guitar chord, reverberating through every pore. Even just living within five hundred metres of her house, knowing she was there, made the masculine hunger roar to life. When he had to pick up the kids, to see her kissing his kids, caring for them, and yet to know, to feel the barriers neither could breach, he ached and burned.

At night he relived their one night out beneath the stars…the night where nothing, yet so much, seemed to have happened between them. Floating toward him in that white dress, soft half-curls escaping her plait. Just the joy of talking with her…seeing her hand over his; watching her smile at him, her eyes touched with desire…

Most nights he woke up in a sweat that had little to do with the current heatwave—on the nights Tim didn't wake him up with nightmares, at least. No wonder they were both short-tempered these days; neither of them were getting much sleep.

Tim rarely spoke to him now, but he kept watching.

He had no idea how Jennifer felt about him. She seemed so serene, treating him as if he was just another day-care daddy, offering coffee the same way she did to the mothers who dropped their kids here—or worse, like he was her uncle.

He swore as a massive splinter ripped through his thick glove and pierced his thumb.

"Noah?"

Hearing the concern in her voice, he reacted with brusque rejection. "I'm fine."

"Here's your coffee."

The gentle care had vanished; her words were neutral, almost too neutral. He looked up. Her smile was calm, determined. *She* would keep her manners; and it made him feel like a schoolboy being rebuked by his teacher, and just as foolish.

He put out a hand to take the cup, but she put it down beside him.

"Jennifer—" he started to apologise, disgusted by the husky note in his voice at using the name. The *neediness* just using her name provoked in him.

Wanting to touch her, if only for a moment. His temper igniting because there was no way he could take the risk.

He turned away. "I have some quotes to do today. I'll be out until Tim's back from school. Is it okay to work on the verandah from four until dark?"

"Of course." Her gaze moved to his gloved right hand, and the splinter sticking out from his thumb at an angle. "I'll get tweezers and antiseptic. I'll send them out with Tim."

"It has to be this way, Jennifer," he growled, hating the distance. *Hating it.*

She turned to look at him for a moment, her eyes not quite meeting his. "I'm not arguing." Then she sighed. "I have to go in. I asked Tim to mind the kids while I brought out the coffee, and it's interrupting his routine. He hasn't got much time before the school bus."

"He's ready for school."

She frowned and tilted her head.

"He's watching us through the glass of the front door," he said quietly.

She didn't make the mistake of looking. "Then he'll be reassured, won't he?"

His left glove flicked away as he tossed it. Wishing he knew what she felt beneath the controlled words, he pulled the splinter from his glove. Wishing she'd go back inside before he did something really stupid.

"It's not just about you and Tim, you know."

The sudden intensity of it took him aback. He looked up again. She stood over him, her fists curled, and a strand of half-curl dancing across her face in the hot morning wind—and so pretty with her cheeks flushed and her eyes flashing with anger. He ached to brush that strand away: it was that bad with him now, just touching her hair would be enough—and he was a whisper away from *really, really stupid* now. "What is it, then?" He winced at the harsh question: such a pitiful mask for the craving.

As if she'd felt the almost violent need in him, she brushed the lock of hair away, but it came dancing back within moments. She tugged it back hard behind one ear. "You don't need to know. You're just the father of three kids I happen to have fallen madly in love with."

Wham.

Just like that, his belief in shared sleepless nights, angst and craving shattered. She'd only spoken truth as she saw it; not how she felt or what she wanted, but what *was*. Why the truth made everything she'd awoken in him rise up in hot rebellion, he didn't know, but he was on his feet, striding toward her without thought, ready to haul her against him and prove she was lying.

A movement by the window stopped him cold.

"Then why say anything, if you weren't going to tell me?" he snapped, not knowing who or what he was most furious about. He'd bricked them inside four walls together, separated by a wall of Perspex neither could batter down.

One brow lifted as she contemplated his anger and obvious frustration. "So you'll stop apologising. I have good reasons why there will never be another man in my life. I won't bother you." She turned her head away, but not before he saw the flash of want in her eyes. "You don't need to worry I'll jump on you. I wouldn't make a fool of myself."

Won't bother him? She did that just by being here, so close, so lovely, so graceful and so tempting…talking about *jumping on him.* Everything about her bothered him to insanity point.

"My bus will be here in a minute."

Tim made his announcement through the window beside the taped-off door. Noah cursed his stupidity; Tim must have heard everything they'd said. Why hadn't he taped the window shut, as well? He could have sworn he had.

A swift glance showed that Tim had slowly peeled the tape away and opened the window to listen in on them.

"Re-tape the window, please, Tim," he said coolly, asserting authority. "And don't peel it back again. You could put the day-care kids in danger if my work isn't taped and roped off from Jennifer's business. If you want to listen to our conversations, come outside and do it honestly."

"Yes, Dad." Tim didn't so much as look at his father, but his voice was filled with trust as he turned back to Jennifer. It was a trust she'd earned with cooking lessons and games of paintbrush wars, his favourite food—and never looking at Noah as if she wanted him. "The kids are watching *Sesame Street,* Jen, so can I go?"

"Of course, Tim. Thanks for your help."

Her voice was just as warm as Tim's. The mutual admiration society had just upped a notch, thanks to Jennifer's blunt statement that she'd never pursue Tim's only security. Tim liked Jennifer; Cilla and Rowdy adored her, and she loved them all.

He was the only one locked out.

He couldn't look at her anymore. Life was too hard as it was. He didn't need the answer, as logical as it was impossible, standing right in front of him, reminding him of everything he couldn't have. "Don't bother with the tweezers. I got the splinter myself. Thanks."

There was no way she could miss the freezing politeness in his voice.

She didn't answer, but the rustling of hot air touching his face told him she was gone.

"Oh, good grief," Jacey's mother Kate muttered the next afternoon, as she stared out the back window. She was the last mother for the day, and she, like the others, married or single, had done the same thing.

Stared at Noah as if he was manna fallen from heaven...

In the light of the setting sun he was tearing up old wooden slats and tossing them behind him. He was wearing only cutoff jeans and work boots; his bare, tanned chest and builder's strong arms were slick with sweat; his legs were muscular and brown. His hair took on the sun's glow, touched at its ends with golden fire.

"Jen, you lucky, lucky girl," Kate muttered, drinking in the sight Jennifer had been studiously avoiding for the past hour. "How on earth do you live next door to *that,* have him here day and night and *not* get into the horizontal tango with that gorgeous man?"

"Shhh," Jennifer whispered frantically, with a quick glance back to where Tim watched a re-run of something, Jacey on his lap, and Cilla and Rowdy played a game of memory cards.

Kate grinned, impudent and unashamed. "Come on, girl, are you dead? Lost your hormones? Coz otherwise you can't tell me you don't spend hours every day looking, and itching." She lifted a brow in cheeky suggestion. "Make me coffee and tell me all. I swear if I wasn't happy with Nick…"

How many more times would she hear the same thing? It wasn't as if her rebel body needed the encouragement!

After she'd eventually ushered Kate and Jacey out of the house, Jennifer sighed. Why couldn't she find the words to shut the mouths of the curious and determined? It was bad enough that every child's mother had asked the same thing, and her mother, alerted by Uncle Joe, was calling from Italy for updates; her quilting friends Veronica and Jessie had also met him when Tim took off last week, and Noah had come over looking for his son. Wearing only a singlet top and denim shorts, his body gleaming with sweat from making her cubby house…

Not one person in town believed they weren't lovers. Not one person didn't fill her imagination daily with visions she couldn't lock out of her head.

Not with him *there,* looking like that…

Like Kate, like Annie and Olga and every other woman with a beating heart and hormones, Jennifer was mesmerised. Through the elusive, shifting colours of her old stained window, he seemed godlike, a glowing being of strength and power…and a rich male beauty that left her breathless and hurting.

Trying to behave, she'd done no more than steal glances as the kids played and she stitched her latest quilt she was making; yet every peek made her feel like a sneak thief in her own home. But she was helpless to stop herself from doing it, over and over.

Quilting was a form of creation she could take anywhere, one she'd learned at the Children's Hospital during Cody's stays. It kept her hands busy and her mind calm and centred, especially when she was tired or feeling negative.

Unless there happened to be exquisite, golden-brown temptation working just outside her window, bending down over lumber, wearing only hugging jeans…

She had to stop it, now!

Sticking the needle into the quilt, she folded it up and put it out of the reach of little hands. "Let's play a game of hide-and-seek before dark," she announced to the kids.

"Yeah!" Rowdy and Cilla bolted from the game of Memory they were playing, straight out the back door to the yard.

She looked at Tim, still watching some rerun of funny videos, with a smile she made deliberately impish. She couldn't show him that she'd suggested the game for his sake alone. Desperately hoping that, by playing the game so often, she could desensitise the issue of his disappearances whenever life overwhelmed him. "If you stay there I'm going to find you pretty fast, Tim—and Rowdy will crow about it all night."

With a chuckle, Tim ran for the back door.

After a slow, loud count to twenty, she walked out the back door after them, calling, "I'm coming to get you," in a way that never failed to make Rowdy giggle.

She always made sure Tim or Cilla won. Rowdy didn't seem to mind; he liked finishing the search with her, and once he'd said, "Timmy likes to win," for which she was awed. That a three-year-old had such self-esteem, and such insight into his insecure brother's needs, was a testament to Noah's rearing of his kids. That Tim and Cilla were healing so quickly—and they were—could only be laid at Noah's door, as well. All her training told her it should take far longer to have gained the kids' trust, and for them to let her in.

It amazed her that Noah didn't realise what a magnificent father he was.

"I'm coming to get you," she cried again, and heard the giggle from around the front of the house. Smiling, she called it over and over, hearing the laughter smothered by a hand, but still constant. Running around the old cubby at the side, she dashed into Rowdy's favourite hidey-haunt: behind the gardenia bushes at the front corner of the house. She dived on him, tickling his tummy. "Got you, bud!"

Rowdy shrieked with laughter, not in the least put out at being found first. "Let's get 'em, Jenny," he whispered very loudly, slipping his hand into hers.

Resisting the urge to kiss the little hand, she circled the yard at a little-kid running pace, crying out, "We're coming to get you!"

As they approached where Noah was tearing down her verandah, he turned his head: the golden-rose rays of sunset fell on his face as he smiled at them.

Jennifer lost her breath—and caught her toe. She tripped over a root and stumbled. Acting with lightning instinct, she twisted Rowdy so he came down on top of her as she fell to the spongy grass.

Seeming unhurt, he cackled with laughter. "We playing Ring Around the Rosie?"

"No," she laughed back, "Jenny's just playing dropsies."

"I thought *I* was the dropsy one around here."

His voice was close. *He* was close…too close. She turned her head, with the vestiges of laughter still in her eyes, to see him smiling down at them. "No." The word came out half-strangled. "I—why do you think I work with kids? I thought I'd put the family's genetic clumsiness to a good use. It entertains the kids no end."

Grinning, he put out his hands to them. "This feels like déjà vu." He lifted her to her feet. "But there are no pots to take off you this time."

And no shirt, either.

On her feet, Jennifer found herself in direct eye contact with his naked, brown chest; her hands, released from his, were a bare inch from touching him. He smelled like earth and grass and wood, and hardworking, raw, sensual male. His bare skin gleamed with honest sweat.

Heart racing, breathless, she didn't dare look up at him.

She'd only make a fool of herself if she did…but she couldn't help it, couldn't stop it. Within moments her gaze lifted to his.

Deep, hot, strangely vulnerable as he took in the desire she couldn't hide…and *tender.* Will against wanting, need against reason…the aching current arced between them, impossible and beautiful—and her hands, with a will of their own, lifted that inch—

"We go finding Timmy and Cilla now?"

The hopeful question roused her from the lovely stupor. She shook her head to clear it, and her hands fell. She couldn't breathe, or speak with any semblance of normality. It was all she could do to smile down at Rowdy and nod.

Noah stepped back without a word, but a tiny smile hovered around his mouth.

On legs that felt like jelly, she took Rowdy's hand again, and headed toward the other side of the house.

And Noah, as off-kilter and damned scared as he knew Jennifer had been, turned back to the verandah, thanking heaven Tim hadn't seen that moment, for once. Thanking heaven for Rowdy's intervention, or he'd have taken her into his arms then and there…

He'd have to work himself into insensibility the next few hours. It was the only way he'd get any sleep tonight.

CHAPTER FIVE

TIM came into the house without his usual passive-aggressive behaviour that disrupted the family—and Noah knew what he was going to say before he said it. "Dad, you got one of those big letters again."

The kids always left him alone to read them. They knew better than to get him going on "big letter" days—they just didn't know what the letters were or why they got to him.

He carried the letter into the kitchen, got a beer out and sat at the table. He knew he'd need it. Phone calls were positive news, a lead or a sighting of Belinda; a letter was always bad.

Dear Mr Brannigan,

It is with regret that I inform you we found the woman in question, and there is no possible way she could be your wife. Her name is Sandra Langtry, and she lives in a bush cabin in Broadwater National Park with her family. She has lived an alternative lifestyle for eighteen years and has given birth to four children in the past twelve years…

The words blurred in front of his eyes.

It was over. The only good sighting in the past eighteen months, and it led to nothing.

He downed the beer in seconds, but it did nothing; no amount of alcohol could douse the pain, the feeling that a chapter of his life should be closed, but the jagged shards of his life remained in the doorway, leaving it open. The cold winds of uncertainty and abandonment, the feeling of being stuck down a dark well he couldn't climb out of, filled him again.

Unless he did something about it; he had to take charge.

Closing off the door to the kitchen, he picked up the phone to make the call he'd been putting off for more than a year.

A week later

She had to stop looking. It was bordering on perversion, the way she kept finding reasons to sit here near this window, or looking every time he passed.

Which was *way* too often.

Dear God, the man was beautiful…like a statue of David come to warm, touchable flesh…

Would this mid-autumn heatwave never end? It'd been nine days now; nine days of endless heat, where Noah pulled his shirt off to work in the early evenings.

If only he'd keep his shirt on, she wouldn't be so—so lost in the sight of him all the time. Lost in the sight of warm golden-brown skin, muscle rippling beneath; lost in the smiles he gave her when he caught her looking. She was beyond counting the amount of stubbed toes or bruises on her legs from walking into things, or tripping over when she stared at him, but she knew she had fifty-two needle pricks in her index finger…

Ouch. Make that fifty-three.

Right. Stop it immediately. Lower gaze and look at your quilt before it's completely unsaleable. Yes, you can do that.

Her gaze lifted again within two minutes. Obviously self-control was not the forte she'd thought it was.

So Plan B: get out of the line of fire.

"I'm going out to the rocking chair," she announced to the

kids. Yes, that was safe—the rocking chair was on the un-touched side of the verandah, on the other side of the house from Noah. Take the kids, even better. A refuge against temp-tation. "Want to put on the hose and cool down on the Slip and Slide before I make dinner?"

During summer she took the kids to the beach, while it was patrolled, but the lifesavers packed up in late March, and she wasn't a strong enough swimmer to risk taking the children there alone. So they'd played on the wet mat every afternoon during the late-April heatwave, cooling down in the burning hour before sundown. Tim especially liked it when all the kids were there, and he was the big one who watched over them and made sure they were all safe.

"Yeah, Slip and Slide!" Rowdy would have run straight out if she hadn't stopped him, putting on his sunscreen shirt and hat. It might be late afternoon, but in heat like this his fair skin would burn.

When the kids were dressed and sunscreen applied, she let them bolt to the back door, and out. She followed, carrying her quilting basket. "Tim, don't forget to wet the whole slide first," she called, knowing Tim would, but he liked to hear again that he was the senior one, and he had the responsibility.

Tim was already hosing it down, his tongue sticking out with concentration. "No, Rowdy, you could hurt yourself," he said, waving his little brother back. "It'll be ready in a minute."

"Okay, Timmy—hurry." Rowdy stepped back and hopped from one foot to the other in impatient obedience.

As she patched in a small piece of curved rag to the main quilt, Jennifer smiled, watching the brothers. Tim was becoming a child of his family again; the past few weeks, he'd stopped running away, and seemed to begin accepting life here.

It had surprised her at first, given the depth of his anger and rebellion against Noah at the start; but if it worked, if his father thought the change was positive, who was she to question it?

If she saw something in Tim's eyes, in the way he spoke, and how he'd become a big brother again instead of verbally attacking Cilla and Rowdy that made her wonder, she could think of no reason for it. Nothing out of the ordinary had happened to bring about the change that she could think of.

"Maybe it's school?"

"What is?"

"Ouch!" She removed the needle, and rubbed at her jabbed finger. "Fifty-four," she muttered, glaring up at Noah—

Would he never put his shirt back on?

"Fifty-four what?" He looked down at her abused finger. "Sorry." He frowned, taking in the amount of pinprick jabs there. "Are you diabetic?"

"No." Embarrassed, she shrugged. "Just clumsy."

"And you chose quilting as your hobby? Did you see it as a challenge?" He chuckled and sat on the rocker next to her. "Why don't you get a thimble?"

"I've had a dozen—I keep losing them." She grinned back. "Quilting was an exercise in patience more than anything at first—a way to pass the hours. Before I knew it, I loved it. I've met a lot of my closest friends up here in the quilting circle."

"It looks very peaceful. Like you," he said quietly. Then he gulped down the tall glass of iced water he'd brought out with him.

The past week or more, he'd been making more of an effort to speak to her, to begin the friendship they'd spoken of the first night. They talked of their childhood, schooling, what made them choose their career paths. They talked of family still living, his brother, her sisters and brother and cousins. She told him about her parents travelling the world in their early retirement, as his parents were travelling around Australia in a campervan. They were currently in Western Australia, discovering the wildest northwest Outback.

It was so good to have an adult to speak to about something other than their children, but if there was two things she was certain of, it was that she couldn't be Noah's friend…and she was far from *peaceful*. Not when something as simple as watching him drink made her heart thunder and her breath seize in her lungs…watching the movement of his throat and small trickles of sweat run down the golden-brown skin…

Fifty-five.

She was quite proud of the fact that she didn't say "ouch" aloud this time.

"That's a nice quilt," he remarked, looking down at it. "It's nice and soft, with all those swirly bits in different shades of brown. What's the pattern? It looks like the spirit of autumn."

"I—" Oh, help, she hardly knew. This quilt had become her refuge from staring at him the past two weeks; she'd chosen colours and pattern at random.

Looking down, she took in what her fingers had been creating the past fortnight—and felt the heat flaring on her face. Double circles intertwining…golden-hearted rose petals…

She rushed into speech, before he asked another question. "It's…um, a traditional pattern, popular since the early twentieth century—and—and since it's autumn…"

Babbling again, she thought in disgust. If any other of her quilting club were here, they'd give her a knowing grin and tease her unmercifully about her Freudian slip. It was a wonder they hadn't noticed it at the Friday night "eat-fest."

It was a traditional pattern, all right, and very popular: a wedding quilt. And what was worse, it was all in the colours of maple and caramel and golden-brown—autumn shades, but also the colours of Noah's eyes and hair and skin.

She hadn't even known until now, when the evidence was right in front of her; but she couldn't deny her unconscious desires, revealed by her creation.

Lust she could handle; she had been, barring a few physical injuries—try a few hundred—but if she was dreaming of everything—of the marriage and babies she couldn't risk—

Come on, Pollyanna, fix this one, she heard a voice taunting her. *What man will want a tainted strain he can't even have kids with?*

Noah already has children. He doesn't need a baby from you, her mind whispered.

But that's not the real problem, she admitted wearily to herself.

All her life she'd wanted just one thing: to be a wife and mother. To be rounded with her babies, feeling them kick, to feed at her breast, reading stories to her children, singing songs. The whole nine yards that went with it, even the hours of worrying about teenagers let off the leash.

Well, she'd had it—and Cody had been the one to pay the price for her dreams.

"Jennifer? Are you okay? Is the heat getting to you?"

When he spoke like that, touched with caring, his voice ran over her with rough sweetness, making her forget everything: the past, her pain—everything but the rush of wanting him.

You can't have him. No touching.

She gulped and blurted out, "I should ask you that question, since you've always got your shirt off these days. I wish you'd put it back on—then I wouldn't have all these injur—" She skidded to a horrified halt, her mouth open to speak and she couldn't seem to close it.

Terrified but unable to stop it, she looked up at him.

He was biting the inside of his lip, but it didn't quite cover the grin. His eyes were warm with laughter and something deeper, hotter and infinitely more masculine. "I didn't realise it was bothering you. I'll keep it on, then."

She had to force her mouth closed, to stop the protest coming out. Now she'd gotten what she'd needed the past couple of weeks, she wished she'd just kept her silly mouth shut.

Nothing short of sudden blindness would stop her staring at him, anyway.

A trickle of sweat ran down her neck. God help her, she was

so obvious it was pitiful! She jumped to her feet, letting the quilt apparatus scatter across the verandah. "Make way, kids!" she hollered, and bolted for the Slip and Slide.

The kids laughed and scattered for her, knowing when she gave that war whoop, she was going for it—a full-on slide all the way down...

Picking up her quilting stuff, Noah watched her run and slide to her hip as she landed on the wet length of plastic, her legs in the air, with absolutely no grace or dignity. He hid a knowing grin. She might be having fun now, but he knew why she'd needed to cool down; and while he couldn't do a thing about that particular heat, the man in him loved his power over her.

The same power she held over him.

Strange, but though he'd always thought her pretty, at first it was in a more ordinary way: the same kind of appreciation he had for the flowers in her garden. They were lovely, but something he could see anywhere. He wanted her; she'd woken him somehow; but surely he could control it.

But the more he saw her, the more she captured him with every movement of her hands and hips, every nuance of her smile, the light in her soft eyes. The beauty no amount of makeup could create, no amount of surgery could buy. Just being Jennifer...

She landed in a heap of arms and legs at the other end of the slide, where she'd set up rubber bumpers to stop the kids getting hurt, and he laughed. She could make him happy with the simplest of acts, her uncomplicated, innate dignity...and she seized him heart and soul with her love for his children, and how she was healing them just by being herself.

Being Jennifer.

She untangled herself and jumped to her feet, yelling, "Let's all go together! A train!"

Noah lost his breath; a sharp lump lodged in his throat, blocking air. Her thin white summer shirt was wet, revealing every curve, each dusting freckle and the glow of her light-fawn skin. Her smile was radiant; she tossed her half-fallen plait off her breast to her back as if it were a nuisance.

Oh, to be that hand, that plait. To be able to touch her so casually…to touch her at all. Just to be free to touch her, to be a man again…

The gulp hurt him all the way down to his chest.

The kids beat her to the top of the slide, which she'd placed on a slow graded hill; they waited in line, Tim holding Cilla, Cilla holding Rowdy. Jennifer plumped down behind Tim, her hands at his waist, and she pushed off, with a loud cry, "Go!"

They didn't make it to the end, but nobody cared. Everyone was laughing too hard. Rowdy gave his cute, choking giggle, but Cilla and Tim were alive with the joy she brought them.

He couldn't stand it anymore. He'd been alone too long. He had to be a part of the fun.

"Let's make a bigger train!" he yelled, and ran for the hill. "I'll beat all of you!"

When he saw Cilla and Tim running to beat him—Cilla was *playing* with him—he choked up again. He deliberately tripped over nothing, just as Jennifer did when she knew they wanted to win, and landed splat on the wet, muddy grass face-first. "Ah, nuts!"

The kids cracked up when he lifted his face, showing it covered in dirt.

"Oh, get up, Brannigan. You're holding up the train!"

Noah grinned at Jennifer, standing over him like an impatient schoolmarm, if somewhat too wet and dirty for the job. An adorable paradox; the miracle he'd never hoped to find. He had to be careful, or he'd fall so hard and deep for her, he'd never climb out of it; but while he had this happiness, he'd grab at what he could.

He put his hand into her outstretched one, ready to help him up; but as he began getting up, she slipped away, letting him fall on his face again. "Ha! I got him, I got him!" she crowed to the kids, who were on the ground, pointing at him and cracking up again.

"Funny Daddy!" Rowdy cried.

"Silly Daddy," Cilla giggled.

"Silly Dad, he can't even get up by himself!" Tim shouted. He seemed to have no problem with Jennifer touching him—at least long enough to drop him on his face.

He looked up at the instigator of the scene, who winked at him, seeming totally unaware of what she'd just done for his family—or of her enticing state of semi-naked loveliness.

"I'll get you for that," he threatened, but his voice was a hoarse croak.

"Yeah, yeah, promises, Brannigan," she chanted, and ran for the slide. "Get in the line, kids. Big train time! I'm the driver this time!"

With a grin, Noah scrambled to his feet and joined onto Tim, who was at the back…and if Jennifer had deliberately avoided his touch by being the driver, it didn't matter. For this half hour, he had his family with him, his *happy* family, and it was a gift.

Another miracle at the March farm.

"Hey, Uncle Joe! We're here!" Rowdy cried, in his usual bois-terous welcome. "We come for Timmy."

Jennifer's uncle came around the corner of the shop leading to the junkyard. "Hoy, little mate," Uncle Joe chuckled, sounding like a pirate. He'd never been on the sea apart from a few fishing expeditions, but Rowdy didn't know that. "And Miss Cilla—how's the prettiest girl this side of Brisbane?"

From behind Jennifer's skirt, Cilla smiled and waved. She wasn't quite sure of this big, bluff man, but if Tim and Rowdy liked him, she'd give him a chance.

"I called. I guess you were out the back." Jennifer smiled at her uncle. "Is he here?"

Joe nodded, his face tender. "He got here about an hour after school. He said he had permission. I gather he didn't," he sighed. "He's in a bad mood, Jenny—he doesn't even want me to help him. He just wants to bash nails into metal for a while. How about I bring him home in time for dinner?"

Jennifer sighed in turn. "Come for dinner—it might help."

Joe looked a bit shifty. "The Swans are playing tonight— St. Kilda. So how about he stays for dinner with me, watches the game, and then I bring him home? It's Friday—no harm in staying up a bit later, eh? It'll give him time to work it off, whatever it is."

After a brief hesitation, she nodded. "I'll check with Noah, and call you either way."

"It does him good being here, Jenny," Uncle Joe said quietly. "And it does me good, too. I like having the boy around. We have a project or two in the works..."

Jennifer touched his hand. "I know, Uncle Joe. A boy after your own heart, right?"

Joe chuckled, and cocked his head to where some strident banging was taking place out the back. "In some ways too old for his years—in others, just a boy. We're soul mates."

Working on her verandah an hour later, Noah saw Jennifer and the kids returning, laughing, and his heart lifted. She'd found Tim at Joe's again, he guessed.

Thank God for Jennifer—because of her and her uncle Joe, Tim had a permanent and safe place to run...and Cilla only disappeared next door.

But when they spilled out of the car and no Tim was in evidence, the familiar fear chilled his body, as if he'd been dropped in ice water. He snapped, "Where's Tim?"

Her face and voice casual—a mask for the tension Cilla didn't need—Jennifer said, "He and Uncle Joe have some special projects going on. He invited Tim for dinner and to watch the first Swans game of the season, if that's all right. He said he'd bring Tim home straight after—or before, if you prefer," she added quickly.

"Daddy, Jenny took me to the dolly museum today," Cilla blurted out, her eyes shining. "Her friend Brenda runs it. She's got more dollies than I ever saw!"

Noah felt the jerk inside him as he savagely reined in his anger over Joe's commandeering his son. Cilla was talking to him of her own free will… "A dolly museum? Wow—I didn't know there was one!" He waited for her answer, hoping she'd volunteer more information.

Cilla nodded vigorously, glowing with the joy of her outing. "Lots of grown-ups gave their dollies there, the lady said. There's really old dollies, and some talking dollies, and dressed-up dollies, and baby dollies that drink from bottles—"

"And soldier dollies, too, Daddy!" Rowdy added, so excited he was bouncing up and down.

Cilla pulled a face. "They got guns and big sticks, Daddy. Not *nice*."

Noah laughed, and laid a hand on Cilla's curls. "Not nice for girls, but boys like them. Boys don't have good taste like girls. They like silly things like guns and sticks."

Cilla smiled up at him, and Noah almost gasped. He could barely remember when she'd smiled, just at him. "Did you like guns and sticks?" Her trusting expression said *of course you didn't*—and he smiled at her faith.

"Back in the Dark Ages of your youth," Jennifer murmured, laughter in her voice.

He shot her a mock-threatening look before returning to Cilla, telling her a truth that would disgust Rowdy if he was old enough to understand; but he was three, and Daddy could still do no wrong in his eyes. "I tried to like them, for a little while. I always liked LEGO and building blocks and drawing—but all my friends in the street wanted to play the rough stuff, so I had to pretend to like them, too."

Rowdy smiled at him in obvious pity. "Poor Daddy." He patted Noah's hand.

Cilla nodded thoughtfully in agreement with Rowdy, her brow wrinkled. "It must be hard to be a boy."

He choked on the laughter. So damn *adorable*. Cherishing the moment that was too rare—having a conversation with his daughter. "It is," he assured her, keeping a straight face and voice.

"You want to come see the dollies tomorrow, Daddy?"

Cilla wanted to spend time with him. Cilla invited him without being prompted!

Hide the emotion. Don't scare her! He nodded and smiled. "It's a date," he said solemnly.

In his peripheral vision he saw Jennifer swiping at her eyes. She knew.

"Jenny, I'm hungry," Rowdy said, with the angelic look he always used to get his way.

Jennifer laughed at that, and held out a hand to him. "Come on then, piggy, let's find something to eat. How about burgers tonight, and oven fries?"

"Yummy!" Rowdy cried, and scooted ahead of her around the side of the house. The screen door banged a moment later. Within moments, after a visible hesitation and a glance at her father, Cilla ran in after him.

Noah smiled after her, torn between joy at their first conversation in too long to remember, and wanting more in case it never happened again.

"Is it all right, Noah? About Tim, I mean? I told Uncle Joe I'd ask you and let him know."

He turned back to Jennifer, knowing he shouldn't indulge in the rare moment of being alone with her without Tim watching. "It's fine." His voice came out rough-edged. "If it makes Tim happy…"

"He's doing so much better." Jennifer half-reached out to him before she let her hand fall. "I know it's hard to see at times, but his teacher says he's settled down in class, and I can see him softening toward the kids here, as well. Before long, I think he'll be working on that cubby house with you."

Not unless Belinda's found. He couldn't blame her for not understanding. Tim might be healing with other people, but he'd only trust his father again if Belinda came back—and he no longer believed it was going to happen. Tim blamed him for his mother's disappearance, and barring a miracle, there was no way to change that.

He turned back to tearing off another plank. "That's great."

The tone of his voice made a lie of the words. *Just go away and leave me be...*

"I know you want more. You want him to be healed, to be able to accept what he can't change. You want him to stop resenting you for losing his mother and everything else that goes wrong in his life. But you're his father—who else can he blame? And no matter how he worries you, you've *got* him, Noah. He's here with you—he loves you dearly, even if you can't always see it. You don't know what a miracle that is."

Noah had looked up by the end of her first sentence, arrested by the taut, restrained passion in her voice. She stood before him, her right hand shaking, her eyes burning with a fire she was obviously about to share with him, whether he wanted it or not. "Are you okay?"

She dragged in a breath, two, before she spoke, yet it still came out choked with emotion, like a river rushing down-tide against a collapsing dam wall. "You lost Belinda, yet you still don't understand. There are thousands of people out there who wait years, and pay a fortune for what you have—a family. You have three beautiful, healthy children who adore you, despite their problems. I'd *die* for what you have!"

She pushed past him, running into the house with a stumbling step.

When the screen door slammed shut, Noah closed his eyes

and dropped the ripped-up plank he still held. She was right, so right he was shocked, shamed by his wilful blindness all this time. His beautiful, healthy children were a gift he should never take for granted—and moving here, having Joe and Jennifer as a safe bolthole for the kids when they needed it, was a miracle he hadn't dared question, in case he woke up back in Sydney, still struggling to make it alone.

He was *blessed,* so much more so than he'd realised.

But it was *why* Jennifer had said it that shocked him the most…all she'd half-said. All the painful hunger, the thwarted passion in her face and voice, which told him so much more than her stark words.

All this time he'd looked at her and wanted her, ached for her, been on-his-knees grateful for her, been amazed by her—but finally he was *seeing* her. Her words ripped away his blinders and showed her, not just as a woman, but as a person: a person whose empathy and strength came from a loss as profound and life-changing as his own.

All this time she'd listened to him, given to him—but she hadn't shared, and *he* hadn't listened. So damned scared he'd get too close to her, he'd missed all the signs.

No more. Right now, with the kids still awake, wasn't the time—but the first piece in the jigsaw of all she hadn't told him had just fallen into place, and judging by the anguish bursting from her just then, Jennifer needed to talk to someone about the tragedy in her past.

Desperately.

CHAPTER SIX

HE WAS watching her, every time he thought she wasn't looking.

Talk about basket cases…!

Jennifer kept her attention on the kids as they ate, and again as she washed up; but it was hard to avoid him when he insisted on helping bath Cilla and Rowdy and putting them to bed. Then he also wiped the dishes before he returned to work.

It was even harder to act normal when he kept *looking* at her as if he was waiting for her to burst out again.

Well, you did before…

I am a strong woman. I do not need to lean on a man. I do not need a family to complete me. I can stand alone. I have a good life!

Her hand might be shaking, but it was a fine tremor hardly noticeable, she thought. She had it under control this time. So what if a few plates fell back into the dishwater? Soap made them slippery. He couldn't make anything out of that, surely.

He was still watching.

Would he never *speak?* She kept waiting for him to go off, like a bomb with a faulty timer. She refused to say a word beyond anything to do with the kids. He was nothing but her neighbour. They had an arrangement to eat together while he worked on her house. An attraction was there, but they'd submerged it. They'd agreed on that—so why did it feel so wrong?

Because you're lying to yourself. It was a truth she couldn't deny. Even now, she had to fight the shiver of pleasure when his arms brushed hers just to pick up a plate to dry. *If this is attraction submerged, how bad would it become if it came out into the open?*

"You need a haircut," she blurted, and almost gasped. Where had that come from? "It—it's a bit shaggy," she added, feeling defensive with the look of hidden amusement he aimed at her.

He shrugged. "I've been meaning to get it cut for a while, but life's busy." He ran a hand through the length of it—and she gulped, following every movement of his fingers through the long, silky mass.

"I can cut it for you, if you like." Good grief. What was wrong with her tonight? But she held her ground when he lifted a brow in inquiry. "I did a year of hairdressing, you know, when I was sixteen. Before I decided it wasn't for me, and went back to school."

"So if it wasn't for you, why should I trust you with my hair?"

He was laughing at her, and it made her smile. "I learned enough to do a wash and simple cut." To her horror, she was almost whispering. What must he think of her? She rushed into speech. "I won't nick your ears or cut your neck…or cut it too short. It's too beautiful to give it a buzz cut…"

Oh, help, she'd done it again. Staring at him like a loon, now offering to cut his hair—calling it beautiful. What an infatuated fool he must think she was!

"Don't worry. It—it was a stupid idea." She stared down at her feet, wishing a black hole would miraculously open up and transport her to a parallel universe. "You have work to do…"

"Actually I'd appreciate a cut if you have time for it?"

His voice was soft, knowing. He'd seen her embarrassment, and was helping her out. Again. Would she never stop making an idiot of herself over him?

Yet, though she knew she should reject his offer and keep what shards of her pride remained intact, she pulled out a chair for him. "Sit." She got the kit she rarely used, but hadn't thrown out. "I can't believe I still have this kit. My friends Veronica and Jessie call me a squirrel, the way I won't throw out anything useful."

He laughed. "We all have our faults." He tipped his head forward while she laid the plastic cloak over his shoulders. "You're not going to wash my hair for me first? I hear it makes it easier to give an accurate cut..."

His tone was pure mischief: the same tone he'd used when he offered to put his shirt back on. She put the Velcro pieces together. "I have a bottle of water," she informed him primly, and began squirting around his head before combing it through.

It was intimate—too intimate. Running her fingers through his hair, touching his scalp—she might as well have washed his hair. Noah made a tiny, masculine sound as he leaned back into the touch. "Mmm, that's good."

"I'm supposed to massage it a bit before I cut, to stimulate your scalp," she said, then closed her eyes. *You idiot, why not just tell him you can't keep your hands off him?*

"It's stimulating all right," he said softly.

Jennifer almost gasped. The meaning was too strong to miss.

"I'm going to cut now. Lean back a bit more."

This was such a personal thing. It had never felt this intense with customers—even with Mark. Threading her fingers through Noah's hair before cutting it felt so sensuous; she felt stark, her desire totally open to him. Trying to avoid nervous babble, she remained silent, except to say "left" or "right," "up" or "down." Hand through again...lift hair...cut. Yes. That's it. Cut. Don't just touch and let it fall...

Her throat began to ache with the constant rushing of her breath. Surely he could hear the way she gulped down air with each touch—a touch that became more of a caress each time?

She couldn't help it...how did she stop? Body and heart were betraying her will. A strong woman? Ha! She was a quivering mass of jelly…aching for him to turn around, look at her, slow and wanting…take her in his arms, and—

"I think you're done," she announced eventually, despising herself for the breathless way she said it. Foolish woman!

He looked in the mirror at every angle, and nodded. "A great job. Thanks, Jennifer."

He wasn't smiling, either…and the *look* in his eyes, dark and lush—

"It's almost dark," she said when she couldn't stand the silence, his closeness, anymore. "Soon you won't be able to work."

"I brought spotlights," he said, his voice rough with all they weren't saying. "I want to keep working until Joe brings Tim back."

"Then off you go. I can sweep up the mess." Turning her face from his, before the temptation clawing at her came bursting to life, she pulled off the protective cloak.

"If you need anything, call me."

"What do you imagine I'll need?" she asked before she could stop herself.

She felt rather than saw his shrug. "Maybe to talk to someone? It's obvious you need to talk to somebody, Jennifer." He stood up.

She spun around to face him. "Why? Because I happened to mention that you've got so many wonderful blessings in your life you're taking for granted?"

"I think it was what you didn't say that needs to come out," he said quietly, his gaze steady on her face: warm and caring, deep with unspoken male empathy in those deep maple syrup eyes. It made her shiver in longing. Strong, beautiful, raw masculinity just a breath away…

And the urge to tell him everything was growing stronger, more unbearable, every time he was near her. The urge to haul him against her, and—

"You think I'm so weak I need to speak to a near-stranger about my personal concerns?" she snapped, to hide it.

"I think you're the strongest woman I've ever known and we've never been strangers. Some people know each other from the start and you can be around others all your life and never get close." His voice was rough-edged, deep and hot, and she ached and burned. Just one step, one touch, and she'd be in his arms. "I also think you're falling down, Jennifer, and too strong and proud to admit you need anyone."

She jerked back in reaction to his insight.

"Even the strongest people fall down sometimes," he went on, ignoring her upflung hand, trying to put distance between them: a pitiful barrier. "We all need someone to give back now and then. I've been there, and I refused help, Jennifer—and you know the consequences. If I'd reached out and admitted my family needed help before Belinda disappeared, when she was ill with depression and I knew she wasn't coping, my kids might still have their mother."

Jennifer repressed the shudder. What he said was true; but though it might hurt Noah like crazy to have this life, she felt sick at the thought of knowing him only as another woman's husband...

He is another woman's husband, until Belinda is found.

She started when he touched her cheek with a finger. "You've given my family so much. I'm not asking for anything more—just let me be here for you when you need someone, Jennifer. I'll catch you. I won't let you fall."

Oh God, he was touching her.

The power of it left her breathing hard and shallow, her body weak and trembling, filling her with hope for what she couldn't have; she knew that. But the tenderness in his face, in his voice, undid her; temptation clawed and bit at her with relentless aching. If he had any idea what allowing him in would cost her...

She couldn't turn away, could only look up at him, half-mes-merised; but still her rebel mouth spoke a truth she'd give anything if it weren't so. "If I'm going to fall, let me fall. You can't save me, Noah. You don't have the right."

His hand dropped from her face.

After a few minutes of a silence that screamed his protest, he said, his voice neutral, "Thanks for dinner and the haircut, Jennifer."

She shrugged, and found her voice. "Just hamburgers and chips, and ten minutes to cut your hair. It's no big deal."

"It means a lot to me, to the kids…they love you, Jennifer. And you don't know what it means to me to see them smiling and—and happy again."

Her mouth flattened. The choked tone, filled with emotion, left her longing to reach out, to touch him. *You can't!* "It's a business arrangement." Refusing to admit the truth—that the Brannigans had become her lifeline to brittle sanity.

There was too much to lose in getting close to him—for them all.

She jumped when his hand touched her shoulder. "I know I have no right to ask for more, and I don't—but at least let me be your friend, Jennifer."

Treacherous currents of warm need flooded a heart and soul empty for too long. She squeezed her eyes shut, allowing one moment, two, of not being alone.

Of being with Noah, who must never mean this much to her. Beautiful, forbidden sweetness and desire…

She stepped out from under his hand, feeling it like a physical wrench, the loss and the longing. "Don't you understand? I can *never* be your friend."

She strode into her bedroom, shut the door and pulled the curtains tight, before he said another word and totally shattered her fragile illusion that she had a life, that she was happy, that life was good.

This had gone too far, and they'd barely touched. She had to sell up and leave this place before—before she started *thinking*…

Dry-eyed and her mind burning-hot, she stared through the curtains onto the night, knowing that he was out there, working. Just because he was there, she was a quivering mess of aching femininity and hope. She'd been doing nothing but *thinking* about it from the moment she'd seen his face.

Lovers. If she stayed here another week without making the change, it would happen—she knew it. He had to know, too. The look in his eyes, the tension in his body when he was near her, told her she wasn't alone in this. One touch, and the un-controlled flight, body, heart and soul came. This was a once-in-a-lifetime, never-again occurrence. She'd loved Mark dearly for many years, and enjoyed his touch; but she'd barely touched Noah's hand, and she was so *alive,* so tuned to him she could think of nothing else when he was near her.

One more touch, and they'd become lovers...

Beautiful, too brief, and soon over. There could be no promises with a man who wasn't officially separated from his missing wife, not divorced and not quite a widower...and Noah still didn't know why she'd never marry again.

She closed her eyes, his words already haunting her. *You're falling down, Jennifer.*

But for the first time, she wasn't grieving for Cody, or her broken marriage.

Noah. Tim, Cilla, Rowdy. Right now, when she admitted to herself she'd give up her hope of life itself just to have the right to be with them a little longer; that she'd give up anything to just touch Noah—she knew she would lose them before long.

And the pain of it was just the same as she'd faced two years ago.

She was absolutely crazy about all four of the Brannigans. They'd taken her heart and soul—and they belonged to another woman: a woman more *here,* more *alive* in her absence than she'd be if she were here.

* * *

Joe dropped a sleepy, grinning Tim home after ten that night.

Smiling, no doubt, because he'd had fun with Joe—and because Noah was working hard on the verandah and Jennifer was nowhere to be seen.

"Hey, Dad." Tim waved at him, his eyes heavy. "I'm going in to Jen."

"Did you have fun, mate?" Noah called as his son half-stumbled toward the front door.

"The Swans won, Dad! It was a cracker of a game to start the Season—a pearler!"

Noah smothered a grin, and lifted a brow in Joe's direction. "That's great, mate!"

Tim waved again, and went inside, calling to Jennifer.

Joe came over to where he worked: a casual stroll that didn't fool him for a moment. "They all treat Jenny as if she's their mother now, don't they?" he asked quietly.

He didn't answer at first; he'd been expecting this for the past week or more. Nodding, he said, just as softly, "They're still so little. They need a mother."

"And you need a child-carer, dinner-maker and the like. Your moving here provided the ideal situation for you all, you might say." Joe's voice was dry.

"Just say it, Joe," Noah said wearily. "I've had a long day. I'm too tired to talk in code."

"Has Jenny told you about herself at all? About her past, and why she came here?"

The blunt question, also, wasn't unexpected. "Only that she's divorced and her ex was obviously into nasty labels about her."

Joe sighed and rubbed his forehead, obviously searching for words.

"Don't break her confidence, Joe," he said quietly, and tore up another plank. Almost the last, and he could start rebuilding. "She wouldn't appreciate you saying anything to me. She'll tell me if and when she wants to." He hoped.

"That's the trouble," Joe snapped. "That's what you don't understand, Noah. Jenny *never* tells anyone anything about her private business. She never even talked to her parents after it all happened, or during. She went to some grief class things, but never told us, her own family. If she tells you—" he thumped a fist against his open palm "—if she does, it's because…" He swore: a long string of words that showed his frustration. "If she tells you, it's because you mean more to her than anyone else in her life. And you might want that…or you might just want to help her. And it might help, for a little while. But when you don't find whatever it is you came here for, and move on— and we both know you will," he added dryly, "when you go, and take those kids from her, she'll break."

Break.

Not *break down,* not *break her heart.* Just—*break.* Not a warning, not a threat; just a statement of fact.

Jennifer would break—and he would be the one to break her.

He didn't know what to do or say to that. How did he say he'd already pushed Jennifer onto that path, because he couldn't handle all her giving, and not giving anything back but a stupid verandah, so she could sell up and leave him?

Leave me?

Was he taking the family life she'd given back to him for granted, even knowing it could only be temporary? When it was over, would he resent her for having her own life and choices, when Belinda had left him with none, trapped and resenting everything and everyone who *did* have a choice in life?

Joe nodded. "It's there, isn't it? You're not just taking all she's got to give you and the kids. You want more. You want something with my Jenny, at least for now—but until you're free to reach out and take it, until you know what happened to your wife and you've worked out things with young Tim, stop messing with my

girl's emotions. You've been to hell and back—but so has she."
He sighed. "The attraction between you is so strong even an old
fool like me can feel it. She's dreaming, Noah…and she loves
those kids of yours so much. Like a mother."

The unwanted insight broadsided him. Joe was right; and
Jennifer was right, too—they could never be friends. The
wanting was agony already, and it was growing every day. He
could easily imagine himself old and grey and still in pain with
wanting Jennifer—but not just in bed. Every small thing he did
with her, every smile or flick back of her plait, every time she
hugged his kids or looked at him with that half-hidden yearning,
he soared with the joy of it: of family, of belonging—of being
a man desired by a woman with so much inner beauty she
made him ache.

And if he took the chance, his family would fall apart.

One or the other. Jennifer or his son; both fragile, both part
of his life and, yes, damn it, his heart. He cared about Jennifer.
So who did he break?

He wanted to hit something, because he knew it wasn't a
contest.

As much as he loved Tim, the resentment had grown from
a tiny kernel to a massive forest inside Noah's heart during the
past couple of weeks. For how many years would Tim's happiness depend on his father struggling alone? Did he have to
give up what remained of his youth for Tim's security? Leaving
Jennifer behind would lead to a lifetime of regret…

You'll break her.

"Uncle Joe, did you want a coffee or a beer before you
head home?"

Noah looked up at the frost in her tone, hidden well beneath
a veneer of polite welcome—but it was there. As her glance
flicked to him, he saw the speculation…the accusation.

She'd heard—perhaps not all of it, but she'd heard—heard
what Uncle Joe said about what he, Noah, might mean to her.

If he'd had any chance of giving back to her, of hearing the story that might take some of the burden from her giving shoulders, he'd just lost it.

No way. *No!* He wouldn't let her withdraw—he needed her too much.

Yet, wasn't that the problem? He needed her—but what did Jennifer need?

*She's been to hell and back...*and he was adding to her pain.

None of this was Jennifer's fault. Nothing could change for them while he was still technically married...and while he allowed Tim's fears and terrors to rule the family's life. While he allowed Belinda's ghost to haunt them all, even people who'd never known her.

There was only one option: closure. He had to find it.

CHAPTER SEVEN

HE HAD to do this. *It's for Tim and Cilla.*

Noah stood outside the door in the children's ward at a private hospital near Lismore, an hour north of Hinchliff, reading the sign in silent loathing. *Maggie Horner, Social Worker And Grief Counsellor.*

He'd thought he'd seen the last of the professionals trained to help him—making him feel like not only a basket case, but a bad husband and a failure of a father. *It's not your fault, Noah, you're only human. You can't take responsibility for everything that goes wrong in the lives of those you love.*

It was just a pretty way of calling him a control freak. How could they know anything? They learned it all from books, got a degree, and thought they knew life.

When had their wife taken off and left them with three kids under six?

This isn't for me. I have to learn how to help Tim and Cilla. I can't keep leaving it to Jennifer. I can't make the kids—or Jennifer—dependent. It isn't fair.

He pushed open the door—and rocked back on his feet in shock when he saw one of only two occupants of the room.

Jennifer gasped and stared at him in turn.

"Well, here we are," a brisk woman in dark blue pants and a striped uniform shirt said cheerfully. "Welcome, Mr. Brannigan.

I'm Rachel Howe, Ms Horner's receptionist. Ms Horner sends her apologies. There was an emergency in the E.R."

"I hope everything's all right," Jennifer said, her voice stifled, at the same time Noah wondered what kind of emergency could possibly require a social worker.

"A baby drowned," the receptionist said, her voice dropping to real sorrow. "It will hit the local papers tomorrow. Maggie will stay with the parents for the next few hours, helping the family through as much as they'll let her."

Jennifer gasped again, her eyes full of tears. A shaking hand lifted to her mouth.

"I'm sorry, Mrs. March," Rachel rushed to say. "I shouldn't have said anything, after your son's death—"

Jennifer paled so quickly, Noah thought she might faint.

"I'm so sorry, Mrs. March," Rachel went on, looking uncertain and guilty. "I didn't mean to break confidentiality—"

Jennifer looked at her, but seemed to see right through her. She looked as clear and delicate as blown glass, and just as easily shattered. "It's all right. It's not a state secret."

"Maggie tried to call you both, but you'd left," the receptionist rushed on. "She left messages on your phones, but I guess you'd turned them off while you were driving. Maggie noticed you two are neighbours, so she thought you might take advantage of the two hours' crèche arrangement for Mr. Brannigan's children, and maybe go for coffee? There's a lovely café just down the road that serves a good lunch under umbrellas in the sun…"

"Thank you," Noah said gravely. "Jennifer?"

The question wasn't a ploy. The words she'd spoken the other night burned in his brain like a bushfire that wouldn't go out. *I'll never be your friend.*

Too much between them, and never enough.

After a long hesitation, she nodded without looking at him. "Thank you for letting us know," she said to the receptionist, still sounding stifled.

Noah's mind was spinning as he opened the door for her. Ever since her outburst last week and Joe's warning, he hadn't tried to get her to open up. He thought he'd known her problem—but now he knew Jennifer could have children. She'd had a son—and he'd died.

I'd die for what you have!

The pieces finally fit.

"Would you like coffee, or lunch? It's almost eleven-thirty," he said, for the sake of something to say.

They stepped out into the bright autumn sunshine. A clear, windless day, warm enough but without the intense dry pulsing of the recent heatwave. The street stretched out, long and straight, with waving banners on the streetlamps, announcing an upcoming festival.

Jennifer didn't appear to notice. "I think I'd throw up if I ate now," she mumbled. "The poor, poor parents. Poor baby, so short a life…"

Filled with compassion like a wave hitting him from behind, he put an arm around her shoulders. "Makes me thank God for my kids," he said, in a low voice.

She didn't shake him off, as he'd half expected; nor did she turn her face to him, but remained looking straight ahead. "That's why you came, isn't it? To learn how to best help Tim and Cilla?" The question sounded blind, as if she wandered in a dark maze, and familiarity was comfort. Asking him about his life as usual, taking nothing in return.

Being Jennifer.

"You know my story, Jennifer. You know why I'm here." He pulled her back as she was about to walk straight into a massive crack in the sidewalk. "I haven't kept any secrets."

Liar. But now wasn't the time to tell her that.

Finally she turned to him. Her eyes were fierce. "Just say it, Noah."

A furious opening, but if it was all he'd get, he'd take it. As he steered her into an open courtyard with tables and umbrellas, he asked, "How old was your son?"

"Three." The word was curt.

He shut his eyes for a moment. He understood so much now. No wonder she'd had that look on her face when she'd first seen Rowdy. "What was his name?"

Something passed over her face; her eyes were cold and dead. "Cody James McBride."

"Cody. That's a nice name." *How lame was that, Brannigan?*

Her smile was no more than a slight curl of the ends of her mouth. "Mark picked it, but I liked it, too."

After a long hesitation, she answered what he didn't know how to ask. "He had Cystic Fibrosis. He choked to death—it was like drowning. His lungs just couldn't keep stretching."

She spoke as if it was something she'd rehearsed for a play, just reading it aloud; and he wondered how many times she'd had to say it, just like that, to get the tone down pat. The tone said, *keep your distance. You know what happened, now back off.*

Joe had been right. Jennifer was not one who wanted her wounds touched.

"How long have you been going to the counselling sessions?" he asked gently, taking her hand in his.

She let it lie there resistless. Her eyes were like pools drained of water…empty. "I began in the hospital in Newcastle, when I first found out about Cody's illness."

I began. Not *we.* That told him far more about Mark McBride than he'd wanted to know—he'd left Jennifer alone with the grief and guilt.

Yeah, you know nothing about male denial and running away, do you? his mind mocked him. *That's why, three years after Belinda ran, you're finally reaching out—but only for the kids' sake; you don't need help from outsiders.*

You'll take it from Jennifer, though, his mind mocked him again.

"And you kept it up when you moved here?" He heard the strange, choked sound of his voice, and wondered if she'd pick up on it.

She shrugged. "A few sessions here and there, when I need to. I've become good friends with Veronica and Jessie from the group. We meet every second Saturday for lunch—we all like to quilt as well, and started a quilting circle." She smiled, but it was remote, untouched by sweetness or sorrow. "They have kids now, and I have my business, so Saturdays or the occasional Wednesday evening works for us all."

He frowned. "But you haven't gone out on a Wednesday since…"

Since I've been taking it for granted she has nothing to do but mind my kids for me, or have my family to stay for dinner.

Selfish jerk! He hadn't thought of Jennifer at all—maybe as a desirable woman, but as a *person* with needs? He'd thought he'd written the book on loss and suffering—but what he'd written was a treatise on selfish need: a blindness to anything but his needs, and that of the kids.

The waitress came then, and took their orders. Once she'd gone, he lifted their hands upward, so their fingers laced through each other's. "Damn, I'm sorry, Jennifer," he said quietly. "You've been putting your life on hold for me, for the kids."

Her eyes weren't empty now, but gentle, eager and shy. "Don't apologise, Noah. It's been nice to be part of family life again." Her gaze landed on their linked hands, and she bit her lip and pulled away. "For a little while, anyway."

"Why won't you marry again?" He could have hit himself for the bluntness of the question, but it had been burning in him since before they'd met. He *had* to know.

A hand scrubbed her forehead, tugged at a lock of loose hair waving in a light breeze just springing up, pushing the hair behind her ear. Then she began twisting her plait around a finger. "You want it all, don't you?" She sounded so tired: a weary Madonna. "After Cody was born, they tested us to see who the carrier was, and why Cody had CF so badly. It seems I'm a freak medical case—the doctors haven't come across it before. There is CF in my family—but my genome is so dominant they believe any child I have would be almost certain to be born with the disease…and I won't play Russian roulette with a baby's life, just to fulfil my desires."

Noah knew he'd never seen anything sadder than this quiet, giving woman, a woman more born to be a mother than any he'd ever known, accepting that she'd always be alone.

It was only when his arms and body were warm and her head was resting on his shoulder that he knew he'd gone to her. "I'm sorry, Jennifer," he whispered, holding her so close she was a part of him; the ache threatening to burst in him.

"It's all right," she whispered, pulling back to smile up at him.

"Couldn't you do IVF? The kind where there's a donor mother?" he blurted.

She smiled again, but with more sadness than any woman as giving as Jennifer should have to know. "I could. My sisters have all offered to be the egg donor. But that isn't the point." She sighed. "As selfish as it sounds, I want *my* baby, not someone else's—and I don't want to be a—"

"Single parent?" he filled in, when she bit her lip. "It's okay, Jennifer. Raising kids alone isn't something I'd recommend to everyone."

"You don't know how lucky you are," she mumbled, low.

Noah flinched. He'd done it again. "Jennifer…"

"Don't." She shrugged. "This isn't a Greek tragedy, you know. I have a good life. I have a wonderful family, friends who care about me, a life that's mostly full and busy. It's not the life I planned for myself, but it's still good."

"You could still marry a man with kids, who doesn't want any more." He stumbled over the words. Damn, it sounded too close to a proposal.

She didn't even seem to notice; she was already shaking her head. "I could never marry a man for his kids alone—I'd have to marry for love." She gave him a watery smile. "And while I'm sure I'd love his kids, it wouldn't be right or fair to them, if I couldn't love them as much as I loved Cody. All I ever wanted was to get married and have four or five kids—but if they weren't mine…" she trailed off, shrugging; but it was eloquent enough.

He frowned again. "You don't think you could mother kids if they weren't your own?" It sounded crazy to him. She gave love to the kids she minded so naturally, so lavishly. It seemed impossible that she could have given more to her own son.

"Not the way a child deserves to be loved." She pulled away, discreetly mopping her face with the serviette. "Here comes the waitress. Just as well I don't bother much with makeup, or I'd look like that sad-faced clown painting right now." She smiled again. "I promise you, I don't cry on people often."

As the waitress put down the coffee and cake and bustled off again, he looked down at Jennifer. So *close*, those wet cheeks, the salty, pretty mouth. He'd never wanted to kiss her more, and that was a big statement, given the hot, sleepless nights he'd endured, dreaming of her face, her touch.

But she moved away, sitting up straight, and smiling again. She'd closed the subject of her past, the life she'd chosen. She'd said enough; she didn't feel sorry for herself, wasn't angry or in the throes of unresolved grief. She had a life, and was moving on.

Then why did it feel so wrong?

"You shouldn't be alone," he muttered, as savage as he felt at the thought of her growing old, still minding other people's kids, spending day after day with reminders of what she could never have. "You were born to be a mother." *And some kids need a mother as good as you.*

She looked away. "The world isn't perfect. Babies all over

the world were born to live, not die. People weren't born to starve or live in war zones. We don't all get our dreams, Noah."

Who was she trying to fool, herself or him? "I suppose you sing 'Always Look on the Bright Side of Life' whenever you feel sorry for yourself," he shot back, furious. Why, he didn't know—but he couldn't stand this quiet acceptance. She should be yelling and screaming at the unfair hand life had dealt her, fighting somehow.

She turned back then, with a lifted brow. "Would you dish out a Pollyanna crack if I said yes?" Her grin was both mischievous and challenging.

Without warning, warm laughter bubbled up and burst out of him. "Probably," he said when he finally got control of himself again.

"Then I refuse to answer on the grounds that it might incriminate me."

He chuckled again, and tapped her chin. "You're an amazing woman, you know that?" How she'd gotten him from grief to fury to amusement so fast was beyond him; but Jennifer could make him *feel* more, and feel it faster, than anyone he'd ever known.

She lifted her coffee cup, and toasted him with a grin. "Even we incorrigibly cheerful types have our surprises."

Obviously, he thought as he crammed some cake in his mouth. She'd done nothing but surprise him from the moment he'd seen her. How her ex had been stupid enough to lose her once he had her, Noah couldn't begin to understand.

Don't go there. It was dangerous enough that his dreams were filled with her; daydreams were strictly off-limits. If things were different…but he was still a nowhere man—and though he'd been trying like crazy to change that, some things were beyond his control.

His vow was still intact, set in stone by the suffering of an innocent child. He couldn't have Jennifer—and that, too, was end of subject.

* * *

"No, don't come and get him just yet," Uncle Joe said with a mysterious air the next day when Jennifer called. "Tim and I are *very* busy right now. Give us until six?"

Jennifer sighed and looked out the window. There was no sign of Noah as yet, but he'd stressed he wanted Tim here when he got home from a quote on a new industrial complex in Brisbane city. Tim had spent every afternoon at Joe's for the past week, taking his new best friend Ethan with him. Tim had an air of hidden excitement the past few days, growing so big by last night he'd only picked at his vegetables.

It was almost time to reveal the secret, whatever it was—so what did she do? Alienate the parent or force the child home, and ruin his big surprise?

Come on, Pollyanna, fix the situation for everyone as always.

She had to take the fall, one way or the other.

Since their talk in Lismore, Noah had been acting strangely with her. She couldn't put her finger on what the difference was—maybe he didn't know it, but it was in the way he looked at her, both with him and with the kids. Something had changed between them that day, and they couldn't go back now, but there was a feeling of—waiting…

As if he was going to just pack up and disappear one day, and never come back.

"Sure," she said to Joe, knowing she took a risk in not following a parent's dictum; she could lose her licence for it. But she wasn't paid to mind Tim; she'd refused all payment for him being here in the afternoons, so this wasn't a professional, but personal matter.

And she knew Noah would never make an official complaint, in any case.

She just hoped he came home after six—

But Murphy's Law seemed to apply to everything that happened between them; and of course he drove in at five-thirty.

"Hey, kids, I'm home—and I have presents for everyone!" he yelled from the car.

"Presents!" Cilla and Rowdy squealed in sync, and jumped up from their painting game and rushed out the back door.

With a sense of fatality she'd felt since saying "sure" to Joe, she followed the kids. She should have known Noah would have a good reason for demanding Tim's return. Now she'd not only disregarded a parent's rule, she'd ruined his joy in present time for his children.

The set smile was already on his face when she came around the side of the house to the pressed-dirt driveway. "I hear Tim's still at Uncle Joe's," he said over the kids' excited chatter: Cilla over her talking, feeding dolly; Rowdy over the big, shiny black water gun that squirted water balls.

She had no right to argue the rightness of her decision at this moment. "I'm sorry, Noah. Uncle Joe said he's almost finished his big project…"

"And you couldn't say no." Noah's shrug was weary; all the happiness evident in his voice moments before was gone.

"I had no right," she said bluntly, unable to stop the half-defensive self-condemnation. "I know that."

"You care for him more often than I do, so let's not go there." The tiredness in him seemed endemic, reaching out to touch her, feeling worse for its not being physical.

"No, you're the guilt specialist. Nobody has as much right to feel bad about themselves as you do." The words popped out before she knew she'd spoken; she stared at him in horror.

He'd stiffened by the end of the first sentence. "I wasn't aware it was a right." He began ushering the kids into his truck. "I think of it more as a life sentence—but by all means, Jennifer, indulge as much as you want, if you like it." He strapped Cilla into her seat.

*That's right, Jennifer, let the man come home with gifts for his kids and destroy it for him…*she groaned to herself. What was *wrong* with her? How many more times would she need to apologise to him before she began getting things right? "I have dinner ready," she said quietly.

He strapped Rowdy in next. He was happily playing with his squirt gun, pretending to hit Cilla over and over. She didn't notice, too busy feeding her dolly. "I think we've imposed enough on you for one day. You haven't had time to yourself in weeks as it is. It's Wednesday—you should call your quilting friends and have some fun. We'll go get Tim."

Peace and quiet…just minutes ago she'd registered how tired she was; now she had the prospect of a night to herself, all she saw was hours of silence, no childish chatter, no hugs, no *family*. Just spending a night alone.

There was nothing to say. She'd infringed on his rights with his children too much lately. It wasn't as if—as if she was anything to them. "Good idea, I will call them."

She made herself smile and wave to the kids as Noah pulled out his phone and called Uncle Joe. "Joe, I'm on my way over to get some dinner, so I'll get Tim…yes, I know, thanks anyway, but I need to get some dinner anyway—what?" The easy tone turned hard. "What do you mean he's not there? Where did he go—?" He listened for a minute, his nostrils flared and his eyes dark. "It's a surprise. I see. How long has he been gone…an *hour?* What happened to him? Was he upset? Did he say anything? Do you know where my son is, Joe? *Do you know where Tim is?*"

The panic in his voice would have been out of place for most parents, but not for Noah—never for Noah.

Feeling sick with fear and wretched guilt, Jennifer was already strapped into the front passenger seat by the time Noah flung himself in the truck.

CHAPTER EIGHT

"I CAN'T tell you—I promised the lad I'd keep his secret," Joe was saying for the fourth time. "I'm sure he's not in any danger. I swear he hasn't run off, Noah."

"Promises. Swearing. What is that supposed to mean?" Noah snapped. "You think it counts for *anything* with me, when it's just about dark and my son's missing?" Noah's voice cracked; he pulled out his phone again.

"Don't do it!" Again Joe reached out to stop him. "The little lad was that excited, Noah. If you call Sherbrooke on him now, you'll ruin it all."

"So you keep saying. Tell me why!" When Joe shook his head, Noah lost it. "Then damn your promises and Tim's surprise! My eight-year-old son is *missing,* it's almost night and you expect me to—"

"To trust your son! Yes, I do!" Joe snapped back. "Give him ten more minutes! That's all I'm asking."

"That's what I did with Belinda," he snarled at the older man. "I trusted her to come home! After my five-year-old son called me to come home because the babysitter had to go and Rowdy was screaming and he couldn't get him out of the cot, I came home to find my wife gone—not her things, just her. I gave her ten more minutes, and another ten, and another, hoping she was just shopping, visiting someone I didn't know—anything but the truth. And then when she was put on the missing persons list, all I could think was, *what if I hadn't given her ten minutes?* What if, in those ten minutes I hesitated, she was abducted, raped or murdered, and I could have saved her? If there's one thing experience has taught me, it's that it's better to have my son alive and mad at me. If I can save my son's life by being *safe rather than sorry,* I'll do it even if he hates me!"

Joe's resistance tumbled down like a house of cards out in the wind; his hand dropped from the phone. Noah flipped it open, finger poised to hit speed dial 1—Police Sergeant Fred Sherbrooke's home number.

"Noah."

The touch of Jennifer's hand on his didn't feel as Joe's had—trying to stop him; it trembled slightly. "Noah, I understand—I want him found as much as you do, and it's my fault this happened. But before we call Fred, why not call his friends' houses? He's just a kid, Noah, and he's been so happy, so settled lately. If he's just playing, and lost track of time…"

The good sense beneath the guilt in her words stopped him, just as he was about to ignore her and hit the green call button. He heard all she wasn't saying: *he's only little, he wouldn't notice the dark coming if he's having fun with a friend.*

"I already called Ethan's house on the way, but I can call Miss Greenwood and get the numbers of Tim's other friends…"

He heard what she was saying. Tim was making friends here; a sign of healing, even if he wasn't ready to admit to that. Here in Hinchliff, the kids either didn't know or didn't care about the family's history. Tim was just a normal kid, one of twenty kids of a single parent.

And he'd thanked God for it.

If he blew it now by overreacting…the story would be around town in hours, and they'd rehash all they knew about Belinda's disappearance, and their theories on why she'd run. Just like in Sydney—a repetition of the reason Tim had begun running away in the first place. *I'm going to find Mummy, then they'll all stop being nasty!*

Everything else Jennifer hadn't said came whispering into his brain. Tim hadn't run away now for almost two months; the change of scene, school and friends, and Jennifer's healing presence, had worked the miracle he'd prayed for when he'd left Sydney and all its memory. One misstep now and he could undo all the progress Tim had made.

But the one thing Jennifer could never understand was the ghost stalking him night and day, the spectre of history repeating—the history that had almost repeated so many times, every time Cilla or Tim disappeared. *Oh God, if his precious boy was truly missing, in danger…*

"I *can't*," he rasped. Feeling the line in the sand shifting with the wind, as it had done almost every day throughout the past three years, he pressed the button, spoke to Fred briefly and then stood there, feeling guilty and lost and angry.

He started when a pair of gentle arms slid around his waist. "I understand. It's all right," she whispered from behind him. She held him close, giving him her caring and strength at the moment he'd never felt so alone with his fears.

Without conscious thought or decision he turned his face. "Thank you," he whispered back, in a tight, halting rasp. Two words hadn't taken so long to say since the time he'd heard four fateful words: *your wife is missing.*

Tonight wasn't about Belinda; she'd been fading from his thoughts for a long time, but now she wasn't here with him at all. Usually she seemed to hover over him like some damned ghost ship packed with sackloads of guilt and regret. But at this moment he was just a worried dad, with a beautiful, gentle woman who loved his son and made him feel like a *man* again. A woman who was looking at him with so much longing in her eyes it turned his fears inside-out; with so much *faith*, he began to believe.

"Tim will come home to us," she mouthed without sound. She was with him...and for the first time in years, he didn't feel so damned alone.

Without conscious thought or decision, he moved across the inch that had been separating them for too long, and brushed his mouth over hers.

Could a first kiss be any more wrong? Wrong time, wrong place, wrong everything. He wasn't free; his son was missing; his other kids were four feet away, playing with their new toys—and Joe, who'd warned him against taking things further with Jennifer, was watching grimly. Noah could feel the anger simmering in him.

But it was all vague, peripheral, technical; it didn't matter. What was real was that Jennifer's breath hitched; he felt her breasts flatten against his shoulder and arm. Her eyes filled with a yearning and arousal so strong, his entire body tightened in reaction.

The current of wanting snapped together. Finally, contact...

One moment in time, that was all; then she pulled back, her face carefully controlled. "Tim!" she called, waving to the left. Noah, lost still in the feeling of being a man, not just a dad, took a few seconds longer to react.

And then it was too late.

The beaming boy proudly riding a slightly lopsided bike— this must have been his project with Joe—vanished in an instant, and the resentful rebel in a child's body replaced him. The slitted eyes, the mouth turned down. The suspicious boy, the guard dog in human form had returned by necessity.

Tim had seen him kissing Jennifer.

"Hey, mate!" he called, going into automatic damage control. "You've got a *bike?* That's a real beauty! Where did you get it?"

Tim threw aside his "surprise" as if it didn't matter. "Let go of her, Dad," he yelled. Rowdy and Cilla, startled by the roar, turned to look at their father. "Let go of her, I said!"

"What?" He looked down at his hand, which was clenching Jennifer's in a stranglehold. It was obvious who'd been doing the touching.

Then he looked at Tim, and an anger to match Tim's filled his soul. It was time he asserted the authority he'd lost more than three years before. If he kept living in the fear of Tim running away, their family would be ruled by the demands of an unwise, unstable eight-year-old.

When he spoke, it was with quiet authority that never failed to get through to his son. "I'm the grown-up here, Tim—you do as *I* tell you, not the other way around. What Jennifer and I do, or don't do, is between us alone. It isn't any of your business."

Tim's control slipped, seeming to shatter on the soft dirt footpath. *"You're married to my mum!"* he cried, his voice rising to the pitch of the small, terrified child he truly was.

Noah closed his eyes. The choice was as clear as it was heart-breaking. He either kept knuckling under to Tim's insecurity in the hope that his son would heal eventually, or he did what he could to give all three of his kids as normal a life as possible.

It was time to move on, whether Tim wanted to, or not.

He released Jennifer's hand and walked over to his son. When he reached Tim's side, he held his shoulders despite the boy's stiffening. "It wasn't me who left the family, Tim. Mummy went away because she was sad—but if she was coming home, she'd have come a long time ago. And all the yelling at me, and all the running away in the world, isn't going to bring her back to us. Do you understand, son? It's just us now."

"No. *No*," Tim screamed, struggling against him, his face white. "She's coming home, she is. She *promised!*"

Noah's heart stalled at the terrible pain his son was in. "She promised to be home in an hour, matey," he said quietly.

Tim's little hands clenched into fists. "It's your fault! We shouldn't have left home!"

Noah closed his eyes for a moment, praying for inspiration,

because his barrel had run dry. "She broke the promise three years ago, mate. She knew where we were all that time, and she never came home."

"You made her sad! That's why!"

Grimly he knew exactly who fed Tim that line. "I know Nana and Pa need to believe that—but it's not true, Tim." Noah faced his son without flinching. "Mummy was sick. She had something called post-natal depression, and she had it very badly. I didn't make her sad. I loved her—I'd loved Mummy since I was thirteen. I wanted her to come home. But the sickness got too much for her, the pills didn't help, and she ran away. But if she comes back to our old house, Nana and Pa live just down the road, right? She'll go there, and they'll tell her where we are."

"No, no!" Tim cried. His poor, thin little body was shaking; he didn't resist when Noah drew him into his arms, cuddling him close. "She can't, 'cause Nana and Pa aren't *there*."

Noah frowned and pulled back. "What do you mean, Nana and Pa aren't there?"

"Get *away!*" Tim suddenly screamed, his face flushed with fury. "Get away from my dad!"

Noah turned and saw Jennifer a few feet away, her face filled only with tender sadness. "Tim, just this morning I was your friend. Just because I care about your dad too doesn't make me the enemy."

Noah's throat tightened with the words. *She does care about me.* He knew it, had known it all along—but hearing the words made it real somehow. Not just wanting, not mere fascination; she cared and he cared.

There was no going back now.

"Your dad was so scared about you, Tim. I hugged him to make him feel better. Can't I be your dad's friend, too?"

Tim turned from her, his thin face white and strained. The emotion so jumpy it was frightening. "Dad." The word was a

plea—begging him to make a little boy's world secure again.
To let him hang on to a faded thread of memory, the vow that
was all he had left of his mother.

For a moment, Noah hovered on the brink of choice: giving
in from pity as he'd done the past three years—or doing what
he must to help Tim heal. Then he said quietly, "Tim, what did
you mean about Nana and Pa not being home in Sydney?" But
he knew exactly what Tim meant, and a grim sense of foreboding
filled him. Peter and Jan would only leave home for one
reason—the only reason for living they'd had from the day
Belinda disappeared.

When Tim shuffled his feet, looking miserably guilty, Noah
said it for him. "They're here, aren't they, mate? They heard
about the lady who looks like Mummy. The one that lives here."

Tim looked up then, his eyes—eyes so like his mother's,
despite the colouring being his—blazing. "You know about
Mummy being here?"

Behind him, he almost felt Jennifer's body stiffen; but he had
no time to reassure her. "Yes, matey, I know about the lady. Are
Nana and Pa up here somewhere nearby?"

If they were, they wouldn't tell Noah. Though they'd known
him all his life, and had been so joyful when he and Belinda
married, they'd distanced themselves from him from the day
the police marked her file Presumed Dead. When he'd accepted
it rather than spending all his time and resources on finding her,
their love had grown cold. When they called, they asked for
Tim, who passed the phone to Cilla and Rowdy.

Suddenly he understood the reason for Tim's settling down
the past few weeks. Peter and Jan had been feeding Tim from
their unending well of hope.

"They're at a caravan park near Ballina," Tim said, his voice
muffled against Noah's shoulder, shuffling his feet again.
"They're looking for Mummy. They've been here a while."

Noah sighed. "I didn't tell them, but the police report about that lady was the original reason why we moved here, Tim. They showed me a photo, see. I didn't tell you all because I didn't want to get your hopes up, but the police told me there were sightings of a woman who looked a lot like her. I've been looking for her ever since we got here." He hesitated before he added, with painful difficulty, "About a year ago, I hired some special people who look for missing people for a living. They're looking for Mummy."

With that, Tim threw his arms around Noah's neck, burrowing close in a way he only had during nightmares for the past two years. The helmet he hadn't yet taken off whacked against Noah's collarbone. "Thank you, Dad," he whispered. "I was scared…"

Scared you were forgetting Mummy.

The words hovered like a spectre between them, the lie unspoken. For Noah knew now that even had the woman been Belinda, he would have tried to help her, reconciled her with the kids and Peter and Jan—but there was little left inside his own heart but memories. A month ago, he'd hired a second, local detective to find this woman, in a last-ditch effort to remember a marriage gone wrong, to stick to marriage vows long abandoned. The divorce papers he'd had the lawyer draw up last week were in his study now. The guilt and the shame and the relief all at once: ending a chapter of his life that seemed never-ending only three months ago.

But thanks to Jan and Peter's need to keep Belinda alive at all costs, his son's suffering just went on and on…

Was this why he'd seen the fear in his daughter's eyes? Why Cilla had been disappearing until they met Jennifer? *What the hell had Peter and Jan been telling his kids?*

It seemed today was the day for too many choices. This hour was an epiphany for them both. He could remain quiet, and let the pain come in its time and way, and have his son close again—or he could give Tim maximum anguish now, and let him find healing.

There really was no choice.

"I know Nana and Pa want Mummy to be alive as much as we do, but I heard from the special people last week. Remember the big letter you brought me?" he asked gruffly, hating to shatter his illusions even though he knew it was right. "They found the woman. Her name is Sandra Langtry, and she lives out in the bush with her partner and four kids. Though she looks a lot like her, she isn't Mummy—she had kids the same age as you and Cilla."

Tim's body went stiff for a few moments; then he gave a tiny cry, lost, soulless, like a dying animal. He broke out of Noah's hold and bolted for his wobbly bike.

And for once, Noah didn't even try to call him back.

As he disappeared down the road, a little hand slipped into Noah's. "We go in the car, Daddy?" Rowdy asked, helpfully. "We find Timmy?"

Noah looked down at his little boy, and a massive lump formed in his throat. Rowdy and Cilla were so completely un-affected by the news that their mother wasn't alive somewhere nearby. It was as it should be, but it also seemed wrong somehow, like he'd let the family down by not keeping Belinda's memory alive and strong in them all.

As if healing was the disloyalty Belinda's parents be-lieved it to be.

It was only now he'd begun to buck the system he'd permit-ted Jan and Peter to create that he realised the damage he'd done by allowing everyone to think Belinda *could* come home after she'd been presumed dead. Tim was a child, and needed to accept reality; he needed to begin the healing process at last. He should never spend his time running: not running *away* as he'd thought, but running around with his grandparents to find his mum, who either couldn't or didn't want to come home. And so his parents-in-law were going to find out before the night was over.

No more status quo. It was time, not just to move on, but to heal.

He watched Tim turn the bike left, toward the coast— toward home, and sighed in relief. It seemed he'd been right. Tim's disappearances had been about trying to find Belinda—or, he thought grimly, to meet his grandparents. "Yes, into the car—but we're going home, Rowdy. Timmy needs time alone."

A risk he wouldn't have thought to take an hour ago now seemed the only option. He couldn't stop Tim; his dream had been shattered, his faith destroyed. He needed time out before he'd accept his world needed to be reconstructed.

As Cilla and Rowdy, obedient as ever to following his dictums on Tim, opened the truck doors to climb in, Noah turned to Joe. "I'm sorry about all this."

To his shock, Joe was wiping tears from his cheeks. "No, I'm sorry, son. I never realised—anyway, you might want to call Fred and tell him Tim's safe," he said gruffly, trying to recover from being caught out.

Noah nodded, and felt his pockets for his phone. Where had he put it after—

A voice said, sounding completely calm and in control, "I've called Fred already."

Jennifer.

The voice had come from inside the junkyard; she must have walked off to make the call.

Already knowing it was far too late, he turned to her. She was holding out his phone to him, with a tiny smile. "You dropped it when Tim came back."

She seemed unruffled. There was nothing on her face to indicate her emotional state. Nothing to gauge how she felt about his reasons for moving to Hinchliff—damn it, it must have sounded so *bad* to her, given what he'd said the first night about Belinda presumed dead—or about his kiss.

A one-moment brushing of lips. How did that qualify as a kiss in anyone's book?

It does when nobody but a kid has touched you in years.

A one-moment brushing of lips meant far more to him than it should, and with a sense of fatality, he knew that wouldn't change. He'd always been too intense. He'd never known how to play the field; for most of his life, his heart and body had focussed only ever on Belinda—then there'd been the years of nothing, where he'd been in limbo-land, over Belinda but not wanting anything with anyone but his kids.

And now the focus had returned: a tunnel-vision centred on Jennifer.

He'd have loved Belinda until his dying breath, if she was still here with him, loving him—and his fascination with Jennifer wouldn't change until then, either. He didn't know what his feelings were yet, but it had all the hallmarks of speeding-down-a-one-way-alley-into-a-wall he'd felt with Belinda all those years ago. He knew every curve and line of Jennifer's face, what every movement of her mouth meant, how her eyes changed and darkened as her moods moved. He knew how she felt by the way she walked.

And he knew when she was in hiding. This time, her placidity was an act she'd put on to cover her pain—to seem stronger than she was. Why she'd begun this cover, he didn't know—yet—but he would find out.

He'd know everything about her, and soon.

"Thanks," he said quietly, allowing her to retreat while they were in company. He took the phone and pocketed it. "Let's get home."

He used the word *home* deliberately, testing her reaction, but she merely nodded. "The kids need their own home, and you need time on your own."

And though she smiled, she couldn't have been more distant from him if she'd climbed the crags overhanging the town behind Joe's house. She might have been talking of the weather, so light was her emotional investment. And somehow he just knew that spelled trouble.

CHAPTER NINE

THEY headed for home as soon as Noah picked up the pizzas he'd ordered.

As they turned into the long driveway leading to her place, Jennifer knew her veneer of serenity was cracking, breaking open to show her vulnerability every time he looked at her, every time he spoke. She was surrendering to the needs of a body and heart too long buried beneath grief—and yes, the anger she couldn't totally bury, no matter how hard she tried.

And she was *hurt*…hurt that Noah had kissed her, awakening her body, only to—

Oh, get over yourself. You've been into him from first sight. The kiss only made it real.

Don't think about it! Just bury the memory. You're good at that.

Thinking about the rage and grief would lead her straight back to the pit she'd lived in too long after she'd buried her son. Acceptance and moving on was the only option.

"I'm sorry, Jennifer," Noah said, a welcome break into morbid thoughts she didn't want to indulge in. "I lied to you about why we moved here, and why I've been gone through the days. I wasn't always at work. I took advantage of your friendship to spend time looking for Belinda."

After a short breath, she turned to him. Barriers in place with a smile. "Don't apologise to me, Noah. It's not my place to know where you go or what you do. You did what you did for your family, for Tim. Never apologise to me for putting your kids first. I'd have done the same." She always had, with Cody.

"Thank you." But the words held a wryness that told her he wasn't buying it. He'd seen inside her soul, and the emotion she'd tried to hide.

She shrugged and twisted around to the kids. "Almost home."

"Are we going to your house, Jenny?" Rowdy asked, smiling through a mouth full of Hawaiian pizza.

She shook her head. "Not tonight, sweetie, but I'll see you tomorrow, okay? Daddy needs to get home for Tim."

Rowdy nodded, with his gift of accepting life as it was, and returned to making a mess of his clothes and the car seat with dripping mozzarella.

Cilla was trying to feed pizza to her new dolly: the gift Noah had probably bought to soften the blow that the woman he'd moved seven hundred kilometres to find wasn't their mother.

Jennifer frowned and turned back to Noah. "What was Tim's present?"

"A bike," he said quietly.

Of course it was a bike, she thought. Her life had become rich in irony since the Brannigans had moved in next door. It was as if she and Uncle Joe were here for the exclusive purpose of wrecking Noah's relationship with Tim.

"I'll keep it until his new bike breaks," he said with a casualness that really seemed genuine. "I'll offer him a trip to Coffs Harbour or Lismore, and he can pick whatever he wants. Within limits," he added with a laugh that again surprised her.

"You don't need to act with me," she said, taking the unspoken bull by the horns. "Surely you must feel some kind of grief or anger over the news about your wife?"

Noah's wife. That's it, Jennifer, keep reminding yourself. Then the kiss will mean nothing to you but helping a scared dad who took comfort where it had been offered. Then you'll stop these ridiculous dreams of being Noah's love...Noah's wife.

Yeah, right—in about fifty years.

He pulled up the truck at the side of her house, and turned to her, taking her hands in his. His eyes were dark, filled with emotion. "It's been over a week since I found out. I can't pretend there wasn't some kind of pain, Jennifer—but it wasn't the kind you're thinking. I—"

"Jen? Jen, is that you?"

The familiar voice wrenched her from the dreaming spell of Noah's sincerity, and his touch. She gasped; her eyes widened as the tall, strong figure came to the passenger side. She wrenched her hands from Noah's, and, as if in a dream, watched him opening the door. In the light of the new moon and the automatic spotlights on her verandah, she saw the features she'd once loved, dark, mysterious, romantic.

More irony, or was her life spinning out of control? "Mark?" Dazed, she stared up at the man who'd been her life and soul from the age of seventeen until the day he'd walked out on her when she'd needed him most. "Mark, what are you doing here?"

The Irish rogue's face—so like Cody's—lit up with a smile; those blue, blue eyes creased in the grin she could never resist, once upon a time. "Where else would I be on our tenth anniversary, but with my beautiful wife?"

He lifted her right up out of the passenger seat and pulled her into his arms, tipping her face up for his kiss.

Noah drove away from Jennifer's house, refusing to watch in the rearview mirror as she embraced the man who hadn't even noticed she'd been with another guy...

Was this Nature's joke on him? The day he realised there was no going back, the day he began to realise just how much Jennifer meant to him, her ex-husband shows up.

No wonder she'd been acting strangely today. It's her wedding anniversary.

So ended the belief that it was something he'd said or done that forced the change in her. She hadn't been thinking of him at all. So what if she liked his kiss? Any woman who hadn't seen her husband in a long time would be open to temptation.

Ex-husband, Brannigan. And she asked why he was here. She didn't ask him to come.

She hadn't known Mark was coming.

Did that mean—?

There were lights on in the house when he pulled up—and there was another car parked in the open garage.

A utility truck big enough to pull a caravan. The truck Peter and Jan had used the past three years to take a caravan to every place where there was a possible sighting of Belinda.

It seemed Tim had turned on his phone this afternoon, and made one call, at least. But wait—Tim hadn't had enough time to come home on his bike, call them and Peter and Jan to be here ahead of him. And that meant Tim either had their number on his phone, or he knew it off by heart.

He got the kids out of their seats, and took them inside.

It was after eleven when Noah finally saw Jennifer walking to him.

How he knew she'd come, he wasn't sure; they hadn't met here since that first night. Maybe it was his frantic hope that made it seem like belief. He only knew that, by God, he *needed* her, and she'd come.

He'd been waiting forty-five minutes, since Peter and Jan finally left—only the lights on in her house fed his hope she'd be here.

If her ex-husband wasn't staying the night…

Then she was coming to him, like the miracle she'd always been.

Like the purple star-flowers, the white dress of summer was

gone; in its place were jeans and a thick windcheater, since the nights had turned nippy in the past two weeks. Her feet crunched dried grass. As she drew closer, he turned the two-bar halogen lantern down to one bar, giving a soft half-light.

She looked as exhausted as he felt.

He held out a glass. "I was hoping you'd come."

"I wasn't sure," she said softly as she sank to the blanket. "I've been arguing with myself the past half hour."

His heart began pounding hard. Was she thinking of Mark? "Was it so hard?"

"I didn't want to make things worse for you and Tim," she said quietly.

"Belinda's parents were here tonight." Why he was telling her, he didn't know.

What a crock. Denial was useless when every pore and cell of him was beating in time to his heart, aching to touch her. He was taking her into his life. He was making her his woman.

"How did they take the news?"

He shrugged. "Badly, of course, but it wasn't as hard as I'd expected. Maybe because I had to confront them about them calling Tim, feeding him and Cilla, too, with their belief that she's alive and coming home soon…and that it was my fault she left. They told the kids I scared their mummy into running away." He blew out a frustrated sigh. "They've been damaging my kids in an effort to keep Belinda's memory alive."

"Oh, Noah." Her hand slipped into his, a natural gesture of comfort he cherished after thinking all night that he'd blown it with her. "No wonder Tim has been punishing you for trying to help him heal."

"And no wonder Cilla's been scared of me. I couldn't work it out." His head filled with her soft scent, the empathy brimming in her eyes, the feel of her work-roughened hand in his. The pretty, shimmering lips so *close*. "They picked a fight tonight in front of the kids. Tim told them about the private detective, and they wanted to know why I hadn't done it earlier. I had to tell them—" He stopped abruptly. There was a line between confidence and betrayal, and he'd been about to cross it. Not even to Jennifer could he say: *Belinda left me in so much damned debt I couldn't afford to pay a detective until a year ago.*

But Tim had heard it, and Noah knew he'd pay for that particular piece of impulsive anger for a long time to come.

And it had done no good. Peter and Jan refused to believe it. They clung to their picture of Belinda's perfection, and their bitter blaming of Noah, like it was their only lifeline.

Maybe it was.

"People believe what they want to, no matter how you show them the truth," she said softly. "Or maybe everyone's truth is different."

"They asked to take the kids away to the theme parks at the Gold Coast for a week," he said abruptly. Peter and Jan had *demanded* it, but they were the kids' grandparents, and God knew he needed a break right now. "They were devastated that the Langtry woman wasn't Belinda—and so is Tim. They all need time out, some fun. I'm sorry for the short notice."

A short silence. "It's all right."

"No, it isn't," he replied, his voice rough. "It's never damned fair the way they operate on guilt, but there isn't a bloody thing I can do to change it. They never listen to me anyway."

"As I said, people believe what they want to." Jennifer walked into his thoughts as if she belonged in his head. "Look at my ex—a classic example. He's been gone three years, and he's been with several other women since he left me, but he was sure I'd take him back. Because I haven't been with another man, he thought it meant I still loved him."

She hadn't asked him to tell his secrets, but it didn't stop him asking. He had to know. "And you don't?"

Jennifer looked at him, and away. Her hand pulled from

his before she spoke. "If you don't know the answer to that, you're blind."

The sudden acerbity in her tone didn't bother him. His heart beat even harder. "Feelings can come back when you see the person you once loved."

She wet her lips, breathing fast and shallow. "Is that what you believe of me, or yourself? If you moved here to be near her…"

"To *find* her," he corrected through a throat so damn tight with desire, it was choking him. "It was a last-ditch thing, mixed with desperation to get out of Sydney, the house we'd built together. My in-laws were making life a misery, but I had to let them see the kids. All they had left of her was the kids, and their unshakable faith that she's alive." He dragged in a breath before he made the confession, took the biggest personal risk of his life. "Then I saw you, and even from a distance, I knew I was in trouble."

The soft, glowing eyes turned back to him at last. She took in his face, slowly, every part of it. Her lips were already parted; her chest heaved with every breath. "I've never been the 'in trouble' kind of woman."

He smiled, a little. "Who's playing games now?" He moved closer to her, until the warm current of wanting grew to heat, fuelling their bodies.

She bit her lip over a grin: the kind of warm, sensuous curving of lips that told a man exactly what he needed to know. "This kind of game is…" Her tongue ran over her lips again, her gaze glued to his mouth. Her hand half-lifted, waiting in the middle of that hot, swirling current.

"Yeah," he breathed, lifting his hand, twining his fingers through hers. "It is."

"I can't do this if you're still married in your heart," she whispered.

He'd expected that. For answer he reached back with his free hand, and passed her the papers he'd signed. "I had to tell you before I sent them. It's for me, not you," he said quietly. "Meeting you made me see the truth. I can't hang onto something that's no more than a memory. Part of me will always love her…but she's gone. I can't keep living a half-life for Tim's sake, for my in-laws. Living a lie doesn't help anyone. It doesn't keep her alive, except in their minds."

She read the divorce papers, and closed her eyes as she let them fall. "This is why you bought the kids the presents."

He nodded.

She gave a little sigh. "Everything about us seems to have irony in there somehow. Is there a message in that?"

He leaned closer to her, and captured her other hand. "There's no timetable, Jennifer. There's no right time or way. It's happening, no matter what we do. We either ignore it and regret it later, or we take what we both want, and accept the consequences."

She looked at him, her eyes shimmering, uncertain. She wet her lips as she gazed at his face. He'd never felt so strong, so glad to be a man in his life as now, when Jennifer looked at him with all that longing.

"I want the consequences, Jennifer," he murmured huskily. "I want you. I want you."

"Noah." Her voice cracked; her eyes drifted closed, and she fell into him. "Don't make me wait anymore."

Jennifer had waited for him. Though he'd known it from the first night, he'd treasure the words until his dying breath.

Tender and a touch clumsy in first-kiss anxiety, they bumped each other's noses. He opened his eyes, drew back a little and smiled at her. Jennifer laughed, low and soft and throaty: a rich, sensuous laugh, and he knew she'd laugh just like that when they made love.

He unlaced their hands and twined his fingers through her loose plait. "Come here," he said huskily, drawing her against him.

For the first time in half a lifetime, the sense of fatality filling him was beautiful. He *knew* this would be the kiss of his life.

Holding her flush against him, he hovered just over her mouth, waiting, teasing, loving the impatient little moan coming from her, the way her hands threaded through his hair and drew him down to the blanket so he was half-lying on her.

She moaned again and moved against him. "Noah," she whispered, aching with wanting. She wanted him so badly she was shivering.

Then her mouth covered his, tender and hungry; and *rightness* filled his soul at the same moment his body's insistent beat took over everything and shut down every other sense.

The responses of her warm, generous body filled him with her sweetness and urgency. She kissed him gently, but when he took it deeper, she went with him; her hands were threading through his hair, fingers trailing down to his neck. The tiny, whisper-soft sighs between each kiss held a half-plea. "More, Noah…more…"

More was fine with him. Right now he never wanted to stop.

"So unfair," she whispered, more a tiny gasp of sound, as he kissed her throat.

He grinned down at her, a brow lifted. Her voice was so full of feminine arousal he knew it wasn't his kiss that was unfair.

Her smile in return was languorous. She pulled him back to her, and mock-grumbled between kisses, "The heatwave's over, and it's too cold to take your shirt off."

The fire burning in him flared higher, hotter. "Touch me all you want." Was that his voice? It sounded like tyres over gravel.

With a little sigh of delight, her hands slipped under his sweatshirt. "Ah, *Noah*…" She caressed him at first slow and soft, then with greater urgency, chest, stomach and waist; then she wrapped her arms around him and drew him back down to her. "More," she whispered.

When she said his name like that, said *more* like that, the thin threads of control snapped. He devoured her like a starving man at a feast, and she was with him all the way, whimpering and arching up to him with all the passion of his summer-hot dreams, and then some.

Touching, caressing with sweet discovery and wild tension; tongues twined and mouths fused. Loving had never been like this for him, never so intense yet so right and beautiful.

In his limited experience, men wanted the touch and play of lovemaking far more than women. Yet Jennifer's passion matched his, and raised the stakes. Her hands on his skin was making him crazy; the stroking of her tongue against the roof of his mouth short-wired every thought but the need to have her, now. Then one of her legs hooked around his, holding him down hard against her, and she moved against his aroused body again, her kiss hotter, deeper, almost frantic.

How had he been so *blind,* refusing to see what was right in front of him for so long? He thought he knew her; she'd reached right down to his soul from the start, not taking but *giving,* and he'd been drowning in her understated beauty and quiet grace from the first night.

Jennifer. Even the name had become beautiful to him.

But this Jennifer was vivid, passionate, raw with desire. She was melting into him like candle wax, making soft, eager sounds, her fingers and palms not just caressing his skin, but gulping it down, as hungry for him as he was for her. Mumbling his name between kisses and touches so *glorious* he lost all sense of time and place. Nothing else in his life had ever been like this. *Jennifer, Jennifer…*

He must have said it aloud, because she pulled back to smile, glowing with happiness and desire. "Noah, oh, yes, Noah," she mumbled, and tugged at him until he was lying fully on top of her—and his brain circuits sizzled. "More, more."

Oh, man, but he loved that word…

He smiled, but she'd pulled him back down before he could speak. More kisses, mouth, throat and at the vee of his sweat-shirt. "I had to throw him out," she mumbled, rolling them over until she lay on him. "He touched me, kissed me, and I just wanted him to go away." She kissed him all over his face, throat, chest. His placid, everyday Jennifer seemed taken over by another being, a wild woman with no thought beyond touching him, loving his body. "He wasn't you, Noah, he wasn't you."

The kiss following her words was even hotter, filled with a need so strong—not a need for any man, but him alone—it knocked him for six.

Torn between masculine triumph at her confession and primitive fury that another man touched her, he growled between kisses on her throat, "Did you tell him about us?"

Suddenly she stilled. "How could I? There was nothing to tell."

He lifted his head and looked down at her, flushed and drugged with his kisses—and just a touch wary. "There is now. Is he still in town?"

The wild passion in her banked down, like a fire after someone stomped on it. She nodded. "He said he'd stay a few days to see if I'd change my mind."

Another irony in their relationship—he'd gone crazy trying to find his wife for three years; she had her ex back and didn't want him. "When he comes back, tell him about us."

"And say what?" she asked with the fierceness of passion thwarted. He wished he'd kept his mouth shut—or kept speaking the language she'd been loving so much. "That we can't keep our hands off each other, despite knowing we have no future? That stolen hours at a café, or meeting on a blanket in the grass in the night fifty feet from your kids is all we can have, but we take it anyway?" She pushed off him and rolled away.

Put with such blunt ferocity, he stared at her, a slow frown gathering between his brows. "Is that what you think? That I'd use you that way after all you've done for me, for the kids?"

"Did I say it was just you?" she snapped. "I've been just as stupid. I *told* you I had my reasons for staying out of this, yet here I am."

"This." She'd called it "This," as if kissing and touching him was a disease she'd tried to avoid by washing her hands. "I remember," he said grimly. "So why did you come tonight?"

Her eyes met his with quiet defiance. "You know why. I'm not going to lie for the sake of some misplaced pride. I'm here because I couldn't think about anything else after you kissed me today. But there's no future for us. You're not divorced, you're not a widower…and I'm—"

"I showed you the papers. I'll be divorced in a month or two. I'm not using you, Jennifer."

She gave a choked laugh. "That's really not the point, is it?"

"Then what is?" But he knew. "Jennifer, I'm not playing here. I want you in my life, not just in bed. I want you, not a baby!"

"But I do, Noah."

In the grip of fury greater than any he'd felt in years, he snapped, "So you're saying I'm not enough for you? My kids aren't enough?"

"You don't understand. It's *me*. It's not just a wish, Noah— it's a bone-deep part of me I can't change. I can't allow myself to fall in love with you—I'll only make you all miserable in the end. Your kids deserve better than the second-best love I can give them…*you* deserve better than a woman who can't give you children, but will never stop wanting them." With a sigh, she got to her feet. "I shouldn't have come here. I'm sorry. There's just too many people who can be hurt. Even if you wanted something serious with me, it's not going to happen. I won't let it."

Noah watched her walk away, her stride swift and determined. She meant every word of what she said.

CHAPTER TEN

JENNIFER knew something was wrong when Noah showed up late the next morning—just before the other kids and parents arrived—and alone. With a brief "good morning, Jennifer," he taped up the west-facing windows.

"Where are the kids?" she asked, frowning.

"With their grandparents—remember? I told you last night," he replied. "Excuse me. I'm starting the actual building today, as you know, so I'll be putting the barricades up to block the kids from coming in." He turned and walked out the door.

She followed him out, too angry to think. "And that's it? You turn up late, don't even bring the kids to say goodbye—"

He just kept walking. "The kids needed time out, away from here."

That silenced her for a few moments. "I see," she said eventually. They were alone…

Burning heat flashed across her cheeks. As if she floated in the sky above them the night before, she saw them entwined on the blanket, kissing as if it were the last night on earth…

The look he threw at her held a tamped-down fire of warning. "There's no other sightings of Belinda left to follow," he said quietly. "Peter and Jan are pretty devastated."

The flat statement broke into her sensuous visions of last

night, and made her take a step back. "Of course," she faltered, feeling as if she was the one in the wrong, and he'd deliberately put her there. "I'll miss them."

"When they come home, I'll be making other arrangements for them." His voice was as hard as the dark wood he was using for the verandah.

Now she really gasped. "Would you mind telling me why?"

He wouldn't even look at her; he put the barricades in place between them, winding the orange cross-over plastic across the posts. "I thank you for all your kindness until now—but I can't let you hurt them."

The words came across the plastic as if it was an abyss... and she knew whatever he said next, she'd hate it; but she couldn't walk away.

"They love you," he remarked casually, as if it meant nothing. "Cilla and Rowdy think of you as a mother. Even Tim adores you and looks to you for security—and as you said last night, you won't even think about it. You say you can't love them as they deserve." He moved away, winding more plastic across the next pole. "They've already lost one mother. I have to separate you from them before it gets any worse."

A shaking hand lifted to her mouth. "I—Noah, I—"

But he shook his head. "Excuse me. I need to work now."

His cool politeness was a barrier higher than any he created physically.

Within a minute he was bent over the lathe, cutting a verandah plank to the right length.

And Jennifer turned and walked back into the house, to greet the children arriving—children she loved, but weren't her heart, just work, and she was filled with a sense of loss so profound she couldn't argue, couldn't even speak.

Damaged, loving Tim. Adorable Cilla. Beautiful, trusting Rowdy. And *Noah*...

She'd made the decision; it was the best thing for them all—

but she hadn't counted on losing them all so soon. She felt as if she'd lost her family a second time over.

The lights were still on at Jennifer's house.

Noah sat at his back verandah, watching a blur of a shadow pass from room to room, which was all he could see at this distance. Lost without the kids to fill his evenings, more alone than he'd ever been, he watched her house, watched her and hated himself. He'd only done what he'd had to do, but he felt lower than a snake's belly for hurting her.

Regrets were useless. It was over. Jennifer's decision left him with no choice. He had to get the kids away from her before it got any worse for them; but he had to fight himself just to keep sitting here, to not go over there, to take her in his arms and comfort her, kiss her until—

His kids had to come first. He could risk his heart, but not the kids'. Not after losing one mother.

Decision made—but it didn't stop the savage argument inside him. He loved the woman so damned *much*. Heart and soul, he belonged to her, to Jennifer—and she didn't want him. Not for life. And that was all he could offer. He wanted forever, could offer nothing but forever, and she didn't want it.

She does want it, his heart whispered. *She's just terrified she isn't enough. She's blinded herself to all that's wonderful about her because she can't have babies.*

The sudden insight didn't shock him. Maybe he'd known it all along. Jennifer thought it was about that *bone-deep* desire for her own babies—but he knew how much she loved his kids. She was a natural-born mother who hadn't yet come to terms with her loss. He had to show her…to open her mind and heart to new possibilities…

He was at her door before he realised he'd made the decision, or even how he'd convince her. He only knew he had to try.

A soft Elvis ballad was playing on the CD player. Scented

candles were lit around the house, as if she expected a lover; but through the screen, he could see her bent over the kitchen sink. Her arms were wrapped tight around her waist; her body heaved and rocked, and she was crying as though her heart had been ripped from her chest.

"Jennifer!"

By the time she gasped and whirled around, trying to wipe her cheeks, she was in his arms. "Ah, baby, don't cry," he growled. "I can't stand it."

Half expecting her to stand stiff and cold in his embrace, or to pull away, he felt her arms wrap around his waist with a surge of joy so strong it was almost pain. "Noah. *Noah.*" The whisper was harsh, violent in need. She hiccupped, gulped down air, and hiccupped again.

He tipped up her face, kissing her wet cheeks, damp eyes, her mouth. "I know, baby, I know." He kissed her again, drinking in each hiccup of grief, giving her the affection and comfort she needed. "It's just you and me. I'm here, Jennifer. I'm here."

Her arms lifted, wrapping around his neck, and winding into his hair…and she kissed him, heartfelt kisses that lasted forever, promised forever, her red-rimmed, swollen eyes taking him in with a look of wonder, as if he'd vanish if she turned away.

She'd never looked more beautiful to him. He knew what he meant to her; she couldn't hide it, not now, vulnerable in her grief for losing him—*him,* not just the kids. If she wasn't in love with him, she was more than halfway there.

But love wasn't the issue; they both knew that.

It wasn't the time to push—but he could make a start. "I sent the papers today. I know that's not the problem," he added, when she stiffened and began to speak. "I don't think we're going to see the real issues clearly until we've spent time together alone. We've had nothing but problems and issues and kids since we met, Jennifer. The past has affected us both too much."

"I know," she whispered, holding him tight. "I've hated that."

"Me, too…but for now it's just you and me, and we have a week. Let's take the time we have. No promises, no issues— let's be just you and me, doing what we want, for once."

Her eyes were so uncertain. Unsure of what he wanted.

He smiled a little. "No, we won't make love—not yet. I want the right to take you out for dinner, for a ride—I haven't taken my motorbike out since we moved here."

"I didn't know you had one." She smiled up at him.

"With two helmets. Are you afraid of riding?"

"I've never done it, but always wanted to try."

"Come with me tomorrow," he whispered, rough and hard-edged with desire, trying to keep it down. "We'll go to the escarpment at the national park after work. No—let's play hooky. Fridays you usually only have my kids, right? So you have tomorrow off. Let's spend the day together, just you and me."

Jennifer didn't even hesitate. She nodded, her eyes shining.

"I want to spend time with you without worrying about anything else." The gravelly tone of his voice almost scared him. This meant so damned much, and she was glowing, her eyes drinking in his face as if he was beyond special to her. "Just you and me."

"For this week, until the kids come home," she whispered back.

She meant to reassure him, but it only sent scalding pain searing through his entire body. He nodded, not trusting his voice.

"I looked up other child-care centres in the area for you this afternoon. There's three in Ballina, and one at Everwood. That's only fifteen minutes from here."

The shock of it hit him harder than it should have. Being Jennifer, of course she'd try to help him, even if it meant losing the kids she adored. "Thank you," he said quietly; but the night-magic was gone. He pulled out of her arms. "I'll pick you up about ten. Bring a thick jacket."

The anxiety was back in her eyes, but she nodded. "I'm

looking forward to it. I always thought I'd feel—dangerous—riding on the back of a motorbike."

Despite the pain, he chuckled and buffed her chin. "You're dangerous enough as it is. Don't get ideas."

"Me? Dangerous?" she laughed, catching his fist in her hand and caressing it. "Nobody's ever called me that before."

"Then they didn't know you," he muttered. His renegade body was getting ideas of its own, just feeling the repressed sensuality in her caress.

"Dangerous. I like it." She grinned at him, and brushed his body with hers. "I like it a lot." Her voice was all gentle and husky, filled with promise.

If he stayed here any longer, he'd end up in her bed. He knew he could make her want it, here and now—she already did. But he was in way too deep. If he made love to her now, he'd want things she wasn't ready to give. He had to wait. An old-fashioned courtship was the surest way to make her see they belonged together—that they could surmount the difficulties she saw as impossible. Yet right now he'd give anything just to touch her, drink in her bare skin with his hands and mouth…

"You're too dangerous for my peace of mind." His voice was all rough-edged and tight. "I'd better go."

"You don't have to," the voice of temptation whispered into his neck.

He felt the shudder rock his whole frame. "Stop it," he growled, aiming for a joking tone that failed miserably. "We have a week. I'm going to do this right."

"At least one date before—"

"Don't say it, Jennifer. I'm on the edge as it is."

Her laughing tone died; she looked up at him, saw the truth of his words, and smiled. "I'm so glad it's not just me that's on the edge. I'm beginning to wonder if I'll ever think about anything else but wanting you." She kissed his shoulder through the thick woollen jumper, and he shuddered again. "See you tomorrow."

She swatted his butt with a grin as he headed for the door. He grinned back at her. "I'll get you for that, woman."

"I hope so," Jennifer whispered as she watched him leap over the boundary fence. Her knees were weak, and her body was flushed and tense with the need for him she couldn't fight, much as she wanted to—no, *had* to.

For Noah's sake, and for the kids, she could have him only for this week. She'd make love to him, and then she'd let him go.

He roared up to her back doorstep just before ten the next morning, looking like pure sin in the dark jeans, boots and black leather jacket. He flipped up the visor, grinned and held out a helmet. "Ready?"

She caught her breath back and even managed an unsteady laugh. "You bet. Where are we going?"

With a wink, he said, "You'll see." He looked her over, taking in the jeans and joggers with approval, but frowned at her long-sleeved pink T-shirt. "You'll be cold during the ride." Reaching into the black container at the back, he pulled out a jacket almost identical to his.

Jennifer flinched.

"It's my old jacket from uni days," he said as if he hadn't seen or noticed that she'd obviously thought it was Belinda's jacket. "See the old political patches?"

She saw, and slowly smiled, seeing a young, renegade Noah on his motorbike…

"Feeling dangerous still?"

She pulled it on, zipped it up and challenged, "Well?"

"Let's go." He moved forward on the seat. She hopped on, fitted the helmet and wrapped her arms around his waist, almost unbearably excited. Her first real date in ten years or more, and he'd made it her deepest secret fantasy without even trying.

"Hold on tight," he yelled, and roared off. Feeling like a girl again, she squealed and held on tighter to him, loving that she had the right—for now.

They flew through Hinchliff, leaving indignant residents in their wake. Jennifer couldn't stop laughing. After years of a humdrum existence, she was a woman again, and she'd snatch every moment of it she could.

Hitting the highway, he headed north, weaving through traffic with easy skill. Jennifer waved at all the kids who waved at them; she grinned at the women staring in envy. Lord knows, she used to feel envy at the glorious freedom of the bikers. She shivered. Until today—until Noah came into her life, she hadn't known she'd been walking around half-dead. She was living now, really living…she was living out a dream with the man of her dreams. Who could argue with her happiness?

"Cold?" he yelled over the thunderous noise of the engine beneath them.

"No! It's wonderful!"

She felt the rumble of laughter shake his frame, and smiled back, even though he couldn't see it. Who cared if she was being a Pollyanna? The feel of his body surrounding her was enough to make her smile for years to come.

They flashed along the highway, with deep bush each side until it seemed to burst into clean lines of sand and the beach on one side, and tall, dark hills on the other. He roared off to the left, up the darkened road through steep hills covered in gum trees and tangled undergrowth.

In her two years in Hinchliff, she'd never been up this way. "What's up here?" she yelled.

"You'll see." He geared down, and the engine became even louder—and she loved it. The cool, clean air, the dark forest, the feeling of mystery and adventure in not knowing where she was going with Noah—just being with him, without others around to monitor them…having fun without counting the cost.

Oh, yes, this was the stuff of dreams. She almost felt young again. She felt *happy*.

At the top of the hills—a crest far back from the first hill—he finally pulled up.

Jennifer hopped off the bike and pulled off her helmet, her eyes wide with delight. "What is this place?"

Noah grinned at her. "You like it?"

"Definitely." Shining-eyed, she turned in a slow circle. The street was cool and shady, seeming almost a part of the forest surrounding it. The houses and stores were in dark wood, looking both pretty and yet ancient. "Where are we?"

"Lindenbrook. It's a heritage-listed town. It was first built around 1902. They say some famous bushranger started the place as his cover. He ran a store when he wasn't bushranging—or maybe his lady did."

"How did you find it?" She was still turning round and round, taking in the old wooden park, the Hollywood-cinema era café, the quilting store.

Her eyes lit up.

Noah laughed, and turned to chain the bike and helmets together. "I thought you'd want to have a look in there. Their range is more extensive than you'd think. I nearly bought you some stuff last time I was here, but the lady convinced me I'd probably buy the wrong stuff for you—she said quilters can be pretty choosy about what they want."

She noticed he'd avoided answering her question about how he'd found the place—and after a moment she knew why. She didn't ask a second time. Why ruin the day with references to his search for his missing wife?

"Do you still want the jacket?" he asked, in the quiet tone that told her she was right. He wanted to forget—and so did she—about anything that reminded them their time together would be too brief for them both.

She shook her head, and unzipped the jacket, holding it out to him. "Have I got helmet hair?"

"Shake it out a bit." He came to her, minus his jacket— wearing a collarless long-sleeved shirt in the colour of storm clouds. "Let me." His hands threaded through her plait, loosening it until the band fell out and her hair tumbled around her shoulders in loose waves. "Much better," he said softly, his eyes deep and dark. Then he kissed her, long, sweet and gentle.

She almost melted into a puddle at his feet. Her hands gripped his shoulders. "More."

"I love that word when you say it," he whispered against her mouth and kissed her again, still with the tenderness that left her a shivering pool of heat and joy.

"Coffee? Tea? *Anything?*" he asked long minutes later, in a taut, hot voice that told her he was close to losing control, out here in a public street.

Without a word, she nodded.

He wrapped his arm around her, putting her arm around his waist, and led her to the café, in the quiet of wanting too much. Afraid one word would break the constraints they'd agreed to.

They had hot chocolate in a shadowed corner, and discovered how it tasted to sip chocolate from each other's mouths; talking inbetween, about their lives and ambitions, about the verandah's progress—nothing that led to awkward silence. She confessed her fascination with old thirties movies; he liked Jackie Chan. She liked romantic novels; he enjoyed biographies and sci-fi. He loved doing up old houses, and planned to make it a major part of his new business, especially since that was fast becoming the number-one query he was receiving from clients.

He'd also found to his surprise that he loved living in Hinchliff. For a city boy, he'd discovered the love of quiet, and he never wanted to go back. "Dural's pretty quiet, anyway. It's a place with acreages everywhere, so it's got the small-town feel, while being close to the city."

She nodded. "It's similar in Swansea. It's small suburbia, half an hour or more from Newcastle. I could never live right in a city. I like knowing most people in the area, and who the local policeman is."

They talked until they were interrupted. "Did you want to order anything else? Another hot chocolate, or maybe lunch?" the waitress asked, smiling as she came toward them.

Noah checked his watch, and his brows lifted. "It's after twelve-thirty." He looked at Jennifer. "What do you want to do? The gourmet pizzas here are pretty sensational."

Surprised to discover she was hungry, she nodded.

"It will take about twenty minutes. Want to go visit the craft and quilting store?"

Her hand was in his already as she rose to her feet.

The quilting store was one of those curio kinds of stores that hold a bit of everything that Jennifer adored. She wandered around twice, and found one or two items she'd been after for a long time. She took them to the counter with a massive smile of pride and happiness; but Noah had already pulled out his card when she reached for her purse. In his hand was the item she always lost: a thimble. In fact he had half a dozen of them. He grinned and winked and she felt the blush touch her cheeks. He knew why she'd stabbed her finger so often…

"Put them all on one purchase," he told the woman behind the counter. His tone told Jennifer he'd brook no denial on this. He was in charge today.

It felt good to be cherished.

While they wandered back to the café, Jennifer suddenly wanted to tell him something. "I sent Mark back to Newcastle yesterday."

Noah's arm tightened around her waist. He turned her around to face him. "Did you tell him about me?"

She laid a hand on his chest. "I told him there was a stubborn man next door with three adorable kids who made going back to him impossible." She smiled and shrugged. "Not that he really wanted it, anyway. I think he was at a loose end between women, and thought he'd get taken care of for a while. Until he was ready to leave, of course."

"I doubt that—" Noah stopped as he thought about her words. There was something…he frowned as he realised. She'd told her ex about him yesterday—before he came to her last night. She'd told Mark about him, even when he'd made it clear he was cutting her out of their lives.

For the first time, hope soared inside him. Did this mean she wanted him beyond this week? To toss her ex out of her life for him, within hours of his ending all connection with her—

"Noah?"

He kissed her: a butterfly kiss, but he felt her quiver and drag in a breath. "I'm glad you feel like that," he growled. Now wasn't the right time to say everything in his heart. She wasn't ready yet. She'd show him in her time and way. He had to believe that, because she'd taken him body, heart and soul. Giving her up wasn't an option anymore, even for the kids. Whatever Tim thought he wanted, all three of his kids needed Jennifer almost as much as he did.

Now he had to make her want a life with him more than her longing for a baby of her own—more than her fears of inadequacy.

The words were out before he'd thought it through. "Tell me what Mark said to make you feel as if you wouldn't be good enough for me and the kids."

CHAPTER ELEVEN

JENNIFER stared at him. "What?" *Mark?* He actually thought—

She frowned and pulled away from him, feeling bewildered and betrayed. "You couldn't even wait four hours, could you? I thought we were supposed to just enjoy the day, to enjoy our week together. But you're pushing for what I've already told you is impossible!"

The waitress arrived at the doorway, looking for them at that moment. "Your lunch is ready," she called, with a smile.

They walked back to the café, but without the tender connection of earlier—and she found herself grieving for what she'd only had for a few hours. He'd promised her a week...

The waitress put the steaming pizza on their table, along with their cutlery and plates. "Enjoy, folks. Would you like something to drink with that? Some sparkling apple juice, or ginger ale, or cold water?"

"No, thanks." Though Noah smiled up at the woman, he had that repressed intensity about him again. The moment she was gone he turned back to her, his eyes burning. "Tell me, Jennifer. Tell me what he said that's so important that you'd destroy our chance at a life together."

Denial was useless at this point; Noah knew she wanted to be with him. She wasn't the kind of woman to play around. She'd never have kissed him, touched him or offered to make love, if her heart wasn't deeply involved. "It wasn't Mark. It was never Mark." She could feel the shaking begin, deep inside. "He didn't care about having more kids. He didn't care about my defect. The only reason he left me was because I put Cody before him, and he couldn't stand the constant sickness." She lifted a slice of pizza onto her plate. "He tried to come back to me after Cody—he couldn't understand why I didn't joyfully welcome him back. He loved me, he said—he just didn't want to come second, even for his sick three-year-old son. He was glad I wouldn't have more kids!"

After a long silence, Noah said, "Don't despise him for hiding from the truth, Jennifer—or for not knowing you. He probably loved you in his way—he just wasn't mature enough to want to put Cody first. Sometimes it's easier to ignore stressful situations, to let someone else deal with them, or to run away, than stay and face the fact that you have to make changes in your life."

The unwilling empathy in his tone took her aback. "Did you run from Belinda? I can't believe you'd ever leave your kids."

He gave her a small half smile. "Thanks for the faith, but there are many ways to run without leaving physically. I only learned to stop hiding my head in the sand when it was too late. I only grew up when I was left alone with three preschoolers and a mountain of debt I couldn't even work off, because I had to stay home with the kids. It was only then I realised that though I'd always loved her, I loved the vision I had of her when we were kids, and when we were first married. I didn't want to face how deep her depression was because it didn't fit the way I wanted her to be."

"That's why you didn't divorce her until now, isn't it?" she asked slowly.

He shrugged. "There's a bucket load of guilt in every direction I look. Things started getting bad for us when she fell pregnant with Rowdy. She didn't want another child so soon after Cilla. When she mentioned abortion, I took it personally instead of seeing it as a cry for help. She was a fantastic mother, and I couldn't see that she wouldn't cope with three as well as two. She did everything for the kids, and I worked to pay the bills. I thought it was how things should be." His face tightened. "I blinded myself to every sign of her depression because, to me, it meant I was going wrong, or I'd have to change something about me to make her happy."

"Is that why your in-laws blamed you for her disappearance?"

"They had to know I was in denial. Belinda called her mother every day, and took the kids to visit three times a week. They would've known more than I did about her feelings, because I didn't listen. I didn't want to know."

She looked in his eyes, and instead of self-recrimination, she saw determination, and hidden purpose. "Why are you telling me this now?"

His eyes remained steady on her face. "So you know the truth about me. I'm no prize. I'll make more mistakes. You saw enough of them at the start. I was falling down when we met—without you and Joe I don't know where I'd be now, let alone the kids." He gathered her hands back in his. "But that's not the reason I want a life with you. You know it isn't." His eyes were dark, intense on hers. "Marry me, Jennifer. Not for the kids, not because I need you, but because you want to spend the rest of your life with me. Because you love me as much as I love you."

The shaking went right down to her bones; tears filled her eyes, and she couldn't breathe. Dream and nightmare met and kissed, and temptation and desperate fear clawed right through her. "I can't, I just can't," she babbled. "I'm sorry, but I told you I couldn't."

Noah didn't seem to be insulted, hurt or even taken aback. "That was a bit sudden, wasn't it?" he asked, with a rueful smile. "I was going to ask at the end of the week."

Unsteadily she replied, "My answer will be the same, now or then."

"Are you saying you don't love me?" he asked, the quiet tone in no way hiding the demand; but she didn't know how she felt about anything right now, except that she couldn't marry him. Helplessly she shook her head.

"Do you know how you feel?" he asked, his gaze on her face: all her turbulent confusion must be very obvious. "I think you do care, Jennifer. I think you're afraid to look at your feelings because it might hurt you too much."

"I told you why I wouldn't marry again," she mumbled, blinking hard, trying to hold in the tears. She hadn't shed a tear since coming to Hinchliff…until an open-hearted man with three adorable kids walked in her back door, and she felt as if she'd been crying ever since.

"You said you wouldn't marry for the kids—or for love, because if you loved a man, you'd want his baby," he said softly, his gaze holding hers. "Do you want my baby, Jennifer?"

Yes! Yes! More than anything in the world!

She gulped the massive hardness in her throat as the truth knocked her silly. The question, and her unconscious answer, made her see the truth far more than his flat-out demand to know if she loved him a minute before.

Love. She'd loved him all along, probably from the first day—but she'd refused to acknowledge it because this moment would always be inevitable, ready to destroy her fragile illusions of control. Because grief was crouching, ready to pounce on her like the monster under the bed that woke her at night when she was little.

Because denial was the only hold on sanity she had.

She loved him more than she'd ever thought to love any man, and she adored his children. She loved them almost as much as she'd loved Cody…

Could it work? Could she make them all happy with *almost?*

Could she mother his children and not long for more—or would she eventually hurt them all with what she couldn't change?

How could *almost* be good enough? This beautiful family deserved so much better than second best…and if he touched her now, if he said he loved her again, she'd—

Break.

The word she'd overheard Uncle Joe use that night, talking to Noah, was more appropriate than she'd have admitted only a week ago. Joe knew her too well; he knew this meant too much.

Because Noah and his beautiful kids had become her world, and that terrified her.

"Jennifer?" His voice, so tender and understanding, walked into her mind, soothing the turmoil just by being there. "It's not as impossible as you think. We can work this out."

She couldn't speak; she just shook her head. Some things couldn't be sorted out.

"Think about it, Jennifer. Why can't this work for all of us? Why isn't love enough? I know you love me, and you *do* love the kids."

Think? There was nothing to think about, but loving Noah and losing him. Yes, she loved his kids, but not as they deserved…they deserved a *mother,* not a woman giving them second-best love, making them a substitute for her own children…

Watching her white face and blank, horrified eyes, he pushed aside the uneaten pizza. He'd blown it. Why hadn't he waited? If he'd given her a week—

He hadn't known quite what to expect when he'd asked her about having his baby, but the look on her face left him speechless—the anguished longing and devastation combined.

Too late, he knew this was something she'd always feel utterly alone with, just as he'd felt about Belinda's disappearance. He could never fully understand her loss, having fathered three healthy children with ease.

He should have *thought* before he'd blundered in. Jennifer did nothing but give to him, and he'd thrown her impossible dream in her face as though he could make a miracle happen.

The look on her face had said it all. Jennifer loved him, far deeper than she'd shown him until that moment. He knew it now, just as she knew. She loved his kids, and they adored her.

No, love wasn't the issue.

Acceptance was the real, core issue: Tim needed to accept his mother was gone, but the most incredible substitute already loved him, and the whole family. Jennifer had already accepted she couldn't have the one dream of her life…but she'd blinded herself to a love that would be there for her for the rest of her life. She couldn't see that the kind of love they shared was more than enough for them all.

They could become a family, if only she'd let it happen.

Changing a lifetime of thinking didn't occur in an hour. He'd been a fool to bowl on in like that; but love and longing overcame good sense. Not needing her so much as wanting to make her happy, his beautiful, giving Jennifer.

He opened his mouth to say something to soothe the moment, to give her space and time. Then his phone bleeped—and he went cold. The bleeping sound was what he'd programmed for the police. Tim—Cilla—Rowdy—

He flipped the phone open. "Fred," he greeted the sergeant tersely. "What is it? The kids?"

What he heard made him go cold all over.

She despised herself…but how could she change the person she was?

Lost in her thoughts, she'd vaguely realised Noah was on the phone to someone, and turned away to give him privacy.

Not thinking wasn't an option, unless she gave herself amnesia—which sounded really tempting right now. To be able to forget all this pain…

You want to forget Noah? Forget the kids?

She knew she would never do that even if she could. The Brannigan family had changed her placid, uneventful, boring life forever. They'd challenged her, made her think and act in ways that she hadn't known were part of her. They'd needed her so much, yet she'd been given so much more than she'd given to them. And Noah—

She closed her eyes, fighting the emotion threatening to overcome her. If only—

"Jennifer."

The shock in Noah's tone jerked her out of her thoughts. "Noah?" She looked up, shocked by his white face and blank, cold eyes. "What is it? Are the kids all right?"

He took his time answering, but it wasn't deliberate. She wondered if he'd even heard her. Finally he spoke, slow, jerky—lost. "They've found Belinda."

The ride back was tense and silent.

Noah felt physically ill. He didn't know what to say to her after that one sentence. What else *was* there to say? He didn't know anything else. Fred had said, "There's been a positive identification this time, Noah. They've found your wife. I can't say more on the phone—I wasn't supposed to say that much, but I wanted you to be prepared. The Sydney people are here, but I convinced them to let me handle it first. I'll be waiting at your place with all the details."

They've found your wife.

The words he'd prayed so long and hard to hear, given in the same hour he'd proposed to Jennifer. When else would it happen?

Jennifer was barely holding on to him, her hands on his waist instead of around his chest as they'd been this morning. A minimal touch—just as she'd touch him if he were another woman's husband…

What if he was?

He almost threw up at the thought. Oh, he'd be happy for her, for Peter and Jan and the kids; but though he was still fond of Belinda, he wasn't the same man-child he'd been only three years ago. He'd grown up, and his heart changed with him— and now he'd given it to Jennifer.

But if Belinda was alive, and wanted their marriage and family back, he knew Jennifer would quietly withdraw, and disappear from his life.

Yet somehow he felt sure his wife wasn't alive. Peter and Jan's faith was the desperate blindness of parents who can't face outliving their beloved daughter, and they'd passed it on to Tim. But Noah had always known. If there was one thing he knew about Belinda, it was that she'd never have left her kids.

She wouldn't have left me either—not without a word.

They'd had their troubles, but he and Belinda had said "I love you" to each other the morning she'd disappeared. Tim's testimony to the tender kiss between his parents—a ritual he'd seen every day—had slowed the momentum on police suspicions. He supposed the lack of evidence, and no other woman in his life, had helped as well.

It was almost in shock that he found himself pulling up outside his house. Lost in the past—in the final, tenuous links to his life with Belinda, apart from the kids—he'd ridden almost an hour without a word to Jennifer.

Her face, when she pulled off the helmet, was white—as if she'd been fighting the same sickness he had. "Jennifer—"

"Fred's waiting," she said softly.

"Come inside with me." He spoke with a desperation he couldn't hold in. "I need you."

Her face slightly averted, she nodded, making a motion with her hand for him to go first.

Fred's lined, honest face looked grim and sad, and Noah knew what he had to say before he said it.

"She's dead, isn't she, Fred?" The words were so damn flat.

No emotional investment at all. Why was that, when suddenly he felt something breaking inside him?

Fred said, with a flicked glance at Jennifer, "Let's go inside, Noah. There's a lot to say."

Jennifer followed the men in without a word or expression. She seemed to drift in, like a small boat listing on a river without its anchor, and sat at the other end of his long, wide living room, her gaze out the window.

She couldn't have stated her protest at being here more clearly if she'd shouted it; but he didn't let her off the hook and tell her to go. Whether she liked it or not she had an emotional investment in this.

Though he'd sat, Fred was twisting his hat in his hands. He looked at Noah, and away. "Yes, she's dead. I'm sorry, Noah. They found her body a couple of weeks ago, but had to get definite DNA evidence to prove it was your wife."

Translation: *the body was too decomposed to be sure...*

Noah's head fell; his voice sounded strange even to his own ears. "Where was she found? Why did they think it was Belinda in the first place? Did—did she leave a letter?" The unspoken question hovered in the air. *Did she kill herself? Did she hate her life that badly?*

"No, she didn't." Fred sighed. "They were sent an anonymous letter by the person who killed her. The dates given and the locale made them pretty sure they'd find your wife."

His head shot back up so fast it hurt his neck. Vaguely he felt Jennifer coming to him; he felt her arm come around his shoulder; but he couldn't think of her now. "Killed? She—Belinda was—" He wanted to throw up again. *Dear God.* All these years he'd blamed her, resented her, and she'd been—

"No, son, it wasn't deliberate," Fred hastened to say. "According to the letter it was a hit-and-run, an accidental death—which is still manslaughter if we find the man or woman who did it. They may show up at a police station one day and confess. Their conscience has been working, that's certain, or we wouldn't have got the letter telling us where your wife was buried."

"Buried?" Noah asked sharply.

Fred nodded. "She was found in the bushland southwest of Dural. She was wearing her wedding ring; dental records and DNA confirmed her identity. It's definitely your wife."

"Dural." The word came out dull, stupid. "You mean…"

"According to the dates given by the driver, she was killed the day she disappeared," Fred said gently. "She never ran off, but according to the letter, she was farther west of the shopping mall than we expected. It seems she must have gone for a long walk instead of shopping. She stepped out onto a crossing as the driver rounded a corner—a young person, we think, and probably speeding. Your wife didn't stand a chance." Fred shook his head. "It was a fairly isolated area, but still, how they got the bod—your wife in the car and took her away without anyone hearing anything, or seeing it happen, is beyond me. There'd be noise, and blood all over the road—"

"Fred," Jennifer interjected sharply.

Fred blinked, and the man re-emerged from the policeman. "I'm sorry, Noah," he said awkwardly. "Stupid thing to say."

Stupid? No, natural—Noah had thought the exact same thing. He guessed he'd never know how it was done, unless the person was caught.

Belinda hadn't left; a damned stupid speeding driver had torn his family apart…

It was curious, the way he felt—everything was spinning slowly around him, yet he was breathing hard and fast, as if he couldn't keep up. His mind felt blank and dizzy, yet the questions kept coming out of the darkness inside him. The only things touching him were the words Fred spoke, and the feel of Jennifer's arm, her fingers caressing his shoulder, like an anchor in sudden storm.

But counterbalancing that, there was only one reality, and the weight of it made it hard to breathe: *Belinda was guilty of nothing but a momentary lapse in judgment in leaving Cilla and Rowdy with a five-year-old Tim and a babysitter.*

For so long he'd almost hated her for leaving him, but she hadn't—she hadn't. Someone had taken her from them all.

"Why do you think the person confessed now?" Jennifer asked from behind him, and he was grateful for it; the darkness had turned blank with the thought. All these years, he'd blamed Belinda, and she was *dead*.

Fred shrugged. "Who knows? The people from the Missing Persons Unit think it might have been a show recently on a Sydney station, a documentary on the families of missing people, and how there's never any closure until the person, or their bodies, are found. If they saw that, perhaps your family in some way became real to them."

Noah nodded. That made sense, he supposed. He didn't know—he knew nothing at this point. "Thank you, Fred," he said, very politely. "Thank you for coming. If you'll excuse me now, I need to make some calls."

"The people from Missing Persons contacted your parents-in-law, and said there was news on your wife. They're on their way back with the kids. Did you want me here when you break it to them?"

Noah went cold all over, as if ice water had been tipped over him. He needed time to get his head together, and Peter and Jan would already be on the road. They took their damned caravan everywhere with them, like a stupid holy grail. It was always perfect, always ready to leave at a moment's notice, even with the kids there. They'd be only an hour or so from here by now. "No, thanks," he said quietly. "They'll want to contact the Missing Persons Unit themselves if they have questions or doubts." And they would. He knew that.

Not noticing his reaction, or tactfully overlooking it, Fred headed for the door. "Missing Persons said you know their number—they'll be here for a day or two if you or any member of your family has any questions for them." At the door, Fred turned back, twisting his hat in his hands before shoving it on his head. "I'm that sorry, Noah—for you, for the kids. I know you were hoping…" He turned to Jennifer, and nodded with obvious awkwardness. "Jennifer."

A hell of a strange situation for all of them, to say the least, but he couldn't hold onto the thought. Closure was finally here, just when he'd accepted it wouldn't come. And now he had to tell the kids, tell Peter and Jan—

The police car revved up, and the taillights disappeared up the driveway toward town.

Silence descended on the house—but it was a cheat. He had to get his head together, and fast, because the kids were on their way here, and he had to know what to say.

CHAPTER TWELVE

"Do you want me to go?" Jennifer asked quietly after a few moments, feeling out of place here, with the man who'd proposed to her this day, the same day he found out his wife was dead.

Noah stared around at her, his eyes blank and unseeing. "No."

The word was plain, stark in its raw emotion. She shivered with the intensity of it. "Are you sure, Noah? Your parents-in-law will hate me being here."

There were many answers he could give to that, firstly that they weren't his parents-in-law anymore, and had no place in his private life. What she didn't expect was what he did say. "Don't go. I need you."

She shivered again, but came around the chair to face him, and slipped her hands into his. After a hesitation, she murmured, "How are you feeling?"

A moment passed, two…ten, twenty; then he finally said, "I don't know. I don't know."

His honesty hurt her. She knew she should be his friend now, to explore his feelings about Belinda since he'd discovered she'd never left him; but Jennifer couldn't make the words come. It was too much to ask of a woman in love.

Swallowing the hurting in her throat, blinking back the tears of pain and half-shame, she tried to smile: a grim travesty of her glowing smiles today. "What do you need?"

He pulled his hands from hers, rubbing his forehead with the weary gesture that had touched her soul the day they'd met. "The right words to say to Tim, and to Peter and Jan."

Throwing up a brief, heartfelt prayer, she kept her distance: he didn't need a lover now. The right he'd given her today had vanished; she must accept that. She must let him go, give him the right to grieve. "There are no right words, Noah," she said gently. "You can't make this better for Tim."

He sighed and frowned—and she felt his withdrawal growing. She understood; she'd been there after Cody's death, sharing her deepest loss with no one.

To understand is to forgive, or so people said—but it didn't stop the heartache blossoming inside her like an evil vine. She moved back, physically and emotionally—slipping back to the role of friend she'd had only a few days ago, and accepted as right. "Would you like a coffee?"

He nodded, lost in his thoughts. "Thank you," he added vaguely.

When she put the mug in front of him, he didn't notice—and her nerves stretched to breaking point. What was she doing here? "You know what, the kids might need some comfort food when they get here. I think I'll just nick home and get the chocolate cake and cookies—"

"No."

It stopped her mid-stride; she turned back, half-inquiring, half-terrified. He was on his feet, staring wildly at her, half-seeing through a blur of tears, his arms wide-open and his face anguished. *"Jennifer."*

It was all she needed. She ran to him, throwing her arms around his neck. "I'm here, Noah," she whispered, holding him close, caressing his face, his shoulders and back.

"I can't feel anything," he whispered, shuddering. "I'm a widower about to bury my wife's remains and I can't even feel grief…I still *resent* her. She went for a walk, and was killed in a stupid accident. What right do I have to feel so much anger against her?"

Jennifer kissed his cheek, his lips: love without passion, giving all the love she had inside her. "I was angry with Cody, too. I wanted him to fight, to stay with me just one more day. But he looked up at me and whispered, 'I'm tired, Mummy'—and he stopped breathing soon after," she choked, feeling the grief swamp her over again in retelling it. "I almost *hated* him for that, a sick baby. He shouldn't have left me alone!"

Her outburst seemed to calm him. He wrapped his arms tight around her. "Not me—I'm angry for the sake of the kids," he rasped. "She shouldn't have gone for a walk without the kids, or gone shopping without me—we'd arranged that the last time I found out about her debts. She coped with depression by spending money we didn't have. She shouldn't have left the kids, even with the babysitter…but if she'd taken them…" He shuddered and buried his face in her throat. "I don't want to be angry with her, I don't want to hate her—but the last three years of hell wouldn't have happened if she'd kept her promise and waited for me!"

Finally she said it. "You're angry for—for still loving her so much when she's not here," she murmured, her heart breaking. He had the right to grieve, to love the wife who hadn't left him but *died*—but it didn't stop the pain; it made it worse.

"Love or anger, I don't know anymore. Everything's jumbled in my head. All I know is, I have to explain this to a little boy who's faithfully kept his promise to her for three years, and waited for her to keep hers and come home!"

"You'll find the words. You're his dad. He loves and trusts you more than you know," she said, feeling helpless to say the right words.

"There's nothing to say. You know that. You said it yourself." He sighed against her throat. "What can you say when you have to shatter the dreams and hopes and faith of a little boy?"

The words, his warm breath, slid over her skin; his meaning touched her like a farewell.

Because it was. It was inevitable. There was too much between them, and yet not enough, not while he grieved and Tim would yet grieve; while she longed for the one thing she couldn't have, even while loving the daily reminder of Noah's love in the past.

Tim, Cilla, and Rowdy—she loved them so much; but she wasn't and never would be their mother. They were Belinda's children: Noah and Belinda's children. A fact as stark as her own: her tainted genetics would always create terminally ill children, and it would be too damn *painful* to raise Noah's kids. The first time she heard Tim say *you're not my mother,* it would break her.

She had to walk away. There was no option.

But when he lifted his face and closed his tear-wet eyes, seeking her mouth in near desperate hunger, she couldn't hold back. She knew this blind need, and let the kiss happen, allowed him to ravage her lips and crush her against him…and when his hands curved over her breasts, she moaned and arched into him. Celebrating life in the midst of grief and despair—oh, she knew that, too; but it didn't matter, nothing mattered but the over-whelming rush of love for him and his need for her colliding.

They fell back onto the sofa, kissing and touching. Wanting to forget all they had to face.

"I need you, Jennifer, I need you," he murmured as he kissed her throat, rough and gravel-edged with desire and pain. "Don't go now, baby, don't…"

"Noah," she whispered back, turning her face to kiss his mouth again. Oh, the rush of beauty and wanting—it had never been like this for her before, and walking suddenly wasn't an option. "I'm here, Noah, I'm here."

"I thought I could take the risk—that I could be near you and walk away later, but I can't." He kissed her over and over, face, lips, throat and the hollow between her breasts; branding her as his with mouth and hands, caressing her in a fever that ignited hers, until her legs felt like jelly and her arms trembled with longing for more, for *everything*.

Longing to say the words that would change everything—then he nipped the corner between shoulder and throat as he caressed her breast, and words fled except one.

"Now," she whispered, arching up to him. "Now…"

He looked down at her, his eyes black and intense with desire. "The bedroom."

"Yes, yes." She got to her feet, then sat abruptly. "I don't think I can walk that far. I'm shaking," she confessed.

He smiled, his eyes softening in tenderness; then he swung her up in his arms, heading for his bedroom. "You're mine," he growled with soft nibbles to the vulnerable corner again, and she went limp in his arms. "I won't let you leave me, Jennifer. You hear me? *I won't let you leave.*"

Where had her gentle Noah gone? He sounded so fierce—and in those dark jeans and shirt he looked like a warrior fighting a battle in darkness. She shuddered in primitive response to it, unable to think beyond this moment; she loved him so *much*. She moaned, seeking his mouth again.

Lights on high beam turned into the driveway. The crunching of tyres over gravel came, and kept coming, as if a semi-trailer had turned in.

"The kids are here," she said, her voice flat and tight with thwarted passion.

Noah stilled, and looked down at her in tender command. "Tonight, Jennifer," he rasped as he slowly set her on her feet.

Sadness filled her; she shook her head. Their chance was gone.

He read her without any difficulty. His eyes burned into hers. "Tonight. There won't be regrets or second thoughts. You're mine."

She shuddered again, and clung to him until she was sure her legs would carry her weight. "I should go now."

"Don't go, Jennifer." He held up a hand as she tried to speak.

"I know you're thinking of Peter and Jan and Tim—but Cilla and Rowdy will be confused and scared by all the emotion. They'll need someone…distanced from it. They'll need someone they love to explain it all to them. Maybe to take them out of it."

Jennifer gnawed on the inside of her lip, but there was no way to discount what he'd said. Cilla and Rowdy had no memories of Belinda, and the raw grief bound to come from Tim and their grandparents would confuse and frighten them.

"I'll stay," she said slowly, "until the children are asleep."

"And beyond," he added in quiet force. "Peter and Jan won't stay the night."

Before she could answer, the door flew open and Tim rushed in, his face alight and eager. "Dad! Dad, we're home. Nana and Pa said there's news of Mummy!"

In a moment, the sensual man became one hundred percent father. Noah watched his little boy running to him, knowing this would probably be the last time Tim *was* a little boy. He knelt down to catch his son in his arms. "Yes, matey," he said, gruff with sadness. "There's real news this time."

At Noah's tone of voice, Tim whitened and began to struggle against him. "No…you're lying. Mummy just went away for a while!"

"Ah, matey." Noah held him gently. "They found her. Mummy never ran away, matey. She was hurt when she went out that day. She was gone all along. She's—at peace, Tim. She's not sad or hurting any more."

"No. No!"

The wail came from the open doorway, where Jan stood, clinging to the handle. She was white and shaking. "No…my girl, my Linnie…"

Tim slumped against Noah, with a high-pitched wail.

Peter was already dialling a number—the number for the Missing Persons Unit, no doubt.

Noah said quietly, "It's true, Peter. It was a hit-and-run. The driver finally got an attack of conscience and wrote a letter, telling where he'd buried her—and they found her."

And for some reason, the emotion overcame him. Three simple words changed his life. *They found her.* The choking ball of tightness cut off his breathing. One gulp, two—and the tears came at last, the tears he hadn't been able to shed since the day she'd gone missing. He held his little son in his arms and they cried together, while Peter yelled at the people from the Missing Persons Unit and Jan kept shaking her head, refusing to believe her daughter was—

But she knew it, just as Noah knew. Belinda was gone.

Peter was rapping out question after question to the person on the phone while Jan's face slowly crumpled, seeing the defeated slump to her husband's shoulders.

The dream was over. Though they'd refused to believe, Noah suspected they'd always known, deep down, because Belinda would never have left her family. She was dead, their daughter, his wife, the mother of his kids—and it was a damned stupid accident. Somebody in a rush to get somewhere, not thinking of the consequences—and a family had fallen apart…

No, you didn't, Noah. You held them together. The kids are okay, thanks to you.

In the midst of sudden, overwhelming grief, Belinda's voice came to him so clearly he almost turned around to find its source. Instead he wanted to thwack his head. He didn't *believe* in life after death, and—

You chose well, Noah. She's a beautiful, loving woman. She'll be good to our kids.

He couldn't help turning his head. She'd gathered Cilla and Rowdy onto her lap on the sofa in the furthest corner of the room, holding them close as Cilla sucked her thumb furiously and Rowdy, frightened by all the grief, was crying too.

Jennifer's face was filled with tenderness as she held them and told them she was here, that it was all right to cry.

Cilla laid her head on Jennifer's breast and escaped the only way she could, falling asleep; and Jennifer held her and caressed her hair, while murmuring loving words to Rowdy, whose tears were already subsiding.

Tim kept beating his fists against Noah's chest, with those sad little wails, slowly descending to hiccups. Noah murmured over and over, "It's all right, matey. She never left you. She loved you—she loved us all. It wasn't her fault—she never left you."

Peter finally hung up the phone and just stared at his wife, his eyes filled with horror and devastation. Jan collapsed on Peter, sobbing.

Tim hiccupped and looked up at Noah. "Nana and Pa said…"

Noah knew what Tim couldn't say. "They needed to believe it was my fault, Tim. I always understood that." He looked up briefly at his mother-in-law. "They needed to believe she was alive. They wanted a reason for her not wanting to come home."

His son nodded. "But…it wasn't your fault," he whispered. "Dad…"

The tears streaking down his face blended with Tim's as he felt him close again. "Ah, don't, matey. I know. You had to keep your promise."

Tim sobbed against his chest, whispering, *"Daddy, Daddy."*

And finally, after three long years, Noah knew his little son would be all right. He'd come home at last. In being found, Belinda had released Tim from the promise that had become an unbearable burden for eight-year-old shoulders.

Closure. It was as if Belinda had somehow given them all her blessing in moving on, in finding healing…

"What is *she* doing here?"

Jan's accusing voice startled them all. Cilla jumped in Jennifer's lap, and started crying; Rowdy wailed again—and Tim noticed Jennifer for the first time. "Jen…my mummy's dead," he sobbed, and ran to her. Somehow Jennifer found a few inches more space on her lap for him, crooning soft words of comfort.

Peter and Jan gasped, as if Tim had betrayed them. Noah groaned inside. They needed to be angry right now, and they'd found the perfect target.

"What is *she* doing here?" Jan snapped. "She's an outsider. She didn't know Linnie!"

But Noah had had enough. "Stop right there, Jan. Jennifer's a close family friend, she minds Cilla and Rowdy most days, and the kids love her."

"She's an outsider. She doesn't deserve to be here!" Peter yelled.

"She didn't know Linnie!" Jan near-screamed, setting off all three kids into terrified tears.

"No, she didn't, but she knows the kids—and for once in three years, I'd like you to put your grandchildren's welfare before your feelings. Tonight isn't about Belinda. This is about my kids' needs—and they need Jennifer!"

"Get out. Get out!" Jan screamed at Jennifer—but Noah stepped into her range of sight.

"This is my home, Jan. I've told you Jennifer's welcome," he said coldly. "I loved Belinda all my life, too. I know you're grieving, but I will not allow you to take it out on Jennifer. Belinda's gone, and the kids love and need Jennifer—and so do I."

Jan gasped and whitened. Peter stepped forward with clenched fists. "Damn you, boy, you only just found out our girl—*your wife*—is gone!" he yelled.

Noah held up a hand. "How many more years do I have to live alone to prove to you that I loved her?" he asked wearily. "You've set Tim up as my watchdog, stopping anyone from getting near. You've reminded him of his promise over and over, keeping the family ready for Belinda's return. You now know it's not going to happen. And despite his best efforts, Tim loves Jennifer as much as Cilla and Rowdy—"

"His real name is Jesse," Peter snarled. "Linnie named him Jesse!"

"—and I'm not going to allow you to damage that for your need to keep Belinda alive. My kids will always know who their mother was—I'll make sure of that. But she's gone, and these kids need a mother. And I need Jennifer. I love her, and I want to marry her."

Jan burst into tears again. Peter stood over Noah, his face mottled with fury…but Noah's focus was on the silent woman holding his kids. What she was thinking about his declaration.

"You forget quickly," Peter sneered. "It shows what my girl meant to you."

"Enough," he snarled, so harshly Peter took a step back. "I won't apologise for putting a new life together for myself and the kids. We've been through enough pain."

He met his father-in-law's eyes without flinching. "I've only got one more thing to say. For three years I've allowed you to blame me for everything. But you've damaged Tim—and I won't allow that anymore. I wasn't responsible for Belinda's disappearance—you know that now. You'll always be welcome here, and be a part of the kids' lives—but I'll never let you hurt them this way again. Belinda would never have allowed it."

At the mention of her name, both their faces crumpled, and he knew it had been a low, if necessary blow. This was the first day of their grief—until now they'd lived in fear and determination, but never allowed grief to be part of their emotions.

"I'm sorry," he said quietly, "but it had to be said. You both need time now to grieve—but the kids and I need to move on. We've done our share."

"I want to go see the Missing Persons people." Peter turned his back on Noah. "The kids' bags will be on the verandah." He held out his arms to the kids. "Nana and Pa have to go now.

Be good for—for Daddy," he said, his voice gruff with tears, "and don't you ever forget your mummy."

He glared at Jennifer when the kids hesitated.

"Go to Pa," she said softly, avoiding Noah's eyes. "Kiss Nana and Pa goodbye, and thank them for your lovely holiday."

As the kids hugged Jan and Peter, Noah thought of the holiday the kids hadn't had, and vowed to take them back to the Gold Coast as soon as the weather grew warmer.

Then he noticed Jennifer, sitting stiff and still on the sofa. She wasn't looking at him—she hadn't looked at him since he'd stated his intentions to Jan and Peter.

She didn't look like a woman in love. She looked as if she desperately wanted to bolt.

CHAPTER THIRTEEN

IT WAS after ten by the time they finally got the kids to bed. She'd sung a dozen lullabies to Cilla, and they'd had to lay on either side of Tim and hold him as he cried himself to sleep.

Rowdy, tired out by his crying, had fallen asleep hours ago, even before dinner.

In the living room again, Jennifer stretched, feeling the bones crack in her back. She was so tired—but there was more to come. There was no way Noah would let her leave without…

The gulp hurt her throat and chest. He had the right to expect *something* from her. If she'd meant her rejection today, she shouldn't have kissed him and allowed him to touch her with such intimacy. She shouldn't have almost demanded they make love.

And oh, how she still wanted to—she ached for him—but could she take him into her arms, spend the night in his bed, and then reject his proposal a second time?

When she heard his step on the floorboards, she almost turned tail and ran. Then she felt ashamed. If Noah could face her the day his proposal was rejected, he discovered he was a widower, confronted his parents-in-law and brought his son to terms with the loss of his mother, what right did she have to be a coward?

So she swung around and smiled at him. "Quite a day, huh?"

He didn't bother with preliminaries. His red-rimmed eyes bored into hers, no compromise, no surrender. "But it's over for us, isn't it? Just tell me the truth, Jennifer. I'm too bloody tired to tap-dance around it."

It seemed this was the week her gentle Noah came into his own. He wasn't going to stop her—but he wouldn't let her off the hook, either. If she was going, she had to do so honestly. She walked over to him, lifted her hands and, seeing the flat distance in his eyes, let them fall. "A lot of things have changed since this afternoon," she said, feeling her way.

"But not your decision, right?" he asked, sounding unutterably weary. "You haven't looked at me since I told my in-laws I wanted to marry you."

She spread her hands wide, praying he'd understand. "I told you why I wouldn't remarry. That hasn't changed. It never will."

"You're turning me down because you want my baby. You love me the way I love you, but you can't have my baby, so all five of us have to suffer the consequences. You don't get one thing you want, so we all miss out on happiness. Is that it?"

The casual-seeming words made her catch her breath, then it got stuck there, choking her. She coughed and coughed, but it did nothing; the stinging came, the tears welled up, filling her eyes. "Noah…"

"Is that everything?" His tone was almost conversational. "You were the one who said we can't always get what we want. So I lose the love of the rest of my life for a genetic defect, and my kids lose the mother they adore because they're not enough for you."

She did gasp then. "It's not that!" It was the other way around…wasn't it? That she wasn't enough for them?

He went on as if she hadn't spoken. "Yeah, it looks like we don't always get what we want—but walking away from me, from us, still isn't going to give you a baby. Nothing's going to do that—but for some reason, you think punishing us all for your broken dreams will work for you."

"No!" It was a strangled croak now. "I never said that, or thought it…Noah, please…"

"Didn't you? Didn't you say that?" Suddenly he was right in her face, speaking with guttural demand. "Because that's what I could have sworn you said. You love me, but I'm not enough. You want my baby, but the three kids I have, all little more than babies, aren't enough, either. They have to have your genetic code, or have come from your body, to be worth a lifetime of love."

The bald fury of his statement knocked her arguments down flat. "It...it's not that..."

"Isn't it?"

A lifetime of longing, of knowledge of what she'd always dreamed of having, withered and died before the raw pain in his eyes. She didn't know what to say. Nothing would make this right. How could she say it? *Tell me it's real—tell me you love me as much as you love Belinda. Tell me the grief I saw tonight wasn't the raw grief of a man still in love with his wife!*

Second best, always second best in her life. A life where she either replaced what she wanted with next best, or she *was* next best. She could never be the woman he'd loved since he was thirteen, but she could be a great wife and mother...a terrific *replacement.*

She couldn't do it. One of them she could handle, but both would break her in two.

"I'm sorry," she faltered, feeling more inadequate, more foolish than she ever had in her life. "There couldn't be a worse day for this..."

"There is no right day, Jennifer." He turned away, his body stiff, his face white. "I have to pull a miracle out of a hat to be good enough for you. The fact that you're leaving me the day I find out my wife's dead is beside the point. My falling in love with you was my decision, my problem. I'm a man and can handle losing you if I have to. But the fact that you made my kids love and rely on you—to look on you as a mother, when you never meant to stay—that I couldn't believe of you."

She stepped back, almost falling over, but found nothing to say. *Do you? Do you love me, Noah, now you know Belinda never left you, but died?* It rang in her mind, but somehow it seemed ridiculously selfish, given all he and his family had been through today.

He wouldn't even look at her now. "Did you ever think of what you were doing, Jennifer, in making three motherless kids love and depend on you? If you never intended to give us a chance, why didn't you keep a professional distance with them, like you do with the other kids?"

Her mind totally spaced on that. Suddenly it wasn't about her, but the kids—if she'd hurt them... "I...I didn't mean to...to—I thought..."

"What?"

"They—needed me more than the other kids," she faltered. "I just wanted to help. I thought of myself as a transitional mother—someone to help them heal. Then when you found them another mother, they'd be ready..."

"Very noble of you," he mocked quietly. "No, I'm sure you even believed it, for a while. But you must have seen how dependent they were becoming? You knew I wasn't playing games, either. I'm not that kind of man. So at what point did you start blinding yourself to the damage you could do to them, because you loved playing house with us? When did we become your disposable family? Did you set a date for when it would end, or was there a plan to introduce me to the kids' new mother at the right place and time?"

It was as if he was holding a mirror up to her face, and she could see herself clearly for the first time since Cody's death. She'd indulged in playing house with the Brannigans, without thinking of the long-term consequences to those adorable, motherless children—or to a man who had struggled for years on his own.

All she'd wanted to do was help, to be close to them; but

without meaning it, she'd played God with the Brannigan family, and it was they who would pay the price.

"Don't come back here, Jennifer. Don't come near me, or my kids, unless you intend to stay for life. Don't play house with us anymore. My kids aren't your dollies."

She'd never heard him so harsh, or inflexible. He meant every word. There'd be no more midnight kisses in her kitchen or on blankets; no more smiles, no hugs or childish chatter to fill her life. *No Noah.* No more words of love, whether she was the love of his life or second best.

It was over. She didn't deserve them.

With a tiny cry she turned and bolted out the door, and even made it to the back field before she started throwing up.

Six weeks later

"Dad, that's hot. You need the oven mitt." Tim raced over from the table to give Noah the protective cover.

"Thanks, mate," Noah said, realising what he'd been about to do. He put on the mitt before getting dinner out of the oven. He served up the food for them, and sat at the table, correcting the kids when they needed it, cutting up Rowdy and Cilla's food—but he didn't eat himself. The kind of kiddie food they liked best had lost its appeal six weeks ago.

He felt Tim watching him, with the same anxiety he'd been watching the past two weeks since coming back home from Sydney, where they'd had the funeral for Belinda. "Tim, you're not eating enough, matey," he said, to distract him.

"You aren't eating at all."

The aggressive tone startled him; Tim had been so quiet since they came home. Noah frowned and looked down at the food and pushed it away. "Just not hungry tonight, I guess."

"You haven't been hungry since we got home," Tim shouted. "You've been all weird for weeks, since you stopped being friends with Jen. If you want her back so bad, why don't you just go and get her?"

Rowdy burst into tears. Cilla sucked hard on her thumb… and they all looked at him like they expected him to make their lives right.

He was failing them all over again. Nothing was damned *right* since Jennifer refused him. His family was falling apart again…

Noah felt the blood drain from his face. "Stop it, Tim," he said, very quietly. "Stop it."

And he pushed back his chair and went outside to run again, up and down the field. He didn't leave them alone, but stayed where they could yell for him, but he ran and ran, and ran…

Five minutes later, Tim climbed out his bedroom window.

Noah was running again.

Jennifer closed her eyes. She had to stop watching the Brannigan house from the window, or she'd go insane…

But moments later, she was looking again. What else did she have to do?

It was only now that, when it was too late to change things, she knew how *empty* her life was without them. She'd gone back to quilting circle, took on more kids, went to church and the fundraising sessions and town improvement meetings, but none of it helped the tightness in her chest and the feeling that she wanted to be sick all the time. Veronica and Jessie had stopped making jokes about the sexy man next door weeks ago. They didn't mention him at all after the first night, when they'd seen her reaction.

There was nothing to say, nothing could help, and the ache in her heart just grew and grew, because unlike Cody, the people she loved were alive. She could be with them all now, if she hadn't been so blind and so stupid.

So go to him, go to them.

And say what? *I'm the world's prize idiot, I don't deserve any of you but I need and love you and please, please accept second best?*

Suddenly she squinted, concentrating. Yes, even from this distance, in the light of a strong full moon, she could see the small figure climbing out his window...

Jennifer closed her eyes, throwing up a brief prayer for him to come to her, and not to run away again.

It seemed she was answered. He came straight to the boundary fence and hopped over it, and ran to the verandah. "Jen! Jen," he whispered urgently. "Jen!"

She was at the door before the last call. Seeing the blazing intensity of his eyes—Noah's eyes—she gathered him into her arms. "Tim, what is it, sweetie?" She drew him inside the house. "Would you like a cookie?"

Tim shook his head, his gaze fixed on her. "Why aren't you our friend anymore?" he asked so bluntly Jennifer caught her breath. "Don't you love...um, Cilla and Rowdy anymore?"

Even amid a pain so strong it clawed at her heart, she wanted to smile; but she kept a straight face and said, "Of course I do, Tim—I love you all."

"Then why don't Cilla and Rowdy stay with you anymore? Why did Dad get someone else to finish the verandah and cubby house while we were gone? Why are you selling the house and going away? Why don't we have dinner here and play now? We—Cilla and Rowdy, I mean—miss it here! They miss you!"

The words were fierce with the pain he was trying so hard to hide—and her heart melted. "If your dad will let you come, Tim, you are always welcome here. Always."

But he didn't let her off the hook. "Why does Dad get so—so *sad* and white when we want to see you? He—he's as sad as Mummy used to be." The glitter in his eyes became full-blown tears and his mouth trembled. "I'm *scared*, Jen!" he wailed. "Daddy's not the same, and I can't make him better. He doesn't eat much and he just runs and runs and is sad all the time!"

Jennifer held him close, rocking him. "Oh, baby. Oh, Tim. I'm so sorry." She hesitated. "Is Daddy really so sad?" The boy nodded, his head against her breast, and she ached with sweetness—she loved this strong, vulnerable boy so much! "Do you think he's sad because of your mummy?"

Tim wrenched himself out of her arms. "No. I *know* it's 'cause he misses you. He won't even *look* over here. Cilla and Rowdy miss you. *Why* don't you come over, Jen?"

There was no way to avoid it; she must be honest. "Your dad wants to marry me, Tim, but I—I thought I couldn't do that."

"Why? Is—is it 'cause of me? 'Cause I've been so naughty?" Pleading eyes turned to her. "I can be good, Jen. I— I promise I'll be good."

"Oh, Tim!" She wrapped him close in her arms, kissing his forehead, his cheeks. "You *are* a good boy. It wasn't that—"

Tim's voice came out all muffled when he finally spoke. "I'm not a little kid anymore, Jen. I know you love Dad, 'cause you always look at him all goofy." Jennifer had to choke back the laughter and tears at once. "Why won't you be our mummy?" he cried again.

She hesitated. "It wasn't you, or your family. It's—it's me. I have a problem…"

"Can't you make it go away?" His voice was half-muffled in her shoulder.

"No," she said, sadness touching her soul at speaking of Cody, but with Tim in her arms, it didn't have that exquisite agony. "I—I lost my little boy a few years ago, you see. Cody died, like your mummy died. He was very sick. I have something wrong with me, you see. If I have more babies they could be sick, too. And—and that made me sad. I thought I'd miss it too much." *But not as much as I've missed all of you,* she suddenly thought.

Tim pulled back to look at her, his eyes desperate. "But that's not fair! Can't—can't Rowdy be like your little boy?

Can't he hug you and—and be like him? And Cilla could be your little girl? We *need* a mummy, Jen!" he cried, trembling all over with emotion. "Dad doesn't smile anymore, and—and Cilla's sucking her thumb all the time and climbin' trees again, and Rowdy just *cries*. He doesn't even wanna play anymore…" His tears spilled, and he dashed at them with a fist. "They *need* you, Jen. Please, won't you be our—I mean, their mummy? And be nice to Daddy again, and make him happy? If—if you want more hugs, I'd even give you some," he finished, his face filled with brave determination. "If you want *two* little boys, I can be your little boy, too."

Oh, the courage of this magnificent, hurting child! Out of the mouths of babes came truth—a truth that did indeed set her free.

She might never have the baby her heart craved, but if there was something the past six weeks had taught her, it was that life with the Brannigans held a joy that stopped it ever being second-best. She missed the hugs and kisses from the children, so much more so than any of the children she minded—

And it wasn't because they needed her: she needed them. From the first day, her heart had known what her stubborn mind refused to see. She'd loved them like a mother all along…and she loved Noah, loved him so much she felt dead inside without him.

She had two choices: she could have almost everything she'd ever wanted, or nothing at all—and nothing meant emptiness and regret for life. Almost everything was far better than second best. Just having Tim with her now, she *felt* like a mother. She felt *loved*.

"So you think your dad's missing me, sweetheart?" she asked softly, her heart racing. *With joy.* She was going home, home to her babies, to her beautiful Noah…

"I know he does. He gets so sad when we want to see you, and—" Tim's face lit up. "Jen?" he whispered, trembling with excitement.

Jen nodded, smiled and kissed him. "Tim, you are the best boy in the whole world, and I would be so proud to have you for one of my boys—but never a *little* boy. That can be Rowdy's job." She laughed at the relief lighting up his expressive eyes. "Can you climb back through that window, and do exactly what I ask you to do?"

CHAPTER FOURTEEN

THE fire had gone out again.

With a savage sound of impatience, Noah got out the box of fire-lighters again, and, giving up on economy, put four cubes under the logs at once, screwed up newspaper as well and put it everywhere, and lit it all. He stepped back, locked the fire guards into place and stood there watching, hands shoved in pockets and kicking at a piece of coal.

How could a life so full, with so little free time, still feel so empty?

Tim's words had been bashing around in his head like a hollow drum for the past hour or more. *If you want Jen back so bad, why don't you go and get her?*

Six weeks—such a short time, yet it felt like a year since he'd seen her.

He didn't look up the hill. He *didn't* look for her lights at night, and wonder if she'd come to him. It was obvious she was avoiding him. He knew better than to look. She hadn't changed her mind. She loved him, but not enough.

He might have looked for her during the first few days after they'd come back from the funeral, but not now.

What funeral? He thought grimly. What he'd done was formally identify his wife from her wedding-ring and rotten wallet, and arranged a travesty of a service because the police wouldn't release the remains for burial. She was still *an open case,* because of the letter...but the kids didn't need to know that.

Now Peter and Jan had begun a new crusade: finding Belinda's accidental killer. He didn't blame them for it. Parents always wanted justice and right for their children, and Peter and Jan's whole life had revolved around their daughter. He had more immediate priorities: his kids. He wasn't going to let his former parents-in-law damage the kids by talking of justice, or say their Mummy wasn't at peace yet, and why.

There were times when the fight just wasn't worth the cost.

He felt that Belinda was finally at peace with the finding of her body—but he wasn't. He'd said he could handle losing Jennifer— but all the way through the ordeal of looking at the wedding ring, the rotten wallet and the skeletal remains, and through a sham service with an empty coffin, a wailing son and dry-eyed, vengeful parents-in-law, all he could think was *why, Jennifer? Why the hell didn't you love me enough to be with me now?*

He'd thought he was strong enough. He'd lost the love of his young life and survived, and brought up his kids the best he could...but the pain of losing Jennifer was getting worse every damned day. He'd done all he could. He'd fought for her, he'd—

Hadn't he?

He blinked, and again. Had he fought, truly fought for Jennifer?

He hadn't been passive; he'd fought to make her love him— but had he left something, anything undone?

The past three or four years had taught him to put the kids above his own needs—they must come first. In submerging everything that made him a man for too long, he'd buried his wants, his desires—his *love*—for the sake of Tim's fears...

Even when he'd met Jennifer, and knew she loved him, when she'd made her decision to walk away, he'd let her do it. He'd let her go rather than risk it all, instead of truly fighting for her, because *the kids* would be hurt—

Rubbish. They were your excuse and you know it. You were too scared to be a man again...

If you want her so bad, go and get her!

With that the man in him roared to life—the man he'd lost to the father three years ago—and he would no longer be denied. What was he doing here alone, when the love of his life was five hundred feet away, loving him as he loved her?

Before he thought it through, he stalked through the door toward Jennifer's house. He'd do whatever it took to make her say yes. Failure wasn't an option.

"Dad!" called an imperative voice from the house. "Dad!"

Noah turned, but only for a moment. "No, Tim. Go back to bed. You're fine, and the kids are safe. I'll be back in fifteen minutes. I've got my phone if you need me."

"But I've got a surprise, Dad—it will make you happy—"

"It can wait," he shouted back, resuming his relentless stride.

"Where are you going, Dad?" Tim yelled, sounding frantic.

"To get Jennifer!" He didn't care at this point if Tim rebelled; his son *needed* Jennifer, even if he didn't know it yet.

But after a moment, a cry of "Waahoo!" came from the house. "Go, Dad, go get her!"

Despite his grim determination, a smile curved his mouth.

Lights were on in her house, but he didn't care if he woke her, or knocked the door down. If she was anything like him, she wasn't sleeping anyway. He hopped the boundary fence—

"Jennifer!" he roared as he strode up the stairs to the back door of the house he'd known as home from the first day. The *woman* he'd known was his the first day. "Jennifer!" He pounded on the door.

Moments later the door swung open, and a breathless woman in the throes of putting on lipstick and combing her hair at once, by the look of the things in her hand, gazed at him. The smile wavered on her lips, fear and joy at once, her whole face filled with love...*with love.* "Noah," she whispered, her eyes drinking him in with wide-eyed wonder and joy, like she was a kid having her first glimpse at Disneyland.

Without a word he scooped her against him and kissed her, deep, drugging kisses filled with demand. "You're mine," he growled between kisses. He moulded her body to his, curving his hand around her waist and hip until she moaned, dropped lipstick and hair comb, completely melted against him and kissed him back with the same insatiable hunger he felt. "I *love* you, and you love me and you're going to marry me. I won't give you up for a dream you can't even have. I won't give you up because you think you're not enough for us. You are—you *love* my kids and they love you, and it's more than enough. We belong together—you, me, the kids—all of us. I'm not asking you to marry me—I'm *telling* you."

She pulled back, her eyes shining. "Yes, Noah," she said softly. "Yes."

He made another growling sound and kissed her again. "You'd better mean it, because I'm taking it as a promise. We're getting the rings tomorrow, and I'm calling my parents to fly home. We'll need them to mind the kids while we're on our honeymoon."

Jennifer gave a low, throaty laugh that made his body tighten even more. "Yes, darling," she murmured with a teasing wink. "And are you going to tell me when the wedding is and where? My brother and sisters and their families might want to come to my wedding, and my parents will need to fly home, too."

He grinned and kissed her again, deep and hot, until they forgot the questions for a while. "Thirty-four days," he whispered against her mouth. "We get the licence tomorrow, and marry the day we legally can. And—" thinking on his feet had worked quite well in the past half hour "—how does the Barrier Reef sound for a honeymoon? We could get my parents to mind the kids on a family-friendly resort, and we could sail around the islands. We could visit them every few days, and be close enough for contact…"

"And still have time alone," she whispered, her eyes shining. "I can't wait." Her kiss was deep, with an urgency that told him the past weeks had been as hard for her as for him. "I love you so much, Noah. I've missed you like crazy."

"I can tell." He grinned down at her, but with a strange feeling inside. He supposed simple family happiness was something he'd have to get used to again—but he didn't think it would be very hard. Not with Jennifer as his wife.

She laughed again, and buffed him lightly on the chin. "Let's go tell the kids."

"I thought you'd make it harder for me than this," he said after the next kiss, as he turned her around, heading for his house.

"You underrate yourself," she said quietly. "There hasn't been a day, an hour, when I haven't wanted to turn the clock back and say yes, or run over to you. I've missed you so much."

He helped her over the fence, not because she needed it, but he wouldn't let go of her for a moment. "You could have come to me." But right now, the past didn't matter; she was where he needed her to be—with him, loving him. It was enough. More than enough.

"I couldn't. I didn't know if you loved me, Noah—not after you knew Belinda didn't leave you," she said quietly. "You said the words, but I didn't *feel* them. Probably because I didn't believe I was worthy of you. I thought—if you missed me enough, if you loved me enough, you'd come to me. And you did…"

He stopped, turned her in his arms and cupped her face in his hands. "Jennifer," he whispered. "Jennifer." The long, tender kiss showed her without words just what she meant to him. "Even if she'd been alive, I couldn't have gone back. I'm not the boy she married anymore—and the man I've become is yours. I knew it even as Fred told me she was gone. I thought you knew it, too."

She shook her head. "That night…what you said. I felt so ashamed, Noah." Her voice quivered with shame through the happiness. "I was selfish, punishing all of us for a dream I can't do anything to change. I didn't feel like I deserved you all."

He nuzzled her throat. "I'll remind you of that every time we fight, or the kids play up," he said, his voice filled with sudden laughter, and she wrapped herself around him, chuckling and kissing him. "But you said 'didn't' deserve me. Seriously, what changed your mind?"

"Not what—who," she murmured through kisses to his throat, making him groan with pleasures to come. "You should be very proud of your oldest son. He proposed to me on your behalf thirty minutes ago—for your sake, and for Cilla and Rowdy. He was worried about you all, and I knew that in punishing myself, I was only hurting us all. He showed me that I *am* their mother already, whether I deserved it or not. He also told me how much you were missing me," she added with an impish note in her voice. "I'll remind you of *that* every time we fight."

He grinned again. "So that was Tim's surprise just now? You were coming to me?"

"Yup. You've raised an amazing boy, Mr. Brannigan."

"He's got a lot of raising time yet, Mrs. Brannigan-to-be," he said, just to hear the sound of it. "Jennifer Brannigan."

"Jennifer Louisa Millicent Brannigan." She rolled her eyes. "What a mouthful…but it'll be worth it, to have you."

And they stopped for another kiss, the passion leaving them breathless and aching.

The door opened before they could knock. Joyful screams came the moment the light from inside the house spilled over them. A pyjama-clad Cilla and Rowdy, tousled, bright-eyed and eager, jumped into Jennifer's arms, squealing and asking when they could call her Mummy and when they were coming back to her place every day.

Jennifer staggered back a little under the combined weight of the kids, her eyes alight with joy. "Right now for both, if you want to," she replied, winking at Tim, blowing a kiss in his direction. "Tim, being a big boy, might want to keep calling me Jen?" She turned to the little kids, hugging and kissing them, telling them how *much* she'd missed them…leaving Tim to make his own decision, in his way and time.

Noah swallowed a lump in his throat at her understanding, loving Tim just as he was without trying to change him. How did he ever get so lucky?

"I woke the kids to tell them," Tim told Noah importantly, with a massive grin. A grin still touched with sorrow—he had some healing yet to do. But after his unselfish act tonight, Noah had no doubt his son would make it—that they'd all make it now. With Jennifer by his side, his family would be just fine…and he'd be the happiest man alive.

The first miracle at the March house had been the woman who lived inside it—and the second, that she'd needed them as much as they needed her; that she loved him as he loved her. He didn't need to ask for a third miracle: he knew they'd love each other, be a family for life.

Jennifer smiled at him, as if knowing what he was thinking, and announced, "It's celebration time—and I have loads of ice cream and cookies in my freezer! We're going to have a late-night snack, just for the fun of it. Go sit at the table, and Dad and I will be there in a minute. Tim, can you get the stuff out for me?"

"Sure, Jen," Tim grinned. "Let's go, kids!"

Cilla and Rowdy hurrahed, and then bolted after Tim toward Jennifer's house, leaving them alone.

A pair of warm, loving arms slipped around his waist. Noah turned in her arms, smiling down into her glowing face. "What is it?" he asked, seeing she needed to say something.

She hugged him, but bit her lip. "I adore the kids—you know that—but I'm not marrying you for them. You know that, don't you?" Her gaze on his was a touch anxious.

He grinned. "With the way you look at me, and touch me?

I know you're marrying me for my body." And he laughed as she swatted him.

"The worst thing is you're partly right. I can hardly wait to get you naked," she murmured in his ear, sending shudders of need, of desire, all the way through him. "I'm going to be a demanding wife, love."

"The kids are waiting for ice cream and you say that to me? You're killing me, woman," he groaned.

"I'll make it up to you." Her eyes shone with promise. "Just as soon as we're alone…"

"Dad! Jen! Ice cream! Cookies, Mummy!"

The cries from three young throats broke the frantic kiss. They leaned on each other's foreheads, smiling, knowing this was life as it was meant to be. Then she whispered, "Race you!" and they headed for the house, toward kids and cookies and ice cream and love.

For home.

* * * * *

The Nanny Solution

TERESA
HILL

Teresa Hill lives within sight of the mountains in upstate South Carolina, with one husband, very understanding and supportive; one daughter, who's taken up drumming (Earplugs really don't work that well. Neither do sound-muffling drum pads. Don't believe anyone who says they do.); and one son, who's studying the completely incomprehensible subject of chemical engineering (Flow rates, Mum. It's all about flow rates).

In search of company while she writes away her days in her office, she has so far accumulated two beautiful, spoiled dogs and three cats (the black panther/champion hunter, the giant powder puff and the tiny tiger stripe), all of whom take turns being stretched out, belly-up, on the floor beside her, begging for attention as she sits at her computer.

To the woman in my life we all call Nannie,
My grandmother, Lurene Haggard,
In honour of her eighty-fourth birthday.

Chapter One

"You look like a nun in that outfit!"

Audrey Graham sighed and turned around to face what might be her only friend left in the world, sixty-something, maybe even seventy-something, Marion Givens, her inspiration, best cheerleader, landlady and now unofficial job counselor.

"Thank you, I think," Audrey said.

She'd wrapped herself from head to toe in the thick, concealing fabric of what she considered a neat, maybe even stylish designer warm-up suit, if there was such a thing as a truly stylish warm-up suit.

"It wasn't a compliment," Marion said. "Although with that face, I have to say you're much too pretty to be a nun, at least. But from the back…"

Audrey frowned at her own reflection in the mirror.

She'd cut her long, brown hair six weeks ago in a fit of…needing to be different, she supposed, different in every way. It was curlier than it had been, now that it wasn't so heavy and long, and it bounced around her face constantly. There was just no taming it, but she didn't really spend any time on it, which was what she'd been going for.

Sometimes she thought it looked cute.

Hoped it didn't look sexy.

She hadn't worn any make-up this morning, not really, just some lip gloss and mascara, and she looked like…

Audrey just didn't know.

Not like her old self, that was for sure.

Younger than she would have thought she could look, although she hadn't been going for that, either.

She'd been hoping for…invisibility or something along those lines.

"I hear nuns have very peaceful lives," Audrey said, grabbing her purse and fishing for her keys. "Peace sounds good to me. Although at the moment, I'm scared to death. I haven't gone on a job interview in nearly twenty years."

She'd been nineteen and looking for a job waiting tables at a place where she was really too young to work, a place where the wait staff wore low-cut tops and little, bitty skirts and the tips were really good.

She'd gotten the job.

Now forty was fast approaching—God, how did that happen?—and she was covering up as much of her skin as possible.

'Bout time, Audrey.

"I don't think the interview process has changed all that much," Marion said, trying to reassure her.

"You're sure he really needs somebody? This is not some kind of favor you called in, some make-work kind of thing?"

"I'm sure. He's desperate. He was practically babbling when I ran into him at the restaurant—and this is a man who does not babble. Not ever. Plus, honey, remember the most important thing—he lives in the perfect place."

Only five blocks from Audrey's daughter.

She hated Audrey at the present, but she was still here.

Audrey hadn't dreamed of being able to be that close to Andie. She never could have afforded it on her own.

"Okay, I'm ready," Audrey said, glancing at her watch. She had to go.

"Relax," Marion told her. "Breathe. He's not an ogre, and he's not brusque. Not really. Just rushed. Always rushed. Don't waste his time. Don't chitchat. He hates it when people do that. And don't kiss up to him. He hates that, too."

"Does he like anything?" Audrey asked, even more nervous now.

"Peace. He told me he just needs some peace and quiet, and you can give him that." Marion looked like she'd surprised even herself. "Maybe the nun outfit was a good idea after all."

Audrey's hand gripped the steering wheel like a woman facing near-certain death.

Much as she desperately wanted to see her daughter, she hated coming to this part of town. In fact, she didn't come here. Dreaded facing the people here.

Well, she'd just have to get over that.

Because Audrey's ex-husband wasn't really interested in being a father anymore, even if Andie was living with him now. Andie would figure out that she really couldn't count on her father before long, and then…

She'd have to turn back to her mother, wouldn't she?

Audrey was counting on it.

Honestly, time and proximity were her only hope.

Andie might not forgive her, but she'd need a mother, and Audrey intended to be as close as possible when that happened.

Which meant, she needed this job.

She took the turn onto Maple Street, gripped the steering wheel so hard she was surprised it didn't snap in two as she passed the entrance to her old neighborhood, then heard nothing but her own heart pounding in her ears.

Breathe, she reminded herself.

You're not that woman anymore, Audrey.

Not that wounded.

Not that angry.

Not that self-destructive.

The pounding eased just a bit.

Nineteen years of careful, predictable, perfectly acceptable behavior, building a good life, what she thought was a reasonably good marriage and a mostly happy family, and she'd thrown it all away in a fit of outrage and bewilderment last fall after her husband walked out on them.

It was as if the nineteen years counted for nothing, and all that she was was the woman she'd become in those raw, painful days and nights. While her husband walking away from her and Andie seemed perfectly acceptable.

Audrey closed her eyes again, breathing.

You're not that woman anymore.

At the end of the block, she turned into the older, more traditional neighborhood of Highland Park. She'd known a bit of what to expect from living nearby for so long. But as she got closer, she realized that Simon Collier lived in the really fancy, older section of the neighborhood, in which the homes were practically estates.

Wow.

Impressive.

She was surprised he hadn't put up a wall with a gate at the entrance, as some of his neighbors had.

The house was a huge, imposing structure of weathered gray stone soaring three stories high, the grounds extensive, if a bit…unkept-looking here and there.

She drove up the long, winding driveway and parked outside the two-story, four-car garage, got out of her car and looked at her watch.

Right on time.

In fact, she was all of two minutes early.

Cutting it too close for comfort, actually, but she'd nearly panicked trying to get out the door at Marion's, and it had slowed her down.

Precisely at 7:00 a.m., the first bay of the garage opened, and standing there beside a sleek, black Lexus convertible stood a man in an elegant, crisp, dark suit, white shirt, blue tie, shoes polished until they shined.

Simon Collier, she presumed.

It was a little scary how he appeared out of the darkness of the garage with the precision of a magician just as the big hand on her watch ticked onto 7:00 a.m.

Still, neat trick.

It helped her to smile just a bit, despite feeling as if she wanted to throw up. As she walked forward, she decided her best bet was pretending he was a very important client of her ex-husband's, coming to dinner at their home, and it was up to her to make sure he felt comfortable and had a good time.

She stuck out a perfectly manicured hand—her one beauty-vice left—and said, "Mr. Collier? I'm Audrey Graham. Nice to meet you."

He took her hand and looked as if he approved, most likely of her promptness and that she'd made no attempt to chitchat, if Marion knew him as well as she claimed to.

Audrey was still just trying to breathe normally.

Her eyes finally adjusted from the brightness of the morning sunshine to the shadows of the garage, and she realized he was a breathtaking man.

He was beautifully dressed, the suit obviously cut to hug a perfectly proportioned body, handsomely groomed, his hand strong and sure as it gripped hers for a moment, then withdrew.

He had jet-black hair, still thick and full, perfectly tamed, dark eyes with little lines at the corners and a polite smile. He managed to look elegant, pampered even, and yet most thoroughly a man.

Younger than she'd expected, too. The more her eyes became accustomed to the light, the better and younger he looked.

She'd never expected this, given the neighborhood where he lived, the way Marion talked about him with something akin to awe and getting the definite impression that the man was worth a lot of money.

Sixty and balding with a potbelly would have been just fine with her.

Great, even.

But not this.

"Ms. Graham. You're right on time. Good. I'm sorry, but I have very little time this morning, which is almost always the case. We should get right to this."

"Of course," she agreed.

"I have four problems in my life right now, Audrey. May I call you Audrey?"

"Please," she said.

"Good. Please call me Simon. As I was saying, four problems. I don't like problems. I make it my business to solve problems, and right now I have four. Four is very bad."

"I'm sorry," she said, not knowing how else to reply to his crisp stating of facts.

"Don't be. I'm counting on you to solve three of those four problems for me. You understand this is a live-in position?"

"Yes."

"Excellent. My first problem is the yard. Marion tells me you used to have the prettiest yard in the Mill Creek."

"I…" What did one say to that? She settled for, "People seemed to like it."

"She gave me the address. I drove by yesterday to take a

look. It was very nice. Not too fussy, not too… regimented. Big, lush, greening up already, even this time of year. You could do something like that, here?"

"Of course. But you should know, I don't have any formal training in landscaping—"

"I don't care," he said, extending a hand in the direction of the front yard, and Audrey took off in that direction with him following her. "I've hired three landscape architects so far. I haven't liked any plan they've shown me, and they've wasted a great deal of my time. You planned and planted the yard at your former home? And maintained it yourself?"

"Yes."

"Good. I want something like that. Something…normal looking. Not regimented. Not odd. Normal and green. Now, I want us to work together like this. I don't want to be bothered with details. I want you to handle problems on their own as they come up. Give me a plan to look at, a budget to approve, and then do whatever it takes to make it happen. Understood?"

"Yes," she said, trying not to sound scared out of her mind at the fact that three landscape architects hadn't been able to please him and yet he expected her to do so, without any of the formal training they had.

And at the way the man issued orders.

Not in a mean way, just…as if he assumed every word would be obeyed, every expectation met without question.

They made it to the front yard, and he moved quickly, almost soundlessly in front of her, grabbing her by the arms to steady her when her own momentum would have propelled her forward.

"Sorry," he said, giving her an exasperated smile, letting her go and stepping back immediately.

Up that close, she thought he definitely wasn't old.

There'd been a flash of an impression of power and the firm, muscular build that few men had once they hit middle age.

And the eyes, with those little, crinkly lines at their

corners... Maybe they'd led her to believe he was older than he actually was.

Was he even forty?

Audrey looked up at him, feeling every one of her thirty-nine years and wishing all the more that he was sixty and balding.

She wasn't doing this again, wasn't throwing herself at a man, thinking it was the way to forget all her problems, to solve them, to make everything right again.

He looked nearly as taken aback as she felt and went still for a second once he'd let go of her, as if he might have actually lost track of the orders he was firing off for a moment.

"Sorry," he said again, recovering before she did. "I was afraid you were going to hurt yourself."

He looked down toward her feet. There, mere inches in front of her, was a narrow, deep hole dug into his front lawn.

"This is my second problem," he said.

"A hole in the ground?" She was lost.

"A number of them, all over the place. You really have to be careful walking out here. I don't want you to break a bone. The last landscaper did. He's trying to sue me right now. One more thing I have no time for."

"Oh," Audrey said. "I'll be careful. You have some kind of...animal problem?"

"A dog," he said, as if the mere word implied something vile. "It digs."

Audrey worked to keep a straight face.

A mere dog could get the best of this perfectly controlled, very powerful man?

So he was human, after all.

He looked as if he knew she was thinking of laughing in his face and didn't believe for a minute she'd actually do it, that anyone would.

Audrey wiped every trace of amusement from her face, and then watched in amazement as his own mouth started to twitch;

he shook his head and swore so softly she wasn't sure she could even make out the words.

"Yes, I know, bested by a dog. I realize how ridiculous that is. Nevertheless, this is the state in which I find myself. I despise the dog. The dog despises me. We have been waging war for weeks, and the dog is winning. You have no idea how much it pains me to admit this—"

"Oh, I think I do," Audrey said.

Once again, the ends of his mouth threatened to curl upward a bit. She could almost feel him battling the impulse, before tamping it down and banishing it completely.

He cleared his throat and went on. "Marion also said you had a very well-behaved dog."

"We had a wonderful dog. She died two years ago."

"She didn't dig up things in your very well-designed yard?" he asked.

"She had a small corner of it where she was allowed to bury her bones. Would that be acceptable? One small, out-of-the-way spot where such things are allowed?"

He sighed. "If it's absolutely necessary."

"I think it probably is," Audrey said.

"Fine," he said, as if he'd just agreed to millions of dollars in concessions on a contract he was negotiating. "The dog belongs to my daughter, Peyton. She loves the dog, much more than she loves me at the moment. I'm not proud of it, but I'll admit, I tried to buy her affections with the dog and to some extent it worked. She's very happy to come here now. The problem is her mother only allows her to come for a weekend here and there, and the dog is here all the time. Because Peyton's mother decreed that the dog could not go to her house with Peyton. I think just to torment me even more than my ex-wife already has, and if that's the case, she's succeeded beautifully because the dog has wreaked havoc on my entire home life."

"I'm so sorry," Audrey said, surprised he'd admitted to so

many of his own weaknesses—the child he indulged and the ex-wife who's needling still got to him—so forthrightly. Most men wouldn't have, would have relished seeming invincible. And there was something in his manner that Audrey imagined could be thoroughly intimidating but she found oddly amusing.

And there was something else. The distinct impression that while the situation at hand was annoying, he knew he would triumph in the end. As if it was a secret he knew, one that kept him calm and able to deal with just about anything.

Except a dog.

"It's here all the time," he complained. "It digs. It eats my socks. It ate my favorite pair of shoes, makes all sorts of noise at all hours and generally makes a nuisance of itself. I'm afraid it hasn't been successfully housetrained, either."

Audrey nodded, hopefully giving the situation the proper gravity he thought it deserved. "I assume you've tried dog trainers with no success?"

He gave her a pained look. "Three."

And they'd all just annoyed him and wasted his time, as had the poor, unfortunate, would-be landscapers. She wondered how Simon Collier acted when he was truly annoyed. If the earth literally shook or something?

"Again, I really don't have any formal training in… training animals," Audrey began.

He shot her a look that said 1) he obviously knew this. 2) they'd covered this point before, and he'd pronounced already that he didn't care about formal training, and 3) he didn't care to repeat himself.

"Okay," Audrey said. "I'm to train the dog."

He nodded, no doubt satisfied that he hadn't had to repeat himself further and she hadn't wasted any more of his time.

"Just so you know, it eats bushes, too." He pointed to an unfortunate azalea, which she assumed was the dog's latest victim. "It eats vines, flowers, everything. The dog eats it, chews it enough to kill it or pulls it out and drags it around the yard, in addition to digging in unexpected spots. Something else you'll have to contend with."

"Does the dog have a name?" Audrey asked.

"I call it any number of things," he said, dry as could be, but amusement flashing beneath the surface.

Audrey was sure of it.

And she wondered for a second, in that flash of humor, if he was even younger.

Thirty-eight?

Thirty-six?

She suddenly felt ancient, envying him the utter confidence, the air of power, the obvious wealth and all the security she imagined it would bring, that he didn't depend on anyone to secure his own future except himself. The kind of security that could not be taken away.

How would it feel to have that and know that no one could take it away?

"What does your daughter call the dog?" Audrey tried.

He made a face, distaste obvious, and reluctantly admitted, "Tinker Bell is its formal name."

Audrey made a choking sound as she tried as hard as she could not to laugh, then covered her mouth and coughed—she hoped realistically—and then finally managed pure silence.

It was hard, but she managed it.

His mouth settled into a hard, straight line. "We've settled on Tink for short. It's the most dignified thing we could come up with, given what we had to work with."

Audrey nodded, afraid to even try to speak.

"I suppose I'll be forced to introduce the two of you before you agree to take this on," he said, then waited and waited.

Hoping she'd say she didn't have to actually meet the dog first?

Should she agree to that?

Did she want the job that badly?

Audrey feared she did.

Then he saved her by saying, "But my business experience tells me to do everything I can to sell you on the job before you meet the dog. Shall I show you the living quarters?"

"Please," Audrey said.

He lifted his arm, gesturing for her to head back the way they had come. "And on the way, I'll tell you my third problem. My housekeeper, Ms. Bee. I adore her."

"Really?"

He liked someone.

What a surprise.

"Yes," he said, one end of his mouth actually curling up just a bit, as if he'd actually thought of smiling. "People may tell you that I'm…difficult. Demanding. Unreasonable. That there isn't a woman alive who could live happily with me. It simply isn't true. Ms. Bee and I get along beautifully."

Chapter Two

So people talked about Simon Collier, too, and he obviously didn't like it. Audrey thought about telling him she understood and wouldn't listen to the gossip.

Except in all of the ten minutes she'd spent with him, she was fairly certain no woman would have an easy time living with him. She'd figured out all on her own that he was certainly demanding, precise to the point of perfectionism, and that from his youngest days, probably wouldn't have gotten the little check mark in the box titled Plays Well with Others.

Women included.

Of course not. He'd have all the power, and they'd have none.

Audrey had been in a relationship like that, and look how badly it had tuned out.

But this was about him and his Ms. Bee.

"I'm very happy for the two of you," Audrey said.

He gave her a wry smile. "We've been together for ten years. Our relationship has lasted much longer than my marriage, and we understand each other perfectly. She's precise, careful, orderly. Runs my house like a machine. Anything inside those walls is her domain. You are not to interfere in the least or question her or bother her, because I can't imagine living without her. I don't want to."

"Okay," Audrey said.

But what did she have to do with his love for his housekeeper?

"Unfortunately Ms. Bee—that's Peyton's name for her—hates the dog, if possible even more than I do," he said.

"Oh." Audrey got it.

"She threatened to leave me if I didn't get rid of the dog. I confess, I considered telling Peyton it ran away and that I couldn't find it or that it got hit by a car. But then she'd cry, and I hate it when my daughter cries. But I refuse to live without Ms. Bee, either."

"I understand."

"I promised her I would find someone to fix the dog, that she would never have to have anything to do with it again. It's the only way I could get her to stay. Which is where you come in. You're to see that the dog never bothers Ms. Bee, which is why I need someone to live on the premises."

They reached the side of the garage, and he led her up a set of stairs on the side of the building that led to the second floor and a door; he unlocked it and stepped back, letting her go inside first.

It was an open, L-shaped space, tastefully, if sparsely, furnished, a living room, small dining area and kitchen, obviously the recent recipient of Ms. Bee's attentions, because it was absolutely spotless. The hardwood floors gleamed, as did the countertops and the appliances.

The walls were a light, cheery butter-cream, and there were tons of windows that looked out over the backyard.

Audrey stuck her head in the door opposite the kitchen and found a bedroom and nicely appointed bathroom.

"The previous owners had a son in college who lived here, I believe, when he no longer wanted to live at home, precisely," Simon said. "I hope it's acceptable?"

"It's perfect," Audrey said.

Much more than she'd expected to be able to afford on her own, given her lack of experience at anything and lack of formal job training.

"So, you can fix the lawn, fix the dog and keep it from bothering Ms. Bee?"

She took a leap of faith.

Either that or told a full-blown lie born of the desperation to be near her daughter.

"I'm sure I can," she said.

"Excellent." He named a salary she thought was more than fair, given the fact that she'd be living here for free. "When can you start?"

"When would you like?" she asked.

"I suppose this instant is out of the question, given the fact that you need time to move your things in. Dare I hope, tomorrow?"

"You don't want any references or a résumé—?"

He shook his head. "Marion vouched for you. That's all I need."

Audrey nodded. "Did she tell you... I mean, you should know—"

"You're one of her strays, aren't you? Had some problems? Trying to get your life back together? And she's taken you in for a while?"

"Yes." He *did* know Marion well.

"Have you ever been arrested?" he asked.

"No, I haven't," she said.

"And Marion wouldn't let you stay at her house unless you were clean and sober now, so... Good enough. I don't need the details. I just need someone to fix my three problems. You're going to do that for me?"

"Yes, I am," Audrey agreed.

"Excellent." He handed her the keys to the apartment, turned and started walking away, still talking to her.

Audrey hurried to follow.

"I'll leave you to introduce yourself to Ms. Bee. She's in the kitchen, expecting you. She'll give you all the details you need," he said, waiting for her to lock the door behind her.

"Thank you. I really appreciate it," Audrey said.

"No, thank *you*. You're going to make my life much easier."

Audrey nodded.

"The dog should be returning any moment. We hired a dog walker, hoping we could survive the week that way. Yes, here they come."

Audrey followed him down the stairs and waited as a young woman in shorts and a T-shirt came up the walk, half-dragged by what looked like a long-haired, mostly black-and-white, wiry but overgrown puppy, maybe six months old.

Although having just returned from its morning walk, the dog looked as if it had just gotten out of bed and was ready to run a marathon, looked hopeful that the opportunity might be offered. Its mouth stretched wide, it appeared to be smiling, happy and eager to take on the entire world, and as it got closer, Audrey could see its beautiful coat was shot through with silver.

He was striking looking.

The young woman said, "Hello, Mr. Collier," and tried to turn over the leash to him, but he waved it off, motioning for her to give it to Audrey.

The dog's tail whipped back and forth madly. It made a happy, yipping sound, then eased up on its back legs until it was standing practically straight up and rested its paws on Audrey's thighs, mouth open, tongue lolling out in greeting.

Simon Collier grimaced and said, "Sorry," then turned his attentions to dismissing the dog walker.

Audrey smiled, looked right into the dog's eyes as she gently pushed it back and onto all four feet. She knelt on one knee, bringing herself to eye level with Simon Collier's nemesis.

"Hello, Tink."

Tink's grin got even wider. The dog put his overgrown paws on her bent knee and then eased up to lick her cheek excitedly.

Simon made a sound of pure disgust.

"We're going to be friends," Audrey whispered to the dog, hoping it was true. Her job depended on it, after all, and the poor baby probably didn't have any friends at all, except for Peyton Collier.

She stood up. Tink reared up and did a little dance of pure excitement but didn't jump on Audrey, which she took as a sign of intelligence and eagerness to please.

"That's nice," Audrey complimented. "You can dance."

"You're not going to change your mind, are you?" Simon asked, as the dog walker turned and left.

"No, but why in the world did you get a border collie?"

"Because my daughter thought it was cute, and the woman who sold it to us claimed it was a smart dog, although I haven't seen any sign of that. Why?" He looked worried. "Border collies are bad?"

"Not if you want an animal that was bred to herd sheep all day without getting tired," Audrey informed him.

He froze for a moment. "You're telling me I need to buy it a herd of sheep to keep it happy?"

Audrey burst out laughing. "No, just that this animal has a great deal of energy, which is why it seems destructive to you. It's bored, probably extremely bored. It needs something to do."

Simon frowned. "What does it do besides herd sheep?"

"Exercise. I'll run with Tink every morning. Maybe in the evening, too, if I have to. The dog will be too tired to cause trouble."

"That's all it needs? To be too tired to cause trouble?"

"That should go a long way toward solving your problems

with Tink. The good news is the person you bought the dog from is right—dogs of this breed are known for being very intelligent."

"This one is not," Simon insisted.

Audrey laughed again, petting the dog, who'd jumped back up and planted its paws on her, wanting to be close and unable to contain its excitement.

"See," Simon said.

Audrey gave a little push against the dog's furry chest and said, "Tink, off."

The dog went down and stood there looking up at her, tail wagging, whole body practically trembling with excitement, but it stayed on all fours.

"Good dog," Audrey said, wishing she had some kind of treat to offer.

"He most certainly is not," Simon said.

"So it's a he?" Audrey sighed and turned from the overeager dog to the all-powerful man. "Well, he is smart enough to know you don't like him—"

"Then he's a genius," Simon quipped.

Audrey fought a grin once again. "And by now Tink probably knows just how to get to you."

Simon looked incredulous. "You're trying to tell me I've been playing mind games with a dog?"

Audrey just looked at him.

"And you think the little devil is winning, don't you?" Simon Collier looked as if she might have just called him a whiny, little girl or something equally offensive.

"I'm saying the dog feels the animosity between the two of you, and it's not helping the situation. Try to be the bigger man here. How about that?" Audrey said, hoping she wouldn't completely alienate him before she even started the job.

"And how," he asked, looking not at all pleased, "would the bigger man behave here?"

"He'd realize this is a battle he doesn't care to fight—"

"You want me to walk away from a fight?" he asked, incredulous again.

"I'm saying that Marion told me you detest wasting time, above all else. Surely you see it's a complete waste of your time to play mind games with this animal. It's completely beneath you. Go take over a country or something. Isn't that more your kind of challenge?"

He looked taken aback and stared at her as if he might be truly seeing her for the first time and found someone worthy of his notice.

Oh, Lord.

Was he furious?

She couldn't tell.

Finally, as snotty as you please, he said, "I don't happen to own any countries."

Then he burst out laughing, and Audrey could breathe again.

"I think we're going to enjoy working together, Audrey. I'll see you Friday evening when I get back into town."

He strode into the garage, got into that sleek, beautiful, black Lexus that looked like a very pretty, fancy toy, whipped it out of the garage and down the driveway and was off.

The dog started crying pitifully and dancing on his hind legs again, obviously feeling he deserved Audrey's complete attention.

Damn, Audrey thought.

What had she gotten herself into?

Simon couldn't get the sight of her out of his head, even though she'd covered herself up from head to toe. Which was a damned shame, he thought, to cover up a body like that.

He picked up his phone as he drove down the road and called Marion.

"You didn't tell me she was gorgeous," he told Marion.

She laughed. "Since when have you needed me or anyone else to tell you a woman is gorgeous?"

Simon put the phone aside and swore softly.

Marion laughed some more.

"I really don't need this right now. I still haven't gotten myself untangled from the last woman I allowed into my life."

"Believe me, you are the last kind of man Audrey Graham wants, which means you're perfectly safe with her."

"And why wouldn't she want me?" he bristled. "I'm a helluva catch."

Any rich man was. Rich, single and under forty made it doubly so. It wasn't his ego talking, simply the facts. There would always be a supply of women who wanted a man with money, and Simon had loads of it.

"I make it a point not to spread tales about other people's business, Simon. You know that. But I'm sure Audrey would be much more comfortable with you knowing that she just got rid of a man like you and doesn't want another one."

"What do you mean, by 'like me'? Sweet tempered and sexy?"

"Oh, yes. Those are exactly the words that come to mind when I think about you," Marion said. "Although, I have to say, you seem to be in a much better mood than usual. Are you feeling all right?"

"It's temporary, I'm sure."

It was the idea of someone taming the monster-dog, making Peyton happy, making Ms. Bee happy and ensuring she didn't quit that was easing all of Simon's headaches.

Or maybe it was just meeting a gorgeous, dark-haired woman with a little attitude who clearly wasn't afraid to go toe-to-toe with him that was causing his good mood.

There weren't a lot of women who'd dare.

Or who could make him laugh as he had with her.

"I just need someone to fix the dog and the yard," he said, maybe to remind himself even more than Marion.

"And that's exactly what I found you," she claimed.

"You wouldn't try to fix me up with her, right? You know better than that."

Ms. Bee probably *was* the only woman alive who could live happily with him. He accepted that, was fine with it.

Life was so much less complicated that way.

"It wouldn't matter if I was. I told you, she most certainly does not want a man in her life right now."

Which was a damned shame, Simon thought, though he certainly shouldn't.

He liked a woman who wasn't intimidated by him, who could spit fire every now and then.

Especially in his bed.

Audrey still couldn't believe she'd actually done it!

She'd gotten a job! One that came with a place to live that was tantalizingly near her daughter.

The first step of many toward getting back into her daughter's life.

Not even meeting the ultrascary Ms. Bee could ruin this day.

And Ms. Bee was ultrascary.

Frosty as a cold north wind, squinty-eyed, rail-thin with a spine as straight as a ruler and if possible, even more adept at firing off orders than her employer.

She'd allowed Audrey entrance into her spotless, cavernous kitchen only long enough to get her social security number and reiterate her hatred of the dog and all that Audrey was expected to do without bothering or causing any additional problems for the man of the house or Ms. Bee.

And Audrey was most definitely not to get any ideas about causing the kind of trouble that involved an unworthy woman trying to get her hands on Simon Collier.

Audrey tried to assure Ms. Bee that she wanted no kind of trouble at all in her life at present. She didn't think Ms. Bee was convinced.

"Whew," she said to herself when she finally escaped the confines of the kitchen and was safely in the backyard again.

Good thing she wasn't here to make friends.

She was headed for her car to leave when Tink, who'd been sleeping under a nearby tree, lifted his head and came bounding toward her as if the dog had experienced more than enough of Ms. Bee and couldn't bear the thought of Audrey leaving him all alone with her.

He promptly jumped up on Audrey, barking excitedly and trying to lick her face again.

Audrey had to work to put on a somewhat stern face and say, "Off," while giving the dog a little push until he was on all fours again.

Then she knelt down beside him and scratched his pretty black head.

"I have to go, but it's only going to be for a little while. I promise. And then I'll be back, and you and I are going to be buddies," she told him.

He made a half-crying sound, as if he understood that she was leaving and thought he might convince her to stay.

"Oh, baby," she said, knowing what it was like to feel all alone in the world and unloved. "I just have to get my clothes and some shoes, a few CDs, some gardening books, maybe some treats for you, and then I'll be here all the time."

More crying.

Pathetic crying.

The dog could really turn on the sympathy cries when he wanted to.

"I'm sorry. I have to go." Audrey kissed him on the snout, then stood up to go.

Tink started barking like crazy.

She couldn't shush him fast enough.

Ms. Bee appeared in the open back door of the house, a

scowl on her stern face, clearly ready to rebuke the dog until she saw Audrey and turned her scorn to the adult in the group.

"Oh," she said. "You're still here."

And then she gave a rather theatrical huff, as if it were an insult that Audrey hadn't left quickly enough, and she stood even straighter, her expression becoming even more annoyed.

"Will you be doing something about that thing or ignoring him until he becomes your responsibility tomorrow?" Ms. Bee asked.

Audrey managed a slight smile and what she hoped was an even tone. "Actually, I thought I'd take him for a walk, that a little more exercise might help him quiet down for a while and…um…make your day a little more pleasant."

If it was possible for Ms. Bee to have a pleasant day.

Audrey wasn't sure it was.

Ms. Bee looked puzzled by the idea of a pleasant day but simply gave another huff, shut the door and disappeared back into the house.

Audrey took a breath, went and got the dog's leash from a peg on the inside of the garage, clipped it to the dog's collar and then unlatched the collar holding his link to the electronic fence around the property. All the while Tink danced with excitement, no doubt knowing he was going somewhere and greatly complicating the entire process.

Audrey didn't even try to correct his behavior at the moment. She just wanted to put some space between herself and Ms. Bee.

She and Tink set off at a brisk walk, which soon became a fast jog. It was that or let the dog pull her along, another bad precedent to set. So Audrey ran, again taking the path of least resistance, telling herself she'd do better tomorrow, when her job started for real.

They ran past the grand, old near-mansions of Simon Collier's neighborhood and then took a turn down the sidewalk along the main road that led from his neighborhood to Audrey's old one.

They ran past the entrance without slowing a bit, nerves

pushing Audrey on, boundless energy and the allure of freedom pushing the dog. She sensed that Tink didn't get to run often and that he really liked running.

They got to the ice cream store on the corner of Maple and Vine, a longtime favorite of Audrey's daughter, and she couldn't run anymore.

There were a lot of dogs in the neighborhood, and the owner kindly left a big container of water out for thirsty ones. Audrey stopped to catch her breath and let Tink have a drink.

He was so excited to be out and about in unfamiliar territory that he couldn't quite decide what he wanted more—to satisfy his thirst or properly explore his surroundings.

He'd take a couple of huge, messy laps of water, then lift his head and dance a bit, checking out cars and pedestrians alike, grinning that silly grin of his and looking at Audrey as if he absolutely adored her for freeing him from the confines of the house and the people there who just didn't understand or appreciate him.

"Aah, you're just a big, sweet baby," Audrey said, scratching his head and giving him another kiss.

He jumped up on her again, as if he just couldn't get close enough to her, and before she could correct him again, an astonished voice to her right yelled, "Mom?"

She turned toward the voice, and there was Andie, holding a chocolate ice cream cone and looking as if she couldn't believe what she was seeing, and Andie's friend Jake Elliott, who'd been there to witness so many of Audrey's sins.

"What are you doing here?" Andie asked accusingly.

"I…" Oh, she'd tried to figure out how to do this a thousand times, and the truth was that nothing would make it easier. Nothing would make this a welcome change to her daughter, Audrey feared. So she just looked her daughter in the eye and said it. "I've taken a job in Highland Park. I'm going to be living there."

Andie looked horrified. Her pupils got big and round, suddenly swimming in tears, and she took a step back, as if even this distance was much too close.

"You can't," Andie whispered, Jake coming protectively to her side in a silent show of support Audrey was glad her daughter had, even if they stood together against her.

"It's true. I did," Audrey said, standing her ground.

"How could you do this to me?" Andie asked, shaking her head. "Haven't you done enough already to ruin my life!"

Audrey didn't know what she would have said to that, but then she didn't have to respond, because Tink saved her. He must have felt the tension between her and Andie and decided to make it clear that he was on Audrey's side.

He started growling at Andie and Jake.

"Tink, no," Audrey said sternly.

He looked at her as if she might be too dumb to understand he was defending her.

"It's all right," Audrey told him. "I've got it."

He quit growling but stood by her side bristling and ready to step in, if need be.

"So, you think you're going to force yourself back into my life? Just like that?" Andie asked.

No, she simply thought she'd live nearby and hope eventually something would change. That Andie would need her.

"I just took the dog for a walk, Andie. I had no idea you were going to be here. How could I? I haven't seen you in two months."

"But here? You had to do it here? Where I live? Well, it's not going to work," Andie told her. "I don't care what you do. It won't work."

And then she stalked away. Jake stood there for a moment, looking as though he wanted to say something, but in the end just shook his head and walked away without a word.

Tink pitched a fit, barking for all he was worth, chasing away the enemy.

"No," Audrey tried to explain to him. "That's my baby. My little girl."

She stood there watching as Andie got into her car and drove away, and then she sank down onto a bench in front of the ice cream store, shaking, the dog practically in her lap and making that fussing, crying sound, not understanding what was wrong but wanting to help in any way he could.

Chapter Three

Andie was still shaking when she pulled into the driveway at her family house, which she now shared with her father. Jake had tried to calm her down all the way home, but it didn't work. He'd wanted to come home with her and talk some more, but she wouldn't let him. Not that he could really do anything anyway.

She was too furious for that.

Plus, it was better to handle things like this on her own. It wasn't as if she could really count on anybody to help, anyway.

Her life.

Her problems.

It was safer that way.

Still, after everything her mother had done last fall, everything the entire neighborhood was still talking about and probably would be for years, her mother dared show her face here?

And planned to live nearby?

Andie couldn't believe it!

She got out of the car and slammed the door, then swiped

away angry tears. Her father's car wasn't in the driveway, which meant he wasn't home, as usual, but judging by the other car in the garage, his embarrassingly young, snotty, blond girl-friend was.

Great!

If only her parents had held things together for two more years, she'd have been gone to college, and it wouldn't have really mattered. As it was, Andie couldn't wait to escape from both of them. How she'd make it through another year and a half living with her father and Barbie—that's what Andie called her because she was like a Barbie doll come to life—and her mother now living nearby…

Well, that just sounded like seven different kinds of torture.

Andie went inside through the garage door, not quite slamming it but shutting it none too gently, and stalked through the house.

She was nearly to her room before she came face-to-face with the new love of her father's life. They nearly collided in the hallway, Barbie wearing a robe, slippers and some kind of green gunk on her face.

She gave a huff of displeasure, stopping short just before Andie plowed on by. "I thought you were Richard," she said.

"At this hour? You're kidding, right? When was the last time he made it home before dark? I mean, it's not easy, making enough money for all the things you need. Your new car, and your home-spa days, Barbie."

Barbie gave her one of those sickeningly sweet smiles that seemed to say, *You won't get rid of me that easily.* Or maybe *I'll outlast you. Just wait and see.*

Andie told herself she didn't care. She went on to her room, fell back onto her bed and pulled out her phone to call her father.

"Please, be there. Please," she whispered. "Just this once."

She got his secretary, of course, who was actually willing to grant Andie an audience with her own father. *This time.*

"Dad!" Andie groaned as he came on the line. "The mos

awful thing happened just now. I ran into mom at the ice cream place. She said she's going to be living in Highland Park!"

He laughed. "Andie, there's no way your mother could afford to live there. Unless..."

Unless she'd found another man to support her.

He didn't have to say it.

Andie knew it better than he did.

Highland Park was as fancy a neighborhood as any in town.

"She claims she got a job," Andie told him.

"Doing what? She's not trained to do anything."

"I know," Andie said.

Which meant...what? That her mother had lied to her? That was nothing new. She'd told any number of lies last fall.

"I can't have her back here," Andie said. "Everything was finally starting to quiet down, and I just can't go through all that again. Will you just call her and tell her to go away, please? Tell her if she really loves me to stay away."

"I... Hang on, Andie. I've got a call on the other line I've been waiting for. I have to take this—"

"Dad, please!"

"I'm sorry—"

"No. Just call her. Promise me, you will. Please—"

And then he was gone.

Andie clicked off her phone, barely managing to resist the urge to throw it across the room.

Of course, he had an important call.

This was only her life, her mother about to ruin it once again, and he had a call. No big surprise there. She was lucky if she could get five minutes of his time in a day, maybe even a week. He'd come back to live in the house these past few months, but he wasn't really here. Not any more than he had been before her parents separated, she realized.

He breezed in, breezed out, did his own thing, and now he had Barbie to entertain in what little time he did spend here.

She really was all alone.

* * *

Audrey didn't have many things of her own to pack.

She'd left her own home three months ago with nothing but the contents of one suitcase and an overnight bag and arrived at Marion's two months ago with the same things. In her time here, she'd accumulated no more than what would fit in two boxes, and they were already in her car. She zipped up the suitcase and looked longingly around the tiny guest cottage of Marion's feeling something akin to sheer panic.

"Now, now," Marion said, coming up to her and putting an arm around her waist. "None of that. It's time, and you're going to be fine."

"I'm glad someone thinks so." Audrey leaned her head down on top of Marion's.

The woman was maybe five feet tall but a dynamo nonetheless.

"How can I ever thank you," Audrey began, choking up.

"No. I mean it. Don't. This is a happy house. I told you that when you moved in, and it's certainly not going to change now that you're moving out. I have adored having you. I will be rooting for you all the way. You're certainly welcome to call and come visit. In fact, I'll be hurt if you don't. But it's time to push you out of the nest, my dear. On with your life. I'm very wise about these things, you know? And I'm always right. You're ready."

Audrey stood up, nodded and worked hard not to cry.

"I didn't think anyone in the world would have given me another chance, except you—"

"No. I mean it. Don't. If you want to pay me back, you find someone else to help get back on their feet. That's the thanks I'm interested in."

"All right. I will," she promised, looking around longingly at the pretty iron bed with the pink flowery quilt, the lace curtains, tiny sitting area and a kitchenette the size of a broom closet. Her sanctuary in her time of need. "I'm going to miss this place, too. So much."

Marion beamed at her. "You're ready to go, my dear. And you never told me. What did you think of Simon?"

"Well, he's not sixty and balding."

Marion whole body shook because she laughed so hard. "How in the world did you get the impression Simon Collier was sixty and balding?"

"I don't know. I mean, you talked about how successful he is and that the man is rich. I just assumed he wasn't…"

Ridiculously attractive?

Audrey hoped she wasn't blushing just thinking about it. *Honestly.*

"How old is he?" she asked, because it was the first question that occurred to her, and she didn't want to even talk about how good the man looked.

"I don't know. I've known him forever. Since he was practically a boy."

"And has he always been so…demanding?"

"Yes." Marion nodded. "And always known what he wants and how to get it. In business, I mean."

Audrey felt a little flutter of panic. "Marion, you're not trying to fix me up with Simon Collier, are you?"

"No. Of course not—"

"Because a man is the last thing I want or need in my life."

"I know," Marion said with an odd look in her eyes that made Audrey nervous. "Now, is this all you brought?"

Audrey nodded, picking up the overnight bag and the handle of her rolling suitcase.

When they got outside, Marion shut the door and said, "Don't look back. Only forward. It's the only way to get to where you want to go."

And Audrey was ready to cry again. "I saw Andie today."

"Really?" She knew how much this meant to Audrey.

Audrey started down the little path that led around the side of the house and to her car out front, with Marion following. "A few blocks from Simon's. She was furious when I told her I'd be living and working nearby."

"Well, you knew she'd likely be upset about that. It's not a surprise, and it's not a setback. It just proves you were right in thinking if you could be close, you'd run into your daughter. Give it time. You'll wear her down."

"Oh, I hope so. I don't know what else to do."

Marion rolled her eyes, then grinned. "She's a teenage girl. They change their minds every thirty seconds, and they find drama in the smallest of things."

"It was no small thing that I did."

"I know, but you're still her mother. A girl her age needs her mother, and it's never too soon to learn how important forgiveness is," Marion insisted. "I'm right about this. And I'm right about you, too. Try to believe me, if you can't believe in yourself just yet."

"I will," Audrey promised.

She got to the car, hefted the suitcase into the backseat, then the shoulder bag. Her cell phone rang.

"It's Richard." Audrey made a face when she saw the number.

"Don't let him bully you. The man is certainly not blameless in all this."

Audrey took a breath and answered, "Hello, Richard."

"What kind of nonsense is this I hear about you moving to Highland Park, Audrey?" He was bellowing, so Marion heard every word, too.

"It's true. I'll be living there. I have a job."

He laughed. "And I can just imagine what you could do to earn your keep in a place like Highland Park."

Audrey saw red but held her tongue. The conversation wasn't anything unexpected. Andie didn't want her there. She wanted Richard to ask her not to come back.

She listened as long as she could stand to, then simply said, "Tell her I'm sorry, but I'm staying."

Richard called her selfish, irresponsible and a bad mother. He was still yelling when she hung up on him.

Marion stood in front of her, looking sad and angry and yet calm as could be. Put Marion in the midst of the worst of emotional storms, and she'd look just like this, as if she was saying to you, *Okay, let's think about how you can handle this without doing anything stupid.*

"You heard him. Andie begged him to tell me to go away."

Marion nodded, wise and confident in a way Audrey thought she could never, ever be again, if she ever had been that sure of herself in her life.

"The surprise is that Richard actually took the time to listen to her and then did what she asked," she told Marion.

"I was thinking the same thing myself," Marion said, putting a hand over Audrey's and holding on to her. "And I'll tell you a little secret, just because it might make you feel a bit better. If you ever wanted him to, Simon could crush your ex-husband with his little pinkie. Businesswise, I mean. If the urge to have Richard destroyed just happened to overtake you and couldn't be resisted."

Audrey laughed, liking the idea of anyone being able to crush Richard.

"If our daughter wasn't headed to college in a year and a half, I'd consider it," Audrey said, trying to hang on to her resolve to do this. "What do I do now?"

"You trust yourself, Audrey. Trust that you know what you're doing, what's important to you. Your daughter. And that you're working to make things right with her."

Audrey leaned down and hugged Marion. "How did you get to be so smart?"

"I made a ton of spectacular mistakes of my own. The trick is learning from them, which you've done." Marion let her go, giving her a big grin. "Now, go get your daughter back."

* * *

Audrey found Simon Collier's house quiet and dark as she pulled into the driveway and parked at the bottom of the steps that led to her quarters. She was unloading the first box when the front door opened. Ms. Bee looked out, and Tink barked like crazy.

"Early, I see," Ms. Bee said, as if she were both surprised and, possibly, actually pleased by that particular trait—someone arriving early for work.

"You can let the dog out. I'll take charge of him now," Audrey told her.

In two seconds flat, Tink shot out the door and across the distance between them, complete joy on his face, as if he were thrilled that she'd returned.

Audrey put the box down and knelt to greet him. He put his front paws on her thighs and practically hurled himself at her chest. She laughed and put her arms around him as he snuggled against her for a moment, then reached up and breathed warm puppy breath on her. Next thing she knew, it felt as if he was trying to wash her entire face with his slightly raspy tongue.

"Okay, okay," Audrey said. "Thank you, but—"

And then she started to cry.

Tink drew back, likely tasting her tears. Puzzled, he cocked his head to one side and then started making his crying sound, too.

"I'm fine," Audrey tried to reassure him. "Or, I will be. I just don't remember the last time anyone was this happy to see me. You're very sweet. A little rambunctious, but sweet."

She fluffed his pretty silvery-black fir and just sat there and soaked up all that happiness that seemed to radiate from him toward her.

Dogs loved lavishly, extravagantly, without holding anything back.

She'd forgotten that in the last few years since her family's last dog died.

When no one else loved you, a dog still would, which Tink proved by licking her cheek some more.

"Okay." She pushed him back gently. "This is going to be hard for you to understand, but a lot of people don't appreciate doggy kisses, Tink. Why don't you come upstairs with me and check out my new place, okay? We'll find you someplace to sleep, and tomorrow we'll go for a nice, long run."

Twenty minutes later, all her things were in. It was quiet, peaceful even, and the little apartment was all hers. She'd never lived any place that was entirely hers, having gone from her mother's house to a tiny apartment she'd shared with a girl-friend to Richard's apartment, then Marion's cottage.

She was scared but excited.

Curled up on one end of the overstuffed sofa, the dog prac-tically in lap, she soaked up the quiet, the comfort of the warmth and weight of the dog, and fell asleep without ever making it to her new bed.

Chapter Four

Audrey woke early to messy, doggy kisses, opened her eyes and found herself stretched out on the sofa, the dog next to her licking her face.

"Ugh," she groaned, having slept on her side on a couch that wasn't exactly uncomfortable but just not so great on her neck.

Tink gave his little cry, then grinned at her, practically bouncing with excitement as he looked at her as if to say, *You're still here!*

Audrey sighed and looked outside to see that it was daylight, but just barely.

"I guess we might as well start our day," she told Tink. "Give me just a minute and we'll go running. I promise."

He slipped off the couch and bounded for the door. She let him out so he could take care of his business, then quickly brushed her teeth, put on her sweats and running shoes and headed for the door.

Tink was waiting for her on the other side of it, grinning like crazy.

"Okay," Audrey said. "Let's find out what it takes to wear you out."

He danced along beside her as she went down the stairs, nearly tripping her twice because he was staying so close, then was beside himself with excitement while she struggled to get his regular collar with the receiver for the electronic fence off and put on a leash and collar they'd use for their run.

He was really puzzled by Audrey's stretching routine, watching every move with his head cocked to the right, then the left, as if he was trying to understand. She bent over and found him sniffing her hair and trying to lick her face, until she laughed out loud and gently pushed him away.

He came right back.

"Okay, we have a lot to work on," she told him, mentally making a list. "First, we're going to run."

She took off at an easy jog, down the street that took her farther into Simon's neighborhood, not nearly brave enough to step back into her own. It was cool but not cold with the sun shining down through the trees. They passed a few other joggers, a few other dogs.

Tink, looking as if he could run all day, was just thrilled to be out.

Audrey kept going, waiting for that feeling. People called it a runner's high, but Audrey didn't need a high. She wanted to get to the point where she wasn't thinking about anything at all. To where the need to breathe—and the sound of her own heart thumping strongly, the breeze on her face and the rhythm of her feet hitting the sidewalk—was simply all there was.

It was like reaching a place in her head that no one else could get to, a place where she was perfectly safe from everything, even her own thoughts, her doubts, her fears.

Some people might call it an emptiness and not understand. But it wasn't. It was peace.

If she ran far enough and got tired enough, she could finally be at peace.

She found it that morning and didn't want to let it go, so she ran some more, ran until she got a nasty cramp and had to stop. She collapsed on a bench in front of the ice cream store, Tink limping on the sidewalk at her feet, tongue lolling out, his breathing as fast as hers. Audrey grabbed her calf, groaning as she tried to stretch it without standing up, because her other leg felt like jelly. Tink roused himself enough to make it to the water dish and start lapping, making a huge mess in his enthusiasm for it.

People were starting to make it out onto the streets now. A couple of kids walking to school stopped to pet Tink. Audrey thought she saw a woman she knew from the PTA at Andie's school but couldn't tell for sure.

Her cramp finally easing, she stood up gingerly to test it out, see if they could continue on now, then winced as she took a few steps.

"We really outdid ourselves this morning," she told Tink, who stretched out on the sidewalk looking as if he could happily go to sleep right where he was.

She'd worn a pedometer to keep track of their mileage but hadn't stopped to look at it until she'd already gone too far.

"I think we'll have to limp home," she told the dog. "So, I hope you're as tired as I am."

He got wearily to his feet, as if to show that he was.

Trying not to make the muscles in her leg any madder than they already were, she moved slowly and hadn't gone fifty feet when a car, an old Buick, pulled to the curb beside her and stopped.

A teenage boy, one of three in the car, got out.

Andie's friend, Jake, Audrey realized.

"Mrs. Graham? Are you all right?"

"Just a cramp, Jake. We'll be fine."

He hesitated, then said, "You're really living around here?"

"Yes, I am," she said.

"You want to get in? We could make room and take you home."

"Jake," the driver called out. "We've got to get to school."

"It's just a few blocks. We have time," he told his friend, then looked back at Audrey. "Really. We do."

She suspected he wanted to talk to her more than anything else and agreed. Jake climbed into the backseat, and she got in front with the dog beside her, sitting on the floor by her feet. Jake introduced her as Andie's mother, which had his friend, the driver, doing a double take but saying nothing. Audrey gave him directions and thanked them all for the ride.

Jake whistled as they pulled into the driveway of Simon Collier's house. "Wow. You live here?"

"I'm working here," Audrey told him as she got out of the car.

Jake got out, too, saying, "She's really upset that you're back."

"I know. I'm sorry about that, but I have to try to make things right between us, Jake."

He nodded. "I don't know if she'll forgive you or not, but...she's really not very happy living with her father and his girlfriend."

"I didn't think she would be," Audrey said. "But thank you for telling me and for being her friend. And I'm really sorry about all the trouble I caused for you last fall. I had no right to draw you into my mess."

She'd gotten drunk at a party one night and made a huge scene. Andie, in trying to get her home, called Jake to come and get them both. Jake, who hadn't even had a license back then, ended up wrecking his uncle's car early that morning while trying to get an unconscious Audrey to the hospital. Audrey still considered it a miracle none of them had been seriously hurt in the accident.

"My uncle says I made my own choices, and they were all

bad. Not in trying to help Andie, but in understanding what I could and couldn't do. Understanding when I needed help myself."

"But I'm the one whose behavior put you in a position to have to make those choices that got you into trouble. And for that, I'm sorry."

He nodded. "I know. We got your letter."

"Well," Audrey said. "Thanks for the ride. If you or Andie needs anything, I'm living right there, above the garage. You can come by anytime."

Not that she thought he would. Still, she was here. She wasn't leaving.

Jake got in the car and Audrey watched them drive off; then, with her leg muscles still cramped tight, she limped across the driveway toward her apartment.

Audrey was sitting under a tree in the front yard, studying the house, the placement of the big trees and shrubs, the existing planting beds, the fence to one side that belonged to the neighbors, thinking of what to do with what was already there and what to add to it, when her phone rang.

Tink roused himself from his spot sprawled out in the grass beside her, but only long enough to lift his head, see that it was nothing but her cell phone ringing, then gave a contented, tired groan and sank back down into the grass.

Audrey was still laughing at him for how tired and complacent he'd been today, since their run, when she picked up the phone and said, "Hello."

"Don't tell me you're actually enjoying this job," Simon Collier asked, with astonishment in his voice.

She felt a little tickle of something run through her.

Pleasure?

At the sound of his voice?

Surely not.

Please, not.

"Is it impossible for you to believe I could be enjoying myself?" she asked, hoping that little fizzle of something didn't come through in her voice.

"I would think it's at least highly improbable, given the tasks involved. Namely, dealing with a certain unruly creature," he said.

"I was laughing at the dog," she told him.

"That I can believe. I think it has the IQ of a shrub."

No way Audrey was going to risk another conversation with him about the dog's intelligence and their battle for control. She feared she'd come too close to insulting Simon on that topic already.

"I was laughing because he's funny and because he's been good all day," she explained.

"Impossible. What did you do, drug him? Because I've heard there are vets who are willing to prescribe things like that, to certain highly troubled canines. I considered trying to find one."

"Don't you dare even think of drugging this dog," she said, rolling her eyes, knowing he was baiting her and still rising to it.

"So, what kind of miracle did you perform to make him... good?"

"I took him for a run this morning and wore him out," she said. "He's been too tired to do much of anything since then."

"I find that very difficult to believe," Simon insisted, then was silent as Audrey heard an announcement of a plane boarding in the background. "That's my flight. I'll need to go. I just wanted to check in with you and make sure you didn't hurt yourself. Or that the dog didn't hurt you."

"No, I'm fine."

"Ms. Bee said you could hardly walk this morning when you got back to the house after exercising him. That you had to get a ride back?"

"Oh, it was nothing. I got a little carried away, and we ran too far. But it was me, not Tink, who did it. I just had a cramp."

"You're sure. Because I won't have that dog hurting anyone—"

So, he was worried about her? Or just looking for an excuse to get rid of the dog?

"Simon, he's just a little rambunctious. That's all. Not a bad dog. And he's smart, but he's not the one who knows how far I can run without cramping up or the one who should keep track of how far we've gone. I am."

"All right. If you say so."

"I do."

"So, how's my yard?"

"Tink and I are studying it as we speak. Or actually, he's lying in the grass half asleep and I'm studying the yard. It looks as if the trees haven't been trimmed in years—"

"You want to cut down those huge trees? I like my trees. Big, lush, green, remember? That's what I want. Surely you can see that the trees are big, lush and green."

"Yes, I see that. But they also have some dead branches in them, and some are dangling over the house. You would be greatly inconvenienced if one of those limbs fell through your roof one day."

"All right. Yes. You're right. Just don't cut them down."

"I just want them shaped up, like a pretty, big, frame of greenery around the house and the yard."

"All right. Do it."

"It means a lot of noise and disruption. Crew of workers, a big truck, limbs being cut and falling to the ground. Limbs being ground up into mulch."

"Then have it done while I'm not there," he said. "Just check with Ms. Bee. She always has my schedule."

"All right," she assured him.

"And take care of yourself," he said, almost like he was concerned.

"I will." Then, without really thinking, she added, "See you Friday."

As if she was looking forward to it or something.

Audrey winced.

He didn't seem to pay any attention, just said goodbye and hung up.

He'd be home on Friday.

She would not look forward to it, and she would not care.

Simon got to the gate and found out that despite the announcement he'd heard only moments before, his plane was not boarding.

How annoying.

Traveling had only gotten worse in the past few years, but this trip had seemed particularly irksome. Delay after delay. Frustration on top of frustration. He found himself just wanting to be at his own office in the city and at his own home, rather than forced to wait to be allowed to board a plane or to take off on a runway or to get into a hotel room.

His phone rang, and he looked at the Caller ID display.

Ms. Bee.

He clicked the phone to answer. "Yes, Ms. Bee."

"Now she's just sitting there in the grass in the front yard, staring at everything. Her and that animal."

Simon wished he was there to see it, the dog miraculously still and quiet, lounging in the grass, and Audrey, probably sitting cross-legged in the shade of one of his enormous trees she planned to tame, bits of sunshine filtering through the new spring leaves. And Ms. Bee, spying on her through one of the front windows, a scowl on Ms. Bee's face.

He had a feeling he'd enjoy the sight.

"What's wrong with that? She's not allowed to sit in the grass?"

"It's just…odd. Did you ever find out exactly what she did to be taken in by that criminal-loving woman you like so much?"

"Criminal-loving?" Simon laughed. Ms. Bee had a talent for making people she disapproved of sound positively evil, and while she'd never admit it to his face, she was highly protective of Simon and especially of Peyton. "You've known Marion for years. And in all those years, I think she's had only one lover who could properly be classified a criminal, and even then he didn't commit a felony, just a few misdemeanors."

"Marion Givens has a talent for finding trouble, and you know it. And now she's gone and convinced you to hire a woman who seems to be casing your house—"

"Casing the joint? You think she's going to rob us?"

"It looks that way," Ms. Bee claimed.

"She's planning to have some trees trimmed, then landscape the yard, remember? Surely you understand how reasonable it seems—no, necessary—to thoroughly study the yard first. We want her to do a proper job, after all."

Ms. Bee gave a huff to show she still disapproved, then said, "I think she's bewitched that animal."

At which point, Simon threw his head back and laughed.

"I don't see any other explanation for how he's behaving."

"You believe in witchcraft, Ms. Bee?"

"Of course not, you wretched man. You know what I mean. She couldn't just snap her fingers and make him behave, although that's exactly what he's been doing since she got here. So how would you explain it?"

"I don't know and I don't care, as long as it works."

"Well, I don't trust that woman," Ms. Bee said. "And I can't believe you do, either."

"What, are you afraid she's going to bewitch me, too?" Simon asked.

As if any woman could after his first experience with matrimony.

Although, he was afraid he'd like to see Audrey try to bewitch him. Simon shook his head, thinking he could get himself into serious trouble here.

"You like her," Ms. Bee said accusingly, then launched into a condemnation of the entire male species and their lack of reasoning and willpower where a pretty woman was concerned.

More mother and sometimes boss than anything else, she was the only woman in the world who'd dare talk to Simon that way.

"I'll try to keep my head screwed on tight in all my dealings with Audrey. I promise."

"And I'm going to keep my eye on her," Ms. Bee promised.

"Fair enough," Simon said, still amused when he hung up the phone.

Surely he didn't need Ms. Bee's protection.

Surely he wasn't that far gone.

He'd had only one brief encounter with Audrey, over a job and the dog.

He couldn't be smitten yet, and besides he was not a man who became *smitten*. He was someone she should be half scared to even talk to, just because he had a reputation for being that way in business. It saved him from so much useless chitchat, saved him so much time and often boredom.

And yet he'd called Audrey at the first excuse he was given, and here he was, anxious to be home rather than out here doing his job, expanding his empire and his already impressive bank account. The way he kept score on his life, because…

Well, because there was no other way to keep score, nothing else really in his life except Peyton.

He wondered how most people kept score.

How did Peyton?

How would Audrey?

He was sure it wasn't a bank account with either one of them.

* * *

He endured another thirty-six mostly unproductive hours on the road and then said to hell with it and came home a day early.

Because he wasn't getting anything done.

Not for any other reason.

He pulled into the driveway sometime after midnight and left the car outside on the far side of the garage, not wanting to wake Audrey or, more likely, the dog, who would then wake Audrey. He knew from Ms. Bee's spying reports either that the dog got Audrey up at the crack of dawn or that Audrey got up then and the dog appreciated it, ready to run for a few miles with her.

Either way, they didn't need to be awakened at this hour.

He slipped into the house, took a quick shower and crawled into bed, grateful that it was his own, thinking he might actually sleep in the next day. It wasn't as if the world would come to an end if he did, and it would probably save him from biting someone's head off from lack of sleep.

He punched his pillow a few times, getting it just right, closed his eyes and dropped off in seconds.

And woke to…

It sounded like a bomb dropped on top of his house!

Simon shot upright in bed, heart pounding.

Surely he'd imagined that.

Because the house was still standing.

Nothing was falling on his head. He didn't hear anything, in fact.

Shaking his head to try to clear it, he eased back down and had nearly dropped back off to sleep when he heard a huge crash right outside his window.

"What the hell?" he muttered, grabbing the pajama bottoms he kept in his bedside table for those nights when Peyton was here.

He stepped into them as he ran for the stairs and then the front door.

Who in the world would bomb Highland Park?

Simon came roaring out of the house to find a bunch of guys in hard hats, a couple of huge, roaring machines and his yard certainly looking as if it had been bombed, with tree branches everywhere. Not quite six-thirty in the damned morning, and someone had bombed his yard!

He stalked toward the nearest guy in a hard hat, ready to raise hell, when he heard Audrey shouting his name, saw her coming at him at a dead-run. She grabbed him hard and tugged him back the way she'd come. He could see her lips moving but couldn't quite tell what she was saying.

"What in holy hell is going on?" he roared. He'd have liked to say something much worse but was trying to clean up his language because of Peyton.

"Get over here!" Audrey screamed.

He heard it again, that bombing sound, as a huge limb crashed to the ground behind him, just missing him. He turned around and just looked at it, mouth hanging open. They'd nearly killed him in his own front yard!

"What the hell are they doing dropping limbs like that when there are people around?"

"They're trimming your trees," she yelled back. "What are you doing here?"

"I live here! It's my house! I thought somebody had started bombing the neighborhood!"

"Bomb the neighborhood?" she repeated, making it sound absolutely ridiculous, which he knew it likely was. Still…

"That's what it sounded like when it woke me up," he said, still yelling. "They could have killed me!"

"I know. I saw. I'm the one who got you out of the way," Audrey said.

One of the hard hat guys came running over to them then, looking as if someone had taken a few years off his life.

"What the hell is going on?" he yelled at Audrey.

Simon stepped in, intending to stop that right there. He might raise his voice every now and then, but he wasn't going to stand by while anybody else talked to her that way and if that made him a hypocrite, well…fine!

Audrey must have known what was coming, because she stepped between them and put up a hand to stop Simon from getting any closer.

The next thing he knew, she had her palm pressed flat against his bare chest.

And that stopped him cold.

Chapter Five

Audrey felt as if she'd been burned.

No, scared half to death and then burned. Burned in a not altogether bad way, but certainly not good, either.

She kept her hand on his bare chest just long enough to stop him, along with a look in her eyes she'd used on her daughter when she was two and stubborn as could be. Then she turned back to the head of the tree crew and told him she'd take care of Simon.

"Tell him to stay the hell out of the work zone," the guy said, then added. "There's no one else on the property now, right?"

Audrey heard Simon growl a bit. She turned back to him. "Please tell me your daughter isn't here?"

"No," he said, like a bear with a thorn in his paw.

And then Audrey had a painful thought of her own. "And you're not... I mean... You don't have some kind of woman inside, do you?"

He arched a brow. "Some kind of woman?"

"Any kind of woman?"

"What kind do you think I might have? I mean, I'm just curious. Part-woman, part...what?"

"Simon, don't be an ass!" she said, too exasperated and still too scared to be diplomatic. "I thought the limb was going to land on your head, and while I'm sure it's a very hard head, I don't think it's hard enough to handle a limb crashing down on it."

"Sorry," he said, not sounding sorry at all. "It's not every day I get nearly killed in my own front yard, and then I'm accused of sleeping with some kind of... I don't even know. Alien creature? I sleep with women. Normal, attractive women. But thankfully, I was all alone last night."

Audrey could have gladly rung his neck right then, but she still had to deal with the tree guy.

"That's it," she told the guy. "Just him. I'll keep him out of the way."

Then she had to turn back and face Simon, gloriously shirtless, still breathing hard and wearing a loose-fitting pair of pajamas hanging dangerously low on his hips, showing off all the beautiful lines of his chest and abdomen.

Audrey had to take a breath, then another.

Then she realized she was staring.

And he knew it, too.

At least she didn't still have her hand on his chest.

Her palm still burned somewhat, as if the imprint of his skin were still there.

Her boss.

Good Lord, he was her boss. He was even more gorgeous than she'd realized. And she'd yelled at him as if he were her kid who'd run into the street in traffic or something.

"You told me to get this done while you were out of town, remember?"

He nodded.

"Check with Ms. Bee. She always knows your schedule. Remember?"

He nodded once again.

"Well, I'm sorry about all of this, but I did what you told me to do, and you are not supposed to be here this morning. You're not supposed to be back until late tonight."

He looked even madder at that, if it was even possible to look madder than he had before. He was still breathing hard, still a sight to behold, all rumpled and sleepy looking and dangerous, all that beautiful skin with the morning sun shining down upon it.

It hurt just to look at him, Audrey decided.

Couldn't she just stop looking at him?

Another limb came crashing down, though not anywhere near them.

"Do you want me to make them stop?" she asked, not knowing what else to say to him.

"No," he growled. "They'd just have to come back another day, and they've already made a damned mess that's going to take them hours to clean up. They might as well stay and finish."

"Okay," she said. "I'm sorry. I was just trying to get it done before you got home—"

"No, you're right. You did what I told you to do." He shook his head. "I just changed my plans at the last minute. I'm…sorry."

And then they just stood there, not happy but not yelling anymore, either. Thank goodness.

She'd hate to lose her job the first week. It would be humiliating, and she'd already been humiliated enough in the past year.

"I'll go back inside and stay out of the way," he said finally, still looking a bit dazed and sleepy.

And just like that, he was gone, and Audrey could breathe again.

* * *

"I really yelled at him!" Audrey told Marion that night on the phone.

"You yelled at Simon Collier?"

"Yes!"

"And lived to tell about it?" Marion sounded astonished.

"So far. I figure he could fire me at any moment," Audrey said, sitting in a chair by the window overlooking the driveway. "I still can't believe I did it. I don't know how it even happened. One minute everything was fine, and the next there he was and we were screaming at each other."

Half-naked.

That had been part of the problem.

He'd been half-naked, and he'd scared her half to death, with that branch almost crashing into his head.

"Well, I'm sure Simon can withstand a little yelling. If you ask me, he gets away with it too often, and no one ever yells back at him."

"Oh, great," Audrey said.

"He was probably so astonished that he didn't think enough to fire you."

"Yeah, but what about when he's not so surprised? I mean, he could fire me any minute, and I can't let that happen, Marion. I need this job so much."

Tink padded over to her and put a gentle paw on her knee, whining a bit, as if he was worried about her.

Audrey leaned over and rubbed his pretty head. "You sweet baby," she told him. "Peyton's going to be here soon."

Tink perked right up and turned his attention to the window, going up on his two back legs, the front ones on the window-sill so he could look out, mouth spread into a wide, pretty grin.

"So you get to meet the golden child. Finally," Marion said.

"That bad?"

"Simon's that bad with her. Or so I hear, but also that she's a sweet child, all things considered."

"I need the dog to behave, Peyton to be happy and Simon to be happy, and I didn't even get to run with Tink this morning because the tree crew got here at the crack of dawn. I had to keep the dog locked inside so he wouldn't get hurt while they trimmed the trees, and then I spent all afternoon spreading the mulch from the ground-up trees. I'm so sore I can hardly walk."

"What are you doing spreading all that yourself? Let the landscaping crew do it," Marion told her.

"I didn't even think of it. They asked what I wanted done with the trees, and I told them they could grind them up. Then they drove away and left me with a huge pile of mulch on Simon's spotless driveway. They said I hadn't arranged ahead of time for a crew to spread the stuff, that the job I hired them to do was done, so it was my problem."

"Oh, honey! All that and yelling at Simon, too? You've had quite a day."

"I have," Audrey said, feeling sorry for herself right then. "And I still have to meet Peyton and hope that everything goes well with her and the dog."

"You need to drag yourself outside and throw a ball or something with the dog. Surely you can manage that. He could probably chase it happily for hours, and by the time Simon's daughter gets there, the dog should be nice and tired. And then you turn the dog over to them and have a nice hot bath and go to bed. Everything will look better in the morning. It almost always does."

Audrey said goodbye to Marion, found Tink's favorite bouncy ball and made her way gingerly down the steps, the dog dancing with excitement beside her.

"Tink," she said to him when they got to the backyard, "I need this to go well, okay? Peyton's coming, and I need for you to be on your absolute best behavior while she and her father are here. Can you do that for me? Please?"

She figured she had nothing to lose by trying to explain it to him.

He cocked his head to one side, as if trying to decipher her meaning, then went back to staring at the ball, which seemed to look as good to him as a T-bone steak.

"So much for our little talk," Audrey said, then threw the ball.

Tink raced after it, fast as could be, and was back in front of Audrey in seconds, dropping the ball at her feet.

"Good dog," she told him, fussing over him for a moment, then throwing his ball again.

She felt sick with anticipation of having to face Simon again and not knowing what he might say or do after the way she'd yelled at him. Every muscle in her body hurt, and she hadn't been on the job for even a week yet.

Way to go, Audrey.

Peyton arrived precisely at six o'clock by private car, hired by Simon at the insistence of his ex-wife, who didn't care for the whole divorced-parents-exchanging-the-child scene.

Not that Simon minded.

His ex was a terrible driver, and Peyton adored Mr. Hobbs, the driver Simon used regularly with the car service. She pretended to be a princess when she rode in the back of the big, black car, and Hobbs obliged her by treating her like one.

Simon had been instructed by his daughter to wait patiently by the car door so Hobbs could open the door for her and even announce her presence, something that seemed to delight his daughter.

So, Simon stood there, waiting as the car stopped and Hobbs got out, tipping his hat to Simon and then to Peyton, as he opened the door and asked, "Will that be all, miss?"

"Yes, Hobbs. Thank you, very much."

"Delighted, as always, miss."

And then she ran into Simon's arms. He lifted her off the ground and swung her around while she giggled and hung on to him, and a moment later the dog came roaring around the side of the house, barreling toward them.

Simon lowered Peyton to the ground and then held his breath, waiting for the dog to stop and sit and act as if he had some manners, which he always had where Peyton was concerned. Still, Simon held his breath every time.

She was his world, and Simon adored her, feeling as vulnerable as he supposed a man could be at the idea of her being hurt.

He glanced up and saw Audrey come around the corner, looking as anxious as he felt, while they both waited and watched. Sure enough, the silly dog slid to a stop at Peyton's feet, sat on his rump and whipped that tail back and forth in a frenzy. But he was calm as could be otherwise, as Peyton wrapped her arms around his neck and greeted him as if he were her best friend in the world. She kissed his snout, and the dog licked her nose, making her giggle and grin even more.

"I missed you, Tink!" she cried. "Did you miss me?"

"Woof!" was the response.

Simon just shook his head, knowing he'd have to share her with the dog all weekend and that he'd come in a distant second for his daughter's attention.

Bested by a damned dog.

Peyton kept fussing over the foolish animal, acting as if she hadn't seen him in ages. Simon motioned for Audrey to come join them so he could introduce her to his daughter, and he noticed she was moving gingerly.

He frowned as she reached his side. "Those idiots with the trees didn't hurt you somehow, did they?"

"No," she told him.

"The dog?"

"No. The dog is not a problem, Simon."

"Then what is it? You can hardly walk."

"I think I just did too much. The mulch had to be spread."

He looked around, seeing that all the trees in the front yard had a thick, fresh coat of mulch, then looked back at Audrey, who might be five foot two on a good day. "You did all that yourself?"

"Yes," she said.

"Why?"

"Because it had to be done."

"Not by you," he said, realizing he was damned close to yelling at her again, and that was the last thing he wanted to do after this morning.

He'd acted like an ass and still hadn't managed to apologize properly for that, and here he was, about to do it all over again.

"I'm not a slave driver, Audrey. No matter what you might have heard. And I didn't hire you to do manual labor."

"Well, I happen to like the manual labor part of the job. I like digging in the soil and planting things and trimming and generally tending to a yard. As for the mulch, it's not my favorite, but I just didn't expect there to be so much of it. But I'm fine."

He looked again and considered the sheer volume of the material she'd moved with those trim shoulders and arms of hers. She had to be aching all over.

"I don't want you working like that," he insisted. "It's too much."

She got that really stubborn look on her face that she'd worn this morning and said, "I got it done, didn't I?"

"And now you're suffering for it—"

"Simon—"

"This is not a discussion, Audrey. When it comes to jobs like that, the ones that take sheer muscle, hire some men with nice, big muscles."

He was trying to do her a favor—stubborn woman—to take

care of her, when she obviously didn't have the sense to take care of herself.

So why had he come off feeling as if he'd both insulted and infuriated her?

Women!

Would he ever learn how difficult they were and that he was better off steering clear of them, except when absolutely necessary?

Honestly, he was doomed where relationships were concerned, and now she looked halfway scared of him. Either that or seemingly about to cry.

Oh, hell.

Not that.

Anything but that!

Now he had something else to apologize for, and he hadn't even made his apologies for this morning yet. Although now certainly didn't seem like the time. He'd probably just end up yelling some more and have to apologize a third time.

He took a breath, tried to wipe the slate clean between them, at least for the moment, and said, "Peyton?"

She finally stopped fussing over Tink and turned her back to the dog.

"This is the woman I told you about, Mrs. Graham. The one who's taking care of your dog when you're not here."

Peyton stood up and smiled, then held out her hand, the way he'd coached her to do when meeting an adult. "Hello, I'm Peyton Alexandra Collier."

Impressive for a five-year-old.

Audrey gave her a beautiful smile and shook her hand. "I've heard so much about you. And Tink has been waiting by the window, watching for you to arrive for hours. I think he missed you."

"Did he really?"

"Yes, he did."

"I miss him all the time!" Peyton sighed dramatically, as if they were normally separated by an ocean or something. "Are you going to love him and be nice to him? Because Daddy and Ms. Bee think he's awful."

"I think he's a wonderful dog," Audrey said. "He just needs some help understanding how to behave. That's all. And it's easier for him to understand if we all expect the same things and treat him the same way—"

"But we're all going to be nice to him, right?" Peyton asked, looking concerned.

"Yes, we're all going to be nice to each other," Audrey reassured her.

She looked a little worried, put one arm around the dog, then leaned toward Audrey and whispered, "You can make my dad be nice to Tink?"

Simon laughed.

"I'll do my best," Audrey promised.

"And Ms. Bee? 'Cause she yells at him when she thinks I can't hear her."

Audrey nodded. "I think when you're not here, I'll just keep Tink with me, so he doesn't bother Ms. Bee."

"Okay. I think that's a good plan," Peyton said, giving her approval after some consideration, then turned to her father. "Daddy, I need to go play with Tink now. He missed me."

"All right, darling." He kissed the top of her head, and she giggled. "Go ahead. I'll be inside when you get tired."

Simon stood there, watching her and the dog. Audrey gave Peyton a ball and told her Tink liked to chase it. She showed her how to be sure to get his attention first, so he was ready for the toss, and then to throw it for him and wait for the dog to bring the ball back and drop it at her feet.

"She's absolutely adorable," Audrey said as they watched Peyton and the dog together.

"Well, I think so, but I admit, I'm biased."

* * *

Audrey had been watching his daughter. Then she turned and saw Simon, glowing with paternal pride, and decided he wasn't just a good-looking man.

He was devastating.

Or maybe she just wished her husband had a fraction of that love and joy in his eyes when he looked at their daughter now. Maybe that's why the look seemed to cut right through her.

Simon Collier absolutely adored his daughter.

Audrey wondered if Richard ever had.

It hurt. It really, really hurt. All that she wanted for Andie, all they seemed to have lost as a family or maybe never had.

"Audrey?" Simon put a hand on her arm and was suddenly in front of her, frowning and looking worried. "You really hurt yourself, didn't you? Dammit, you said you were fine—"

"I am," she claimed, blinking back tears. "I mean…it's not what you think, Simon. It's nothing. Just the way you look at her. It's beautiful, and I hope you never lose that. I hope you always feel that way about her."

He frowned. "How could I not? She's my daughter."

"Exactly," Audrey said, trying to smile through her tears and standing too close to this powerful man who was her boss, letting him touch her.

"You have a daughter?" he guessed, his eyes never leaving her face, as if it were a puzzle he could solve if he just tried hard enough.

"Yes."

"And she's…okay?"

Audrey shrugged one shoulder. How to answer? How much honesty to include? "Andie lives in the house you saw with her father and his girlfriend and goes to the local high school. The last time I saw her, she was fine."

Furious at Audrey but fine.

"Okay," he said, looking like he had a million other questions about the situation, but was hoping she'd explain without his having to ask.

Which she didn't want to do.

"I'm sorry about everything," she said, rushing into another subject. "For yelling at you this morning, and the tree branch almost falling on you—"

His hand slid up to her shoulder and gave it a gentle, reassuring squeeze. "I told you, it's not your fault. It was mine. I shouldn't have yelled at you like that. I can be a bear at times, but honestly, that's no excuse. I really am sorry."

Audrey sniffled while wiping away a tear. "So, we're okay?"

"I'm okay. Are you sure you're okay?"

She nodded, feeling foolish and overwhelmed at the moment. "I have to talk to your daughter. We have to go over some things about the dog—"

"Later. Go inside. Take a break. Come to the house when you're ready."

Audrey nodded. "Okay. Thank you."

And then she practically fled up the stairs to her apartment. When she turned around to close the door, Simon was still standing there watching her.

Chapter Six

Peyton was a good listener and a fast learner, Audrey discovered later that night, once she'd gotten herself together.

She joined Simon and his daughter on the covered patio at the back of his house, after they'd finished their dinner, to give Peyton some lessons on how to get the dog to become a model member of the household.

Peyton quickly got Tink to come when she called, sit for her, fetch, lie down and, for a few seconds, stay when he was told to do so. He never jumped on Peyton, so that wasn't an issue between them, and he ignored Simon completely when Peyton was nearby. The dog was even starting to understand he needed to wait to be invited before trying to climb into Peyton's lap or brace his front paws on her while he stretched up to lick her.

"Okay," Audrey said. "That's pretty good."

"Daddy said he's not a smart dog, but I knew he was," Peyton said.

Simon, who was standing on the edge of the patio, holding

a drink in one hand and watching their every move, met Audrey's eyes for a moment, then shook his head.

Audrey grinned, unable to help herself. "Now," she told Peyton, "let's talk about tonight. Does Tink normally sleep with you?"

Peyton nodded. "In my bed. He likes that. Ms. Bee doesn't, but…." She shot her father a worried look.

"She knows he sleeps in your bed, Peyton."

Peyton just grinned.

"So you want him with you tonight. That's fine. You just need to make sure you take him outside, so he can go to the bathroom before you two go to bed. Tell him he has to go, and he will. Make him wait to be invited before he jumps onto your bed, and then… He wakes up early. About six o'clock, he needs to go outside again and then he wants to run. Do you get up that early?"

Peyton shook her head.

"I'll be up," Simon said. "I'll let him out. And then?"

"I'll be ready to take him for a run," Audrey told him.

"What about me? Can I run with him?" Peyton asked.

"I don't think you could go as far as he wants to go. But it would be good if you could exercise him, too. How about you and I work on some ways you can do that for him tomorrow, after you get up?"

"Okay," Peyton said.

Tink licked her, making her laugh, and the little girl looked up at Audrey as if Audrey had just given her the moon or something as amazing and wonderful.

Which made Audrey think of Andie and the days when Andie thought her mother was amazing. Audrey worried her daughter would never feel that way again.

Audrey was great with his daughter, Simon decided. And a miracle worker with the dog, as far as he was concerned.

Peyton was thrilled to have someone she considered a friend

and a fellow dog lover in the house, and Ms. Bee hadn't voiced one word of complaint about the dog since Audrey had moved in.

Simon was pleased.

Very pleased.

He just wished he knew what had put that haunted look on Audrey's face when she talked about him and Peyton and why Audrey's own daughter wasn't living with her.

On top of that, he'd screamed at her this morning and then she'd done the work of three men this afternoon in the yard. She could barely walk at the moment without something hurting, and she planned to get up at the crack of dawn and run with the dog?

No way.

As Simon saw it, she was due a little rest and an apology.

He left Peyton in the backyard playing with the dog, with Audrey explaining how she'd taught him various things so Peyton could work with him on reinforcing them.

Ms. Bee caught him a moment later in the kitchen on the phone with Natasha Warren, the owner of a downtown salon and spa. Simon was one of her best customers, thanks to his often-short temper. He was just making the arrangements.

"So, how bad were you?" Natasha asked in her normal, easy, sexy voice.

"I'm thinking a ninety-minute massage—"

"Ninety minutes?" Natasha sounded surprised.

"She's sore," Simon said, then, when Natasha gave a throaty laugh and Ms. Bee shot him a look of outrage, explained, "Not like that!"

"If you say so, honey," Natasha said.

"Yard work, Natasha. Too much yard work."

"Yard work? Could there possibly be some completely new move I haven't heard of, because, honey, I thought I knew them all—"

"Oh, hell. I'm talking about working in the yard and nothing else."

Simon swore, and Natasha only laughed harder.

"Ninety minutes on the massage table. Fine. Will that do it?"

"I don't know. What do women like these days?"

"When Simon Collier doesn't know what a woman likes, we're all in trouble," Natasha purred.

"From your spa," Simon explained, rapidly losing his patience to the point where he'd soon be sending Natasha a gift certificate to her own business.

"All right. If she's truly slaving away in your yard, I'm sure she needs a manicure, but if she's going to keep doing that kind of work, it won't last. How about a pedicure? Maybe a haircut and some highlights?"

"Don't mess with her hair. Her hair is perfect," he said, then caught Ms. Bee's look of disgust at what he'd said.

Oh, fine.

He didn't care.

He liked her hair. So what?

He didn't want anyone messing with Audrey's sexy curls, except him. He liked the way they looked so natural and free, the way they framed her face and sometimes danced around it.

Surely he was allowed to like a woman's hair.

"Okay," Natasha said. "I'll let her pick—manicure, pedicure or facial. How about that?"

"That sounds great. I'll send her in a car." To make sure she actually went and because, well, just because. Pampering was pampering. "And she gets up early, so let's say seven-thirty? Can you do that?"

Natasha groaned. "Only for you, honey. Only you."

Simon thanked her and then hung up, with Ms. Bee waiting for him.

"I knew you liked her," Ms. Bee said.

"I like her hair, okay? The woman has great hair," Simon remarked.

"Sure you do. Did you ever find out what she did to end up here, living above your garage and playing nanny to a dog?"

"No. Did you?" he asked, because he was sure she'd tried, just because Ms. Bee liked to know everything about everybody.

"Not yet. She acts like she's afraid of me—"

"I wonder why?" Simon quipped. Most of his employees were terrified of Ms. Bee, and she knew it, enjoyed it, even.

"I haven't done anything to her," Ms. Bee said. "Actually, I think she's afraid to let that dog get anywhere near me in case he annoys me. Which, I have to say, I'm very happy about. But since the dog hardly ever leaves her side, I haven't seen much of your newest em-ploy-ee."

She dragged out each syllable.

"I'm fully aware of the fact that Audrey works for me."

"And that she has perfect hair," Ms. Bee said, as she walked out of the kitchen, leaving him gazing out the window at Peyton, the dog and Audrey.

"She does have perfect hair," Simon muttered, too softly for Ms. Bee to hear, because he didn't want to fight about it anymore tonight, and Ms. Bee never gave up on a good fight.

It was just hair.

Surely he could resist something as simple as perfect hair.

Simon was not so happy when his alarm went off at five forty-five on a Saturday morning, but he got up, got dressed for a run and was in Peyton's room by a few minutes after six.

Then he ended up standing in the doorway just watching her sleep.

She had what she called a Princess Bed, a fancy white bed of swirling iron and hot-pink sheets. She was lying in the middle of it on her side, her arm around the dog, who was lying beside her, his back to her chest, and they both looked comfortable as could be.

The dog lifted his head and squinted at Simon for a second

or two when he walked in, then gave a little groan and put his head back down, as if to say there was no way he was leaving that nice, comfortable spot in the bed at this hour.

Simon swore softly in the darkened room, the first rays of the sun just starting to peek through the window shades.

Now what?

Wait here for the dog to decide to get up?

"It's a good thing Peyton adores you," Simon said to the animal, who was starting to stretch at least, as if he might get up soon.

Now they had him talking to the dog.

"No," Simon told him. "I'm up. Audrey's up, I'm sure, so you're definitely going to get up. Come on."

Tink looked truly annoyed, and he took his time but finally got off the bed and trotted over to Simon, looking up at him as if to say, *Fine. I'm up. What now?*

"As I said, it's a good thing my daughter adores you. Come on. We're going out."

The dog followed him downstairs and out the kitchen door, promptly relieving himself and then looking up the garage stairs toward Audrey's apartment and whining.

"Yeah, I know. They both think you're great, don't they?"

Simon grabbed a leash from just inside the garage and took off the dog's link to the electronic fence. Then he followed Tink up the stairs to Audrey's. She opened the door before he even got there, dressed in a loose-fitting T-shirt and what he thought was nice, tight biker shorts. Not that he could really see anything. Her T-shirt was too long and loose.

Damn.

Her face was completely bare, her hair a little wilder than usual and cute as could be. She looked soft, sleepy and inviting.

If she was his, they would not be getting up this early to run.

"Any trouble with him last night?" she asked.

"Not a bit. Except when I tried to get him up a minute ago. He looked quite comfortable in my daughter's bed."

Audrey bent down and greeted the dog, asking him if he was a good boy and then telling him she'd heard he was. Silly thing ate it up, as if he hadn't been admired and praised by another female all evening long.

Audrey stood up and looked at Simon in his exercise clothes. "You're going running?"

"I run," he said. Did she think he looked like he couldn't manage a few miles? "Granted, not that often. I'd rather play basketball at the gym at my office, but when I can't do that, I run."

"Okay." Audrey hesitated. "You're coming with us?"

"No. I'm taking the dog, and you are taking the day off."

She looked worried at that. What was there about the idea of her having a day off that could worry her? Women could be absolutely bizarre at times.

"You did too much yesterday. I know it. You've got to be sore this morning, and you don't need to be taking this dog for a run—"

"I can do it," she insisted.

"I'm sure you can." He laughed a bit because she sounded insulted, when all he was trying to do was apologize. "I'm saying you don't have to, that I don't want you to."

"But, this is my job—"

"I know." He was the one who hired her after all. "And as I tried to tell you yesterday, I'm not a slave driver, contrary to anything you might have heard about me. Audrey, I'm trying to apologize. I lost it with you yesterday morning. I screamed at you—"

"I screamed right back," she reminded him.

"I know. I was there."

And then she looked worried again.

Damn.

He didn't want her to be afraid of him.

He didn't want her to be afraid of anything, he realized.

"I just don't want you working this hard, and I don't want you doing anything today. I have a car coming to pick you up in—"

"A car?" She looked completely baffled.

"A driver with a car, coming to pick you up in exactly—" he consulted his watch "—forty-seven minutes to take you downtown to Morton's—"

"Morton's?" she asked, looking like a kid headed for the candy store.

Finally, he'd done something right with her.

"You know it?" he asked.

She nodded.

"Good. You're going to Morton's for a little pampering."

"You can't do that," she told him.

Simon laughed. "I'm certain I can. In fact, I already have. It's all arranged."

"But… No."

Did the woman not understand? No one argued with him, except Ms. Bee. "Why not?"

"Because," she insisted. "Simon, you're my boss."

"Yes," he said, deciding to agree with as much of her argument as he could. Maybe that would work and she'd listen.

"So, this is not really…appropriate."

"Why not?"

"Because you're my boss," she repeated.

"And you've made remarkable progress with the dog. Amazing progress. I couldn't be more pleased. I even like the trees and the way they look. Tamed a bit, and the way the trimming opened up the view of the house. And I lost my temper. And the mulch was way too much for you to handle yourself, so…here's a little thank-you and an apology all in one. Okay?"

"It just doesn't seem…right. You sending me to a spa?"

"Why?"

"Well, I just…it doesn't seem like the kind of gift that a man who happens to be someone's boss gives to a woman who happens to be his employee."

"Why not?" He thought it was a fine way to say he was sorry.

He let himself take a nice long look at her, all soft and rumpled and still sleepy, telling himself it was about figuring out what was wrong and nothing else. But he got distracted pretty fast and just started thinking of how good she looked like this.

How inviting.

How ridiculously attractive.

He caught an odd glint in her eyes, narrowing in on his.

Uh-oh.

This was probably not going to be good. He'd made her mad somehow.

"Simon, if you're thinking that… That…"

"Yes?"

"That there's going to be anything else between us—" She blushed furiously.

He thought about how very much he wanted there to be something else between them and wished it could be as easy between them as the dog disappearing, his pushing her back inside, closing the door behind him, peeling off every stitch she was wearing and taking her back to bed for a good, long time.

And he couldn't say any of that to her.

At least he really shouldn't.

He made a habit of not messing with the women who worked for him. He'd been tempted before, but he'd always resisted.

Of course, he'd never wanted to break all the rules as much as he did right then.

The dog whined, saving him maybe or maybe just doing it to spite him.

Simon really hated the dog in that moment.

But Audrey looked well and truly scared and sad and vulnerable as could be, and life seemed hard enough for her already. He didn't want to make it more difficult.

"Audrey," he said, not letting himself look at her anymore. He looked at the wall, at the sofa, at the tiny kitchen. "I do this all the time."

Her mouth hung open, and she just stood there, waiting.

He thought back to what he'd just said.

Oh, hell.

"Morton's, I mean." He stepped back, trying to act as if nothing had happened, nothing had been between them in that moment or any one before. "I have an account there. I send my people there all the time. You know, I yell more than I should, and I'm trying to cut down. Really. But until I can manage that, I try to at least apologize nicely afterward. Morton's has proven to be a favorite form of apology among the women on my staff."

She looked confused, disbelieving, and then hopeful. "Really?"

He nodded. "It's all arranged. They're waiting for you. You have forty-five minutes until the car comes to get you. Enjoy your day."

He went to leave before he said anything else he shouldn't, but the dog didn't want to go. He stood in the open doorway, whining pitifully and looking up at Audrey as if he couldn't bear to be parted from her.

"It's just for a few hours," Simon told the dog. "She'll be back."

If it was possible for dogs to pout, this one did.

"Oh, for God's sake. If you want to run this morning, come with me. If not, we can both go back to sleep."

"Go on, Tink," Audrey told him. "Go with Simon. Run."

Run seemed to be the magic word. The dog looked disgruntled at his change in running partners but went, down the stairs and off into the neighborhood. Simon wondered how many miles he'd have to do to forget everything he'd like to do with Audrey, but doubted he could run that far if his life depended on it.

* * *

If Audrey had been Cinderella, in her version she'd rather have gone to Morton's any day of the week instead of a silly ball. It was a real treat, even in her old life. Expensive and sinfully indulgent, like being transported to a private beach on a perfect summer day, without ever having to pack or leave town, and without getting a bit of sand on her.

A car and driver came to get her instead of a coach and white horses, which was fine with her, and the whole thing carried an air of fantasy with it.

She had to be dreaming.

Which meant she hadn't accused Simon of trying to buy her affections with a trip to the day spa. Surely she hadn't done that!

Audrey groaned, utterly confused, and sank back into the buttery-soft leather of the car seats. She got to Morton's, and it didn't even look as if it was open. Why would it be at this hour? But just as she was worried she was about to wake up, the front door opened and she was practically handed from the driver of the car, who was holding open the car door for her, to the beautiful, smiling woman who held open the front door.

"Ms. Graham. Welcome," the woman said. "I'm Natasha Warren, the owner. I promised Simon we'd take good care of you."

She was ushered into a beautifully serene room in all different shades of cream. Lush, soft, quiet, perfect. A virtual oasis.

"He suggested we start with a massage and then…whatever you like? Manicure? Pedicure? Facial?"

Audrey closed her eyes and wished fervently that she got to enjoy the massage and a facial before she woke up from her dream.

"Facial," she said. "Please. I've been spending too much time in the sun."

Natasha made tsk-tsking sounds about the dangers to a woman's face lurking in the sunshine, as if that had a chance of even registering on Audrey's list of worries until this very moment. She'd been too worried about keeping her job and getting her daughter to stop hating her.

But not now.

For now Audrey let herself float along, to the nice, quiet, dimly lit room where she took off her clothes and got under the soft, expensive cotton sheets and stretched out on the heated massage table, closed her eyes and let herself drift, her mind slowly emptying of everything except how good this felt.

Vaguely, she heard Natasha making worried sounds about the state of her hands, which were swathed in a soothing cream and then covered in big, warm mittens. More hands, starting on her head and working their way down her neck to her poor shoulders.

She didn't do anything but roll over when told to do so and didn't say anything resembling words, just moaned with happiness every now and then for the next... She didn't even know how much time.

The idea of someone else taking care of her was completely foreign to her. She was always the one taking care of everyone else, so it was heavenly just to lie there, relax, rest and enjoy.

Her warm mittens came off eventually, and someone rubbed her poor, tired hands, then tucked them under the sheet where they could get warm again.

Warm, gooey things went on her face and stayed there, and she dozed a bit, she thought, too relaxed to even care or know for sure.

She felt like warm putty when they were done and wasn't even sure she could get off the table or if her legs would hold her up.

"Good?" Natasha asked from nearby.

Audrey opened her eyes, blinked once, then again, slowly coming back to the present. "So good," she said.

She had to be dreaming.

Reality couldn't be this good.

Natasha laughed and said, "Don't tell Simon, but I swear some of his women try to provoke him, just so he'll send them here to make up for it."

"Simon's women?" That woke Audrey up.

She was not one of Simon's women.

She couldn't be.

"The women who work for him," Natasha said. "I tease him and say I'm going to create special packages just for him. Simon Collier's Standard Apology, Simon's Really Big Apology and Simon's Ultimate Apology. What do you think of that?"

Audrey thought maybe she wasn't dreaming after all, that maybe she wasn't going to wake up.

"He does this a lot?"

Natasha shrugged elegantly. "He should own the place for all the business he sends me."

"So…" There was nothing special at all about this, just Simon being Simon.

And she'd accused him of coming on to her!

"Oh, no!" Audrey said.

"What? What is it?"

"No," Audrey cried.

How could she have said that?

Thought that?

Just because she thought he was incredibly attractive didn't mean he thought anything like that about her, and to just come out and tell him what she thought and that it wasn't going to work with her…

"Oh, no!"

Natasha took her by the arm and made her sit back down, fussing over her and trying to figure out what was wrong.

"How can I ever look him in the eye again?"

Natasha tried, but Audrey absolutely refused to tell her any more. She fretted silently about it all the way back to Simon's house, her body heavy and warm on the soft car seat, her mind muddled and troubled and still really hoping she was going to wake up.

The car stopped. The driver came around to her side and opened her door, and she feared she had no choice but to get out and hope Simon wasn't here.

"Enjoy yourself, Ms. Graham?" the driver asked.

"Yes, thank you," she whispered, sad as could be.

She stood in the driveway, afraid she heard footsteps behind her. Strong, masculine, self-assured footsteps.

Yes, that's what she heard.

When she opened her eyes again, he was standing in front of her, an absolute model of healthy, confident, attractive male.

"You didn't like your day?" he asked.

She groaned. "Simon—"

"What is it?" He held her by both arms, closer than he'd ever been to her, seemingly truly concerned. "What's wrong?"

She closed her eyes, dipped her head down low, unable to look at him, and just blurted out. "You really do this all the time for people. That's what Natasha said."

He took her chin gently in his hand and tilted her face up to him. "So?"

She let him force her face up and opened her eyes, but she wouldn't look at him. Instead she looked at the blue sky just above his right shoulder. "Please tell me. Please—"

"What? Anything," he promised her.

"That I didn't accuse you of flirting with me by sending me to Morton's for the morning. Or…no, worse…accuse you of thinking you could buy my affections with a trip to Morton's."

He laughed, just a bit, then took a breath and let it out ever so slowly. "You want me to tell you that you didn't?"

"Yes, please!"

"Okay. It never happened," he said, looking as agreeable as could be and very un-Simonlike.

She looked away, definitely not needing to see him looking like that or spend her time trying to figure out what it meant.

But she accused him of those things, and she couldn't forget it.

She most certainly couldn't throw her arms around him.

"I am so sorry," she said.

"Why?" He sounded puzzled.

"Because, you weren't flirting. You weren't even thinking of flirting. You were just being…you. Like you said, you do this. It's no big deal. It didn't mean anything."

Especially not that he wanted her.

Not that a part of her didn't really love the idea of him wanting her.

She just couldn't have that.

Him.

Wanting her.

She couldn't.

She'd had enough trouble with men in the last year to last her a lifetime.

"I wanted you to have a nice day," he said. "And not to work so hard in the future. And to say I was sorry."

"I know. Thank you. It was lovely there. Just lovely."

"Good. I'm glad," he said, still too close and coming closer as he spoke. "And maybe I shouldn't say any more because you were so worried about it, or maybe I should say this because you were so worried. Or maybe I'll say it just because I want to say it…."

"Say what?" she said, instinctively wary.

"I'm sorry, Audrey. Really, I am, if this makes things harder for you. I know I'm not supposed to do this, and I tried not to. I really did. But if you thought I wished this morning that there was something between us…"

Oh, no.

His nose brushed past her hair, his warm breath on her ear. "You were right."

Chapter Seven

Audrey thought about slapping Simon out of sheer frustration. Then she just stood there, mouth hanging open, unable to say a thing.

He backed away, studying her face, then said, "I really am sorry. I don't want to make things difficult for you—"

"Difficult?" she finally got out.

"Yes," he whispered.

"Difficult?" she yelled.

Dammit, she was yelling at him again.

"Yes," he said, even more quietly than before.

For a man known to have a temper, he was coming off looking as if his was better than hers.

"Oh, Simon," she said, and then the tears really started to flow.

She hated that.

Just hated it.

Simon looked completely baffled, as if he wasn't sure

whether to flee or grab her and hang on to her and wished she'd give him a clue.

"You don't understand!" she cried.

"Then explain it to me, Audrey," he said, coming back to her and very carefully, very slowly, wiping her tears away. "Because I want to understand. I want to help, and I want to make things better for you. Tell me what you need, and I'll do it."

"I just need this job. I need it so much—"

"And no one's going to take it away from you, no matter what happens or doesn't happen between you and me."

She nodded, then got to the hard part. "And I need for nothing to happen between you and me."

"Why?"

He didn't make it sound like a command.

Anything but that.

Just a quiet request for understanding.

"Because I want my daughter back. I want that so much, and she lives five blocks away from here. So it means everything to me to be here, to be that close to her."

"And you can stay. I told you that. But, the rest of it, I don't understand. You can't be with me, even if you want to? Because I think you want something to happen—"

"I want my daughter back," she said again, more forcefully this time. "That's the most important thing."

"And you think us being together would interfere with that?"

"I know it would."

"Audrey, you're a grown woman, you're not married anymore, and yet for some reason, you're not allowed to have a man in your life—"

"You don't know," she told him, crying again. "You don't know what I did. You don't know how awful it was. How much I hurt so many people, and I just can't do that again, Simon. I can't."

He appeared to want to argue more, but then all the fight

went out of him. He put his hand to the side of her face, as if it hurt him to see her this miserable, and then he folded her into his arms and held her so gently it made her want to weep all the more.

He was so big and solid, his body so reassuring against hers.

For a moment she felt safe again, as she hadn't in so long, as she'd longed to feel ever since her marriage fell apart.

What was wrong with her that she thought she needed a man to feel truly safe, when the truth was a woman wasn't truly safe with any man, only herself? Surely she'd learned that by now. And yet there she was, sobbing against his broad chest, enveloped in the warmth of his arms.

"You shouldn't be so nice to me," she protested.

Laughter rumbled up from deep inside him, and she was sure she could feel a smile on his face, which was bent down low over the top of her head, his hold infinitely gentle and reassuring.

"But I so seldom am nice," Simon said.

"No. You are. You just try to hide it."

She snuggled a bit closer, if that was possible, trying to pull herself together. Trying to make herself let go.

It was so hard.

She felt his lips brush against the side of her face, which was wet with tears. Felt him kiss her cheek, then the corner of her mouth, slowly, giving her plenty of time to object and to move away.

And like a fool, like a woman who hadn't learned a thing in the past year, instead of moving away, she turned her face up to his, her mouth opening beneath his, welcoming the intoxicating pleasure of kissing Simon Collier, slowly, sweetly, as if they had all the time in the world.

He groaned, a hand at her waist pulling her body closer to his, his lips, his tongue teasing, arousing, promising all sorts of pleasures.

Audrey wrapped her arms around his shoulders, arching her back and pressing her body against his big, powerful one.

Kissing him was sheer bliss, she found.

And it had the power to push every single thought out of her head.

Andie was at the ice cream shop Saturday afternoon, looking around warily to make sure her mother was nowhere nearby.

She hadn't talked to her mother since the day they'd run into each other here, her mother with that dog, but Andie knew her mother was around. Half a dozen so-called friends of Andie's claimed to have seen her running through the neighborhood regularly or at the nearby park, again with the dog.

Could her mother really be working as a dog sitter?

And even if she was, how much time could that take? What kind of a living could a grown-up possibly make taking care of a dog?

It didn't make sense.

Which had Andie thinking it was probably just another lie.

Not that it really mattered.

She heard a car pull up to the curb in front of her and saw that it was Jake. He had that goofy grin he always wore around her, and she tried very hard to ignore how silly it made her feel.

Happy and warm and tingly inside.

Honestly, it was ridiculous.

He was a man, after all, and not to be trusted.

Neither should the feelings he brought up in her, because Andie was sure they wouldn't last.

"Hey, need a ride home?" he asked.

"I was going to walk," she said.

Actually, she was just killing time, trying to stay out of her house. Barbie and her father had been fighting, and she just didn't want to be there.

"Come on, I'll drive you," he urged, that grin simply huge now.

Andie got up, telling herself she was going to turn him down just because it was the smart thing to do and she was trying so hard to be smart.

Jake really was cute, but honestly he was like an overgrown puppy—big feet and too much hair and still awkward inside his own skin, as boys his age tended to be. Still, he'd been really nice to her these past awful months, despite the mess he'd gotten into because of her and her mother.

She still felt awful about that.

"Come on," he said, pushing open the passenger door to let her in.

"Well," she said, "I guess it would be better to get out of here. This is where I ran into my mother, and I certainly don't want to do that again."

"Yeah? I saw her here again the other day," Jake said.

"You didn't tell me you saw her again," she said, as if accusing him of something awful, but she got into the car anyway.

"I thought it would only upset you, so I didn't say anything."

"Well, what did she say? What did she do? You can't let her get you into trouble again," Andie said.

"She didn't say much of anything, and she didn't try to talk me into anything," Jake said, pulling out of the parking space and into traffic. "Actually, I had to talk her into letting us help her. She'd hurt herself while she was running with this dog, and we drove her home."

"We?" This was worse than Andie thought.

"I was getting a ride to school with Jordan and a couple of his buddies. It was no big deal, Andie. She was in the car for like two minutes," he claimed. "You didn't really want us to let her limp home, did you?"

"I don't care what she has to do, as long as I don't have to see her or talk to her," Andie told him.

Still, she hurt herself?

Andie pushed that thought away.

Instead she asked, "So you saw where she's living?"

Jake nodded. "Place looks like a mansion."

"Of course, it would. She's obviously found some man to take care of her again. It's all she knows how to do."

"She said she's working there," Jake claimed.

"Well, you can't trust anything she says. You know that."

"I'm just telling you what she said." He sighed, shook his head, then stopped the car in front of Andie's house.

She sat there, not wanting to go in. Not wanting to do anything, really.

"They're fighting again?" Jake asked.

Andie nodded.

"Want to come to my house? You know my uncle and Lily don't mind."

"I know," she muttered.

She did like being at Jake's house. It was nice there, and everyone in it was nice. It was just that they knew all about her mom and all the bad things that had happened, and she hated getting those looks from people. The smirks, the whispers, the laughter were one thing, but the kindness and understanding were almost worse.

As if they felt sorry for her.

She hated that.

Still, she hadn't been at Jake's in weeks, hadn't let herself go there.

"Andie, what's the big deal? We'll look over the AP Bio stuff. I can't wait and do it Sunday night. I promised I'd baby-sit the girls for Lily, so she and my uncle could go out," Jake coaxed.

"Okay," she said finally.

It took only a couple of minutes to get from her house to his. Andie got out of the car to follow him inside but ran into Mrs. Richards on the sidewalk. She hoped the woman would walk on by, but no such luck. She'd once been someone Andie's mother considered a friend but was now someone who seemed to revel in every bad thing her mother did.

"Andie, honey, imagine running into you today. I could swear I just saw your mother coming out of Morton's today and getting into some fancy car with a driver to take her away."

Morton's?

"That fancy spa next to the Westin?" Andie asked.

Mrs. Richards nodded. "Expensive as can be, too. I guess your mother landed on her feet again. Someone told me she'd taken a job as a dog walker, but believe me, you don't go to Morton's on what you earn walking dogs. So, there must be a new man. Have you met him yet?"

Andie shook her head, biting her bottom lip to keep from saying anything. Honestly, what was there to say?

"Well, it was nice to see you, honey. You take care," Mrs. Richards said, then walked on by.

Andie sank back against the side of Jake's car. He stood on the sidewalk beside her, waiting, probably trying to figure out what to do.

"Morton's," Andie said. "She's living with some rich, old man in Highland Park and spending her days getting pampered at Morton's. That's perfect. Just perfect."

"You don't know that," Jake insisted. "People will say anything about your mother these days—"

"You're right. I don't know," Andie said. "So let's find out. You drove her home that day? So you know where she's living. Take me there—"

"Andie, you don't need to do this. Not right now. You two don't need to fight anymore. What's it going to do except make things even worse?"

"Jake, take me there. Right now," she insisted, going back around to the passenger side of the car and getting in.

He looked for a moment as if he was going to refuse, but

he finally gave in. "Just try not to lay into her the minute you see her, okay? Give her a chance—"

"Why?"

"Because she's your mother and because your father's a jerk and you hate his girlfriend and you're miserable living with them."

"I'm just fine there," Andie insisted.

"Oh, yeah. You're thrilled with the whole situation."

"It's not like I have a choice, Jake!"

"Yeah, you do. Some of us don't, but you still do," he insisted.

And she fell silent, instantly ashamed of herself.

Jake had lost both his parents in a car accident last year. That's why he'd moved here, to live with his uncle.

"I would give anything—anything—to be able to talk to my mother again," Jake told her. "To see her. To have her get on my case about something. To live with her. But I can't. You still can."

"I know. I'm sorry."

"Andie, the thing is you might not always have that choice," he said softly, sadly.

"I'm just…" She couldn't tell him, didn't want to tell anyone.

She was terrified of depending on her mother like that again. Of depending on anyone.

Jake, even.

She had to fight hard not to let him any closer than she already had, and yet the relationship still made her uneasy.

Did he not get that?

Hadn't he learned anything from his parents' deaths.

Andie was terrified to trust her mother again.

"Will you just take me to that house where she's living? Please?"

"All right." He sounded disgusted with her and all her problems.

Fine, she thought.

He was mad. So what?

It was better this way.

He liked her too much already.

Simon wasn't quite sure how he'd gotten to this point—having Audrey in his arms, that luscious body of hers pressed up against him, her arms clinging to him, her mouth open beneath his—but he sure was glad.

One minute they'd been arguing, and then she'd been crying, and then she was here. He intended to make the most of it because he had a feeling it would be a while before she let herself be here again.

He held the side of her face to his with one hand, let his other slide down her back and to that sweet curve of her derriere, settling her even closer against him with a groan of frustration and pleasure all mixed into one.

He'd dreamed of having her spitting fire at him one minute and clinging to him the next, but the reality was even better.

She smelled good enough to eat, and her skin was whispery soft, her hair a little bit crazy and sexy as could be. She was trembling in his arms but hungry for him, too, kissing him as if her very life depended on it.

He was wondering if he could get away with carrying her upstairs and into her apartment without anyone seeing—especially his daughter, who was napping on a lounge chair on the back patio with the dog.

If the damned dog heard them, Simon didn't stand a chance of getting her upstairs alone.

And he very much wanted to be alone with her, behind a locked door, preferably in a room with a bed, because he'd like to stay there for a while afterward, and he feared this was really not the time.

She wanted him, but she was scared.

He wanted her, selfishly despite her fears, whatever they might be.

They could work through them, he decided.

He wasn't a man who let things stand in his way for long.

He could fix this, and then he could have Audrey in his bed.

"Come upstairs with me," he whispered urgently against her mouth.

"What?"

"Upstairs. With me. It's okay. Peyton's asleep."

He felt resistance slipping between them, could tell she was trying to summon the will to pull away.

"No," he said. "Don't do that. Don't think of all the reasons why. We'll deal with those later, and everything will be okay. I promise. I'll handle it, whatever it is. For right now, just be with me. I know that's what you want. It's what I want, too."

She groaned and stood on her tiptoes to kiss him even more desperately. "Simon, I can't."

"Of course, you can—"

She was trying to disentangle herself from his arms when Simon suddenly realized they were not alone. There was a car he didn't recognize in the driveway. An old Chevy with a teenage boy behind the wheel.

A tall, blond-haired girl had obviously just gotten out of the passenger seat and was staring at them with pure outrage in her eyes.

Audrey gasped and seemed to wither before his eyes.

"So, you're working here?" the girl said. "That's what you call it now? Working? No pretense that it's even anything else?"

Simon didn't care for the inference at all. He barked out, "Who are you?"

The girl's eyes flashed fire at him. "Who am I? Who are you?"

Great.

A furious teenager with a smart mouth.

He went to roar right back, not accustomed to anyone

taking that tone with him, but Audrey put a hand against his chest to stop him.

"Simon," she said. "This is my daughter. Andie."

Oh.

This was *so* bad.

He wasn't sure why, but he knew it was bad.

"Andie," Audrey began.

"Oh, save it, mother. I just came to see if you really were working here, and I got my answer," Andie said. "I heard someone was pampering you with a trip to Morton's this morning, and I thought it must be a new man. Looks like I was right. Judging by the house, I'd say he has a lot more money than the last guy you threw yourself at. How nice for you."

Simon had a flash of Audrey with another man and saw red for a moment but held his tongue, somehow. He slipped his arm around Audrey, not caring how it looked to her daughter, because she was trembling and hurt and worried.

The girl turned to him, fire flashing in her eyes. "Please tell me you're not married, because that was such a mess the last time when my mother went after another woman's husband."

Simon's jaw clenched even more tightly, as he said nothing more than, "No, I'm not married."

"Well, that's something. I hope you will be very happy together," her daughter said. "Just be sure to lock up your liquor cabinet. Mom has a little drinking problem. But you probably knew that already, didn't you?"

Simon saw that the teenage boy had gotten out of the car at some point. He looked embarrassed and weary and apologetic all at the same time. "Andie," he said putting his arm around the girl. "Come on. I'll take you home."

The girl looked vulnerable and hurt for the first time when she stared at him. "I don't have a home anymore."

But wasn't she living with her father? Simon didn't have time to figure it out because the stupid dog picked that moment to burst onto the scene, whining and barking and then standing guard between Audrey and her daughter.

Did he not think Simon could take care of this and protect Audrey?

Annoyed as he was, Simon almost missed the fact that Peyton was now hovering on the edge of the ugly scene, looking like she did when Simon had lost his temper with his ex-wife or his ex had lost her temper with him.

"So, this is the dog, I guess?" Audrey's daughter said. "You really expect people to believe you were a glorified dog walker—"

Simon stepped in then, ready to end this no matter what it took. He let himself tower over Audrey's daughter, drawing himself up into the biggest, baddest, most intimidating version of himself he could manage, something he would normally never do to a girl her age but was willing to at the moment.

He leaned over the girl and whispered to her, "That is my daughter. She's five. And she doesn't need to hear any more of this. Do you understand?"

"She understands," the boy said, showing more guts than most men would by being willing to nearly put himself between Simon and the girl.

Simon liked the kid, gave him major points for that and for working to diffuse the situation.

Audrey's daughter still looked defiant and furious and reckless in a way he feared many teenagers were, something that scared Simon half to death, thinking he'd one day be parenting a girl like that.

"Peyton," he said, without turning around. "Everything's all right, promise. Just take the dog and go to the back porch. I'll be there in a second."

"But—"

"Peyton, go. And take the dog."

He waited until she left with Tink.

Then he feared he was about to have a stare-down contest with Audrey's daughter.

"She ruins everything," the daughter said. "You should know that about her."

Could that actually be true?

Simon just couldn't make himself believe it.

"Andie, come on. Let's go," the boy said.

And finally the girl gave in, letting him turn her around and steer her to the car. She glared at her mother one more time, then let him put her inside.

The boy looked at Audrey. "I'll make sure she gets home okay."

"Thank you, Jake," Audrey whispered.

And then they were gone.

Audrey stepped away from him, eyes wet with tears and said, "That is why I can't have anything to do with you."

And then she turned, walked up the stairs and closed the door behind her.

Chapter Eight

So, she drank?

And chased married men?

Expensive men who could take care of her?

Simon stood at the bottom of the stairs to her apartment, on his own driveway, now silent and empty, hating all that he'd heard about her.

Was he just one more expensive man capable of giving her a good life in exchange for having her in his bed?

Surely he wasn't that.

Surely she wasn't that kind of woman.

He'd swear she wasn't.

But the girl was her daughter, and if anyone should know, wouldn't it be a teenage daughter? All that hurt he'd seen in the girl…that had to be real, didn't it? Dramatic as teenagers were known to be, he didn't think the girl could fake that kind of outrage and hurt and make it look so real.

And Audrey hadn't denied any of it.

Surely she would have, if she could have.

Which reminded him, his daughter had heard the whole thing. He had to make sure she was okay before doing anything else.

He walked around the back of the house and found her curled up in a big lounge chair, with Tink beside her, appearing concerned and trying to either distract or entertain the girl.

Maybe the dog was smarter than Simon thought.

He shot Simon a worried look and whined a bit.

Simon actually scratched the dog's head, because Simon appreciated anyone who was kind to his daughter.

Even a canine.

He sat down on the end of the lounge chair. Peyton was curled up in a ball and hardly taking up any room at all.

"Is the mean girl gone?" she asked.

"Yes, darling. She's gone."

"I don't like her. She's mean. And you're not supposed to fight like that. It's bad, and it scares people."

Simon brushed his daughter's pretty, blond hair back from the side of her face and saw that she'd been crying, something that had the power to nearly crack his heart in two.

"I'm sorry you had to hear that, Peyton. I don't want anything to ever scare you. Or worry you."

And he knew there'd been times he'd done both of those things during the breakup of his marriage.

"Who was she?" Peyton asked, her bottom lip sticking out in an adorable pout.

"That was Audrey's daughter."

Peyton sat up at that. "She fights with her mother like that?"

Simon nodded.

"She's not supposed to do that."

"I know," Simon said. "People shouldn't treat others like that. Especially not people they love. But I'm afraid we all do it sometimes. We try not to get upset and yell, but…we do. We should all try to do better, to be nicer to the people we love."

Peyton looked very serious then. "Do you think she still loves her mother?"

"Yes," Simon said, reasoning to himself that it took caring deeply to stir up that passionate a response.

"Do you think her mother still loves her?"

"I know she does. Audrey told me so."

Peyton laid back down, hugging the dog. "Tink loves me, and I love him."

"And I love you," Simon said. "And your mother loves you, too."

"Did she tell you she did? Because…sometimes…she gets really mad at me, too, daddy."

Simon closed his eyes and told himself to breathe. That he'd just told her everybody yelled, and that it was true, and that he was as guilty as anybody.

"Well, people get mad sometimes, and they get tired, and sometimes they're just really worried and scared and they yell. Like that time you almost chased your red ball into the street and a car was coming. Remember that?"

Peyton nodded. "You scared me."

Okay, so he had yelled at her before.

"I know. I'm sorry. You really scared me. I thought you were going to get hurt, and I had to stop you. I don't want anything to ever hurt you, darling."

"But I haven't run out into the street since then," she said.

"That's good. That's very good."

"But still…"

"Peyton, I want you to know you can always come to me if you have a problem. You have my phone number, right? You still remember it? You can call me any time, and I'll come help you. I swear, I will. And I'm sorry we don't all live together anymore. I miss you so much."

"I miss you, too, Daddy." She sat up and flung her arms around him.

He held her tightly, searching for the right thing to say.

The dog whined and tried to nose his way in between them, and then Peyton giggled and sat back down and hugged the silly dog.

At least, she was happy again.

That meant the world to him.

"Peyton, I'm trying to make things better for us, okay?"

"Like…how?" she asked. "Us all living together again?"

Ooh.

Not that.

"Maybe…you and me living together? All the time?"

"And Tink and Ms. Bee, too?"

"And Tink and Ms. Bee," he said. "Would you like that?"

Her whole face lit up. "Can you really do that, Daddy?"

"I'm trying," he said. "I'm doing everything I can."

"But you can do anything! I know you can!"

The faith of a five-year-old. Simon was humbled by it, in awe of it and certainly hoped he'd prove worthy of it.

"I'm going to do my best," Simon promised. "Now, what do you and this dog want to do with our afternoon?"

"Do you think Audrey's okay? 'Cause me and Tink are worried about her."

"You and the dog?"

Tink whined, as if to say, *Yes, he was worried.*

Simon was sure the dog couldn't be that smart.

Still, he gave a good impression of being worried.

"We don't like it when people fight with us, and we don't think Audrey liked it when that mean girl yelled at her," Peyton said.

"The girl was her daughter, remember?" Simon thought at first that would make Peyton worry less—that there wasn't some random, angry stranger here yelling at someone. But maybe it was worse that it was Audrey's daughter.

"Me and Tink think we should go see if she's okay," Peyton said.

"Darling, I don't know if she wants to see anyone right now. I think she might want to be alone."

"Nobody wants to be alone when they're sad," Peyton claimed.

Simon took a breath. "Okay, if you really want to do that."

Tink barked happily and took off running for Audrey's.

"There's no way he could understand what I just said," Simon claimed.

"Of course, he did," Peyton said, as if there wasn't even a question about it. "He's going to find her."

She got up and went after the dog, Simon following reluctantly after her.

He was sure Audrey didn't want to see him.

Audrey wasn't crying.

What was the point?

It didn't change anything.

And she couldn't make herself blessedly numb by drinking, as she had before when things had gotten so bad, because she didn't do that anymore. It had only added to her problems.

Which meant she was stuck, sitting here, feeling awful and sad and upset and lost and alone.

Which was the worst feeling in the world.

She closed her eyes and curled up on her sofa, remembering the lessons of her recent stay in rehab.

Don't try to run away from your problems. You can't.

Don't try to minimize them.

Don't try to deny them.

Don't try to numb them with a few drinks.

Just let yourself feel them.

Right.

Just feel awful.

How could that possibly help?

She sat there feeling awful until she heard a knock on her door.

"Simon, not now, please?" she begged. "I'll tell you whatever you want to know, just—"

The door opened, and the dog shot inside, jumping up on the sofa beside her and licking her face worriedly.

"Tink," she said, pushing him away with a gentle hand against his chest. "We talked about this, remember? This is just too much."

He whined but stopped licking her and settled for just staying close.

She looked up wearily and saw Simon and Peyton, too.

Which was a surprise.

"Peyton was worried about you," he said.

"Oh." Audrey hadn't suspected that.

"And Tink," Peyton added.

"Well, that was very sweet of both of you," she said.

"We didn't like the mean girl—"

"Peyton, remember who I told you that was?" Simon jumped in.

Peyton frowned. "Is she really your daughter?"

"Yes," Audrey told her.

"Why is she so mean to you?"

Audrey let all the breath go out of her at once, leaving her exhausted and clueless as to what to say.

"Peyton?" Simon put his hand on his daughter's shoulder. "This is something for Audrey and her daughter to work out between them, not for us to get in the middle of."

"But I don't want that girl yelling at Audrey," Peyton insisted.

"Peyton, honey," Audrey said. "I'm sorry you had to hear that. Really sorry."

"I don't like it when people fight," she said.

"I know. I don't, either," Audrey said.

"Are you really sad?"

"Yes," Audrey told her. "It made me really sad."

"Well, me and Tink could try to make you better," Peyton

said, in all seriousness, coming to stand by Audrey and lay a hand on her arm.

"You know, that's the best offer I've had in a long time." Audrey gave the girl a big smile and then leaned down so Peyton could hug her.

Little arms wrapped around Audrey and squeezed her tightly, making her think of her own daughter being this little and sweet and loving her the way she had back then. The innocence of her love hadn't survived, but it had been so pure and complete it was enough to break a mother's heart when it was lost.

Audrey hugged the girl back, and then Tink tried to lick both their faces; Peyton giggled and hugged the dog, and Audrey laughed a bit herself.

She looked up to find Simon still in the doorway, watching them with a hooded expression. He had to have a million questions for her. She dreaded answering them, but she would.

And then if he asked her to leave, she'd do that, too.

Audrey really couldn't think much beyond that point.

It was just too hard.

She'd have to explore those feelings a bit later, no matter what they'd taught her in rehab.

"You wanna come to the park to play with me and Tink?" Peyton asked.

"Peyton, no," Simon said. "We're going to give Audrey the day off. She worked really hard yesterday, and she's had a tough day today."

"But everybody's happy at the park. It's a happy place."

If only the world were that simple.

Go to a happy place and be happy.

Audrey was all for a world that worked like that.

She looked up at Simon, asking if he wanted her to go with them, and he shrugged his shoulders, as if it didn't matter to him one way or the other.

"Please," Peyton said. "We can't leave you here when you're sad."

"All right," Audrey said. "I'll go."

Andie couldn't go home. Not in the shape she was in. Not with her father and Barbie there, fighting,

No way Andie wanted either of them to even know what was going on in her life, much less how upset she was in that moment at her mother.

So she let Jake just drive, and he finally pulled into a parking spot in the park by the lake. She got out of the car and sat down on the hood of the car, leaning back against the windshield. The car engine was warm from both the drive over and the sunshine, and the air was nice and cool. Perfect, almost.

The lake was a lazy blue and quiet and peaceful at the moment.

Andie just laid there and stared at it, Jake standing by her side, throwing a rock into the water every now and then and trying to make it skip across the surface. He wouldn't try to make her talk, which was nice. He'd just be here and give her some time, and when she was ready, everything would come pouring out. As if he knew all along how to get her to open up to him.

It was so annoying!

She'd get herself all set to insist that she didn't want to talk about anything, and then the longer they sat there in silence, the more the words fought to come tumbling out.

How did he do that?

Andie would rather try to figure it out than to deal with the jumble of feelings inside of her.

But eventually, Jake's method of waiting silently won out. Either that or her own anger.

"Can you believe she did that again?" Andie yelled.

Jake shrugged, as if he wasn't surprised, but he wasn't mad, either.

"I mean, didn't she learn anything from the last time?"

"She didn't seem like she'd been drinking," Jake said. "Not today or the last time I saw her."

"The last time you saw her was at seven o'clock in the morning, before school started," Andie pointed out.

It would have to be really bad if her mother was drunk then.

"I'm just saying, maybe she's quit drinking, at least."

"Which is such a good quality in a mother. She doesn't seem to be drunk at the moment," Andie said with as much sarcasm as she could muster. Although, no amount of sarcasm would be enough to express how bitter she felt about the matter. "And the men? What is it with her and men? Is she just incapable of being without one?"

Andie knew teenage girls who felt like that, desperate to find someone new when they'd just gotten rid of someone else who hadn't been that good to them or had made them miserable. What made them think the next guy would be any better? Or were they just desperate not to be alone?

"I mean, there are some girls my age who do that. Run from one guy to another. But she's thirty-eight! She's a grown woman. She should be able to take care of herself."

Andie would never be that needy, that desperate, that weak. She promised herself that.

She looked over at Jake, who was calmly throwing another rock that he managed to skip across the surface of the water.

"What? Nothing to say?" she asked, all wound up and ready to fight with him, too, if he was willing.

"I don't know, Andie. I don't know what she's thinking. I don't know if that place she went to, to dry out, helped her or not. And I don't know what to tell you to make you feel better. I just wish I did."

"You're going to defend her, aren't you?" She sat up and glared at him. He hadn't yet, but she felt sure he would, for reasons she couldn't begin to understand. "She told us she was working there—"

"And maybe she is. Everybody who's seen her has seen her with that dog."

"And we saw her all over that man."

"Well, she could still be working there," he tried.

"And fooling around with her boss already. After…what, a week? She works fast, my mother."

To which, Jake couldn't seem to come up with anything to say.

"Couldn't she just stop making a fool of herself? Chasing after men, like she's desperate to find one? Couldn't she just get a normal job and find her own place to live and be respectable again? Is that too much to ask for from your own mother?" she cried.

"Andie, if you want to talk about being respectable, your father walked out on you and her, after they'd been married for almost twenty years. Just walked away and didn't look back. Did you even see him after he left?"

"Once or twice. I don't know. I saw him."

"In how many months? Eight? Ten? Almost a year?"

"Well, he must have been really unhappy with her," Andie said.

"That's no reason to leave you," Jake insisted.

"He's there for me now—"

"Is he? Because it seems like he's never there—"

"He has to work," Andie told Jake.

Jake just looked at her at first, challenging that notion without a word.

"He does! He works hard, to take care of us."

"He hardly even makes time for his girlfriend. You told me that. And it looks like he moved her into your house hoping she'd take care of you, which you say she does a lousy job of. Not that it's surprising given the fact that she's…what, only eight or nine years older than you."

Andie's mouth fell open and she glared at him. "If you're trying to make me feel better, you're doing a great job! Thank you, Jake! I'll be fine now!"

And then she'd done it. She'd just blasted him, and sometimes it felt as if he was the only person in the world who still gave a damn about her.

Way to go, Andie.

She got off the car and took off in the direction of her house.

"Hey," Jake called out to her. "Where are you going?"

"I'll walk home," she said.

"Andie, don't be like that," he called out.

But she just kept on walking.

Lately she wasn't fit company for anyone.

Audrey wanted to walk to the dog park to help burn off some of the dog's energy before they got there. She didn't want him being too rough with any of the other dogs or their owners in his exuberance and excitement.

When she decided to walk, Peyton wanted to, as well, and then Simon decided if they walked, he would, too. So the three of them, plus the dog, set out together, Peyton chattering all the way, the dog barely able to contain his excitement over being out and about with all three of them.

He was practically bouncing from one to the other as they walked. Or at least from Audrey to Peyton, yipping and tangling up his leash, wanting to check out every bush and tree as he went.

"Damned nuisance," Simon muttered under his breath as the dog lunged ahead to catch up with Peyton.

Audrey risked looking at him, trying to gauge just how angry he was at what he'd learned and at the scene that had played out in part in front of his daughter. She wouldn't be surprised if he asked her to leave, no matter what he'd said before he'd taken her into his arms.

She steeled herself not to think about that. Not now when she had so much at stake. Not why he had kissed her or why she had let him or anything about how it had felt. What good was a man who was interested in her, as fleeting as that could be, when her whole life was at stake? And she considered this job and its proximity to her daughter her whole life right now.

Audrey took a breath and tried to calm down, to simply put one foot in front of the other and hold on to the dog.

Of all the times for Andie to show up, why did it have to be then? To see her with Simon like that? As if Audrey hadn't already suffered enough for her own stupidity. Did she have to keep paying and paying, and keep making the same mistakes? Hadn't she learned anything from the debacle of last fall?

Today made it seem as if she hadn't learned a thing.

She was sure her daughter thought so, and that was the worst of all. Audrey wanted nothing more than to show her daughter she had changed, that she had learned, that things would be different now.

And she couldn't even blame Simon entirely, because much as she'd told herself to be smart, to be careful and to concentrate on getting Andie back, Audrey was attracted to him. She had wanted to have his arms around her, his mouth on hers.

How could she still want that, after all the trouble the last two men in her life had caused her?

"There it is! The dog park!" Peyton cried out, beaming as she looked back at them.

Tink must have caught sight of it, too, because he started barking like crazy, trying to lurch ahead, causing the leash to jerk hard on Audrey's right hand and shoulder.

She winced but held on tight.

Simon must have seen it because he swore softly under his breath and grabbed the leash from her.

"Damned dog," he said again. "He's too much for you."

"He's just excited, and he's still a puppy," Audrey said.

"Which means he'll be dragging you down the street when he's full grown," Simon argued.

"No, he'll be calmer and better trained by the time he's full grown." She hoped she could accomplish that with the dog, given time.

If she was given the time.

She glanced over at Simon again, but he was concentrating on trying to control the dog, giving her no clue about whether she'd be around to civilize Tink.

She waited to remove his leash until they got inside the enclosure, and was happy to see that there were only a half-dozen other dogs within the fenced area and no really small children, because Tink still liked to jump up on people when he got excited, and he could knock a small child down. She let Peyton take the leash off him, and he sprinted off to meet his playmates, sniffing them and barking a bit in greeting and then bouncing back and forth, trying to entice a young black Lab into playing with him.

She saw Tink playing rather nicely.

Peyton was petting a prissy, white toy poodle in the corner and was happy as could be, and Simon...

Simon was waiting.

She had to explain.

Audrey let out a shaky breath.

God, help her.

How could she explain?

Audrey sat on a bench beneath a tree in the farthest corner of the dog park, with Simon following her, and tried to figure out what to say.

"You can fire me if you want," she said, once he sat beside her and the silence stretched to the point that she couldn't stand it anymore. "It's okay."

"I told you I wouldn't."

"But you didn't know what I'd done then. Now you do. So...it's okay." She'd accepted that now. This had been a pipe dream, anyway. Coming back here. Being close to Andie. The two of them somehow working out their differences and Audrey reclaiming her daughter at least.

She had self-destructed.

Old life over.

No going back.

She heard Simon sigh heavily, could feel his impatience coming off him in waves and, she thought, him struggling for control.

Peyton giggled as the poodle got up on its back feet and danced for her. Tink was rolling on the ground with the Lab, but they both looked happy, so everything was fine.

Audrey said, "I'm just so tired. I can't fight with anyone anymore. Not you. Not my daughter or my ex-husband or your housekeeper. Not anybody."

Chapter Nine

Simon felt like an ass then.

She looked all done in, worn out, too sad even to say anything to defend herself or to explain.

"Aw, hell," he said, sliding across the bench to her, stretching his arm out behind her and gently encouraging her to rest her weary head against his shoulder, which she finally did.

She seemed so tiny then.

Much too petite to have that fool dog pulling her around all the time or to be spreading loads of mulch. Or to have a daughter she clearly wanted so badly who seemed to hate her.

Way too many troubles for someone so weary and small.

"Tell me what happened," he said.

"Does it really matter? I did what Andie said. She didn't lie."

Simon closed his eyes and absorbed that.

The other man.

The other rich, married man.

And the drinking.

He couldn't be surprised by this, not with her being one of Marion's rescues. And it wasn't as if he was a saint—not by any stretch of the imagination.

Who was he to judge?

He just didn't want this to be *her*.

And it stung. The rich guy stuff stung.

"Why did you come to me for a job?" he asked, his ego still smarting from how much he'd liked her from the start and never gotten that desperate-for-a-rich-husband feeling from her. He usually spotted that a mile away.

"Because Andie lives only five blocks away from you."

He winced. "That's the only reason?"

"Because Marion knew you, and it sounded like a job I actually had a chance of being able to do. Dogs usually like me, and I like them. And I've always liked working in my yard." She sniffled. "It's not like I'm really qualified to do anything, Simon. I was nineteen, waitressing in a bar with a fake ID when I met Richard. I married him, had Andie, took care of them both. That's really all I've ever done. It's not exactly the kind of thing that fills out a résumé."

He nodded. "Okay."

"I'm not trying to make you feel sorry for me. God, that's the last thing I want. I'm just…that's what happened. I had a husband, a home, a daughter I loved. A life. I had a life, and I thought my husband and I were…not thrilled to be together anymore but not unhappy. I thought we had a family and a partnership that was going to last. I mean, it's hard, you know?"

"I know." He certainly hadn't been able to make his marriage work, hadn't wanted to, once he saw what his wife really wanted, and it wasn't to be a mother, just to be a rich man's wife.

Simon looked up and saw Peyton talking to another girl about her age who seemed to belong to the white poodle but was willing to share. He hadn't quite known what would be best—to stay with his wife for Peyton's sake, make that life as good as it could be and go on from there or get out and pray he could get Peyton to himself most of the time.

He still hoped for that.

He wanted it more than anything.

But he was finding himself lonely, too, at times. The deep-down, aching kind of loneliness he didn't quite know what to do with. He didn't think he trusted himself to pick another woman to bring into their lives, and yet he didn't really want to be alone, either.

He was a man who truly hated to make mistakes, and his first marriage had been a whopper, one he was still paying for, one his daughter was paying for. He hadn't chosen the divorce, his ex-wife had. Not that he'd tried that hard to talk her out of it, either. His wealth gave him a huge bargaining chip, and he'd hoped to use it to get Peyton, but that hadn't happened.

He still hoped it would one day.

Which meant he and Audrey were fighting for the same thing.

Daughters they both loved.

What were the odds?

"So, it was the drinking," he asked, "that made you lose custody?"

"No. I wasn't drinking when we divorced. I mean, I had a glass of wine with dinner, went to cocktail parties and threw them at our house for my husband's business connections. Things like that. But I wasn't getting drunk. After Richard left, I had custody of Andie."

"He left you?"

Audrey whispered, "Yes."

"So...another woman?" He guessed.

"Twenty-five years old," Audrey said. "I have trouble thinking of her as a woman, but, yes, that was the reason Richard left. He walked away from me and Andie, and he never really looked back."

"Bastard," Simon said.

Audrey laughed just a bit. "I thought so, but then I'm biased."

"You weren't…seeing anyone, too?"

"No!" She stared at him with weary eyes, seeming hurt that he'd even asked. "I was married. It meant something to me. I didn't do that."

"Okay. Sorry," Simon said. "Your daughter said—"

"Later, I did, and it was stupid and wrong. I know that. I…I was just so mad and scared and hurt. Richard had just found someone else and gone right on with his life. He seemed happy as could be, and there I was, trying not to fall apart for Andie. To hang on to the house without any money. Richard's an accountant. He knew just how to hide everything we had, and he was hoping the longer he could drag out the divorce settlement—with him hardly paying anything in support during the process—he'd get me to agree to the divorce on his terms."

"Bastard," Simon said again.

"Yeah, he was. I just never thought he'd treat me like that. I was sinking faster and faster into debt, and I just kept thinking Richard had to come around, be reasonable, for Andie's sake. Even if he didn't love me, he loved her."

Simon knew men just like that. Out for all they could get in a divorce and never looking back.

"I tried to hang on to the house," Audrey said. "Just until Andie could finish high school. Maybe that was a mistake. I don't know, because we really couldn't afford it once Richard left. But it was our house, our neighborhood. Something familiar in a crazy situation. We'd raised our daughter there. It was our home, and I just got so mad."

"I would have, too," Simon agreed.

Audrey met his gaze for a moment, then hid her head against his shoulder, as if she couldn't stand for him to see her anymore. "It was like it was all on me, to pretend things were okay, to hide how angry I was and the fact that I didn't know what to do. I started not being able to sleep at night, and I'd have a drink or two to help me sleep. And then I figured out that if I drank enough, I wasn't scared anymore. At least, not for a while. I didn't really feel anything, and it was so nice not to be scared or mad."

Simon hated thinking of her being so scared and so alone, and he could imagine her trying to be so strong and trying to hide everything from her daughter. That's who he thought she was.

"Tell me the rest," he said.

Audrey shook her head, sighing against his shoulder.

"It was like taking a vacation from everything lousy in your life, and I needed it. I didn't think I could make it without those times when I wasn't feeling anything at all. I drank because it made me numb, and then I wanted to be numb more and more, and then…for some reason, I decided finding another man was the answer."

He stiffened at that.

That other man.

"I mean, that's what Richard did," she said "And everything seemed fine for him. He seemed happy, so why shouldn't I do the same thing. It just…I don't know. It seemed like a way to…not feel so lousy all the time."

"Who was he?" Simon asked, hoping he didn't sound as jealous as he felt, however irrational that was.

"A guy in the neighborhood. He'd been coming on to me at parties for years, and I'd always turned him down. Although, I have to admit, it was nice thinking someone else wanted me, at least, even if he was married. I'd heard rumors at times that he was seeing another woman, but I didn't really know for sure, and he and his wife stayed together, so I thought maybe they weren't true. And then…I just stopped caring, I guess. I drank to feel nothing, and then I chased after him, thinking if Richard could do it and be happy, I could, too. And at least I wouldn't be all alone anymore."

"So, what happened?"

"His wife found out, at a charity fund-raiser with half the

neighborhood attending. I got drunk. Really drunk. She got very mad at both of us, and the next thing I knew, everyone knew all about what I'd been doing with her husband."

"Ouch," Simon said.

"The worst part was that Andie had followed me there because she was worried about me. She saw the whole thing. Parents of her friends were there, so all her friends heard about it. She ended up dragging me out of that party." Audrey winced. "Can you imagine? I'm the grown-up. I'm supposed to save her from things like that, and there's my sweet Andie, trying to save me."

"Yeah, that would have been bad."

"It got worse. She called her friend Jake, the boy who was with her today, to come pick us up. He didn't even have his license at the time. I'd had so much to drink that night that I passed out and they couldn't wake me up. They got scared and tried to rush me to the hospital, but Jake lost control of the car and wrecked it. It's a miracle neither one of them was really hurt."

"You weren't hurt?" Simon asked.

"Not physically, not from the accident, but I almost managed to drink myself into a coma that night. For a while the doctors weren't sure I was going to wake up, but I did. And then Richard moved back into the house with his girlfriend and Andie. I went to rehab and then met Marion at…" She stopped suddenly, looking at Simon.

"I know she's in AA," Simon told her.

"Yeah, I met her in AA. She took pity on me, took me in for a few months, something I understand she's been doing for years. And here I am."

Simon sat there with her, hating thinking of her having to go through that, of her daughter having to, of Audrey being lost and hurt and scared. And then he didn't know anything for sure except that he wished she'd never had to go through any of that.

And now he'd made it worse for her because he'd ignored

what she said, had told himself she wanted him despite that and had taken her in his arms, just in time for her daughter to arrive.

"I am really sorry about what I did and what your daughter saw. I had no right, Audrey. And I don't even know if it's something I can make better."

Audrey shook her head, which was still resting against his shoulder, her face completely hidden from view. She took a shaky breath, as if fighting to keep from sobbing, and he let his hand rub gently along her shoulder, aiming for comfort and nothing else in his touch.

"Maybe I'm kidding myself. Maybe I just have to wait her out and hope that if enough time goes by, she'll come back to me. Marion thinks she will. So I came here, to put myself in her neighborhood, where she'd have to see me and hopefully deal with me eventually."

"It was the right thing to do. At least, I think so," he said. "I always fight for what I want. I don't know any other way except to fight for what I want."

"So, I have the Simon Collier seal of approval, at least for what I'm doing now?" She lifted her head finally, eyes sad and wet, her nose a little red, and once again the thing he wanted most was to make everything all better for her.

Then he wondered if that's what that other man wanted to do, too. If he thought she was adorable and…not helpless but in need of help, and he just wanted to make everything all better?

Simon bristled at the thought.

"What happened to the other man?" he asked, unable to help himself.

Audrey frowned. "I'm not sure. He and his wife sold their house and moved, but I'm not sure if they're still together. I tried to get an address, so I could apologize to them, but the people I asked weren't inclined to help me find them. Which I understand perfectly. I probably should have tried harder to get in touch with them, because we're supposed to apologize, it's part of the program. I guess I was relieved, really, to not have to face either of them or even know what kind of damage I'd done."

So, she didn't want anything to do with the man.

Simon, ludicrously felt better about that part. Still, the woman had issues. Serious issues.

"What about the drinking? Do you worry that you'll fall back into that?"

"I'm not one of those people who loves to drink. I mean, I don't see a glass of wine and crave the taste of it. It was about how bad I felt and how scared I was—and not being able to face that anymore. Needing to numb myself to all of that. So I worry that life might get really bad again. That even knowing drinking won't solve anything, that it only made things worse for me, I might still feel so bad I'd crave that kind of numbness again. I can find peace when I run sometimes. If I go far enough or long enough, nothing else matters but to just keep going. Everything else falls away for a while. I just hope that's enough for me now."

"So the dog is like therapy?"

Audrey tried to force a smile, tried and failed, tears filling her eyes once again. "He is. He's my best hope because he loves to run, too. And he'll behave if he gets in a good, long run every day. So I'll run. And keep hoping that something I'm doing will work with my daughter and she'll come back to me. Beyond that, I have no idea what else to do."

He still had one arm stretched out along the back of the bench, and he let that hand cup her shoulder, giving her a little squeeze and a nod, inviting her back into a loose embrace. She let her forehead fall to his chest. He let his other hand cup her cheek and laid a gentle kiss against the top of her head.

"You keep doing what you've been doing. Keep fighting for what you want. And hope that tomorrow's a better day."

Andie was walking home through the park when she saw them. She wasn't sure it was her mother and that man at first, but then she spotted the dog, barking and playing with the little girl who'd been at the man's house.

Then she looked back at the bench, not really able to see her mother's face pressed against the man's shoulder that way. But she was pretty sure that was her mother's hair, dark and curly and a little bit wild at times, and that it was the same man from the big house in Highland Park.

They looked…close.

Not happy-close, but he appeared to be trying to comfort her.

Well, that was the way her mother did it, wasn't it?

She played on a man's sympathy, tried to get him to take care of her.

Which meant her mother was up to her same old tricks, just as Andie suspected. A few tears, a few kisses, stolen afternoons spent in bed….

Andie saw the man touch her face, kiss her gently on her forehead.

The gesture was intimate and oddly sweet.

Another man taken in, Andie thought, disgusted.

Then the little blond girl and the dog ran over to them, the girl looking puzzled, then concerned.

Audrey watched as her mother lifted her head and put on a bright smile, the little girl smiled back and the dog started prancing with excitement at her feet.

They almost resembled a family together like that.

New man, new daughter.

She hadn't thought it was possible for her mother to hurt her any more than she already had, but Andie absolutely hated the sight of her mother with that man and his little girl.

Simon wasn't sure whether it was the right thing to do, but since he decided he'd helped make this mess, he had to try to help clean it up.

He waited until Peyton was asleep that night, with Audrey

upstairs in her room, he supposed, then got in his car and drove to Audrey's former home. He remembered the way from when he'd gone to check out the job she'd done with her yard before he'd hired her.

It was a little after nine o'clock when he pulled into the driveway, lights still on both downstairs and up, an older-model sedan in the driveway and a little convertible. Neither of which he suspected Audrey's ex would drive.

So at least he wouldn't have to see that man.

He got out of his car, went to the front door and knocked.

From the music he heard coming through the front door, he was certain a teenager was in there somewhere.

Three tries at the doorbell and Andie finally answered, looking ready to lay into him the moment he opened the door.

"What do you want?" she asked.

"Three minutes of your time," Simon said, not waiting for an invitation before he walked inside.

"Hey!" she protested.

"Three minutes and I'm gone," he promised, stopping just inside the doorway and not trying to go any farther, looking around the warm, comfortable atmosphere of the home and knowing without a doubt that Audrey had created this room.

Her daughter pushed the door hard enough that it closed with a smack, then stood there, arms crossed, glaring at him, but the tear tracks on her face softened the whole look, and then he realized how tiny she was, tiny arms, tiny shoulders, just…tiny all over.

So fragile looking, despite what she wanted anyone to think.

And Audrey's daughter.

"Look, I don't care about anything you have to say to me," she claimed.

"Fine. I'll say it anyway and then I'll go." He looked at his watch, set it to count down from three minutes, showed it to her and then punched a button to start it. "I hired your mother to work for me and nothing else—"

"Right—"

"Hey, it's my three minutes. I hired her to do a job, and she's been doing it. And I told her tonight that I was interested in her, and she told me in no uncertain terms that she wanted nothing to do with me, beyond doing her job."

"Well, I hear women get paid for that sort of thing—"

Simon blasted her with a blistering glare. She held up frustratingly well beneath it, but at least she shut up about her mother for a moment.

God help him if he ever had to resort to this with his own daughter. He didn't think he could stand it.

And the clock was ticking on his three minutes.

"She told me she wanted one thing and one thing only right now and that's to get you back into her life."

Andie laughed, a disgusted sound.

"That's what she said. That's what she wants. She came to work for me because I live in the right place. I'm only five blocks from you, and she's dying to be close to you in any way she can. Me, I can be a little stubborn and a little conceited. I'm used to getting what I want from women. I kissed her anyway."

"Really?"

"Yes, really. And I shouldn't have, and I'm sorry for that because I have a daughter, too, and I wouldn't be able to stand it if she wanted nothing to do with me. I would be furious at anyone who got in the way of me winning her back."

"How touching," Andie said.

Simon bit back a curse, barely.

Were teenage girls the most infuriating, stubborn creatures on earth? He'd heard they were. He began to fear his own daughter turning into one.

"I'm lucky your mother isn't furious with me, but in truth it's almost worse to see what she is. Which is hurt. Devastated, even. She doesn't think she has a chance of making things right between you."

"Done?" Andie asked, not relenting one bit.

"I understand your anger. Really, I do. She hurt you. She became someone you couldn't count on for a time, and it frightened you."

"I don't need her. I don't need anybody," Andie claimed.

"Oh, yes, you do. Your life will get a lot easier once you realize that. Tell me something, before your parents split up, which one of them was really there for you day after day? Who fixed things when you had a problem? Who listened to you? Who did you think would always have your back? Because judging by how angry you are and how betrayed you feel, I'd say that person was your mother. Otherwise, it wouldn't matter so much that she let you down."

Bingo.

He'd finally said something that got through to her.

"Now, you've been through a rough time, and you're very young. I understand that, and I'm sorry. But we all go through tough times, and we all get disappointed by people we love and count on. It's just a part of life. The important thing is what they do afterward. Do they walk away and give up on us? Or do they fight to make things better? Your mother is fighting for you, and she's not going to stop. So the question is what do you want? I know you think you want to keep punishing her, because you're still mad and still hurt, and that's fine for a while. You're entitled to be mad."

"Gee, thanks. I really need your permission to be mad at my own mother."

Simon sighed, more frustrated than he remembered being in years. Time to change tactics one more time, take a chance.

"Look, if everything's fine here, and your father's taking good care of you, giving you all the parental attention and support that you need, great. Go on being furious at your mother. But if your living situation isn't so great and you're missing what you used to have with your mother, you should know that you can have it again. She's right down the road, waiting for you, hoping that you'll let her back into your life. Think about that. It's yours for the asking."

"No, it's not. She's not the person I thought she was!"

"Right. She's human. She messed up, Andie. She spent nineteen years with your father, and he walked away from her and you. That's what happened, isn't it? He walked away and left her to try to pick up the pieces and take care of you. You think that was easy? You think she wasn't scared? And every bit as mad as you are? You think she didn't try for as long as she could to take care of you and everything else?"

"I don't know!" The words practically exploded from the girl. "I don't know what happened to her! I don't know why it happened. I just know it did, and it's not something she can take back!"

"No, she can't," Simon said softly. "But she still loves you."

Finally, more hurt than anger showed in her expression.

"She does. She loves you, and it's nothing to dismiss lightly, that kind of love."

"I can't trust her," Andie insisted. "I can't. But it's fine. I'm fine. I can take care of myself."

"Sure you can," Simon said, frowning, worried that he'd only made things worse.

His watch beeped, three minutes gone.

He took a breath, couldn't think of anything else to say, then settled for, "I'm sorry I made things worse between you tonight. It really was my fault, and I'd hate to be what stands between the two of you."

"There's so much more standing between the two of us," she said.

Simon nodded.

His time was up. He let himself out without another word.

Chapter Ten

Audrey kept her head down, took care of the dog, planned Simon's yard and did very little else in the next few days.

Although she did manage to watch Simon every day as he walked from the house to the garage to get into his car and drive away. And most days she managed to catch him as he came home and walked from the garage into his house.

"There must be something wrong with me," she told Marion one day on the phone as she watched him.

"Honey, there'd be something wrong with you if you didn't appreciate a man as fine looking as Simon Collier," Marion said. "You're a young, beautiful woman—"

"I'm ready to be a smart woman. And the idea of getting in line and becoming one of Simon's women…" Surely she was too smart for that.

Marion made a scoffing sound. "I know he looks like the kind of man who'd keep women on a string, ready to come when he crooks his little finger, but he's not like that now. He made his money at a very young age, and he's always had women after him. He made his mistakes a long time ago, and he learned from them. Believe me, a string of women is the last thing he wants."

Marion sounded as if she believed that, and when Audrey thought about it, she had to admit, she'd never seen him with a woman, except Ms. Bee. But Simon was out of town as often as he was here. Maybe he just restricted that sort of activity to his nights on the road, an idea Audrey absolutely hated.

"Ask me what he wants," Marion prompted her.

"It doesn't matter what he wants. I can't give it to him."

"Of course, you can. But you're going to have to figure that out on your own. For now, I'm just going to say that the man is as solid as they come. And I'm not talking about those pretty muscles of his."

Audrey sighed, giving everything away in that one sound, she feared.

Marion laughed, as if she'd known all along anyway. "Remember what you want."

"I do. It's all I think about. I want my daughter back."

"And then you'll let yourself have a life?"

Audrey frowned, caught off-balance. "I had a life. I blew up my old life."

"So, maybe now you can have something better. Think of that."

"Marion—"

"Oh, fine. How's the dog?"

"Tink is great." He was sprawled out on the floor and lifted his head as Audrey said his name. "He's like…my only friend. Besides you."

He was always happy to see her and slept beside her in bed no matter how many times she shooed him out. By morning, she woke up with him beside her, usually with her arm around him, happy for the comfort of a warm, furry body next to hers.

"And how are your plans for Simon's yard coming?"

Audrey made a face. "I have to…get some input from him on that."

Which she was dreading, because it meant she had to face him, talk to him, when she'd been avoiding him since that scene with Andie.

And she was still nervous about being equipped to do the job he wanted with his lawn. Truth was, she was nervous about everything.

"Just keep moving toward what you want. That's all there is to it," Marion claimed.

If only Audrey could believe it.

Simon knew Audrey was still here because someone was taking care of the dog, but Simon hadn't seen her since that night her daughter caught them together. It had taken every bit of willpower he possessed to leave her alone, to not apologize again or make sure she was all right. He was afraid if he pushed, she might not stay, and he very much wanted her to stay.

So he'd left her alone, gone to work, getting through one day after the next, waiting, hoping, feeling more alone than ever.

Finally, he walked out of his house one morning to go to work, and there she was in the garage, waiting for him, the dog by her side.

Simon had the ridiculous urge to ask the dog to take good care of her because she wouldn't let anyone else do it.

But he just shook his head, hoping she wasn't there to tell him she was leaving, hoping he wouldn't do anything to make the situation worse.

He walked up to her and gave himself a moment to study her. The faint, bruised look under her eyes that told him she wasn't sleeping well. The way she held herself, as if she had the weight of the world on her slender shoulders, told him she was still beating herself up about everything. The way she seemed a little bit afraid to even say anything to him, when she'd never seemed that way before, worried him even more.

"What can I do for you, Audrey?" he asked.

She held out a notebook she was carrying. "I need just a moment of your time. For some things to do with the yard."

"Okay," he agreed.

She put the notebook on the hood of his car and opened it up to a photo from a magazine of a pretty yard. A bit fussy for his tastes, but…fine.

"Just tell me what you like and what you don't like," she said.

He did, and she circled things and crossed other things out. They flipped through the notebook of photos in under a minute.

"Okay," she said. "Thank you. I just…needed a little guidance. I hope to have a plan for the front yard to show you in a few days."

Simon stared at her, baffled.

"What?" she asked.

"Do you know how much information you just presented, how much feedback you got from me and how little time it took you to do it?"

She looked puzzled. "I was just trying not to take up too much of your time. I know you're always in a hurry."

"I have MBAs who couldn't come close to making a presentation that effective or getting that much information from me in return. You could give them lessons."

"Simon, don't be ridiculous."

"I'm not," he told her. "I'm seriously impressed."

She grabbed her notebook and hugged it to her chest. "Don't do that."

"Don't do what?"

"Say things like that."

"Why not?" He frowned. "It's true."

She gave him a look that said he was making things worse

with every word. Did she think he didn't mean it? Or that he was flirting with her?

He sighed, digging for a patience that was in scant supply inside of him. "Fine. I have to go. I'll be back Friday afternoon. Peyton's coming for the weekend."

Tink perked up at that name. Silly dog even looked as if he was smiling.

Audrey wasn't. She looked...

He couldn't really decide what she was feeling.

He shook his head, fought the urge to kiss her goodbye, which he had no right to do, and settled for saying, "Try to miss me, will you?"

And then he was gone.

Miss him?

How dare he?

Audrey was so furious she spent the day tearing old, ugly, scraggly bushes from the front yard, even though she should-n't have until she was ready to put something in their place.

Tink thought they were playing some sort of game, as if it was okay to dig holes again and demolish plants. She finally convinced him he could chew on the ones she gave him but no others, and she thought he understood.

She dug until her whole body ached and she had dirt all over herself, even in her hair, and she was still mad when Simon came home on Friday.

He came to find her at her spot in the side yard, where she'd decided to take out a bunch of scraggly half-dead hawthorn bushes, and just stood there staring as she worked.

"What?" she asked, not at all nicely.

"Ms. Bee said you've been mad as hell since I left."

"So?"

"I just wondered if you could tell me why," he said, sounding much too reasonable.

She was instantly suspicious.

Was he smiling at her? Was he enjoying this, her being this mad?

She grew even more furious.

"Miss me?" she said.

"Immensely. And don't bite my head off for it. If you didn't want to know, you shouldn't have asked."

"I wasn't asking you if you missed me!" she yelled, worrying the dog and obviously amusing him even more. "I was repeating what you said to me when you left. You asked me to miss you!"

"And that's some sort of crime?"

"In my life, yes. I thought you understood. I can't do this—"

"Why not?"

"Because this is exactly what everyone expects from me. They think I'm weak. They think I'm going to go find a man, a rich man to take care of me and go back to being another man's wife, totally dependent on him. They think I'm not capable of taking care of myself. God knows, I never have, and it's long past time I did, don't you think?"

Simon took a breath, then another.

He was a rich man. He couldn't change that. And he really wanted to take care of her. Not with money, although that would certainly be a part of life for any woman he brought into his world. But in every way there was. He wanted to fix everything for her, wanted to protect her and hold her and comfort her and make everything all better.

How did that get to be a bad thing?

Although, he had to admit, he understood her need to be independent. Hell, he even admired it.

It was just so damned inconvenient, given how he felt about her and what he wanted to do with her, for her.

He backed up, frustrated beyond belief. "All right. I'm sorry."

Simon thought she was still fuming as he walked away.

* * *

Audrey felt a little guilty about how mad she was at Simon. It wasn't his fault that her life was a mess, and he was her boss. It was odd, too, that she'd let herself get that mad at anyone. She was normally the one who smoothed everything over for everyone, who tried to keep everything normal and happy and flowing along. She would never have talked to Richard that way when they were married, and he'd done much more than Simon ever could to make her mad.

And the truth was, she missed Simon. Missed him desperately. He'd spent a quiet weekend here with Peyton and then left again.

It didn't help that he was doing as she asked, staying away, honoring her need to have nothing between them, and she missed him so much she could have screamed if she'd let herself.

Still, she kept going, coming up with a plan she was mostly happy with for the front yard, then coming up with another while she was trying to work up her nerve to show him the first.

She'd read a book on landscaping that suggested photographing your house, blowing up the photo and then tracing the house, the driveway, any trees you wanted to keep onto tracing paper, then drawing in the new elements of your landscaping plan. She'd gotten a set of colored pencils and gone to work with the obsession of a painter trying to get a beautiful landscape just right.

Then she put her drawing on the opaque paper over the photo of the house and...voilà—Simon's house the way it would look with either plan.

She thought they both looked great, but then she was probably biased.

Maybe she'd show them to Marion first, and then maybe Simon.

He was due back this afternoon, having a fancy dinner party at the house for some business executives of a company he was courting, hoping to form a partnership on a project in Michigan. Audrey knew that much because she'd received instructions from Ms. Bee on doing what she could to spruce up the yard for the evening and keeping the dog out of sight and hopefully not barking at the guests as they arrived.

She'd run him extra hard this morning and might just take him out again during the time the guests were supposed to arrive. He couldn't bark at them if he wasn't here.

He was doing so well with his training. Not digging. Not jumping on anyone anymore. Not eating the bushes. Responding beautifully to voice commands and hand signals.

Tink followed her around the house to the patio and the door closest to the kitchen. Audrey ordered him to sit, then lie down on the patio while she went inside, and he did it without complaint.

She found Ms. Bee in the kitchen, where she normally was this time of day, and asked what time Simon's guests were due to arrive, so she'd know when to take the dog away.

Ms. Bee turned around from her spot near the sink, and Audrey gasped. The woman was a ghastly shade of white, a pained expression on her face, her hand clutching her stomach as if she was in a great deal of pain.

"What's wrong?" Audrey asked.

Ms. Bee shook her head, unable to answer, then she pitched forward, and Audrey somehow managed to catch her.

Simon got home just after four o'clock in the afternoon. His guests were due to arrive at six for cocktails, and Ms. Bee would serve dinner precisely at seven.

He didn't do this often, not liking to make extra work for her and unable to talk her into bringing in help for such occasions. She didn't like having outsiders in her kitchen, and that's how she saw it. *Her kitchen.* She didn't really like having other people messing with the house at all, so all the work fell to her, and as strong and as tough as she was, she wasn't as young as she used to be.

Not that he'd ever dare tell her that.

But he walked into the house that afternoon and felt like Goldilocks in the fairy tale.

Someone had been in his house.

Things were subtly different.

Very nice, but different.

He could tell Ms. Bee hadn't arranged the fresh flowers—white roses with lots of greenery. Definitely not her style. The table setting was different, too. Different china, different crystal, different everything. It was nice, very nice, but different. The wet bar set up in the family room was somehow different, too.

Even the food—rack of lamb, he thought—while it smelled terrific, was different.

He walked into the kitchen, spotless save for the food being prepared for the dinner party, and saw Audrey, wearing black slacks, a white shirt and a big, white apron, looking ready to serve dinner, the dog lying forlorn in the far corner of the room and being ignored.

That was odd.

He wondered for a moment if he was dreaming.

If thinking of Audrey had addled his brain.

Here he was, coming home from a long, often-frustrating trip, to a beautiful home and a beautiful, welcoming…partner.

Even in his dreams he shied away from the word *wife*.

Still, she delighted in his daughter, tamed that wild beast of a dog, made his home look elegant and comfortable without ever seeming fussy; he could imagine her being the ultimate corporate hostess, charming guests, flattering them, buttering them up for any sort of deal Simon might propose, throwing dinner parties like this with ease.

And waiting eagerly for him in his bed at night.

Simon frowned.

He'd never gotten a welcome home like that from his ex-wife.

He hadn't even known he wanted a welcome like this.

But it just looked so damned good.

Oddly like a 1950s fantasy, he knew, but still…he wanted it.

He was tired, frustrated, missing his daughter, missing… so much it seemed.

Simon wondered oddly if he'd been hit on the head or had really been working too hard.

Was any of this real?

He cleared his throat, just to see what woman of his fantasy-life would do at the sound.

She was handling a big kitchen knife, and he didn't want to startle her. Plus, he was hoping she wasn't as mad at him as she'd been over the last few weeks.

She turned around, indeed looking like someone who might be serving dinner at a fancy party.

"Where is Ms. Bee?" he asked. "And how did you ever get her to allow you into her kitchen? Much less actually prepare food here?"

That more than anything else had him wondering if he was dreaming.

No one cooked in Ms. Bee's kitchen.

"It was the only way I could get her to leave," Audrey said. "I promised to carry on as she would have. Not up to her high standards, of course, but to do my best in a pinch. She was adamant that she couldn't let you down by not being here to pull off this very important dinner party."

"Get her to leave?" Simon was still, trying to make sense of that point.

"With the paramedics," Audrey claimed. "Don't worry. She's fine, I promise. Her gallbladder is acting up, and she had a high fever and was dehydrated. But she's got an IV pumping drugs into her, and it seems to be calming everything down. The doctors might not even have to operate to remove the gallbladder, but even if they do, I've been assured it's completely routine. She'll be good as new in a matter of days, restoring order from chaos and tending to your every need."

He frowned. "Ms. Bee is ill?"

"Simon, I know you think she's invincible and she does, too. But she is human, and I think when the paramedics asked her age, she whispered that she's seventy-one."

"No way," Simon said.

"Really. I think that's what she said. Although she was feverish at the time. I walked into the house this morning just in time to catch her as she collapsed. When she came to, she was mad as could be that I'd called the paramedics and that her gallbladder dared try to interfere with your dinner party. The only way I could get her to agree to go to the hospital was to promise to take care of everything here. I wanted to go with her, to make sure she was okay, but the paramedics were telling me to agree to anything she said as long as she let them take her. So, I did."

"And you didn't call me?"

"She made me promise not to. She thinks it's imperative that you are not inconvenienced in any way—"

"Damned stubborn woman." He really did adore her.

"I know. I was going to call you anyway, once I knew for sure what was wrong with her. It seemed cruel to call and say she'd collapsed and was on her way to the emergency room when you couldn't do anything but worry. And by the time I knew she was okay, you must have been on a plane already, because your cell phone was off. I thought it seemed kinder not to tell you until you got home."

So, Audrey was trying to take care of him by not calling sooner? *How odd.*

No one took care of him. Except Ms. Bee.

"She's fine, I promise," Audrey said, smiling reassuringly. "I talked to her nurse twenty minutes ago. She's ordering the staff around and miffed that they're not listening to her. The nurse said anyone with the energy to be that forceful with her complaints couldn't be too sick."

"Well, that sounds normal for Ms. Bee," he said, trying to convince himself of it.

For the longest time, it had been just him and Ms. Bee, an odd kind of family, but it worked for them. And now here was Audrey, stepping in, making him think that as much as he wanted to take care of her and make things better for her, she might do the same thing for him. She was even trying to take care of Ms. Bee today, by being here, doing what she was doing.

"She's awake," Audrey told him. "If you hurry, you should have time to check on her yourself before the party."

Which he very much wanted to do.

"I'd have canceled the damned party," he said.

Audrey shrugged. "I thought you probably would have, but that would have just upset Ms. Bee even more. And we don't want Ms. Bee lying in her hospital bed fretting because she messed up your dinner party."

Simon's gaze narrowed onto her face. "You like her!"

Audrey scoffed at that. "She's a nit-picking, outspoken, scary old woman—"

"You do. You actually like her." Most people never got past being afraid of her, and they never really understood her. He was ridiculously pleased.

"I've simply been indoctrinated into Simon Collier World, where everything works out precisely as he dictates and, in his absence, as Ms. Bee dictates."

Everything? Not quite.

He didn't have Audrey. Not the way he wanted.

Calming down, finally, at the idea of a sick Ms. Bee, of his world without Ms. Bee, he was back again at the thought of how happy it made him to see Audrey here like this, as if she belonged here, in his house and in his life.

She even liked Ms. Bee and was working hard just to make an old lady feel better.

"You really didn't have to do this," he said. "Although I appreciate the fact that you did. I hope this wasn't all too much for you."

"Simon, what do you think I did for the past twenty years? I could throw a dinner party like this in my sleep."

He could see that she probably could. She'd told him once she thought she and her ex-husband were partners, both working toward his business success.

"The house looks beautiful, and dinner smells great."

"Don't tell Ms. Bee, but I dared change her planned menu just a bit. I felt more comfortable using some of my own recipes."

"I'll never tell," he promised. "Now, what is this outfit you have on?"

She glanced down at her shirt and slacks. "Best impression I could do of a caterer on short notice. Someone has to serve dinner."

"No. No way. You are not going to act like the hired help in my house."

"I am hired help."

"Not for this. I'll find someone. A good friend of mine has a restaurant. I'm sure he'll loan us a server for the evening."

"Why? I'm perfectly capable of serving dinner."

"I'm sure you are." But he had a much more appealing idea. He wanted her by his side tonight. "I want you to put on a little black dress and heels, put another place setting at the table, and act as my hostess."

"Why?"

"Because it's what I want. Simon's World, remember?"

She shot him a look that said she might throw something at him in a moment. "They'll all think that we're... involved."

"So what? They're all from Michigan. Who are they going to tell?"

She was going to argue with him some more. He knew her well enough to see that. "Please," he said. "Stand beside me for one night and look beautiful and help me make sure my guests have a good time."

And he'd have a night in fantasyland. Him, the ultrarealist. He'd let himself imagine that this was his life. Their life together, and it was ridiculously good and happy and satisfying, having her beside him, understanding him, accepting him and all his quirks and flaws, making everything in his life better.

"Simon, I don't even have a cocktail dress anymore. I mean, I guess I do, somewhere, if Richard didn't throw out all my things when he moved back in. It just wasn't the kind of wardrobe I needed in rehab, so I left them all behind."

"So, go get a dress."

"I don't have time."

He shot her a look that said he was getting seriously annoyed. "Then I'll get you a dress on my way home from the hospital. What are you, a size six? Petite? What's your favorite dress shop?"

"I haven't been shopping for dresses in months."

"But you have a favorite shop. Every woman does."

"Simon—"

"It's business, Audrey." It wasn't, but she didn't have to know that. He could have some secrets. "You know how to do this. Be charming, which I know you can do. Flatter them, flirt just enough to make them happy, and then I'll swoop in and convince them to agree to anything I want."

"Business?" She frowned at him.

"Yes, business." She'd buy that much easier than the idea that it was simply what he wanted. And he wasn't arguing with her anymore. He was leaving. "Thanks. I've got to run. I'll be back in an hour. Call me and tell me where to pick up the dress. Oh, and you're going to lock up the dog, right?"

Tink lifted his head and whined an objection.

Simon had his back turned, so Audrey couldn't see how happy he was about something as mundane as a business dinner at his house, all because she'd be at his side.

Chapter Eleven

Simon checked on a grumpy Ms. Bee, so grumpy he was reassured that she was indeed going to be fine, then stopped by the dress shop Audrey had selected and quickly picked three little black dresses from the half-dozen the clerk pulled off the rack. Audrey could take her choice this way, he decided. He then asked for shoes and at the last minute, at the register, a hair clip with diamonds set into a little slash mark.

A rather expensive hair adornment. He decided he wouldn't admit the stones were real, would just say he thought they'd look pretty in her hair if she pulled it back on one side the way she sometimes did.

Then he thought he was being a stereotypical rich man, dressing a beautiful woman he wanted in his bed, throwing diamonds her way.

He hated being thought of as typical in any way, but he bought the dress, the shoes and the diamonds anyway.

When he got home, Audrey picked the plainest dress of all,

which had him wondering about her taste in clothes, until she walked into the room in that dress.

He was certain it had been the most basic thing he'd ever seen on the hanger at the store—solid black, sleeveless, with a square neckline, not low by any stretch of the imagination, formfitting but not at all tight or revealing.

But with her in it… It set off her pale skin and dark hair to perfection. She had pulled her hair back on one side and used the little diamond pin, probably dressing so fast she didn't even look at it that closely. Her skin was absolutely beautiful, smooth and creamy as could be. The dress was short enough to show off a pair of very shapely legs and all of her curves.

She looked compact, elegant as could be, a perfect lady with a subtle hint of sexiness simmering just beneath the surface.

Watching her that night, effortlessly moving into the role of perfect hostess, he wanted her more than ever and told himself there had to be a way for this to work. He'd always found a way to make most anything he truly wanted work out.

She could be a perfect partner for him. Strong, intelligent, not afraid of him or Ms. Bee, helping him like this in his business life, bringing an ease and a genuine pleasure to his home life, loving his daughter, because he was sure she would.

Why couldn't he have that?

He didn't believe anything was impossible.

Simon stood at her side that night, a hand resting lightly at her waist, watching her work the room, proud as he could be of her and what she'd done here on very short notice, eager to get her alone when it was done.

Simon paid off the server, giving her extra to clean up so he could get Audrey out of the kitchen. They stood side by side at the front door, saying goodbye to the last guest to leave, and then he steered her through the house, refusing to let her back into the kitchen or the dining room, and to outside on the terrace.

It was a beautiful night, balmy and star filled.

She wanted to let the dog out, but he insisted that she sit while he did it for her, and when the dog had bounded down the steps and into the backyard, Simon made himself comfortable on the outdoor sofa beside Audrey, who suddenly looked a bit unsure of herself.

"It was a perfect evening," he said.

"Thank you."

"You even seemed like you enjoyed yourself."

She considered for a moment. "I suppose I did. It reminded me that I'd always thought I was good at things like that, and that there was a time when I'd forgotten I was good at anything."

"It's obvious that you were very good at what you did."

"Just not at anything you can put on a résumé. Believe me, it was a rude awakening when Richard left."

Simon put his arm along the back of the sofa, not touching her but wanting to. "You know, I could make his life very unpleasant, if you wanted me to. I'm willing. I think I could enjoy it immensely."

"Don't tempt me. I'm trying not to even think about him, because I'm sick of being mad all the time, usually at him. Marion says we have to learn to let go of our anger, not bottle it up but express it in some way and then move on. Otherwise, it owns us. I don't want to be mad forever. It's exhausting and just no fun at all."

"Would me ruining your ex financially qualify as an expression of anger?"

"I don't think that's what Marion had in mind. Plus, we have a daughter who'll soon be in college. Ruining Richard financially is not what our daughter needs right now."

"Okay, I'll wait," he offered.

Audrey laughed. Beautifully.

He was happy, he decided.

Right now in this moment, he was so damned happy.

He had to figure out how to hang on to this. He couldn't let her out of his life.

Simon thought of what he could say.

Stand beside me. Be my partner. Be my lover. Mother my daughter. Warm my home and fill it with joy. Take care of me, and I'll take care of your every need and your daughter's. You'll want for nothing.

Exactly what she didn't want from anyone.

How could he fight that? It was like fighting himself and who he was. He could take care of her in every way. He wanted to, and she wouldn't let him.

Hell, he respected her for wanting to be independent and take care of herself, inconvenient as it was for him.

"Tonight was nice," he began. "Very nice. I liked having you by my side, you feeling like a partner to me. I never had that with my ex-wife. That kind of give and take—"

"Simon, please don't say what I'm afraid you're about to say," she began as she started to pull away.

"That I like this? That I'm extremely comfortable sharing an evening with you in this way, and extremely uncomfortable with you in so many other ways. That I think about you when I'm gone. I count the hours until I can be back here, see you again. That the toughest time is when I'm alone in my bed at night, wishing you were there—"

She looked shocked, then hurt, then furious. "I thought you understood—"

"I understand that you think you can't have this. That we can't. That you're letting an angry, hurt sixteen-year-old girl dictate the way you live your life—"

"She's my daughter!" Audrey yelled at him.

"So…what? You're going to be alone your whole life, just to make her happy?"

"I don't know, but I have to be alone now. I mean, surely I can manage without a man in my life for a few months, a year, if that's what it takes."

At which point, he fell silent, angry at the whole world and the difficulty of the circumstances in which she'd found herself, knowing how hard she was working just to get back into her daughter's life.

He had to understand that much, at least. He was trying to do the same thing. He wanted Peyton living here with him, and he was prepared to change his life, if need be, to have that.

How could he make it harder for Audrey to do the same?

"I don't even know how to fight this," he said, hurting and hating to let her see it.

"Fight what? Surely you don't happen to get every woman you want, when you want her. I mean, I know who you are. I'm sure you get most everything you want, but hasn't any woman ever resisted you? You just move on, Simon. There's always another woman, right?"

Audrey actually slid away from him, as far as the sofa would allow, as she watched a hard, dangerous glint come into his dark, stormy eyes.

She'd never really been afraid of him before but now was starting to see that maybe she had pushed him too far.

"That's what you think this is?" he finally whispered. "My poor, overly inflated ego raving at you this way? All because there's a single woman I can't have? That's what you think of me?"

He was practically screaming by the time he was done.

And hurt.

He looked hurt.

Audrey just sat there, stunned.

She liked him. She really did.

He felt so strong, solid as a rock. Solid as in grounded, unmoving, unwavering, unrelenting. Someone a woman could trust.

But he was absolutely gorgeous and rich and, she was sure he could have most any woman he wanted.

Why would he want her?

A thirty-eight-year-old woman with a messy personal life and such messy little problems as drinking too much and making a fool of herself by throwing herself at another man who happened to be married?

She was just the latest woman to cross his radar.

Wasn't she?

"You can't tell me you want some kind of lasting relationship with me?" she insisted.

"I can't?" he shot back. "You know that? You're absolutely certain? And why is that? Because I'm not capable of those kind of feelings? The ones that last? Or relationships that do?"

Audrey winced at the bite in his tone.

"Let me tell you something," he said, leaning closer, the words blasting past her heated cheeks. "I am not your ex-husband. I didn't cheat on my wife, and I am not the one who walked away from our marriage. I wasn't happy in it, but I married her and we had a daughter I adored. I would have stuck it out to be there with my daughter for as long as I thought her mother and I weren't hurting her by living together. My wife left me, not the other way around."

"Okay. I didn't know. But still—"

"Am I just an image to you, Audrey? A stereotype? A fairly young, rich man who thinks he's entitled to anything he wants. Is that really what you think of me? Because I thought you knew me better than that. I thought you felt something for me, the man, not the image."

She was stunned.

Honestly stunned.

She didn't just like him. She admired him. And fought nearly every waking and sleeping moment not to think of him or to want him.

Not now.

God, just not now!

"I'm sorry," he said, the fury finally gone and sadness creeping in. "My mistake. It won't happen again."

Simon was at the hospital first thing the next morning because when he called to check on Ms. Bee, she was insisting on being released and her doctor wanted to keep her at least until the end of the day on IV antibiotics.

His ex-wife called as he pulled into the hospital parking lot to say that she and her new boyfriend, some Italian she'd met last month, were planning a two-week cruise of the Mediterranean and Peyton didn't want to leave her dog for that long. She wanted Simon to talk Peyton into going.

"Two weeks? Doesn't she have school?" Simon asked.

"She's five. What are they going to teach her? Her colors? She knows those. She's the smartest child in her class. She's already reading on a third-grade level, Simon."

He grimaced, frustrated beyond belief and determined not to let it show. He tried to never sound annoyed or mad when his ex-wife called, to never show her how much he wanted more time with his daughter. If she knew how much it mattered to him, she'd just make it that much harder. That was the kind of woman he'd married.

He could only hope the Italian had a ton of money and was dying to move back to Rome soon with Simon's ex and wouldn't want to take a five-year-old with him.

"Well, I don't know what to tell you. She loves that stupid dog," Simon said, though he loved Tink more every day for the joy he'd brought his daughter and because she couldn't wait to be with the dog. Which meant, she was with Simon. "Maybe you could take the dog with you."

"On a boat for two weeks!"

Simon rolled his eyes, knowing how outrageous that suggestion was. "Just an idea. I mean, we want her to be happy, don't we? Because if she's miserable and missing the dog the whole time she's gone, you know what it will be like to be around her."

"The dog was a terrible idea," his ex complained.

"I know. I've been trying to get rid of it ever since we got it, but… Peyton loves him now. I can't do that to her." Simon tried to sound overly burdened and uninterested. "She could stay with me, of course, but Ms. Bee was put in the hospital yesterday with a bad gallbladder. So, it's really not a good time."

There.

That ought to do it.

If his ex thought she could inconvenience him, he'd have Peyton for sure.

"Simon, she's your daughter, too—"

"Sorry, I have to go. I'm at the hospital, and Ms. Bee's doctor's here." The doctor looked completely exasperated. Ms. Bee was as set in her ways as a mountain. "I'll call you later."

He closed the phone, introduced himself to the doctor and conferred with him while Ms. Bee glared at them both, insisting she go home immediately.

When the doctor was gone, she let him have it, too.

What was it with the women in his life lately?

Every one of them doing nothing but making him want to scream.

And he'd actually done it—screamed—at Audrey last night, all while supposedly trying to tell her how much he cared about her.

Simon laughed miserably.

Ms. Bee actually stopped complaining at that and stared at him. "What have you done? Besides tell your ex-wife that ridiculous bit about this not being a good time for us to have Peyton for two weeks? You'd never turn down time with that child, and I'd certainly never let you use me as an excuse. I'm fine."

"Don't worry. Peyton will be with us. Her mother has a new boyfriend. They're going on a cruise of the Mediterranean."

"And your dinner party?" Ms. Bee asked.

"Went off without a hitch. You'd have been proud," Simon said. Of everything except what had happened afterward.

She snorted her displeasure or maybe disbelief that things had gone perfectly. "If that's the truth, you certainly don't look very happy about it."

"I swear to you, it was a beautiful party. Not what you would have done, of course," he told her, because she'd never believe anything else and he was perfectly willing to flatter Ms. Bee to make her happy. "But it was lovely."

"Then it must be that woman who's made you so angry."

"It's every woman in my life right now," Simon said. "You on top of the list. If you dare try to leave this hospital before the doctor says it's okay, I'll—"

"You'll do what? You know I don't respond to idle threats. Honestly, Simon, you should have figured that out years ago. Why do you even bother?"

"If you leave too soon, I'll call all three of your children, and they'll be here fussing over you for days."

"You wouldn't," she said, sounding as if there was nothing frail or weak about her, despite her recent medical difficulties.

"Try me," he growled. "I have a meeting, but I paid off the nurse outside. If you try to leave, I'll know about it before you even find your clothes."

She made a disgusted sound. He turned to go, immensely relieved. Ms. Bee was in fine, fighting form. She'd be okay.

"Well, I just can't wait to come home to you," she called out. "Happy and sweet as you are this morning. I may stay another night."

"Idle threats," he said. "I don't respond to them, either."

"You must have fought with Audrey," she said, reading him as well as always. "I can tell."

Simon sighed, wishing he'd made his escape before they got to this.

"I have to admit it, but I may have been wrong about her," Ms. Bee said.

That was an astonishing revelation.

Simon turned back around and waited, frustration warring with his own long-standing habit of trying not to show anyone how he was truly feeling, unless he was trying to be intimidating or he was mad.

"I have to say, she was very…competent in handling things yesterday when I became ill."

"Competent?" Simon grinned. That was high praise from Ms. Bee.

"And, I have to say, even kind to me, when I haven't exactly been kind to her. So I can't imagine why she was nice to me, except that…maybe…she's simply a nice person who's been through a very hard time."

Simon nodded. "I'm glad she was there to take care of you."

"And of you last night," Ms. Bee added. "What did you do to ruin it?"

Said too much, he thought.

Felt too much.

Needed too much.

"She just wants her daughter back," he confessed. "How can I not understand and want it to work out for her? How can I make it more difficult for her when I want the same thing for me and Peyton?"

"You can't," Ms. Bee said. "You wouldn't."

"Yeah. You'd think so, wouldn't you?" he said bitterly.

"She cares about you," Ms. Bee claimed.

Simon lifted his head and stared at her, at that, knowing Ms. Bee wouldn't have said it if she hadn't thought it was true. She'd always been a fine judge of people. Oh, she'd been skeptical of Audrey at first, but she was like that with any woman when that woman first came into Simon's life. Now that Ms. Bee had gotten to know Audrey, Ms. Bee thought Audrey cared?

"I hope you're right," he said.

Although, what the hell was he supposed to do about it if Ms. Bee was right?

"I'm always right," Ms. Bee said.

Simon shook his head, then turned once again to go.

It would almost make it worse if Audrey did really care about him.

Because he couldn't figure out how to make this work.

For the first time in his life, he had no idea, no plan, not even any confidence that he could make it work.

Chapter Twelve

Ms. Bee came home, and Simon and Audrey, working sep-arately but with the same purpose, managed to keep her off her feet for a whole forty-eight hours, which they both con-sidered a victory.

And she was being suspiciously nice to Audrey.

Audrey had no idea what to make of that.

Ms. Bee hadn't even tried to kick Tink out of the house recently, which everyone found puzzling except the dog. He acted as if he'd always know he'd win over the woman.

Peyton came to stay for two full weeks while her mother was on a cruise, and Audrey knew Simon was extremely happy about that. But he was home almost all the time, too, which meant they had to work even harder at avoiding each other.

He couldn't be serious about wanting a relationship with me, Audrey told herself over and over again.

But Simon was either very, very mad or very, very hurt, and the mad part didn't make sense. If he just thought he'd been rejected and wasn't used to it, mad would be normal for a while, but not this long. But if he was truly hurt, that meant he must truly care about her, and she couldn't make herself believe that, either.

And she missed him.

Terribly.

She worked as hard as she could over those few weeks, exhausting herself and the dog on their runs and finally coming up with a landscaping plan Simon approved of. She showed it to him one morning before he was to go into the office for a few hours to get some work done before coming home around noon and spending the rest of his day with his daughter.

Audrey placed the photos overlaid with the drawings she'd done of the plans in place on top of the hood of his car, ready for him when he came outside, and he took a moment to study each one.

"These are beautiful," he said, sounding surprised, studying her anew. "You drew these?"

"Just the new landscaping. There's a photo of the house and the existing yard underneath." She lifted the tracing paper and showed him.

"I kept having to look at graph paper with little circles on it when the others showed me their ideas. Couldn't figure out what the hell they were planning. I like this much better."

Audrey nodded. They hadn't said this much to each other in weeks.

True to his word, he'd left her alone to do her job, and he'd done his.

"So, do you like any of them?" she asked.

"I like them all but this one most of all."

He pointed to the one she'd done with all different shades and textures of green, broken up by lavish flowers and bushes that bloomed in white. It was a nice contrast to all the green and, Audrey thought, gave the yard that simple but lush look, maybe even a bit elegant.

"How much do you think it will take?"

She named a figure she thought was adequate without being extravagant, much more than she'd spend on her own yard, but he would want only the best and he'd want it now. Which meant he wouldn't wait for small plants to grow in and give him the look he wanted in several years. Which meant spending more.

"Fine. Do it," he said, reaching into his wallet and pulling out a credit card he extended to her. "Put anything to do with the dog and the yard on this. The bill will come to the house, and Ms. Bee will give it to you. Just make a note of what the expenditures are on the bill and give it back to her. As long as you stay under your budget, I don't need to know any more than that."

Audrey took the card from him. "All right."

He let out a long, slow breath. "I'm sorry about everything, Audrey. I know I was out of line."

She looked him in the eyes, trying to read what she saw there.

Regrets?

Anger, still?

Impatience?

What?

"Want to go back to Morton's?" He gave her a forced smile, then added, "It's what I'd offer you if you were any another employee I'd treated badly."

"I know. Natasha told me that with as much business as you send her, you should own the place."

He frowned, his face taking on that hard, carved-of-stone look. "I know I'm not an easy man by any measure. But I'm trying to let you be here and do your job without having to see me."

"I know you are," she said, surprised by how serious he sounded, how impossibly controlled.

"And I just want you to know, I'll do anything I can to help you get your daughter back. The offer comes with no conditions, no time limit. If there's anything I can do, all you have to do is ask."

Audrey stood there, stunned.

By his generosity.

His kindness.

The way she believed absolutely in what he'd said.

He would do anything, at any time, to help her get Andie back.

Her eyes filled with tears in a rush so unexpected she had no hope of stopping them. Honestly, she hadn't thought she'd ever trust anyone that way again, hadn't wanted to, but she trusted Simon to do what he said, had no doubts at all that he would.

"I...I don't know what to say."

"You don't have to say anything at all. You don't have to do anything. It's just... I just wanted you to know that."

She took a shuddering breath, took a step toward him, to touch him, maybe. She wasn't sure. But he put a hand out to stop her, shaking his head wearily. She looked at him, not understanding, questioning.

"I told you I'm trying, but it's not easy for me. And if you get any closer to me, I'm going to touch you. I'm going to pull you into my arms and hold on to you, and it's not going to be easy for me to let you go. And I don't think that's what you want," he said, "so I'm going now."

He gave her a smile that was painful to watch, that made her want to cry right there in the garage.

"Simon—"

"And don't you dare do all the heavy work on this yard yourself," he said, trying to sound annoyed with her as he walked away. "Hire some men with big muscles. They need to work, too."

Andie got home a little after three, surprised to find her father's car and another she didn't recognize parked in the driveway.

She got inside to find the house looking unusually perfect, as if there was a new cleaning lady or something and she'd gone all out to impress her father. They'd never had household help before, until her father moved back in with Barbie, who did not cook or clean or do much of anything except spend Andie's father's money and complain.

Maybe it was just a new cleaning lady.

Andie walked into the kitchen, knowing she should eat something, something bland such as crackers, to try to settle her touchy stomach.

It was always a little off these days, but at the hint of something being up, something about to change, it twisted itself into knots.

Maybe she could head it off this time with a little bland food.

Her father was in the kitchen talking with a blond woman in a business suit, clipboard in hand.

"Andie, what are you doing home?" her father asked, looking as if he'd been caught at something.

Her stomach lurched, anger soaring along with the fear.

"It's three-thirty. I'm always home at this time," she said, then let the anger talk. "New girlfriend already, Daddy?"

Barbie showed up in the doorway to the dining room, glaring at Andie.

Okay. Apparently not a new girlfriend.

Her father shot her a warning glance. "This is Ms. Ballantine. She's here to see the house."

"See the house?" Andie repeated. "Why?"

"Just to give us some information," her father said.

Lying.

She could tell.

"What kind of information?" she tried.

"About the current housing market. Some updates we might make. That sort of thing. Nothing for you to worry about," he claimed.

Andie didn't think so. She thought it was definitely cause for worry.

Things kept changing. They never stayed the same.

And lately, all the changes had been bad.

She thought she'd prepared herself for that, but maybe she was wrong.

This one had certainly come out of the blue.

Then she saw the little pin on Ms. Ballantine's lapel, one she was trying to hide behind that clipboard, but Andie caught a glimpse.

"You're a real estate agent," Andie said.

The woman just smiled.

Barbie came to her father's side and took his arm in a way that said she thought she owned him, that Andie did not. "You might as well tell her, Richard. She'll know soon enough anyway."

"Know what?" Andie demanded of her father.

Ms. Ballantine excused herself, saying she'd look over the upstairs and give them some privacy. Andie's father asked Barbie to show the woman around, and with a very smug look toward Andie, Barbie left, too.

"You're selling the house?" Andie asked, incredulous.

"I'm exploring a number of possibilities," her father claimed.

"Like selling the house. And doing what? Going where?"

"I'm not sure. Maybe just to the other side of town. Bethany used to live on the west side, and she's always talking about how nice it is there—"

"You're moving us because Bethany wants to?"

"Andie, this house is getting older. You'll be going off to college soon, and it's much too big for two adults alone—"

"I'm going to be a senior next year! I've gone to school in this district my whole life. Everyone I know is here. You can't take me away for my senior year!"

"The schools on the west side are excellent and much newer—"

"But they're not my school. They don't have my friends."

Not that she had a ton of people left that she considered friends. Many of them had turned away from her in the last year, and she'd turned away from a lot more who hadn't really been her friends at all. But still, her whole life had been spent here. Everyone she knew was here.

And Jake...

She couldn't lose him.

She couldn't.

"Don't do this to me," she begged. "Not now. I've lost too much already. You can't take this away from me, too."

"Andie, you're being ridiculous. Nothing is certain yet—"

She didn't even listen to the rest.

If Barbie wanted this, Andie's father would give it to her. He gave her anything she wanted.

Andie didn't stand a chance against Barbie with her father.

She'd tried not to think about that, who he would choose if it came down to a choice. She tried not to get into that kind of confrontation with him. Truth be told, she was afraid she'd lose, and then where would she be? Who could she count on?

No one?

And now, here it was.

Barbie wanted a house on the west side, one of those newer subdivisions with younger people and the kind of nightlife Barbie was used to, and she didn't give a damn about how Andie felt. So what if they were an hour away from where they were now? New county? New schools? New house?

In fact, if Barbie thought it would mean Andie was gone, it would make Barbie want the move even more.

"You're going to do it, aren't you?" Andie said, feeling as if she might throw up at any moment. "You've probably already picked out the new house, right? Done everything but sign the papers to put this house on the market."

"Don't be so dramatic—"

"Dramatic? This is my life! It's already been turned upside down. Now you're kicking me out of my house and taking me away from all my friends!"

"Andie, honestly. The way things have been…I know you're not happy here," he said. "The tension between you and me, and you and Bethany… It's not good for any of us, and I think it's time we addressed that."

Addressed that?

"What does that mean?" she cried.

"If you don't think you'd be happy with us when we move, we should explore some other possibilities," her father said.

She gaped at him, feeling as if she'd just taken a blow to the stomach.

"You're not trying to move me across town. You're trying to get rid of me!"

He sighed, looking like a man completely misunderstood.

She wanted to hit him, actually wanted to smack her own father.

Andie whimpered. She was hurt, shocked, scared like she hadn't been since she figured out how out of control her mother's drinking had become.

"I'm saying we're clearly not happy here together, and we should try to fix that. Now, there are several excellent boarding schools I've contacted. I think you could be happy at any one of them."

"Boarding school?" She laughed, then sobbed.

"Or if that doesn't appeal to you, I know you've talked about wanting to learn Spanish—"

"Three years ago," she said. "I'm taking Spanish right now. I'm in my third year of Spanish."

"Well, there you go. A year in Spain, in a Spanish-immersion program, you could finish the credits you need to graduate and come back fluent, ready to start college. I think that would be an excellent opportunity for you."

"You're willing to send me to Spain for a year, just to get rid of me?"

"Andie, no one's trying to get rid of you—"

"Right. Bethany wants me gone, and you're more interested in pleasing her than taking care of your own daughter!"

She couldn't deny it now. A woman he'd known for a year or so was more important to her father than she was.

She sat down hard on a kitchen stool, her legs just going out from under her.

First she finds out she can't count on her mother.

Now her father.

What was she supposed to do?

Audrey returned from the dog park with Tink one afternoon a few weeks later and found Simon and Peyton in the garage. Peyton lit up when she saw the dog and held her arms open wide to Tink, who went eagerly to her once Audrey released him from his leash.

Simon was on the phone, looking none too happy and as if the commotion was making it hard for him to hear.

Audrey got Peyton and the dog out into the yard to give him a moment alone, not that it was any hardship to be with Simon's daughter.

Peyton was very sweet, obviously raised by two overly indulgent parents but not ruined by it. Very intelligent, inquisitive and funny. She'd been here more and more since her mother's Mediterranean cruise, and Audrey knew Simon was happy about that. And she was happy for him.

Envious, but happy.

She saw Andie every now and then around the neighborhood, and though they weren't exactly friendly to each other, they hadn't had any ugly fights, either. Which Audrey tried to tell herself was progress.

She was doing her job, working hard, taking one day at a time, feeling…not comfortable exactly but not afraid all the time, like she had been when she first came here. Simon had been good to her. Very good to her, she had to admit, and had kept his word about keeping his distance.

She missed him, missed him a lot, was still at war with herself over exactly what he might want from her and what she wanted from him but was afraid to let herself have.

He walked out of the garage a moment later and said, "Thanks. I'm trying to keep the office stuff at the office, but sometimes things come up."

She was actually amazed at how much he'd cut back on his travel and his work hours. Ms. Bee was, as well. When he said he wanted more time with his daughter, he meant it and was making it happen.

"Trouble at work?" Audrey asked. "Because if you need me to take care of Peyton for a while, I'd be happy to."

Simon smiled, watching her and the dog. "I know she keeps showing up where you are—"

"She says Tink misses me," Audrey explained. "But I miss him, too. So it's fine."

"Peyton loved it when you did her nails last week," he told her.

Audrey laughed. "We treated ourselves to spa night upstairs. She was so cute with her tiny, hot-pink toenails. I used to do that with Andie when she was little. We could have another spa night, if you have something you need to take care of tonight."

"No, it's tomorrow. I'd already told Peyton I have to work. I have a guy coming in to interview, someone I hope can take over some of my own duties. You met him. One of the Michigan guys at the dinner party. The guy with the twins who were Peyton's age."

"Of course. He seemed very nice. So, what's the problem?"

"His wife wasn't supposed to come—some family thing—but now she can. We have a real estate agent who normally shows spouses around town while I interview job candidates, but I didn't think we'd need her, and now she's out of town."

"Oh. Would you like for me to show his wife around, Simon? Because that's not a problem, either."

He turned to look at her, obviously trying not to overstep.

"I'll be taking the two of them to dinner tomorrow, but we could make your excuses for that. If you could just handle the day with his wife…"

"Show her around, lunch, tell her about the best schools, show her some nice neighborhoods?"

"You know the drill," he said. "If you could be ready at nine in the morning, Hobbs will pick you up and take you any place the two of you want to go. Our dinner reservations are for seven. Thank you, Audrey."

"You're welcome."

Much as she enjoyed being outside, digging in the dirt or running with the dog, there were times when Audrey missed the life she'd left behind.

She slipped back into the role of Corporate Wife, feeling a bit nostalgic and a bit sad. Managing a man and his career and their home, old-fashioned as it sounded, had given her a good deal of satisfaction. She'd worked hard and had enjoyed both being there for her daughter and feeling as if she'd had a hand in her husband's success, as well.

Maybe she should have gone out and started a business of her own, but then, there'd always been so much to do to keep her busy at home.

Audrey sighed, sitting in the back of the town car, wearing the most dressy slacks and blouse she had. Betsy Montgomery seemed ridiculously young to Audrey but happy and easy to talk to. They saw a bit of the downtown area, had lunch at a little French bistro and talked about schools, then some neighborhoods, including the one where Audrey used to live.

She could drive through it safely behind the smoky-glass windows of the limousine. As long as they didn't get out and see any of Audrey's old neighbors, they'd be fine. And even if they did…what was the harm, really? It wasn't as if she was going to be attacked on the street or anything.

"It's lovely here," Betsy told her, obviously interested in the area.

"Yes, it is. My own daughter attends these schools, and we couldn't have been more pleased with the education she's received in this district."

She worked up her nerve to ask Hobbs to drive down her street, thinking she was fine with that, that she'd moved past so many things recently.

And then she saw the For Sale sign in her front yard.

Chapter Thirteen

It wasn't necessarily a bad thing. Audrey tried to reassure herself after the initial panic set in.

Richard could be moving out of town. He'd always talked about wanting to be in Florida, especially after his brother moved there five years ago. They talked about retiring there together. Not that Richard was at retirement age, but he might be moving anyway.

But Andie wouldn't want to go. Not if it meant missing her senior year.

So she might end up with Audrey by default. It wasn't as if Andie was old enough to live alone, and if Richard wasn't here, what else could Andie do?

That made sense.

Audrey started to get excited, happy, thrilled, even.

This could be what she'd been waiting for!

Oh, please. Let this be it.

If she could just get back under the same roof as Andie, she knew she could make this work, given time.

Betsy Montgomery started asking how fancy the restaurant where she'd be having dinner would be.

"Definitely a dress," Audrey said. "A dressy dress."

"Oh, no. I didn't bring anything that dressy. I mean, you don't wear things like that when you have twins in preschool, and when I pulled one out of my closet, it was all musty, and I didn't have time to get it cleaned."

"Want to go buy something?" Audrey offered. "My favorite store is two blocks away. We'll shop and run. You'll make it to dinner on time."

So Audrey found herself at a dress shop where the owner knew her well, helping Betsy pick out something and then finding herself tempted as well.

"You know you want it," the owner said, holding out a particularly pretty little black dress.

Not the elegant, ladylike sheath she'd worn to Simon's dinner party, but a little black dress. Beaded in black, shot through with silver here and there to make it really sparkle. Short, not tight but hugging every curve, with spaghetti straps to show off her shoulders and arms.

Audrey let herself try it on, walked out of the fitting room to oohs and aahs from Betsy and the store owner.

"You must be living at the gym," the owner complimented her. "You're as toned and fit as I've ever seen you."

Audrey was surprised. Her new wardrobe was not at all form-fitting, so she really hadn't noticed, but running like a mad woman with the dog every day and unloading truckloads of mulch had obviously done good things for her figure.

"You cannot leave that dress in this store," Betsy said.

And Audrey realized she didn't want to.

She wanted to wear this little black dress and go out to dinner with Simon and the Montgomerys because she was happy and excited and couldn't stand the idea of sitting at home alone waiting for Andie or Richard to return the calls she'd put in to both of them from the fitting room, trying to figure out exactly what was going on.

But she really thought this was it, that she'd gotten what she wanted.

Even if Richard was only moving across town, Andie wouldn't want to go. It would mean a different school for her senior year. No teenager wanted that. If Richard was thinking of their daughter at all, he'd understand and not try to move Andie now. Surely he could have waited a year.

Although Audrey was selfishly glad he hadn't.

She looked at the price and winced.

Audrey used to spend this much on an outfit without even blinking. And she'd need shoes, too, because she didn't have time to go home and get some. But she hadn't bought anything in the longest time, had hardly spent any of what Simon paid her. She had almost no living expenses, living above his garage.

And this might well be a night to celebrate.

The night she got another chance with Andie.

Who would she celebrate that with, if not Simon?

"All right. I'm splurging," she told the two women and bought the dress.

They went back to Betsy's hotel room and freshened up and dressed there. Simon looked surprised but recovered quickly when they both walked into the restaurant that night.

"Audrey, I'm so happy you were able to join us after all," he said, then as he seated her, whispered, "Is everything all right?"

She nodded, beaming at him and whispered back, "I might have something to celebrate."

"Andie?"

She crossed her fingers and held them up for Simon to see. "I'm not sure yet. But I think so."

"That's wonderful." He held up two crossed fingers of his own, then held her hand for a moment. "I'm so happy for you."

She had the almost-impossible-to-resist urge to kiss him then, right there at the restaurant in the middle of a gathering with a man he was trying to hire.

Not at all the time or place for what she wanted to do. Still...

And Simon must have figured out what she was thinking because he went still for a moment; then his gaze locked on her mouth.

It was as if the temperature in the room went up ten degrees in an instant.

Remember what you want, Audrey told herself. *You can't mess this up now. Remember.*

And she gave him a polite smile and backed away.

Audrey was absolutely radiant and sexy as hell.

Simon couldn't keep a thought in his head, other than the fact that she looked like a completely different woman.

Oh, she'd always been beautiful.

But sad.

A sad, beautiful woman.

Nothing could compare to Audrey, happy as can be and all dressed up.

Heads had turned when she walked in. He was sure more than one wife in the room was annoyed as hell at her husband, because he was still looking, appreciative and likely envious as could be of Simon.

She sparkled, and it wasn't just because of those little beads on her little black dress.

He'd never seen her in anything that showed off her figure like this, either. Tanned, toned as could be, the trim thighs, the little defining lines of the muscles in her arms, all those intriguing dips and swells of her throat and collarbone, nothing but a hint of the curves of her breasts.

Her hair was wild and dancing around her face, her eyes flashing, her smile never wavering.

If he hadn't been completely smitten before, he was now.

And if she was getting that chance she so wanted with her daughter, did that mean she was leaving him?

He didn't even want to let himself think that way. She could have this time she needed with her daughter, and they would make their peace, and then, surely, she could do what she wanted with her private life.

Surely she'd want to be with him.

Simon knew he ordered dinner that night and ate it, but he wasn't sure what. He knew he'd ordered a bottle of wine and then worried that might be a problem for Audrey, but she didn't seem bothered by anything. Just drank her sparkling water and charmed the Montgomerys completely and every man in the room.

The pianist in the corner started playing, the Montgomerys went to dance and Simon finally had a way to have her in his arms.

He stood up, took her by the hand and led her to the tiny dance floor in the corner. She fit in his arms as if she belonged there, as he'd known she would, and he tried not to do anything he really wanted to do. He told himself holding her would be enough.

If he could ignore all that glorious skin of her all-but-bare shoulders and how good she smelled, how soft and warm she was. He did his best, too, trying to ignore every slight brush of her breasts against him, of her thighs against his.

"So," he said, bending his head down to hers, so they could talk softly. "What happened?"

"My old house is for sale. It scared me at first, but then I thought...whatever Richard's up to, Andie won't leave now. She starts her senior year in the fall. She won't go. I'm almost sure of it. So, she'll have to be with me, won't she?"

"I would think so," he said. "You haven't talked to her?"

"No. I called as soon as I saw the sign when I was showing Betsy Montgomery my old neighborhood. But all I got was voice-mail at Andie's number and Richard's. I'm so excited I can hardly stand it, and…I just couldn't stand the idea of being at home, alone, waiting to hear from them. So here I am."

He took a breath, squeezing her to him for a moment, then stepping back. "I'm glad you came."

She looked up at him with pure happiness in her face. "I couldn't have done this without you."

He shook his head.

"No, really. I couldn't. Not just the job and a place to live, but…you've been so kind and understanding and supportive. Simon, I…"

And then she reached up and pressed her lips to his, a quick, bittersweet moment he didn't want to ever end.

He was so startled that it was over before he fully realized what was going on.

"Thank you," she said.

"You're very welcome," he said, hoping he didn't look like a lovesick schoolboy, crazy about a woman who wasn't crazy about him in return.

Grateful but not consumed with wanting her, needing her, never wanting to let her go.

How did that happen? When he'd sworn it never would again. That he wouldn't let himself, wouldn't take the risk. It was the last thing he'd ever expected to happen at this point in his life.

And there just had to be a way to make it work between them.

They took the limousine back to the hotel to drop off the Montgomerys, Simon deciding to leave his car at the restaurant.

For now, he wanted to be in the darkened, private backseat of the limousine with Audrey. It was enough just to watch her in her excitement over getting her daughter back. Watch her in that little black dress, needing every bit of willpower he had not to touch her, not to pull her back into his arms and kiss her until neither one of them could breathe.

She still hadn't heard back from her daughter or her ex-husband, and she could hardly sit still she was so excited.

"Shall we drive by your house?" Simon asked.

Her face lit up. "Yes. Please!"

Simon hit the intercom in the back of the limo to tell Hobbs to drive through the neighborhood Audrey and Mrs. Montgomery had visited that day. Beside him, Audrey sat, having a hard time being still, grinning like crazy.

Simon decided he'd bribe the girl to stay if he had to, just to see Audrey this happy.

They got to her house and rolled down the window; Audrey leaned over and around him to get a better view.

"I think I needed to see it again just to believe it was real," she said, then frowned. "No lights on inside. And Andie always parks in the driveway. She's not here."

Simon looked at his watch. Ten-thirty. Then he asked, "What time's her curfew? We could stake out the place. Or we could go home and leave Hobbs on stakeout. He likes you. He'd do it."

Audrey laughed. "Maybe we could just drive around a bit? Most of Andie's good friends live nearby. If she's not there or at the movies, she's usually at one of those restaurants near the movie theater."

"Then we'll search," he agreed.

Anything she wanted tonight was fine with him.

They were making their last turn out of the neighborhood when Audrey yelled, "Wait! That's Jake's house. That's his car. Andie would tell him what's going on."

Then she took a breath and started trembling.

He opened the door, then held out a hand to help her out. She stood up, looking even more nervous. "Wish me luck."

He squeezed her hand and resisted the urge to give her a quick kiss, not sure if he could make it quick and then let her go again.

She'd just started to walk down the driveway when a group of three boys came outside and headed for one of the cars.

Audrey stopped, waited until the boys spotted her and then called out, "Jake? Can I talk to you for a moment?"

He did not look happy. In fact, he looked miserable, but he motioned for his friends to stay where they were and walked up to Audrey.

Simon had a bad feeling about this and went to stand by Audrey's side, hoping he was wrong.

"I saw the For Sale sign," Audrey told him. "What's going on?"

Jake looked as if he'd lost his best friend in the world. "Your husband…. Sorry, ex-husband is moving to Florida with his new girlfriend—"

"Florida?"

"Yes, and Andie—"

"She wouldn't go," Audrey said, as if she could make it true. "She wouldn't. It's her senior year."

Jake shook his head. "She's not going to Florida. Honestly, I don't think her father wants her to go. He found a Spanish-immersion program in Barcelona for her. She's going to spend her senior year abroad."

He looked as if he could have cried just saying it.

Audrey took it like a blow to the abdomen, her breath rushing out, her whole body seeming to collapse. Simon caught her close with an arm around her waist.

She whimpered, gasped, then started to sob. "She can't. She can't do that!"

"She is," the boy said. "She's leaving in three weeks."

Simon got Audrey in the car, and she curled up in his arms, sobbing.

He told Hobbs to take them home, then just held her and let her cry.

If he could have gotten hold of her daughter in that moment, he might have tied the girl up and hid her in the pool house until she agreed to stay. Whatever it took.

He'd swear from the one private conversation they'd had at her house that she wasn't happy living with her father, that Audrey, for much of the girl's life, had always been the one Andie Graham counted on and trusted, that what happened after the divorce was an aberration. Which meant the girl was just too damned stubborn to admit she was unhappy and wanted to be with Audrey. Either that or she was still too hurt and angry and wanted to punish her mother.

Either one, it had to end sometime. Simon was voting for sooner rather than later.

Much sooner.

They got to the house and Hobbs parked the car. Audrey's sobs hadn't lessened. When Hobbs opened Audrey's door and saw what was happening, Simon told him, "Would you mind driving the SUV home tonight and coming back for the limo tomorrow morning?"

"Of course," Hobbs agreed, looking worried about Audrey.

"Thank you." Simon pulled his key ring out of his pocket, found the one for the SUV and said, "Here's the keys. Don't worry. I'll take care of her."

And then he and Audrey were alone in the virtual darkness of the limousine. He pulled her onto his lap, and her body curled against his, her head on his shoulder, a small, soft, trembling mass of absolute misery.

"I can't believe it," she said. "I just knew if I tried hard enough and I did everything I should, I could get her back."

"You still can," he told her.

She shook her head. "No, this is it. If she goes to Spain, then she comes home and goes off to college for four years, maybe even grad school. And I need time to make this okay. Time with her. Simon, there's no more time after this."

"She hasn't left yet. You don't know that she will. This could all be frustration and anger talking."

"Of course, she's angry. She has a right to be angry. I blew it. I blew everything, and now I'm not going to have time to fix that."

She sobbed some more.

Simon held her close, his head bending down to hers, kissing her cheek, his nose nuzzling her hair. He felt as powerless as a man could be, and he was a very powerful man. What good was that if he couldn't protect the people he cared about? If he couldn't make this better?

Audrey started to quiet, making little hiccupping sounds, her breathing ragged but slowing.

He laid his cheek against hers, finding it wet with tears.

She lifted her head, with watery eyes downcast.

He kissed her forehead, brushed her tears away as best he could and then bent his head and pressed his cheek to hers.

"I was so sure this was it," she said. "That she was coming back to me. It's what I always thought would happen. That Richard would get tired of playing devoted daddy and she'd have no one to turn to but me. I didn't even see another scenario except her turning to me when that happened."

And Simon was going to do everything he could to see that it happened just that way. But he didn't think he could convince Audrey of anything that night.

She wrapped her arms around him and held on tight.

He put a hand to her back, one to the top of her head and pressed her even closer, determined to do nothing but comfort her, calm her down and go to work to try to fix this the next day.

And then she kissed him.

A nothing little peck on the cheek, as she had at the restaurant. Gratitude and nothing else, he told himself.

Then he opened his eyes and through the dim light of the back of the limo saw her legs. Curled up in the seat beside them, her dress having slid way up onto those pretty, trim thighs.

Aw, hell, he told himself.

He'd been just fine until then.

This playing the understanding, undemanding hero type was just hell.

She put her lips to his, almost, stopping just a breath away, her cheeks still wet, her hand on his face, holding him there, seeming to want so much, need so much, but he feared it wasn't this, that it wasn't anything he could give her. Not tonight.

She kissed him anyway, soft, sweet lips pressed to his, pretty breasts nestled against his chest and her bottom...that gorgeous, sweetly curved bottom of hers pressed against his thighs.

He'd been doing well to put all of that out of his mind until right then.

But...damn, it was so sweet to touch her this way, and he'd waited so long.

He wasn't a man who normally had to wait for any woman.

He kissed her back, because he was only human. Her mouth opened with no resistance at all, yielding to his touch beautifully, and then he was inside of her in this small way.

Which made him instantly want to be inside of her in every way.

He put a hand on her bottom, pressing her against his erection, and felt her breasts swell, nipples peak.

She moaned and squirmed, trying to get closer, then shifted against him, up on her knees, spreading them wide to straddle his hips, her dress hiked up, nothing between him and her but his clothes and what he suspected were a tiny scrap of panties.

He slid both hands lower until he hit skin, glorious, soft, rounded skin, then slid them up, cupping a hip in each hand. She was completely bare, he thought at first; then he came to a narrow band at her waist.

A thong.

She was wearing thong panties, and he had bare skin in his hands. He pulled her even more firmly against him, the pressure exquisite, the feel of her soft skin cupped in his hands. He dipped his head and nuzzled her neck, the collarbone he'd watched longingly all evening and then the top of her breasts.

"Simon," she said. "I've wanted this for so long. I wouldn't let myself tell you, but I have."

Triumph surged through him as he heard her finally admit it.

He'd been all but certain she did indeed want him, but he found he still needed to hear the words. He let himself go on kissing her, pressing her hips to his, more than ready to lose himself in her.

Here in the back of the limo?

Why not?

The sooner the better, he thought.

He just had to get inside of her, now. They could take their time later, savor later, tease later, do whatever they wanted to later.

All this time she'd stayed away and he'd made himself do the same, but now...

Now, when she'd given up on what she wanted most of all...

Her daughter.

Now she was ready to give herself to Simon.

But, *damn,* he knew he couldn't let her.

Not tonight.

Not like this.

He wouldn't be a man she turned to in despair to make her forget what was wrong with her life. She'd done it once before, and he knew she regretted it and was ashamed of it.

He wouldn't let her make that mistake with him.

Chapter Fourteen

"Audrey, honey, we can't do this," he whispered.

"You mean, not here? Not in the limousine?" she asked, still kissing him.

It was so wonderful to let loose and devour him this way.

Simon.

Her rock. Kindness personified and sexy as hell.

What a combination that was in a man.

"No." His hands slid up to her arms and pushed her away, just far enough for her to see his face. "I mean, you had a lousy night, and I'm afraid what you're really trying to do is forget about that. Which means, you'll probably regret this come morning, and I don't want us to be something you regret. It's too important to me. You mean too much to me to let that happen."

And then, just like that, she was right back where she absolutely didn't want to be.

Thinking about Andie.

About losing Andie.

Being sad.

Hurting.

Needing for it all to go away.

Simon knew her so well that he saw it all.

She felt like a balloon that had sprung a leak.

All desire drained out of her.

She went to lean back away from Simon, then realized she was sprawled out across his lap and kind of fell off him instead. He saved her from landing on the floor of the limo and guided her to the seat by his side instead.

That was Simon, always saving her.

"I thought you wanted me," she said.

"You can't possibly doubt that I do. Or how much I care about you. If I didn't, I wouldn't have stayed away all this time. Believe me, it wasn't easy. But I want you to be happy, Audrey, and certain that this is what you want. If that means I have to wait for you, I will."

He sounded so sincere, so kind, so understanding.

And she just wanted to lose herself in him.

It would feel so much better than the things she was feeling now.

Embarrassment being one of them.

She wished she could just disappear, not because he was wrong but because he knew too much about her, everything about her.

"You don't want to be like that man I spent my time chasing last fall—"

"Last fall? What do you mean by 'last fall?'"

"I told you about him," she said. "Or Andie did. You know this, Simon."

"I know about the man, but you never said it was last fall? All this—your falling apart and drinking and chasing after another man—this was just last fall?" He sounded incredulous

"Yes," she whispered.

"So, how long did this go on, Audrey? The drinking? The guy?"

"I don't know." She shook her head, not really clear on exactly where it started to go so bad, but knowing when it ended. Right before Thanksgiving. "Four or five months, I guess."

His mouth actually dropped open and he stared at her. "You fell apart for all of four or five months, and then it was over?"

"Then I went to rehab, then stayed with Marion for a few months, then came to live here. Yes. Why?"

"Oh, honey!" He grabbed her and hugged her close to him, pulling her across his lap again and cradling her like a little girl. "That was it? Four or five months? Out of years of what I suspect were wonderful mothering on your part? You're getting this kind of grief over what happened over the course of a few months?"

"I..." She didn't know what to think about that. Oh, she'd thought about it, that it did seem unfair. She had been a good mother, at least, she thought so. Then it all fell apart. "But when it was bad, it was really bad."

"I know. You told me so."

"And you just don't get to fall apart when you're a mother," she said, her words muffled by the way she had her face pressed against his chest. "I was all Andie had. Every bit of security and support, and I blew it, and she was only sixteen, Simon. It was awful."

He nodded, still holding her. "I'm sure it was. But it doesn't negate fifteen-and-a-half years of being a great mother."

She lifted her head, wanting to see him, needing to know that he meant it, that he believed it.

"You know it's true," he said, his hand cupping her cheek.

"I want to believe it."

"Then believe it. Step back and get some perspective on this. Stop beating yourself up for it. You've paid."

"No, I'm still paying. I don't have Andie and right now I can't have you." Which meant, she was alone again.

"You can have me any time you want me, starting tomorrow, as long as it's for the right reasons, just because you want to be with me. All you have to do is say the word, I promise."

She hoped so. Still, it stung, having him push her away.

"No," he said. "You don't have to say a word. Just be waiting for me. I have to go to D.C. just for the day. I'll be home by nine, and I can't think of anything I'd like more than to come home and find you waiting in my bed."

"You want me to just climb into your bed and wait for you?"

He nodded. "Peyton will be fast asleep, and her room is all the way at the end of the hall. And Ms. Bee's room is downstairs behind the kitchen. We'll have all the privacy we need. Plus, I've spent hours already imagining you there. In my bed. Waiting eagerly for me. Make it happen for me, Audrey. Please."

The eagerness with which he made his plea soothed her hurt feelings and her embarrassment, and the sheer sexiness of the idea—her waiting there, eagerly, for him in his bed…

She could tell he had thought of it. She'd tried not to, but she'd thought of it, too. She was a woman who'd been alone too long.

She'd spent too long as Richard's wife when he hadn't really wanted her, and that other man, last fall…she could hardly even remember being with him. It was mostly a blur and all about forgetting, not about honestly wanting him.

It would be different with Simon.

He insisted on it, and it was what she wanted, too.

"All right," she said. "I'll be waiting for you."

He shook his head and swore. "Don't tell me that now. It's hard enough to wait without you telling me that."

But they did wait.

And probably he was right to insist on that. For her to be sure and to not come to him out of sorrow, but truly wanting him, caring about him.

She couldn't let herself love him. She wouldn't. That would be way too dangerous and scary. But she was going to let herself have him and let him have her because it was what she wanted. How long had it been since her life had been about what she truly wanted?

She'd had a family she loved, and she'd taken care of them, loved them, guided them, held them together for as long as she could. And she didn't regret those years. She couldn't. But surely it was time she had some things in her life because that was what she wanted.

It was her life, after all.

Audrey let Simon lead her upstairs to her apartment that night.

"Get ready for bed," he told her, turning her around and carefully unzipping her dress.

Puzzled but exhausted, she caught the dress' bodice with her hands before it fell away and turned back around to look at him.

"Go," he said, smiling softly. "Before I forget I'm not that easy."

"I'm sure you've never been easy," she said, still standing there with the black dress around her, thinking of how happy she'd been to wear it for Simon, the way desire had flared in his eyes when he'd caught sight of her. It had started out as such a wonderful night, until she had found out about Andie leaving.

Sad but exhausted, she turned and went into her bathroom, put on a pair of comfy pajamas, brushed her teeth and cleaned off her makeup.

When she came out of the bathroom, he'd turned down her bed and was waiting for her to climb into it. Which she did, then let him tuck her in and sit on the bed beside her.

"Are you going to be okay?" he asked.

She nodded.

And then he kissed her forehead and left.

It was so odd having someone else take care of her for a

change. He was so sweet. Loud sometimes, stubborn at times, but sweet and kind, and she knew she could count on him.

Audrey realized that for the first time she wasn't alone anymore.

Audrey slept like the dead that night and woke—groggy and a bit confused—to full daylight coming in through her windows and Tink sprawled out on the bed beside her, looking relaxed and perfectly content. She looked at the clock and was shocked to find it was after eight; then she rolled over to the other side of the bed until she was nearly nose-to-nose with the dog.

"You never sleep this late," she told him. "What happened?"

He whined a bit, admitting nothing, seeking only someone to rub his silly snout, she realized.

"I bet it was Simon," Audrey said, rubbing nose, then chin, then when the dog rolled over onto his back, his silky soft belly. "I bet Simon took pity on me and let me sleep in today. I bet he got up early and took you for a run and then let you in here so you could be here to keep me company when I woke up."

Simon would do something like that.

Audrey lay there and tried to get used to that idea. That she'd allow this man to become important to her, to care about him, to depend on him, to trust him to be kind and supportive and just…here, by her side, when she needed him.

It was the last thing she wanted to do—trust another man.

And yet, it felt so good.

She did trust him. Maybe not to stay forever… Because, really, who could promise forever with any kind of assurance it would truly come true? She didn't believe in forevers anymore.

But she believed in now and in Simon being here for her now.

"He's such a good man," she told the dog, who yawned dismissively at the idea. "A really good, kind, strong man."

Who'd have thought the combination even existed anymore?

Certainly not Audrey.

Trying to keep her mind off Simon and her own nerves, she attempted to stay busy that day. She and Peyton took Tink to the dog park at midmorning and let him play with the other dogs until he was exhausted.

Peyton announced that she was going to a birthday party at the water park that afternoon. Audrey suspected she'd come home exhausted and ready to sleep soundly, which made Audrey a little nervous, because her evening was shaping up exactly how Simon suspected it would.

Sleepy daughter. Sleepy dog. The only thing left to get in their way was Ms. Bee. Not that Audrey expected any trouble from her.

Oh, Audrey was a little embarrassed at the idea of walking into the house, having Ms. Bee ask what she was doing there and having no idea how to answer that, then somehow making herself comfortable in Simon's bedroom. As if there could be any question of what she might be doing there.

Maybe Simon would send Ms. Bee away, too.

Then Audrey was down to nothing but her own insecurities and nerves.

This wasn't going to solve anything, because she knew very well that a man wasn't the answer to any of her problems. It was just about her wanting Simon and Simon wanting her. She was an adult. So was he. They were both unattached and… Well, there really didn't have to be anything else, did there?

They could take comfort where they found it. They'd already done that. And they could take pleasure where they found that, too. With each other.

Because her life could include some pleasure. She was allowed. She was ready to look at what she had rather than didn't have. Because she didn't know when or if she'd ever have her daughter back, and she couldn't just drift along, waiting forever. She had to make some decisions, had to stop feeling so empty and sad all the time. She was ready to stop concentrating on the past and all that had gone wrong and instead think of the present, knowing that at least one part of it seemed very, very right.

Simon.

Still, nerves were eating at her as the clock rushed closer to the time when he would be home. Did he really just expect her to climb into his bed and be waiting for him? Because she didn't have a thing to wear.

Audrey laughed a bit at the thought.

Nothing to wear. That would work, too, she was sure, if she had the nerve.

In the end, Peyton showed up at around seven, excited and chattering about her party. Audrey ate dinner with her and Ms. Bee, then offered to put Peyton to bed, the dog with her, something Audrey often did.

Stories read, hair brushed, pajamas found, she tucked them both into bed, then closed the door to Peyton's room. And there she was, right down the hall from Simon's bedroom. If she didn't leave, she wouldn't have to try to sneak in later and maybe see Ms. Bee and maybe have to try to explain what she was doing.

Audrey really didn't want to do that.

So she tiptoed down the hall to Simon's room, shut the door behind her, then took it all in. The space was a study in chocolate and creams. Polished walnut-colored floors, a cream rug. Dark, plush, leather headboard and matching footboard with a crisscross-patterned, nail head trim. Billowing, cream-colored curtains along a bank of windows, matching nightstands and lamps, two leather chairs and a table.

That was it.

A comfortable, easy elegance she'd come to associate with Simon. The room even smelled faintly of his cologne.

Her gaze kept returning to the huge bed, and in trying to avoid looking at it, she found an opening to the dressing room with Simon's things on one side, the space where the lady of the house's things would go entirely empty. She definitely had closet-envy. There were cubbyholes, built-in drawers and spaces just for shoes and hanging clothes of every size, plus a built-in dressing table, the only feminine-looking thing in the room.

Just past that was a huge bathroom, with his-and-her sinks, a shower big enough for two, probably more, and, most interesting to Audrey, a big, pretty reproduction claw-foot tub.

She glanced at her watch.

An hour to go.

What better way to spend it?

Because despite what Simon had said, she couldn't bring herself to just hop into his bed.

She snooped under the cabinets, found an almost full bottle of shampoo and decided Simon must have rejected using it himself because it smelled too flowery.

She emptied a generous portion into the tub, which she filled with steaming water. While the tub filled, bubbles formed and the scent drifted through the room, she dimmed the lights, found two candles and a lighter and lit them. She also found a set of controls for a hidden sound system and turned on some soothing jazz; then she stripped off her clothes, laid them in the corner and climbed into the tub.

It felt heavenly.

The water and the bubbles came up to her chin when she sank down a bit, every tight, sore muscle in her body practically purring with pleasure in the steamy bathwater.

Audrey let her head fall back against the tub, closed her eyes and immediately saw Simon in her mind, watching her with those smoky eyes, saying he wanted her, saying how hard it had been to stay away. Telling her to be here in his bed waiting for him when he got home tonight.

There was something positively Victorian lord and master about it. Was she to do whatever he asked of her once he was in that bed, too? She suspected she would, if that's what he wanted. Or would he be as generous as she knew he could be?

And want only to use what she suspected were his enormous talents and experience in order to please her?

She shivered at the thought, shivered with pleasure, anticipation and need, thinking of his hands all over her, his mouth, his big, hard body, wishing he was here already, that first time done, her nerves, her doubts, her fears all gone.

She'd let herself have this time with him for as long as it lasted, and then she didn't know what she'd do.

Simon talked to Peyton on her way home from her birthday party, hearing how excited and tired she was.

Perfect.

Then he called Ms. Bee, waiting for her to give him a lecture on letting any woman into his life again and maybe telling him he was a fool for letting it be Audrey. But he couldn't very well have Audrey waltz into the house and into his bedroom and explain that to Ms. Bee herself. This was what he got for being more like a son than a boss to his housekeeper. He had to explain little things about his private life like this and hear her unsolicited opinion about it.

He made the call just after eight, saying only, "I have a guest coming over later. I told her to let herself in, in case you were already in your room."

Ms. Bee laughed. "A guest?"

"Oh, hell, you'll know by morning anyway. You'll be watching for her to leave. It's Audrey."

He waited, ready for the lecture, the skepticism, the unsolicited advice. And got nothing.

"You can't possibly have nothing to say," Simon told her.

"I'm just surprised it took you this long," Ms. Bee said. "Or have you been sneaking off to her bed at night without me knowing?"

"No, but I might be there tonight, if she won't come to me."

"Your bed is much more comfortable than hers. And much bigger. I furnished her apartment. I should know."

"Thank you. I'll tell her you said so. I'd much rather be in my own bed."

"And we can hope you'll be in a better mood afterward," Ms Bee said.

Yes, we can hope.

Assuming Audrey hadn't changed her mind.

He told Ms. Bee goodnight, then decided he couldn't wait any longer and headed home. He made it in record time, pulled into the garage and thought for a minute at the odds of Audrey actually being in his bed, waiting for him. And that he could have had her there last night in the backseat of the limousine.

Simon sighed, shook his head, and then debated about looking for her in her apartment or heading straight for his room. He didn't see a light on in either one and finally decided to be an optimist and start in his room.

The door was closed, definitely no light on in there.

He opened the door to find...a perfectly made bed, perfectly empty.

He threw his head back and just wanted to swear.

Fine.

He'd just have to convince her.

No more waiting or wanting.

He turned to storm out of the room, downstairs and into her apartment, then heard a sound from the bathroom.

Water rippled.

Hope soared.

He walked toward the faint light, into his bathroom, lit only with candles, and Audrey.

Chapter Fifteen

She was lying in his bathtub, covered mostly with bubbles, head leaned back, eyes closed, skin like ivory and beaded with moisture, the ends of her hair damp and following the curve of her delectable-looking neck.

He didn't care how long he'd had to wait for her.

He was a damned lucky man.

"I have to say, this is even better than finding you waiting in my bed."

She smiled but didn't open her eyes until he walked all the way into the room and stood over her and the tub, finding the water a cloudy, pale pink, her body some combination of promise and illusion beneath it.

"You're going to stand there and stare at me?" she asked.

"For a moment. Then I'm going to touch you."

Her eyes widened, watching him as he slowly, methodically stripped off his clothes, never taking his eyes off her. Jacket, which he hooked on a towel rack, tie undone and on the hook with the jacket, shirt, unbuttoned, uncuffed and tossed across the clothes hamper in the corner. Shoes, socks, slacks. Her eyes came up to his as his slacks fell to his feet, this after she'd watched every move his hands made, unbuttoning, unbuckling and unzipping, something he found wildly erotic.

He couldn't tell if he was making her more nervous or turning her on.

Not that his biker briefs left anything to the imagination at the moment.

He let them be, walking back into the dressing room with his shoes, socks and slacks, leaving the briefs on for now.

She didn't turn around to find out.

Simon took a moment to consider exactly what he wanted to do with her first. Because he intended to get to everything he wanted and she wanted eventually. So really, this was just about priorities, daydreams he'd had for months, promises he'd made to himself about him and her.

"You haven't washed your hair," he said finally, returning to the bathroom.

"No," she whispered. "I haven't really washed anything...."

"I can't tell you how happy I am to hear that," he said.

Even with her skin flushed from the heat, he could sense a different kind of heat coming into her cheeks.

Embarrassment and desire.

What a beautiful combination on her.

He knelt on the floor behind her, heard her quick, gulping breath, saw her shoulders tense.

"I think we'll start with your hair," he said, letting his fingers brush through her hair, drawing it back and away from her face, rewarded with a happy-sounding sigh from her.

He kept stroking her hair, digging deeply for a patience that didn't come easily. Not after all these months. He'd have to remember to comb his fingers through her hair more often. She obviously liked it.

"Simon," she began nervously, "I want you to know, that other man—"

"Audrey, I can't think of anything I need to know about that." Didn't want to think about or be jealous about it, which was ridiculous given the fact that they hadn't even met then. Still, he hated thinking of anyone else's hands on her.

"Honestly, I don't even remember much of it," she said.

"Okay." If she wanted to talk about it, they'd talk.

"And I'd never done anything like that before. I was faithful to my husband for all those years, and anything that happened with anyone before I met Richard was so long ago it feels like another lifetime now," she said. "I just… I feel like… I'm a little nervous."

He kept stroking her hair, thinking that was probably the best thing he could do right now—move even more slowly than he'd planned.

He was ridiculously pleased by her admission, even though he still knew he had no right to be.

"Do you trust me?" he asked.

"Of course, I do."

He kissed the top of her head. "Then everything will be fine."

He stroked her hair some more, then guided her to sit up a bit, then sink down into the water until her hair was immersed.

He made sure it was thoroughly saturated, then helped her back up. She curled against one side of the tub, and he found shampoo on the countertop, emptied a dab into his hand and then went to work lathering her hair.

This was one thing he'd never done for a woman, and he was surprised at how good it felt, rubbing her scalp, playing with her hair, pampering her in this small way.

She closed her eyes and made little, sexy sounds of pleasure, and he found himself thinking he might be able to ease all the tension in her body just by working with her hair this way.

"That feels so good," she said, her voice low and sexy.

He felt it deep in his belly, tingling, tightening desire.

"Okay," he said. "Now, rinse."

When that was done, she leaned back against the tub, the way he'd found her, her back to him from where he was.

Shy, my Audrey?

Okay.

He could deal with that.

Simon settled himself in behind her and the tub, deciding he was going to be there for a while. He reached out with only one finger and traced the side of her face; then he kissed her temple, her soft, warm cheek and then her collarbone, which had teased him so the night before in that sexy, little dress of hers.

She gasped, shivered, but let him do what he wanted.

He decided her neck had to be next, just because she had a beautiful neck and he was betting it was so sensitive. He wanted her begging him before he took her, shivering, moaning, grabbing at him, pulling him to her, demanding that he come to her and take her.

Yes, the neck.

He could feel the heat of the water on his face, the sweet smell all around him and her, just waiting for him and whatever he decided to do.

He put a hand on both her shoulders, skin on pretty, soft skin, finally. Found a bar of soap, soaped up his hands and started to wash her, her shoulders, all the way down one arm, to her hands, and then back up again, taking his time, wanting to be very thorough and cover every bit of skin he found.

She watched him wash her, and he decided he liked it. That he wanted her watching him later, watching everything he did to her.

Simon got more soap, moved across her delicate collarbone, teased that little triangle at the base of her throat with his tongue and then he just couldn't wait any longer.

He had to have her breasts, sliding his hands down into the water, the sliding sensation of the soap and the water and the weight of her breasts making him ache, setting his whole body to throbbing.

She started breathing hard. Her breasts seemed to swell in his hands. He guided her to sit up just a bit more so that her breasts were out of the water. Then he got more soap on his hands and, reaching around her, started soaping along her rib cage, her belly.

She moved restlessly then, her breath coming in gasps.

He couldn't wait much longer.

It had been too long.

He bent his head over one of her shoulders, teasing at her nipples with his tongue, then sucked hard.

She cried out, then tried to muffle those cries. Her hand came up and out of the water, grabbing his hair, and he couldn't tell if she was trying to hold his mouth there to her exquisite body or if the sensation was too much for her and she was trying to push him away.

"What do you want, Audrey? Tell me."

"You," she whispered.

And then he let one of his hands slip between her legs. He had to hold her up with his other arm then, or maybe he was holding her still.

It didn't matter, because he had her, whimpering, crying out, sobbing. "Simon, please. Please."

And then she was gone, her body going all tense, holding there on the edge, holding. He kept her there for as long as he could by varying the pressure of his fingers and his mouth, still at her breast.

And then she tumbled over, her whole body convulsing.

He could feel the power of it in the hand between her legs, feel the heat, the throbbing there.

He let himself have her mouth then, trying to both soothe and arouse.

"There you go. It's all right. I've got you. You're mine now."

* * *

He wished he could have let her come down from that first climax and then start arousing her all over again as slowly and patiently as he had the first time. He'd planned to start by washing her toes and working his way up. But his patience was done.

He disentangled himself from her, grabbed a bath towel from the rack behind him and held it open wide in front of him, then watched as she rose from the tub, gloriously naked. Slightly pink, soft skin, water running off of it in rivulets, pink-tipped breasts, nipples hard and making him want them in his mouth again. All those pretty curves, those dark, serious eyes of her watching him.

He folded the towel around her, then lifted her out of the tub and set her down to stand on the bathroom rug. From somewhere, he found the patience to dry her himself, taking a moment to pause only long enough to drop a kiss on her belly, nuzzle the triangle of dark curls between her legs.

"Oh, Simon," she said, her voice all breathy and low, her hand in his hair again. "I don't think I can stand up on my own for another minute from what you've already done to me. And this…this would make it impossible. Not that I don't want you to, it's just…"

He thought about laying her down on the rug and doing more than that, but his bed was only a few feet away, and more than anything, he wanted to get into it and not leave it for a long, long time.

So he lifted her into his arms and took her to his bed.

He meant to wait.

Honestly, he did.

But the feel of her, naked as the day she was born, against him, was too much.

He rolled her over onto her back, her legs parting easily, finding her wet and ready for him, grabbing a condom from the nightstand a moment later than he should have, and then settled himself on top of her, looking down into her eyes, watching him.

"Do that," he said. "Please. Watch me. Let me watch you."

And then he pushed, as slowly as he could make himself go, deep inside of her.

Her pupils flared as the first bit of him made its way inside her. She started to breathe in these quick, short bursts, her breasts nestled against this chest, hands clutching him to her.

She was wonderfully tight and wet but still yielding easily to him, raising her hips to take him even deeper, her inner muscles tightening to hold him there. So strong, those beautiful thighs of hers toned to perfection by miles of running.

Her body deep inside gripped his.

It was exquisite.

Maddening.

He dipped his head, touching his forehead to hers. "I want you to know that I haven't done this since the first day you walked into my life and told me what a fool I'd been with the dog. So forgive me if this doesn't last. I promise, I'll make it up to you."

"No one?" she asked. "Why?"

"Because I didn't want anyone but you," he said, then took her mouth again, all patience, all restraint gone.

He surged into her, then rocked back, tried to make it last with quick, shallow, little thrusts, but she wouldn't have any of that, her body coming up to meet his, demanding more.

He tried to be as still as he could while he was deep inside of her.

No way.

Her body was throbbing around his, clamping down, letting go, clamping down again. It felt so good.

And then, he was gone, clutching her to him as tightly as he could, thrusting deep into her and just giving up, letting go, his face buried against her neck.

"Audrey."

This was Audrey.

She was his.

No more denying it.

No more waiting.

Just his.

He felt every shudder that moved through his body, felt an answering response in hers. She cried out, whimpered, maybe even cried. He couldn't tell for sure because the whole thing just felt so good and blocked most everything else out.

He lay heavily on top of her longer than he should have, still buried deep inside of her. Little aftershocks rocked through her body, making him remember exactly how good it had felt.

Mind-blowing, he decided, exhausted and spent.

Somehow he found the strength to roll to his side and went into the bathroom to get rid of the condom, then was back in the bed, reaching for her, pulling her to him and settling her in his arms.

"Tell me you don't regret this," he whispered, steeling himself to hear that maybe she did.

"No. I couldn't."

"I can't tell you how happy I am to hear that." He took her chin in his hand and tilted her face up to his. "I know you have doubts. I know you're worried about what all this means for us. We'll deal with it. All of it. Tomorrow's soon enough, all right."

She nodded.

"Stay with me? Peyton doesn't get up until eight-thirty or nine. I'll call and make sure you're up and out of here before then, all right?"

"Okay."

He took a deep breath and let it out slowly.

He finally had her here, where he wanted her, in his bed, silky, bare limbs entwined with his, her breasts pressed against his chest, her head on his shoulder. He was utterly exhausted and as relaxed and happy as a man could be.

Now he just had to figure out how to keep her here.

* * *

Audrey dozed, stretched out on her belly, her body pleasantly warm and heavy and relaxed, imagining someone stroking her leisurely with a hot, heavy hand. Stroking her bottom in little circles, soothing the long muscles of her back, combing through her hair.

She remembered his touch in her hair.

Simon and the bath.

Was she dreaming?

Had she dreamed the whole thing?

She took a breath and let it out with a heavy sigh.

Those hands were back, rubbing her bottom.

Then she thought she felt a warm, slow kiss at the base of her spine, teasing there, all the nerve endings in that region of her body storming to life, tingling, sensations zipping along to her brain.

He kept stroking her, kissing her there.

"Simon," she gasped.

"Yes," he said, his voice deep and slow and rumbling through the big, warm body pressed against her side.

He had his tongue teasing the small of her back, and it felt so good she could hardly believe it.

"What are you doing?" she asked. Because no one had ever touched her like that.

"Waiting for you to wake up," he whispered, as he got on top of her, nudged her legs apart and settled himself heavily between her legs.

She yielded to him, feeling him hot and hard between her legs, nudging until he found her, already wet and aching, and pushed himself inside.

She whimpered, dropped her head down and buried it in the mattress.

"Too much," he groaned.

"Maybe." He thrust just a bit, testing. And she gasped. "That… That feels so good."

At this angle he was so deep inside of her, she felt that if there were any more to him, he wouldn't fit inside at all.

She felt his hands on her breasts, his mouth open on her neck. It was all just too much. She wriggled beneath him, trying to get away, the sensations just too powerful, but he held her fast with his body, all heat and power, over hers.

He set a slow, steady rhythm, rocking gently back and forth while he was barely inside of her, and then surging fully back to the point where she wasn't sure she could stand it. Then back out and rocking ever so gently again.

"Simon." He was going to make her beg. She knew it. "Simon, please."

"What do you want, Audrey? You know I'll give you anything you want."

"I want to be able to touch you."

"Honey, I'm all over you. We are touching."

And they were. She could feel the muscles of his thighs, flexing, advancing, withdrawing, against hers, the muscles of his abdomen, pulling his body up and into hers. His arms beneath her, his hands on her breasts.

And that maddening pace he'd set, in, barely, rocking, barely, and then buried inside of her. Giving her just a bit of what she wanted and then pulling back.

Her whole body started to tremble with need. She sobbed once, then again.

His arms tightened around her as he settled himself deep inside of her and rocked hard. She nearly screamed, remembering only at the last moment to press her face against the mattress to muffle the sound. Her whole body throbbed against his, wave after wave of it, and she felt him shudder above her, heard him groaning out her name.

He collapsed heavily on top of her, then rolled to his side, taking her with him, still holding her close, still inside of her, the aftershocks still pulsing through them.

They didn't move for the longest time.

She knew he nuzzled her cheek, then kissed it, knew at some point he slipped his arm from beneath her and got up. She rolled back onto her belly and drifted back to sleep, limp and satiated.

Audrey woke to the sound of a phone ringing.

Groggy and more than a little confused, she reached for the phone by her bedside—then only, once it was in her hand, remembered that she didn't have a phone by her bed in her apartment at Simon's.

Still, there was a phone in her hand, and she whispered, "Hello."

"Tell me you're still in my bed?" Simon's deep, sexy voice asked.

Audrey's eyes flew open, the night coming back to her in a rush. Simon washing her, stroking her, kissing her, carrying her to his bed and...

She gasped, groaned, just thinking about it.

"No. Don't... Not that." He swore. "How the hell am I supposed to work when you sound like that? Audrey, you're killing me here."

"I was just...remembering," she confessed sleepily, rolling over in soft, soft sheets that smelled of him and her bath and sex.

He groaned.

She laughed.

"I will make you pay," he said.

Feeling adventurous, she asked, "How?"

"I have all day to think about how."

"Well, I'm not scared," she said, feeling happier, younger and more carefree than she'd been in years.

Simon Collier was her lover, and a wonderful lover he was. And she was an adult, completely unattached and sober and absolutely free to be with him, to enjoy him.

Free.

"Last night was…"

"Don't tell me here," he said. "Just…wait. I'll be home. I want to hear everything. Just not now. Besides, you have to get up. It's almost eight. Peyton will be awake soon."

"Oh," Audrey said, remembering.

Simon's daughter didn't need to know anything about this.

"The dog's probably right outside the bedroom door," Simon told her. "I tried to get him back into Peyton's room, but he seemed to know you were in my room. And he really didn't understand why he didn't get to climb into my bed with you. I am not sharing you with the dog."

"So, you plan on making a habit of having me in your bed?"

"Yes, I do. Please tell me we're not going to argue about this. It's pointless anyway. I'll win."

He sounded absolutely convinced about that.

"Although," he added, "Now that I think about it, I really wouldn't mind persuading you night after night, if that's what it takes. Remember, I'm a man who knows how to get what he wants."

"Yes, I think I've heard that about you a time or two. That and your modesty—"

"Just saying—"

"Last night was incredible," she said, because she needed to say it to him, needed for him to know.

"Yes, it was," he whispered.

And she was in trouble.

Lots and lots of trouble.

Because she believed every word he said. She was more vulnerable now with him than she'd ever been with Richard, knew all the risks and yet…she wanted to trust him completely. To give him her heart. To believe in all those things she swore she never would again.

As if she'd never had her heart broken or her life torn apart.

"I'll be home early," he said.

"I'll be waiting."

Chapter Sixteen

"Your mom came by my house last night," Jake said. "She saw the For Sale sign and wanted to know what was going on. She was really upset when I told her you were going to Spain."

Andie looked at him. He'd hardly spoken to her since she'd told him, and she'd missed him. She couldn't imagine not having him nearby to talk to when she needed someone.

Much as she'd tried to push him away, it had never worked.

Until the whole Spain thing came up.

"She's still living with that man?" Andie asked, easing into a recessed doorway at their school so they could talk.

"I think so. He was with her last night. He was...he seemed nice, like he was going to take care of her."

"Of course. That's what she gets men to do," Andie fired back.

"No. Not like that," Jake insisted. "Like he knew she'd be upset, and he was worried about her. That kind of caring."

Andie shrugged. So, there was a new guy, and maybe he was

nicer than that guy from the neighborhood and he wasn't married. So what?

He was just another guy.

"I can't believe you're really going," Jake said. "And I know it's not what you really want."

"It's Spain," she said. "A year in Spain."

"So what? You don't know anybody in Spain. You don't have anybody there waiting for you, anybody there who cares about you. What good is it, if there isn't even anybody there who cares about you?"

"Jake—"

"I know your father's a jerk, and I know you're still really pissed at your mother. But you don't fix that by moving to another country. You'll just be pissed and all alone. Did you even think about that?"

"Of course, I did. But I can't stay!"

A teacher passing by shushed them, and when Andy turned around, she realized kids were staring, probably listening to every word she and Jake said.

She hated that. People staring, whispering about her, knowing every rotten thing that was happening to her.

"There's nothing for me here," she said, turning back to him.

He looked mad enough to breathe fire for a second, then incredulous and then hurt.

"Right," he said, throwing down the big textbooks he carried so that they landed with a huge bang.

Andie gave a start.

"You're right. There's nothing and no one here who gives a damn about you!"

And then he stalked away, with a teacher following and demanding that he stop, come back and pick up his books.

Jake just kept walking, down the hall and out the side door, which he wasn't allowed to do and which the teacher following him was trying to explain to him.

Jake looked like he didn't care.

Andie watched him charging off across the school lawn.

It looked as if she'd finally done it.

She'd driven him away.

She was finally, completely alone.

Audrey felt as if she was blushing the entire day and that anyone who looked at her would know instantly she'd spent the night in Simon's bed.

He was a wonderful lover, generous and at the same time demanding, powerful, intense, patient and then not patient at all. She felt her entire body glowing, and she just couldn't stop smiling.

Tink looked at her as if he knew she had a secret and he didn't like it. He really didn't like knowing she'd slept in Simon's room last night, but he hadn't been allowed inside.

"Sorry," she told him. "Simon is not going to share his bed with you. You'll have to be happy in Peyton's."

Tink whined, looking both sad and offended.

She took him and Peyton to the park that afternoon to play, and when they were walking back home, Audrey had the oddest sensation that they were being watched. She turned around and searched the road and the sidewalk, thinking she might see Simon, but he wasn't there.

They got back to the house, and she got a phone call from Richard.

Audrey made a face. Calls from Richard were never good. He sounded oddly pleasant on the phone, saying only that he needed to see her right away. Richard's being pleasant probably meant he wanted something from her, Audrey decided. Probably something she wasn't going to like.

She told Ms. Bee, Peyton and the dog that she was leaving for a few minutes, then drove to her old house, finding no cars but Richard's in the driveway. At least, she wouldn't have to face Barbie. Richard must have been waiting for her, because he opened the door before she could even knock, thanked her for coming and then asked if they could talk in his study.

No way this could be good. She sat, thinking there couldn't possibly be anything he could do to her now. He'd already done it all. There was nothing left.

She looked up to find him staring at her. "What have you been doing to yourself, Audrey? You look great."

Which had her thinking again that every delicious thing Simon had done to her was showing clearly on her face today, and that left her grinning like crazy, in front of her ex-husband to boot.

He looked even more puzzled.

"Just happy, Richard. That's all," she said.

He didn't seem to understand that she was saying she was happy without him, but Audrey honestly didn't care.

"Well, anyway," he said, "I guess you've heard Andie wants to go to Spain for her senior year?"

She nodded, not bothering to question the way he made it sound as if it was Andie's idea when she knew it had been his.

"Well, I've been looking into it, and it's much more expensive than I first realized. There's a separate payment for room and board that's outrageous, then the plane tickets, spending money, books. I just don't see how I can do it."

Which, on the one hand, made her want to jump up and cheer. Andie couldn't go! Richard wouldn't pay for it!

"Wait, you're the one who came up with this whole idea," Audrey reminded him. "And now that she wants to go, you're going to tell her she can't?"

"I just can't do it," he said.

"What about the house? The For Sale sign's still here. Are you still selling the house?"

He nodded. "I've bought a business in Florida from a retiring CPA. It's all set. We're moving."

"So, you think you're going to force Andie to go with you?" Audrey didn't think that would go over well with Andie, either.

"She doesn't want to move to Florida with me—"

"You mean with Barbie and you," Audrey said.

"Bethany. Her name is Bethany—"

"Fine, you and Bethany. So what are you planning to do, Richard? Are you just going to move and leave her here?"

"Look, she's just not happy with me. We tried and it didn't work. And you keep saying you want her with you, so…it's time she was back with you."

"I would love to have her back with me," Audrey told him. "You know that. She does, too. But she doesn't want to be with me."

"Well, maybe she doesn't get to decide anymore," Richard said. "We'll just sit her down and tell her that we've discussed this and have decided she should be with you again."

"Oh, I get it. You're ready to walk away from her. Because it's a little harder than you thought to play daddy, or because Bethany doesn't like sharing you with your daughter. So you want out, and you want to make it look like it's our decision. Like you did with the divorce. You left, and then you blamed me for it and I got to stay and deal with our daughter's anger and hurt and resentment."

Audrey glared at him.

He looked decidedly uncomfortable and she was glad.

"Nice trick, Richard. But it's not going to work this time. I'm not going to be the bad guy while you escape from all the hard stuff. If you're too cheap to send her to Spain, you tell her. And if you aren't willing to take her to Florida or to stay here for another year so she can finish school, you tell her."

"We're both her parents," he tried.

"When it's convenient for you, we're both her parents. You bastard!" And then she got her temper in check enough to think about poor Andie. "Richard, it's only a year until she graduates. We've disrupted her life enough, already. Give her this year."

"I told you. It's already done. I have to go. And I don't understand. I thought you'd be happy about this."

"I can't be happy if she's going to be miserable. She already feels like she can't count on me. If you do this to her, she'll feel like she doesn't have anybody. Can't you see that?" Audrey was practically begging him. She'd do that for her daughter. "Just give her this year."

He shook his head. "I can't."

"Richard, who are you?" Audrey asked him. "Because surely I didn't marry a man who could be so indifferent to his own daughter and her needs—"

"Now you're just being melodramatic. Are you going to help me explain this to her or not?"

"No. I'm not. If she wants to be with me, I'll be thrilled to have her. But I won't force her. I won't pretend this is part my doing, and I won't try to pretty up this plan of yours to abandon her for a second time."

"Abandon!" he yelled. "Audrey, don't be ridiculous!"

But she was already walking out of the room. She was walking out the front door when she spotted Andie's car in the driveway.

It hadn't been there when Audrey had arrived.

Did that mean Andie had walked in while Audrey and Richard were fighting? Had she heard the whole thing?

Audrey took a breath and went back into the house, searching the first floor for her daughter but finding only Richard.

"So, you've come to your senses?" he asked.

Audrey made a disgusted sound. "No. Andie's here some where. Her car's in the driveway."

"Fine. Let's get this over with. Let's tell her together, that it's our decision, and we can all move on with our lives."

But Audrey wasn't listening to him anymore. Her daughter was slipping out the back door to the deck.

"Andie!" she called after her, then took off to follow her.

* * *

Andie was in the driveway, trying to get her car unlocked and having trouble seeing through her tears when her mother found her.

"Oh, honey," Audrey said, reaching for her, but Andie jumped back away. "I'm so sorry."

Andie shrugged, trying to make it look as if it didn't matter in the least, even as the tears fell freely. She couldn't help it. It was all too overwhelming, too awful.

"Honey, I know this hurts. I know you're still hurt by what I did to you, too, and it must feel like there's no one in the world you can turn to right now. I just hate that for you. But I'm here. I'll always love you, and you'll always have a place with me. I know there was a time when I let you down, badly, and I can't erase it. I can't undo it. I would give anything if I could."

"Well, like you said, you can't—"

"But I'm here now. I'm not going to give up, and I'm not going to fall apart again. I'll be here whenever you're ready, whenever you need me."

Andie scoffed at that. "You're with that man. That man and his daughter. Your own new little family."

"No, that's not my family—"

"I see you with them. Him and his daughter." She'd spied on them, seen her mother looking very happy, which made it even worse. "I know what you're doing. You're starting all over again, and that little girl… She's so cute, and she doesn't know what you've done, so she doesn't hate you. She's probably a lot less trouble than I am—"

"She is cute. And five-year-olds' lives are much less complicated than teenagers'. But she's not my daughter. You are. And a daughter isn't something a mother can just give up or trade in for another one. No one takes the place of your own daughter, and you're mine. You always will be."

Andie took a breath. It came out like a long shudder. She

had no bravado left and was as raw and vulnerable as a person could be.

She'd hated seeing her mother with that man and his little girl, and it was even worse seeing her father with Barbie, having Barbie here in this house and now forcing Andie out of this house.

This house!

Her house!

She'd known it would come down to this, eventually. Her father had to make a choice, and he chose Barbie.

Which left Andie with no one.

"You think about what you want now," her mother said. "And if you want to stay and finish school here but not to be with me, we'll… I don't know what we'll do, but we'll work something out. Maybe one of your friends' parents—someone I know and trust—will let you live with them for the year."

"Pawning me off on a friend's parents now? That's great!"

"No, I am not trying to get rid of you. I would never do that. I just didn't think you'd want to be with me—"

"I didn't say I would," Andie insisted, and maybe it was still true.

She didn't know anymore.

She'd never expected to walk into a conversation like that. Her mother defending her that way, giving her father hell about the way he was treating her and even telling him he needed to stay because that's what Andie wanted. Even if it went against what Andie thought her mother wanted.

"Okay, you just take some time and think about what you want. If it's to stay with a friend, we'll find someone. We'll make it work so you can have this last year of school here," her mother said, showing a patience and a kindness Andie hadn't expected from her. "And if that doesn't work out, there's the little apartment I've been living in above Simon's garage. You'd be close to all your friends here in this neighborhood. I don't think you're old enough to live on your own completely, but if you wanted to, you could live there and I'll...go somewhere else."

Andie just looked at her, having trouble believing that offer.

"We'd have to have rules, about a curfew and things like that," her mother said. "And I'd be right there, working at least every day, and Simon has a live-in housekeeper who's always there. So you wouldn't be alone, but you wouldn't exactly be living with me, either."

"You really live above his garage? I was sure you were living with him."

"No. I'm not. I'm..." Audrey sighed, trying to sort out her feelings. "I don't know what's going to happen with us. But he knows how important you are to me, and he's already told me he'd do anything he could to help me get you back. If I asked him, I think he'd let you live there."

"But I thought you couldn't wait to force me to live with you again," Andie said, swiping away tears.

"I want you to be with me, but I can't force you to, just like I can't force you to forgive me. Your forgiveness is something only you can give, Andie. I just wanted to be close and to have a chance with you again. And maybe be able to have a halfway peaceful conversation with you now and then."

Which didn't sound nearly as awful as it had felt to Andie at first.

Still, a chance?

Could she give her mother another chance?

"Now, don't mistake me. If your father's gone and I'm the one here with you, that doesn't mean you can just do anything you want. I'm going to have to approve of where you are and what time you come home, make sure you're in school and doing well. That's a mother's job, and I'm going to do that, whether you're mad at me or not. But you don't have to live with me. I think we can come up with some kind of compromise that we can both accept."

Andie had almost managed to stop crying, and her breathing wasn't so ragged. She still felt so sad, so alone.

She really couldn't count on her father.

She knew that now for certain.

"So, I guess I'll let you think about what you want," her mother said. "And don't you dare drive when you're this upset. Promise me you won't?"

"Okay," she said, hating the way her voice sounded, so lost and weak.

"Would you like me to take you to one of your friends' houses? Maybe to Jake's? So you don't have to be alone?"

"Jake…" She thought. She needed Jake! He would listen, he'd let her cry and he'd be nice to her, no matter what. Then she remembered…. "I don't think he wants to see me. We had a fight."

"Well, I don't think he could stay mad at you for long."

"No. This was different. It was awful. I was awful to him." Andie started to cry again.

"Want to call him?" her mother offered.

"I can't. I'm scared of what he might say. I'll… I have to think about it."

"All right," Audrey said. "Then, if there's nothing else…"

She waited. For an invitation to stay?

Andie wasn't ready for that.

"Okay, I'll go, but when you decide what you want or if you just want to talk about things, you know where I'll be. I love you, baby. I always will."

Andie stood there, mute.

Always?

Really?

Did anything really last forever?

She didn't think so.

Chapter Seventeen

Simon didn't get much of anything done that day, alternately remembering his night with Audrey and trying to figure out how to get her daughter to stay here so Audrey would stay, too.

He had an awful thought of Audrey getting on a plane and following her daughter to Spain; then he tried to convince himself it would never happen.

But hell, it might.

He told one of the moms who worked for him, "I need to get a teenage girl to do something she doesn't want to do."

"Good luck," she said.

"It can't be that bad," he insisted.

"Peyton's five, right? You tell me in ten years."

The only useful idea he got was that bribery was sometimes effective.

Which made him wonder, what did Andie Graham want? Other than to punish Audrey some more?

Which led him to Jake. He went to the kid's house; then on

a tip from a little girl playing in the yard, he tracked Jake down to the lake in the park. Jake was lying on the hood of car, staring at the water, looking as miserable as a guy could be.

The Graham women could do that to a man—twist him into knots.

Simon walked over to the kid, who sat up, looking puzzled.

"Simon Collier." He stuck out his hand. "I don't think we were introduced a few nights ago or that day at my house. You must be Jake."

The kid shook his hand, looking a little scared.

Simon remembered growling at him the last time they saw each other and smiled reassuringly. "Jake, I think you and I have a mutual interest—"

"You mean, Andie?"

Simon nodded. "I think it's time we started working together to make sure she doesn't end up in Spain. Help me out. Help me to understand this girl."

Jake looked skeptical. "My uncle says nobody really understands women."

Simon laughed. "He's probably right. So…how about this? Tell me what Andie wants. Please tell me it's not a year in Spain and that she's just too stubborn to admit it."

"I thought so. I hoped so." Jake shook his head, bewildered. "But if she does feel that way, she won't tell me. She probably won't even talk to me anymore, and I'm not even sure I want her to. We had this huge fight today at school, and I just walked out. They're probably going to suspend me for it. But I was so mad I just kept walking."

Poor Jake.

Simon felt for the kid. He really did.

And he was obviously crazy about Audrey's daughter, and she either hadn't noticed or wouldn't admit she cared.

Simon put a friendly arm around the boy. "We're in this together now. You and me. We're going to fix this."

"You think?" Jake asked.

"I think we have to, because if Andie and her mom are miserable, you and I are going to be miserable, too."

Andie worked up her nerve and called Jake.

He didn't answer. His phone went straight to voice mail, so maybe it was just dead. She called his home, but his uncle didn't know where he was; then she called three of his friends, and still nothing.

What about the lake? He always took her to the lake when she was upset. Maybe he was at the lake.

She dried her eyes completely, took a breath and then, before she got in the car, thought about what her mother had said, her own promise not to drive while she was upset.

Odd to think of her mother still trying to take care of her, even now.

Of her mother's insistence that she still loved her, always would.

That no one could take the place of a daughter.

Andie pushed away every thought except the one about driving. She'd promised. So she walked to the lake. It wasn't far. And sure enough, there was Jake's car and Jake.

And what looked like her mother's boyfriend.

Why would her mother's boyfriend be talking to Jake?

She hung back, trying to decide if it really was the two of them, trying to decide what she was going to do, but then they saw her and just stared at her. She was too stubborn to turn and run away, so she went over to them, even though Jake didn't look very welcoming.

Andie finally said, "What are you two doing together?"

"Talking about you," the man said, sticking out his hand. "Andie, I'm Simon Collier. I'm hoping we can start over with each other."

She shook his hand, puzzled. "Why are you two talking about me?"

Simon studied her a moment, as if he was trying to figure out how to approach her. "I was hoping Jake could help me understand how to get you to stay here instead of going to Spain."

"So, you haven't…" They hadn't heard her father wasn't willing to send her. "I mean, why would you want me to stay here? If you really want to be with my mother, your lives will be much easier if I'm gone."

The man shook his head. "Your mother will never be truly happy while you're still this angry at her. No matter what I do or what happens between us. And I want her to be happy, which means there has to be some way to work this out. I asked Jake to help me figure out how."

"And I told him I was no good at making you happy," Jake said, not giving an inch. "So there's no way I can help him."

Andie winced. He'd never talked to her that way. No matter what she'd said or done, and she'd done a lot to him. He'd put up with so much from her, more than he should have.

Simon glared at Jake, who stopped talking. Then Simon stepped in front of Jake, blocking Andie's view of him.

"I think what Jake means is that we've all had some tough times lately, and it's time for everyone to try to make things better. Maybe you could think about that, Andie. What would make your life better? What would make you happy?"

"Happy?" He had to be kidding.

"Well, it beats thinking about how you can punish your mother or Jake or anyone else who cares about you. And, understand me, I'm not saying you don't have reason to be mad, at least at your mother. I'm just saying that after a while anger gets really old. And the thing is, you can punish other people all you want, but you're usually miserable while you're doing it. So the longer you spend punishing them, the more miserable you are."

"You want me to forgive her for my sake?" Andie scoffed at that.

"I'm saying maybe you could think about what you want, rather than who you're mad at. I think you'd be a lot happier that way."

"Easy for you to say—"

"Hey, if you're happy with your life right now, you can go right on living this way. But I don't think you're happy. I think you're miserable. When you're ready to stop being miserable, call me." He handed her one of his business cards. "I told you, I want your mother to be happy. I'll do anything I can to help make that happen."

She took the card, knowing he was right about one thing, at least. She was miserable, had been for months. And it only seemed to be getting worse.

He turned and said something quietly to Jake that she couldn't make out, and then he was gone.

Andie stood there, waiting for Jake to say something, to give her some opening.

He didn't. He just sat there, looking as miserable as she felt.

Come on, Jake. Something. Just say something.

But he didn't. Maybe she had pushed him too far.

Maybe there was no forgiveness to be had from him.

Audrey was so happy and so excited that she stayed outside on the porch so she'd hear Simon's car as soon as he arrived. And in the meantime, she called Marion and told her the great news.

"She talked to me! She really talked to me. Didn't yell. Wasn't mean. Just talked! I think there's going to come a day when she actually forgives me for this!"

"Oh, Audrey, I'm so glad. I knew you'd get there. I knew it."

She thanked Marion again, profusely, then heard Simon's car, got off the phone and ran to meet him.

He got out of the car, and she launched herself into his arms. He caught her close, laughing, and swung her around. She laughed, too, and when she was on her feet, reached up and framed his face in her hands and gave him a big kiss.

"So?" he asked. "Andie called here?"

"No, I saw her at my old house. Richard called and… You know, never mind about him. I'm too happy. The bottom line is that he's too cheap to pay for her year in Spain, and I don't think she wants to go, anyway. And when she was upset and needed someone to talk to about that, she talked to me! Really talked, Simon! It was like she needed me for the first time in…months. It was like I was her mother again."

He gave her a beautiful smile, pulled her close and kissed her cheek. Then he whispered, "I told you that you'd get her back. I knew it."

Audrey was smiling through her tears. "She's not ready to live with me again, but I told her we'd work something out. If not her living with a neighbor… Well, I need to talk to you about that. I kind of…made her an offer."

"Of what?"

"My apartment above your garage, maybe? If it's all right with you? Just until she goes to college? If she's not willing to live with me until then? Please?"

He hesitated, not looking upset but as if he was thinking. "And if she's there, where will you be living?"

"I'm not sure. You have a lot of empty bedrooms in your house. Maybe…I could have one of them?"

He considered. "You know I make my living by negotiating, right?"

She nodded.

"And that I'm very, very good at it?" He looked as smug and satisfied as could be.

"I thought you must be. That you're good at everything."

"I am, and I have to tell you, a room of your own in my house is not an option. But I would be more than happy to share my bedroom with you on a long-term basis."

"Really?"

"Yes. There's just one condition. I have a very young, very impressionable daughter and an ongoing custody issue with my ex-wife, whose Italian boyfriend wants to take her to Brazil. Which is fine because Peyton will be here with us. But I'm going to want to file for primary custody of her, and since I've been so willing to help you with your daughter in any way I could, I think it's only fair that you do the same for me when it comes to my daughter. Don't you agree?"

"Of course, I'll help you with Peyton."

He looked incredibly pleased with himself. "So, to live in my house and share my bed on a long-term basis...I think you'd have to agree to be my wife."

"Oh, Simon." He took her breath away.

"You had to know that was coming," he insisted.

"One day. Probably. Not today. Not so fast. Just...because of Peyton?"

"No, I'm using that as an excuse, using this whole thing as an opportunity to get what I want. A good negotiator is always looking for ways to get what he wants. And I want you, and I know you want me." He kissed her hard. "And I know you're scared. And I know this has all happened so fast."

"It did. All of it," she told him, resting in his strong arms.

"I know you had a really bad end to your first marriage, and you know that I did, too. And I know you weren't looking for anything like this right now. Neither was I. But there you were. You just showed up at my house and seemed to fit here with me like nobody else ever has, in ways I didn't think anyone ever would. And I can't imagine my life without you. I don't even want to try."

She kissed him, quickly, then told him, "And I can't imagine my life without you, either. I'm just... I feel like my head is spinning. I can't... You want an answer right now?"

"I'd like one. But if I can't have it, I can wait. I think I've already proven that. And I'm not opposed to taking some time to show you how very pleasant it could be to share a bedroom with me. And a bathroom. Don't forget the bathroom. That great bathtub. I never will."

Audrey smiled. "You think you're so good in bed you can make me forget every doubt I have?"

"I'm saying that I'm a very determined man, and I'm willing to devote myself to trying to do just that. I love you, Audrey." The look in his eyes said that, too. All teasing aside, the words came from deep in his soul. "I think you'll find that I can be as stubborn as you and fight just as hard for you as you've fought for your daughter. It's the first thing I loved about you—how fiercely you love her, how you wouldn't let go of her. I'm not going to let go of you, either."

"So, you're going to wait me out? Sure that eventually I'll give you what you want?" she asked.

He nodded, grinned. "It's worked really well for me so far. I got you in my bed, didn't I? You just take whatever time you need. I'll be right here."

Andie showed up eight days later. Audrey was planting camellias by the giant tree in the front yard, Tink sunning himself in the grass beside her.

Audrey sat down in the grass, waiting for her daughter to come to her, trying to calm herself by fussing over the dog, who stretched, sighed heavily, then laid his head against her right knee, obviously wanting some attention.

Andie walked slowly to her, a troubled look on her pretty face. "You're still working in the yard?"

"Another part of my job," she said. "Simon's yard was a mess when I came, thanks to this dog."

Tink licked her knee, then rolled over onto his back and presented her with his furry belly to rub. Or maybe for Andie to rub. He turned his head toward Audrey's daughter and whined, as if to ask how she could possibly ignore him.

Andie sat down and obliged him, still looking sad as could be.

"The house sold. We have to be out in three and a half weeks," she said, tentatively. "And I thought I might take a look at the apartment here, if that's okay."

Hope surged inside of Audrey. This day had been so long in coming. "Of course, you can."

"You talked to Simon about it?"

Audrey nodded.

"And he's okay with me being there?"

"Yes. He said you and I just can't fight in front of his little girl. We scared her the last time she saw us together."

"Oh. I can do that," Andie said. "I think I'm tired of fighting anyway. I'm tired of everything. Simon said I should—"

"Wait? You talked to Simon?"

"Yeah. That day I heard you and dad arguing at the house. Simon didn't tell you?"

"No. Where did you see him?"

"With Jake. He was with Jake, talking to him about how to get me to stay here and not go to Spain. He told me I should think about what I want, what would make me happy, instead of how mad I was. And I didn't want to hear it then, but the last few days I keep coming back to what he said. I'm so tired of feeling this way. It's exhausting. I've been miserable and making everyone around me miserable, and I don't want to do it anymore."

"Oh, honey." Audrey wanted to grab her and hug her but resisted the urge. "That's good. That's a big, hard lesson to learn."

"And I'm afraid I learned it too late, because I was so awful to Jake, and I don't think he's going to forgive me. He won't even talk to me, Mom."

"Well, it's only been a few days since your big fight, right?"

Andie nodded. "But it feels like forever. He's been my best friend, ever since everything started to fall apart…since you started to fall apart. He's the one who got me through that, and I hurt him. I really hurt him, and… What if he doesn't ever forgive me?"

"Honey, the way he feels about you… That just doesn't go away."

"I hope so. You know, I started thinking about what I could do to show him how sorry I was," Andie said, with tears falling. "And I thought I'd just keep showing up where he was, keep trying to tell him I was sorry. That I'd refuse to go away and refuse to give up on us, and that eventually he'd see that I was really sorry."

Audrey reached out and took her daughter's hand, unable to help herself, and Andie didn't pull away.

"And I realized I was going to do the same thing you've been doing all these months with me," she said. "I remembered how many times I screamed at you and walked away and made you leave me alone, and I don't think I could stand it if Jake treated me that way. I think if I'd been you, I would have given up months ago. And then I knew that all this between you and me had to be really hard for you, but you just kept going. You kept fighting for you and me, and I guess I just understand things better now."

Audrey was crying, too. Tink was whining and making his crying sound, trying to figure out what was going on.

"Andie, I could never give up on you," Audrey said. "Never. You're my daughter."

"Will you help me with Jake? Because, I just really need you."

"Of course, I will. Now, come on. I'll show you where I've been living, and you can tell me what you think of it."

* * *

When Simon got home that night, he found Audrey lying in the hammock in the backyard, Peyton curled up asleep against her, the dog lounging on the ground beside them.

He leaned over and kissed his daughter's cheek, ruffled her hair. She was all warm and limp in sleep, layered against Audrey like a blanket and looking so sweet.

He turned to Audrey and gave her a slow, lingering kiss, then said, "There's a car I don't recognize in the driveway."

Audrey nodded.

"Andie's?" he guessed, and by the way Audrey's smile widened into all-out joy, he knew he was right. "Did she happen to bring anything with her? Suitcases, maybe? Boxes of her things to move in?"

"Not yet. But she spent some time looking over the apartment, and I think she's excited about having her own place, kind-of. She has a tape measure right now, trying to figure out which pieces of furniture from our old house will fit in those rooms."

Simon felt a slow, easy satisfaction rolling through him. "So, that means you'll be needing a place to live."

"Yes, I will. Thanks to you."

He gave her a blank look.

"You didn't tell me you and Jake teamed up to try to keep Andie here. Or that you talked to her that day she found out she wasn't going to Spain."

"Just trying to do my part to help." He pulled a chair over to the side of the hammock and sat down so he could be close to her. "Audrey, I'm always going to do everything I can to make you happy, to make our life together everything we want it to be. I promise."

He took her hand in his, brought it to his lips for a soft kiss. "Now, can we go pick out a ring for this hand and find a minister and a church? Do you want a minister and a church? Or there's the pavilion at the lake in the park. We could get married there. The dog could even go if we did it there, and I know you and Peyton love that silly dog."

She laughed, with tears on her cheek. "You're willing to have the dog at our wedding?"

"I just want a wedding, and I don't want you to make me wait too long for it. Those are my only conditions. I'm happy to let all other decisions on the matter be yours."

"Terms?" she asked. "You have no other terms? What kind of a negotiator are you?"

"One who knows what he wants and is about to get it. Say you'll marry me, Audrey? Make me the happiest man in the world."

Audrey leaned back, looking at him, reality suddenly sinking in. "I can't believe how much has changed since I came here. How wonderful my life is, when I thought I'd never be happy again, that I'd never be able to make everything right again, and I didn't really deserve to be happy anyway. And you… I never thought I'd trust a man again, Simon. I never thought I'd let myself love one, either."

"You still haven't said it," he reminded her, a man focused, goal-oriented and determined as always.

"I still have trouble believing it's all real," she told him.

"It's real. Say it. Now."

"Yes, Simon, you sweet—"

"No."

"Kind—"

"I deny it completely," he insisted.

"Patient—"

"I'm all out of patience. Right now. Say it."

"Yes." She finally gave him what he wanted, what she wanted, too. "I'll marry you."